MYSTIC FIRE
A Bonanza Novel

by Monette Bebow-Reinhard

𝕮𝖆𝖒𝖇𝖗𝖎𝖉𝖌𝖊 𝕭𝖔𝖔𝖐𝖘

an imprint of
WriteWords, Inc.
CAMBRIDGE, MD 21613

Cambridge Books is a subsidiary of:
Write Words, Inc.
2934 Old Route 50
Cambridge, MD 21613

ISBN 1-59431-712-7 or 978-1-59431-712-5

Fax: 410-221-7510
Bowker Standard Address Number: 254-0304

Dedication

To my own Bonanza family –
Joe, CarrieLynn, Adam, and Bennett.

To David Dortort, with many thanks for talking
with me on the phone as this book's outline emerged and
for his enthusiasm for a Bonanza / Civil War novel.

And to good friend Martha Gilmore, who read the book
in early edits to let me know if the story held together
and helped identify potential gaping holes.

To Nadine
August 2011

It was so wonderful having
you in the front of the
audience because you looked
so interested!
Thanks!
Martha Ahlstrand

Acknowledgements

Slave photo courtesy of: U. S. Army Military History Institute, Carlisle Barracks, PA

Lincoln photo courtesy of: Abraham Lincoln Art Gallery.Com, photo by Matthew Brady, January 8, 1864.

The Ponderosa Map watermark is an official licensed product of Bonanza and is used with the courtesy of Bonanza

INTRODUCTION

There will be some readers who don't appreciate radical politics in their Bonanza reading. But my decision to write my second Bonanza novel with some real 'meat' to it is, in part, due to David Dortort's vision, and with his approval, this novel emerged.

But this book began simply with the desire to make it as different as possible from *Felling of the Sons*, which reflected the TV series in its first year, when the four Cartwrights pulled together against all adversity. Here the four Cartwrights are separated into four storylines. They remain connected to each other through remembrances. In the later years of the show, while Adam was still there, the general tendency was to feature each with a main storyline. Here, then, are four episodes rolled into one book.

In order to create intriguing and gritty separate storylines, it became necessary for me to suspend my own belief that the Cartwrights always ran off in search of each other. Think about some of your favorite later episodes, when it seemed a Cartwright, alone, was in trouble, and none of the other three were in sight to rescue them. That's what I capture here.

Also, with the complicated four-part storyline, it was difficult to keep the passage of time straight. For the most part the time line is correct following Hoss and Joe around the ranch, and for Ben and Adam, well, in order for it to keep the action going, it becomes like entering another dimension.

I've tried to retain historical integrity with more intense focus on the Civil War and included some of the Victorian spiritualism of the age, which, I was surprised to learn, began during the Civil War. And, in making the Civil War a primary focus, I also gave voice to Abraham Lincoln and some of his staff, heavily researched to keep accurate but at the same time, weaving him into an imaginative tale of what could have happened. And I couldn't resist having Mark Twain represent the media here, which also played a role in the Civil War period.

So you should notice that this book has a different feel than *"Felling."* This is intentional. I can only hope some of you will highly approve. And the rest should at least enjoy it

A Note About Reading

Unlike *Felling of the Sons*, where you found a few footnotes at the bottom of the page, here you'll see them at the end of the book. This is for reference only — if you're curious about whether an issue is true or something I just conjured. Here only the most important issues are footnoted. I suggest reading *Mystic Fire* the first time through without reference to footnotes, which are there to mark where I've done my research. Instead, immerse yourself into this complex world as though it is *all* true. That's how I like to read fiction, anyway. And then go to the sources and if you're curious at all about what you've just read look at the nonfiction books mentioned in the footnotes to see more on a particular topic. That's the best use for footnotes in fiction. For many readers, this could be your first real introduction to events in the Civil War, and I can imagine some might believe I made all this up!

CHAPTER 1

The wagon rocked, shaking the three runaways into clutching each other as Tobias jumped out.

"Tobias! You's leaving us here alone?! You promised to keep us safe!"

Tobias turned back to his sister. "They're catching up to us now, Sadie. We have to split. One of us will get through. You keep going. Don't stop. You know what to do."

Sadie clung to her children as Tobias sprinted up a rock cliff and looked for a route of escape. "You be careful, Tobias! I'll find us a Cartwright, like we planned. You just be careful!"

"We'll make this right, Sadie, we has to. Lincoln has to. Hurry!"

* * *

With his ranch house waiting cozy and firelight-warm behind him, his sons finishing dinner, Ben Cartwright walked outside to watch the sun fight the coming darkness over Lake Tahoe. No color in the sky, no clouds, no moisture. This was about the driest weather he could remember. Carson Valley was normally dry most of the year, but on the mountain they should have a little rain by now. He couldn't shake the warning in his gut, a half-grown fear not ready to be shared with his sons. Once he figured its source…

The door opened behind him—his son Adam came out, by the sounds of the stride. Ben grinned. They've been together too long. He could tell his three boys apart by the sound of their boots. Maybe because each son was so different. Three wives, all who found life with him too hard. Whenever he caught himself wishing he'd had a daughter, he remembered losing a wife.

But a daughter-in-law might be nice.

Adam stood silent next to Ben, allowing Ben's thoughts to ramble on. Adam, the oldest, and, Ben allowed a moment of ego, far more attractive than he'd ever been by his early 30s, was still single and tied to the ranch. Ben would be happy to have all three sons hitched. Each of them knew a portion of the near thousand acres of the Ponderosa was theirs to work as they saw fit, as their legacy. All the work Ben's done here, cattling, timbering, mining, has been for them—his hope for a better future, for grandchildren, and sons' wives who would live longer than any of his own wives had.

3

Three wives, three sons—even if his darkest grief, he didn't mourn knowing any of his loves, all true, honest, sincere. All giving him another part of his legacy.

A better future. Something good must emerge from that secession war raging out east, giving the world a torn-apart feel, all the way out here. President Abe Lincoln's speeches to the army made Ben shudder. Just keep throwing bodies at the South, that's what winning demanded? Lincoln didn't say as much, but telling the soldiers that they held the responsibility to save the Union made Ben very glad his sons were this far away.[1]

Ben faced his eldest. Adam stared into the same dull dry sky, a brooding look on his darkly handsome face, lips pursed as he wrangled with an issue. His mother, Elizabeth, had laughed when Ben remarked that she had been an Arabian princess in a former life. Adam picked up her darker features, especially visible after the summer sun had its way on him. Adam could have his pick of any woman in town, but there just weren't that many single women out here, even now. That blasted "civil war," now over a year old . and bloodier than ever, kept women from coming west, because few traveled unaccompanied by fathers or brothers. Adam was particular about women. Ben supposed he wanted the same romance he'd heard his father share of his three marriages.

Adam spoke under his father's steady gaze. "No sign of rain yet."

"No, and I am plenty worried about the section up north."

Adam crossed his arms and fixed his intensity back on Ben. "What about a windmill?"

Ben sighed. "That's not an overnight chore, son, and I don't know if we can spare the time or the men."

"I'm more worried about the land. And now we're seeing the worst brand of men running this way from the east, no telling the trouble they can cause with a careless smoke."

"I know." Ben tried to stay calm because he knew how worry looked on his face, with his dark eyebrows furling under stark white hair. He didn't want to get Adam more worked up than necessary, and tried to smile as he laid a gentle hand on his son's shoulder. "Lucky we got the cattle sold when we did. But we could sell off some winter stock locally rather than trying to keep them fed up here."

"I'm going to ride to town in the morning and send a wire to San Francisco. I can get the windmill designs here in a week. We can only hope to get it built and drawing water before we have a major fire."

"I've had all the lakes prepared—"

"We don't have enough lakes for 800 acres, and what we do have are seriously low. Even the water wagons we have filled and stationed at every cattle ground will only carry so far. I've got in mind to build it where the lakes are too far to help."

"Doesn't matter what I say anymore." Ben shook his head. Since that other

4

windmill trip Adam had tried to make went sour, he'd not been able to get the idea out of his head.

"Guess not." Adam looked around. "Wonder why the first crew hasn't returned yet. Mind if I ride out and see if there's trouble?"

"No, go ahead." Ben watched Adam walk to his still-saddled horse. He shook his head at his son's stubbornness and penchant for hard work as he walked back in the house. He'd seen Adam go weeks with four hours of sleep a night and without any seeming ill effects. If only that New England character had rubbed off on his other two sons!

Ben knew, though he didn't like to remember, the real reason for Adam's new somberness and distance from other people of late. A few months back he'd gotten robbed and left on foot to die in the desert, rescued and then tormented by a deranged miner. Ben hated the memory, and figured Adam did, too, but the truth was, that torment at the hand of a madman had changed his son in some irreparable ways. Ben still felt relief just looking at Adam after coming so close to leaving him for dead coyote meat. But for awhile after they'd found Adam dehydrated and deranged, they weren't sure they were going to get him back at all.[2] This windmill project could be the thing to bring him all the way back from that frightful time.

Inside the door Ben took off his hat, as Joe laughed at a checker move he caught on Hoss.

They were embroiled in their usual after-dinner pastime. While Adam might be reading or drawing up designs for improving work flow or building new shelters, his brothers had checkers, cards or girls on their minds. Of course he couldn't expect the boys to be that similar. But Adam could have the ladies on the mind once in a while, or Hoss and Joe concentrate on the next day's chores. After all, they all had the same hard-working, back-breaking father—who encouraged them all to break their backs often enough.

But not tonight.

"Boys," Ben strolled over to them, hands in pockets. "I'm in the mood for a little matchmaking."

Joe's lazy smile fell as he scratched a hand through his brown wavy hair. "Oh boy."

"Now wait, Pa, I done asked that Becky Sue on a date, just last week. Ain't my fault if she turned me plum down flat." Hoss, his biggest son, didn't often attract a girl for his looks but got plenty of attention for being the kindest and gentlest man of his size around—pretty much the size of a mountain, next to Joe. Gentle, too, at least until he was riled. "I think she's just playin' hard to get—so I'm doin' a little of that, too."

"Relax, not for the two of you. But your brother's been working too hard. It's time for a social, what do you think? We can feel the chill in the air, and the cattle are off to market without any of us for once. And before long the passes will be closed by snow."

5

"A social?" Joe winked at Hoss. "Well, that ain't so bad, Pa. I thought you wanted us to find some women to parade around Adam." Ben didn't figure he'd have trouble convincing Joe, a natural ladies' man, as well as an all-round playful tease—which at times could be unfortunate. "I thought we were gonna have to pay them to be nice to older brother."

"Yeah, ha!" Hoss joined in. "Don't think you have enough money for that, Pa."

"All right, that's enough." Ben stoked the fire and threw on another log. He stared at the embers flaking up into the chimney. If he could make one wish, just one…Adam would be settled and with children by now.

"Hey, Joe, when do you reckon was the last time Adam asked a girl out?"

Joe had to think about this. "You know, I don't know."

"Me neither."

"Pa, you know," Joe walked over to Ben and slapped him on the back. Ben recognized the conspiratorial tone but allowed Joe his fun. "I get to feeling that older brother has just given up, you know, when a fellow's been single as long as Adam has, well, they just give up. Figure maybe they just aren't attractive enough to women."

"Hah!" Hoss snorted. "Exceptin' women they don't like!"

Joe pointed a finger like an empty gun at his brother. "That's right. So we just have to find the right girl and the right moment. You have that social and leave the rest to me." Joe winked at Hoss, who chuckled for a moment, then frowned in confusion.

Ben watched the fire and his feelings of half-grown fear returned. Something itching at him, some problem left untended. He instead drifted back to the need for a social, after how hard they had all worked this past summer, Adam more than anyone. Over the summer Adam tended to go off riding without saying anything and came back the same way. One day Ben took him to task, reminding him how they'd all suffered looking for him. Adam, looking like a little boy when scolded, told Ben that he should start treating his sons like the grown men they were.

Ben turned back to Joe, lost in plotting thoughts, while Hoss studied the checkerboard. "Now, wait a minute, Joseph, I only plan the partying and expect the rest to happen naturally."

"Oh, don't worry, Pa." Joe winked at Hoss. "It will."

"And remember, one topic is always off limit at these gatherings. We will not start or get into any discussions about that conflict back east. Nevada and Cartwrights do not take sides in state's rights or that war. The fighting is not in Nevada Territory."

"It *will* be." Joe met his Pa's eyes and shrugged. "I won't start. I never do."

Hoss's mouth puckered as he stood and jammed his hands in his pockets, a habit of his when he felt cautious and needed to talk it out. While others most often thought with their brains, Hoss thought with his heart. "Pa, don't you think maybe we got too much goin' on right now for a social? Adam might think so, too."

"Well, that's true. Now he's planning to build a windmill in the north section that's the most vulnerable to fire."

"Hey, where is Adam?" Joe walked to the door and let in some of the cool night air as he stared out into the dark night.

Ben waited until Joe came back in. "He went to check on the logging crew, they should be back by now. Unless there's trouble." Ben went to the desk, avoiding Hoss's look. Hoss had hired Frank and they'd had nothing but trouble ever since. Hoss defended the man, who'd lost his parents in a mine accident, but how much time does a man need to recover? He braced himself for Hoss's further deliberation on the matter, but Hoss took his time gathering his thoughts as Joe sat on the edge of Ben's desk and picked up the photo of Adam's mother. Ben took out his guest list and made a mark or two of changes.

Hoss came up behind Joe. "Frank still drinkin' too much?"

"It's worse than that."

Three heads turned in surprise. They hadn't heard Adam come in.

Adam tossed his hat on the rack and unbuckled his gun belt. "More trees are down than can be accounted for. And they're cutting trees in sections we didn't mark. One area has been cleared and all that debris not cleaned up makes an even worse fire hazard."

"Adam, you couldn't'a made it there and back, not in the dark," Hoss said.

"No, I met up with Salzar and some others. They were looking for Frank. Nobody saw where he rode off to."

Doubt filled Joe's boyish face. "How do you know about the timber?"

"Al keeps the books and he's upset. Says more timber's being cut than he can account for as being sold. He doesn't know who, or where the extra timber's going. And Salzar saw Frank directing two men to protected sites."

"Salzar?" Joe snorted. "He's just a busybody who sees more than what's there."

"Joe," Ben put a hand on his youngest son's shoulder, "Just because he's German and new to this country doesn't make him suspect."

"And..." Adam took a deep breath as Joe registered brief chagrin. "There have been several men on site that are not part of the team. Not just passing through, either."

"That fool. How does he expect to get away with it?"

"Pa, I can't believe that about Frank." Hoss looked like he'd been punched in the gut. "Sure, he may drink some, but he's honest. You cayn't find men who don't drink anyhow."

"Gambling. That'll do a man in." Adam spoke with the pain he knew Hoss felt.

"Oh now, Adam, come on—"

Ben put up a hand to Hoss. "Quite the accusation, Adam. Have any proof?"

"No, but I intend to ask around when I ride to Virginia City in the morning."

Hoss put a hand on Adam's shoulder. "Pa, I think I oughta find out about Frank."

Adam's jaw clenched but he refrained from responding.

"No, Adam's going to town anyway. It's too long a ride and we've got a lot to do."

"Like planning a social," said Joe to brighten the conversation.

Adam looked back at his younger brother. "What social?"

"Just a consideration." Ben went back to his desk and straightened papers. "Our socials keep us in touch with the neighbors and increase our business contacts. And the three of you need to have a little fun every now and then."

Adam tensed when his two brothers grinned. "Not now. There's too much to do."

"You know, Adam," Joe tried to stop grinning but failed. "Sometimes problems go away when you ignore them."

"Not this time."

"Maybe not," Ben said. "But my mind's made up, Adam." He took the latest Territorial Enterprise to the settee and made himself comfortable. "This social ought to help us clear our heads a little. We can solve problems and still have fun, Adam. You know that. I'm thinking of next Saturday, if Hop Sing's agreeable."

Hoss looked around. "Where he is, anyhow? He's gotta be in on these family plans."

"Oh, he's out back, digging another hole."

Joe's face wrinkled. "Ugh. His favorite job. Why at night?"

Hoss laughed. "Cause then he cayn't see what he's doin'!"

When the kitchen door slammed, they exchanged glances. They never much spoke it, but sometimes Hop Sing spooked them. He seemed to know what they were thinking and anticipated what they needed before they did. Adam thought once his Oriental upbringing played a role, but none of them ever asked Hop Sing what kind of upbringing that might be. They knew he didn't have much interest in being Christian, or American, and even talked about the day he'd have enough money saved to go back home. They didn't underpay him but none of them looked forward to that day.

"Mr. Cartlight?" Hop Sing bounded into the dining room like a panther after prey. "Hop Sing no got time for foolishment!"

"What now, Hop Sing?" Ben sighed, knowing Hop Sing took offense to that which offered none. Their cultural misunderstandings were lessening but would never fully disappear.

"We aglee, best to do one's plivate business far from living quarter. We aglee, we dig in certain area only."

"That's true."

"Why I come back to house I tlip! See foot? Smell foot!"

Even in the glowing embers of the fire and lit lanterns Ben could see that Hop Sing had stepped in something foul. But no one had to see what filled the air with rancid fumes.

Adam frowned. "A hole close to the house?"

Hop Sing nodded, round face narrowed in anger.

Hoss sniffed the air as Joe groaned and held his nose. "It don't smell human."

Ben shook his head. "I don't know why a hole would be close to the house, Hop Sing."

Hoss stuck his thumbs in his vest pocket. "Oh, I plum forgot to mention the guest I had."

Adam crossed his arms as a sly smile crept across his face. "What's her name?"

"Huh?"

"You wouldn't dig a special privacy hole unless it was for a lady. Who was she?"

"Well, now, I don't rightly know."

"Oh, come on now," Joe said. "You had a woman here and don't know her name?"

"Oh dadgummit, I know it sounds kinda funny. She shows up here, all lost and forlorn and looking like she's gonna die. I try to ask her what's wrong but she just shushes me. Wants me to let her rest and then wants food and water, and then wants….you know. And then she just…went missing. Didn't hear no horse ride off neither."

"She just disappeared?" Adam folded his arms, amusement trying to hide on his face.

"Just like that. Narry a sound."

"Sounds like you met a ghost, Hoss," Joe said, chuckling, outright laughter not far behind. "A pretty smelly one."

"Ghosts?" Ben had mentioned the Lincoln séances to the boys but the news didn't have any impact on them. "Sounds like all that eastern spiritualism is making an unexpected western call." He'd had a brush or two with specters as a lad back east, but never mentioned these to the boys because he didn't believe in ghosts—not then, not now.

"No dead lady do this in hole." Hop Sing held up his foot for emphasis.

"All right, Hop Sing, go get cleaned up. At least we've had our explanation." They watched again Hop Sing's peculiar bounding walk, related to his hope of having just a shoe to clean and not the whole floor. Ben grinned at his two chuckling sons and one chagrined one. "Not ghosts, of course, but an unexpected, and slippery, visitor. We don't doubt your story, Hoss."

"Actually, Hoss, some pretty learned people believe in ghosts. That should tell you there's something to it. Even Lincoln, like Pa says."

"She's not a ghost, Adam, I'd swear on my mama's birthmark."

"Dickens is another. He's even been credited with creating the so-called

9

Victorian ghost craze over in Europe."

Joe bit back a laugh. "Yeah, in Europe, that's one thing. But over here?"

"Now Joe, let's give Hoss some credit." Adam said. "He says this isn't a ghost but somehow she just…went missing. Sounds a little crazy…." Adam winked at Joe.

Joe pointed at Hoss. "Even coming from you!" He chuckled with a wink at Adam.

Hoss cast a stormy frown at them both.

"I suppose this isn't a good time to ask Hop Sing about some partying next week." Adam realized he still had his coat on and removed it. "Which is fine, because we don't have the time."

"Don't worry, I'll talk to him." Ben put a hand on Hoss's shoulder. "Son, do let us know if you see her again. Even if it's just for a second."

Joe burst out laughing.

No one noticed as the figure in shadowy pink slipped past the window outside.

CHAPTER 2

"Hey, Adam." Joe poked his head into Adam's room without rapping. He'd been doing that ever since he was a little kid, hard as Adam tried to teach him respect over a person's privacy. "You're not dressed yet?"

Joe took to this habit of entering, Adam realized, just to see his eldest brother get riled. So Adam stopped getting riled. But Joe never did start rapping. Some things, Adam decided, were more important to fight over. Instead Adam began to enter Joe's room without rapping, figuring that eventually Joe would realize his own need for privacy.

That hasn't happened yet.

"You're just dressed early." Adam didn't look up from his journal, where he wrote stretched out and relaxed on the bed. He'd been running water buckets to the herd all week and had applied some liniment to the muscle soreness. He wouldn't admit to Joe that he looked forward to easy hours before a social. Journaling reassured him that as a human being he still progressed in the right direction—or caught himself in those times of regression.

"Oh, sorry, should I wait til you finish?"

"Nope, I heard you coming and wrote "and now Joe's coming so I better stop before he barges in.""

Joe laughed. "And my feet are faster than your hand."

"I won't debate that."

"Nope. Cuz you can't."

They debated often and mostly on subjects that tended to divide them, like the war out east. They met a couple of drifters a month ago and Adam felt sure they were southern deserters but Joe took care of them like long lost brothers. Adam was right about them being Rebel (*excuse me, Joe, Confederate*) deserters, and Joe finally sent them packing, telling Adam that he didn't care if they were North or South, deserters were deserters. When Adam chided him about turning on them only after hearing they'd left ole Bobby Lee, Joe took a swing at him but Adam grabbed both his arms and reminded him where the war was.

When he let Joe go, Joe surprised him by apologizing, so Adam apologized for teasing him. Knowing they differed didn't stop the conversations. Adam

11

felt they wanted to understand each other and all they needed was a single key word.

Adam realized he had time for contemplation because Joe was in no hurry to state the reason for the interruption but stood staring at the Indian blanket on Adam's bed. Adam cleared his throat. "And?"

"Thought we could talk before we get surrounded by people. You've been busy all week." Joe pulled his shoulders back. "We both have."

"Lots going on."

"What did you do about Frank?"

"Oh, I brandished him for drinking and allowing the illegal cutting, which he claimed came as a surprise to him. I've found no trace of them anywhere, so I suspect they fled. And I couldn't fire him, Joe, because he looked so doggone contrite and apologetic for drinking. Promised to give up the bottle."

"Gotta give a guy a chance when he says that."

"Yeah, for Hoss's sake, at least."

Another long silence settled between them.

Adam sat up and looked out the window. No sign of guests yet, though some, and he could name them, tended to come early for more drinking time. "So, what do you think about Lincoln freeing the slaves, Joe?"

Joe sat on the other side of Adam's bed, resting one leg up on a chair. "I never said I believed in slavery, Adam, but Lincoln's trying to make the South look bad. If he'd leave them and their economy alone, they'd find a way to end slavery."

"Actually, the Emancipation Proclamation addresses each Rebel state's economic concerns by encouraging them to return to the Union, where their slavery will be protected."

Joe laughed. "Oh, he's a conniver, that Lincoln."

Adam thought Joe would get upset by this. Maybe Lincoln found a way to heal the country that would also heal wounds inside divided families. Giving him and Joe less to fight about, well, that's a start, anyway.

"So." Adam waited as Joe had no inclination for further war talk. "Did you want something else?"

"Ah, just thought I'd—"

"You want to see how I look so that you could try and look better?'

"Well, doggonit, Adam, you're always getting more girls to dance with you."

"I could help you out. I could whisper sweet 'dance with Joe's' in their ears."

"Now, look, you don't have to get uppity. I can hold my own around you."

"Want to bet?"

"Ha! I'll take you on anytime."

"You're the one who came in here all insecure."

"I'm *not* insecure. I just want you to remember you have two brothers, that's all. You know your appeal? You're the oldest. Maybe the girls around here don't know yet, but Pa doesn't plan on leaving everything to you."

"Oh, so I'm only as good as the land I keep? Well, we'll just see about that."

"Yes! Good! Now get dressed!" Joe turned smartly, hit the doorframe, and walked out of Adam's room, letting the door slam behind him.

Adam shook his head. A slow smile swept across his face. He sat down and picked up his journal. "Joe thinks by egging me on I'll have a better time tonight?" He sighed. "Guess I've been a bore. I'll show 'em how good a time a fellow can have."

* * *

Joe kept his giggle hidden as he strode casually from Adam's door. He felt good, blood all warmed up, and he and Adam knew how to do rile each other, too. Adam was fun to rile, like Hoss was fun to play pranks on.

Like with the deserters a month ago. He knew they were southern deserters but didn't let Adam know he knew. They were tired and hungry and didn't want to fight. They didn't need to be condemned for their fear. They told him that they just wanted to go back home and take care of their ma and sisters. He'd sent them off packing as a ruse, knowing they were on their way back anyway.

Some things his older brother just didn't need to know.

CHAPTER 3

Grumbling, Hoss put work clothes back on after his bath and, still grumbling, walked to the corral. Sure enough, Cinnamon, the newly broke filly, stood with one leg in the air. Hoss gave it a "hyah" to see if it limped. "Dadburnit. Nothing gets past ole' Hop Sing." He'd ridden the horse quite a bit the past week, checking on the herd and the timbering, because he wanted to show her off. But then with everyone running behind the gun, trying to get work done for the social, including all the working he'd done with Frank to make sure he didn't let anyone down again, Hoss got to the house in time to jump into the cooling tub of water. Hop Sing must have noticed the horse limping while Hoss soaked of the week's worth of dirt.

He grabbed the horse's neck rope. "Gonna find a good buyer for you, that's for sure. Made me miss Chubby this whole week long, right enough." The horse threw its head back in protest but learned quick enough that Hoss was in no mood to be gentle. "I know you ain't used to having your hooves cleaned. And I ain't used to horse-tending before a social, neither. So let's just both get this over with."

Hoss tied the horse's neck rope to the fence inside the corral with very little lead rope so the horse wouldn't have room to move. He grabbed a hoof but the horse managed a good kick, clipping Hoss alongside the head.

"Confound it, Cinnamon, that'll be enough of that!" Using the extra length of rope he tied the one front leg to the fence, and leaned against the horse as he picked up the other. The red-headed and tempered horse flared its nostrils and whinnied as it tried to jerk the foot away from Hoss's grip. "You may not got weight on me, but you got temper. I'm getting just about ready to match it." He kept talking to the horse, angry words said in a gentle manner, as he cleaned the hoof that kept jerking about in his steady hand.

Just the two today, and the other two he'll do tomorrow. "I got me some partyin' tonight and now I'm gonna need another bath, and am gonna be too plum tuckered out to hold a little lady in my arms for dancing, and even if'n I try to dance my legs are just gonna fall off. And it's your fault, Cinnamon!" His breath burned with the anger in his chest but he kept his words soft and gentle as he untied the leg. He didn't like taking a chance that the horse might twist wrong and break a leg tethered like that, but sometimes there just wasn't any other way, that he'd found, anyway, to get them used to being picked.

Hoss looked up at the sound of galloping horse hooves in time to see Amos Burnsby from across the lake riding in at a fast gallop.

"Hoss!" Amos said as he rode over to the corral. "Got a problem heading your way. You hiding any niggers here?""

"Any what?"

"Niggers, you know, from back east."

"Well, I don't much like that term, Amos. They preferred colored, don't they?"

"I don't care what they prefer. If you're caught harboring one, free territory or not, you'll be in for a peck of trouble, I'll tell you that."

"Hello, Amos, what's going on?" Ben came out of the house still in the process of tying his elusive tie. "Our social's today, you know, you can stay if you like."

"Well, now, that's sociable of you, Ben, but I—"

"Amos here thinks we're hiding a runaway slave."

Ben laughed at Hoss's concern. "If I had a cent piece…why do you think so, Amos?"

"Ain't me thinking this, Ben. There's a wagonload of southern scavengers combing the countryside, said they was on a trail of a whole family of runaways."

"That legal, Pa? Now that Lincoln made that proclamation and all?"

Ben studied the ground as though wondering if it could still support him. "His proclamation has nothing to do with the any Union slave state, I'm afraid. And Lincoln has yet to repeal the Fugitive Slave Law. But a couple months back Congress passed a law that says slavery is illegal in the western territories, and the army no longer has to return any runaway back to their masters. Any slave that crosses into free territory or into Union army lines is also free. This means that those southern slavers are encroaching on our land illegally. Amos, if we find them we have every right to chase them off. We'll harbor all the slaves we want on our ranch."

"Yeah." Hoss ginned at Amos. "Yeah, that Mr. Lincoln knows what he's doing, Amos, so you don't fret none about us."

"Law also says, Ben, that if the slaver gives valid cause why the slave belongs back in custody, like owing his labor rightful, he's got to go back." Amos grinned and spit a tobacco wad into the corral over Hoss's head, wide off mark but Hoss ducked lower anyway and frowned at him.

"That true, too, Pa?" He wanted his Pa to take this fellow down a mark. Never much thought of him as being that smart.

Ben sighed. "Yes, Hoss, that's true, too."[3] Ben turned a biting eye back to Amos. "I'll take care of my own. We have nothing to hide."

"Yeah. We all wanna say that, eh?" Amos laughed. "Hey, Hoss, don't forget, I'll have that corral full of wild 'stangs for you the first of the month. You come get 'em or I'll find me a more reliable buyer."

"I'll be there, Amos, you can bet your hat on that." Hoss said as he worked a kink out of his shoulder.

"Don't think I will, I'll just look for you on the 1st." Amos tightened the reins, bent on delivering his message of warning across the countryside. "And if I see any niggers, Ben, I'll drive them off yer land for ya!"

Ben stepped forward as the horse and rider rode off. "I don't need...I don't..." He threw up a hand and turned back to the house. "Blame fool."

"Couldn't do it, could we, Pa? If we saw one of them colored people, we couldn't turn 'em away?" Hoss waited as Ben contemplated this idea but the horse snorted so he turned back to finish the hoof.

Ben watched Hoss fussing in the corral. "I don't like the idea any more than you do, son. But during that trip I took to Missouri last year, I ran into a fiery storm of hate I never expected. I didn't tell you boys because I never expected to see the hate reach us here."

"But Pa, if someone comes here looking for help..."

"We will help with food, money and safe passage to California." Ben winced. "This is a terrible time, but something good *will* come of all this blood-shed. We have to be patient. Lincoln's taking steps, small maybe, but he's taking them."

"Is that somethin' you get when you're older, Pa?"

"Patience?" Ben chuckled. "Yes, I guess so."

Hoss leaned his big shoulder against the horse tethered to the corral fence. "Confoundit, Cinnamon!" Hoss wiped a sweaty arm across his forehead, his iron poker a comfortable distance from his face. "You still worried, Pa?"

Ben raised his voice to be heard over the snorting. "It's unsettling to get reminders of how close that war is. Why, if any of you boys were to head out east to get involved..."

"You just tell them brothers of mine, Pa. You ain't gotta worry about me none, you keep me too busy!"

Ben turned, his attention to fixing his tie, and walked back to the house.

Hoss watched, jealous of his father's unruffled look until the horse jerked its leg in Hoss's steady grip. "Dadburnit, Cinnamon, you ain't in more of a hurry than me."

* * *

When the first guests arrived Adam walked to his window. Still not ready to go down, he felt a disturbance in his chest, a ghost digging a different sort of hole. He sighed as he buttoned his shirt, unable to cast the unease away. But they required his presence, whether or not he felt up to the task.

"Some consequence, yet hanging in the stars…Let he that has the steerage of my course, direct my sail." Forcing steely determination in the lingering fondness of Shakespeare's words—although wishing a less pathetic play had come into his head—Adam finished his tie, opened the door and walked downstairs.

CHAPTER 4

The music had started before Hoss walked down the stairs, cleaned and shined up, with a dab of grease on new hand sores from his horse struggles. He swore to himself that he'd never seen so many people in one room before and now pairing to dance. Looked like old Charlie was going to lose out and sure enough, started dancing on his own as he always did. And there was Sam Clemens chowing down.

"Doggone if this social ain't gonna end up in the Territorial Enterprise." Hoss had been surprised to learn Pa invited Sam, who had started signing his crazy articles as Mark Twain. They'd not always gotten along. Even after the Cartwrights came to Sam's rescue, Sam had a tendency to write things in the paper that sounded so doggoned real. Like the time Adam and Joe went fishing and Sam wrote how they were catching eels that were five feet long and tasted like chicken, except that these eels could also run on the ground and so Adam and Joe spent a day chasing them around on the rocks. Ben confronted Sam after one story about how the Cartwrights liked to go rock climbing and toss rocks down on travelers to keep them off their land. Hoss had go along that time and figured he must have turned red several times at the language his Pa had used, but in the end they had a good laugh with several of the City folks who knew better than to take Sam's tales seriously.

From a stopped position halfway down the stairs, Hoss tried to spy if Lizzie had come as she'd promised, and there she was, dancing with a dandy who loved to court every woman in town, never far enough to marry any of them. He and Pa got on well, and Pa didn't like to slight anyone, but Hoss kept his distance because of the hearts the fellow was said to break. Made Hoss want to break him, sometimes. Hoss counted in his head ten ladies and twenty-two men, a rough estimate because he didn't want people to guess he was counting. At least four women, from what he could tell, were of the already married variety.

Adam and Joe were both dancing, and Hoss chuckled to himself as he finished walking the stairs. Joe had told him how he made this like a contest with Adam so that Adam would spark with a certain little lady tonight, a gal Joe had arranged to come. A former sweetheart. Hoss wondered if that could be trouble, as Joe's plans sometimes were.

Hoss angled himself into position so Lizzie could see him. He didn't figure he could compete with a dandy, being only willing to dance a waltz, but any lady should have a hard time resisting his biggest charm—his helpful nature. Or so he reassured himself. A guy doesn't always have to be a charmer to be appreciated.

* * *

Joe felt like the world could end at that moment and he'd never notice. There was nothing in his mind better than dancing to good music with a pretty girl in his arms. And Angela was pretty! He'd never seen her before and found her appeal instant. He thought he might have a little trouble because at first she talked with Adam, but then Adam caught the eye of Margaret across the room, that gal he'd spooned with until she'd on the spur moved to San Francisco years ago. Joe had feared Margaret would change her mind, even just the day of the social, by getting cold feet, because of how shivery she got when he found her and asked her. When she walked in, Margaret took Joe's breath away. Fortunately he had Angela in his arms now. He and his brother wouldn't compete *that* way.

Joe had ridden to Sacramento on a phony errand and found Margaret more than willing to come to a social. Bringing her in as a surprise for Adam seemed perfect. He'd had a fluke of luck running into her there last year on a visit and doggone if he didn't forget to give her regards to Adam. Then Margaret surprised him by getting in a stagecoach with all her worldly goods and moving to Carson City, but that could be for the best, too, if they spark as they seemed to.

And now Angela—her name suited her!—turned her attentions to him.

For a few minutes Joe feared that she had turned her head for Adam, because she asked questions about him and how he drove the cattle—how one gal could want to know so much?—but finally they just talked about each other as they danced and between dances she had the most wonderful laugh. Heck with the competition with Adam, which was just a spur, anyway.

* * *

Adam still couldn't catch his breath and for some reason, one he understood well, the room was very hot. He wondered if he could get Margaret interested in a moon-filled walk, since he could well remember the last time he took her outside during just such an occasion as this. She seemed as happy to be with him as he was holding her to dance, but so much had changed between them.

He remembered the hate that developed when he rode to her place one day and found her gone. Just like that, without a word. Hating her even so many years later, until today, seeing her face light up when their eyes met, now as adults. That hate had diminished in those eight years to some feeling of gratitude for the friendship they had shared. But the hate never fully disappeared, until today, when she smiled at him.

Nine years back, before Comstock, when Carson City was still Eagle Station, Adam had been both stunned and delighted at seeing another family living so close to them out in the middle of nowhere. They were trespassers, but Pa had struck up a friendship with the father. Pa was lonely, too, Adam figured, even though Adam felt his loneliness had mostly left him once Adam returned home from college.

Adam first mistook Margaret for a boy, the way she dressed, and had even tackled her when he caught her stealing a pig. How embarrassed he had been scrambling off her after touching those parts of her that didn't belong on a boy! And how delightful her laugh had been. She made him easy and got him laughing right along with her. He let her keep the pig.

She got him laughing, in that first instant of conversation, by calling herself a party-crasher and did he mind? He couldn't even think, nor has he breathed, so great was his surprise.

They had so much talking to do, but he felt he couldn't say more than two words without choking. He wasn't sure she ever knew the effect she had on him all those years ago. He hoped that she could read his eyes, feel his warm fingertips against her back and read his thoughts, because he could muster so few words to say.

The music stopped at just the right moment, because he'd just asked her if she was still single and she had laughed. They walked to the punch bowl where several of Adam's neighbors begged to make her acquaintance. Adam introduced her and stood aside, but as desire fueled like flaming timber inside him while he watched her chat with others, he took her arm and pulled her to the door. She had become even more charming than he remembered and a sudden jealousy as she talked to another man stoked fiery embers into a breathless tornado of flame.

"Let's walk outside for some air."

"Oh, Adam, yes, I'm wilted!"

Finding courage to take a woman in his arms in the moonlight never used to be this difficult. He wrapped an arm around her waist as they walked, which slowed them down, but in their silence and slow movement she responded as though a part of him. Still, he felt as insecure with her as when he had been less experienced, and the feeling of all those years of hatred threatened to douse the flaming embers.

Adam walked her over to the corral to show off a few horses, but before he could stop himself, he had her braced against the fence, leaned over, met her approval with his eyes, and kissed her.

The moment, he felt, must stay like this forever. Because both of their worlds were about to change. This time, though, he would keep control and not let her get away again.

* * *

Ben came out of the kitchen with a fresh platter of food. He tried to cajole Hop Sing into joining them but no matter how much they tried to make him feel like family, he kept to what he felt was his place. Ben knew that when it was just the five of them, he felt as much a family member as any of them—who cooks, rather than who herds or timbers or goes to socials.

Hop Sing was smart, but also gentle and sensitive. He reminded Ben that he would never wish to cause trouble for the Cartwrights by trying to rise above what others saw as his 'station in life.' Nor, he would add, did he want his own people to see him as getting "uppity" by acting like white folk. He knew, he told Ben, why these Americans didn't like his people. They came here for opportunity but they continued to send money home to provide for their extended families rather than investing locally.

"Someday," Ben thought, "someday this country will understand differences and allow all of us equal right to happiness. Someday slavery will be gone, for good—everywhere." He felt that the Chinese, too, were treated like little more than slaves.

But then, weren't they all, in some respects?

Ben left Hop Sing to his kitchen chores and smiled when his guests cheered the new plate of food, some exclaiming over Hop Sing's culinary talents.

Hoss grabbed a handful of apple dumpling.

"Where's Adam?" Ben watched Joe swing Angela around on the floor. He kept his eye on the floor, too, to make sure the spittoons were being used. Ben had been so disgusted by his male guests at the Cartwrights' first social that ever since he instructs every male guest where the spitting corners of the room were.

"I dunno." Hoss wiped the crumbs from his mouth with the back of his hand, having already half-eaten his dumpling and accepted the napkin Ben handed him. "He ain't said a word to nobody since Margaret got here." Hoss could latch onto new foods Hop Sing brought out, when all Ben could smell was ripe tobacco mixed with whiskey and onions.

"Nothing short of a miracle, having her show up again. I remember Adam had been upset for months after she moved away."

"Oh, I don't know nothin' about no miracles, Pa. Seems to me God sometimes needs some cowboys to do the work for him."

Ben grinned. "You didn't, did you?"

"No, not me. But Joe told me all about it. You ain't mad, are ya?"

Ben laughed and put an arm around his big son's shoulders. They watched the social play on, but Ben never fooled himself. An occasion such as this often disguised the worst of troubles that lie ahead. He lived in the present, but always with an eye on the future.

Lizzie approached the food and smiled at Hoss while reaching for an apple dumpling on the table behind him.

After a moment, Ben stood alone, smiling with pleasure at the happiness of his sons. At long last, he thought to himself, Adam will understand the saying that a man curses himself a fool for having stayed single for so long.

With this thought pounding through his head, and elsewhere, Ben cast about for a reason to leave his single life behind, as well.[4]

CHAPTER 5

Margaret forced her moan of pleasure deep back down her throat during the kiss, the intensity of which she'd never felt—the passion, the desire from Adam felt so necessary to her life and breath that she wanted to cry at the thought of the kiss ending. When Adam pulled back and watched her face, hoping for a response, all she could do with the honesty in her soul was huddle deeper inside her coat and shiver as she looked at the treetops. How dare she hope he'd take her back, now, after all that's come between them? This coming here, she feared, would prove to be a mistake.

"It's so beautiful out here, Adam. Even at night."

Adam took her hand and led her down a wooded path to the bench Ben put there for swooning and spooning moments. "Especially at night. If you're into watching the sky." They sat ever so close but not touching, and looked skyward together. "Until the trees get in the way."

"That makes spotting the sparkles through the leaves an adventure. I remember the first time you showed me the stars, Adam, out on the open prairie. How close they were—I thought I could almost touch them. They don't seem as close now."

Adam grabbed her hands and begged her with his eyes to see him as he saw her. "They don't need to."

Margaret molded into his arms and returned the kiss, until, breathless, she pulled away. "I was only a child, but I never forgot the good times we had."

"You were more than a child," Adam whispered. "You knew your own mind."

"But not old enough that I could argue with my father about leaving. Oh Adam," she kissed him and stroked his chin, tracing his cleft. "Leaving you...devastated me."

"You never wrote, not once. I sent three letters, each time wondering if they were getting through."

"You did? No, Adam, I never got one of them." Margaret pulled out of his warm arms and stood. She knocked on a strapping Ponderosa pine, and wrapped her arms around its cool trunk. "I remember reading Shakespeare. Remember? We'd each take a part. *Oh, swear not by the moon...*" Margaret laughed. "And you taught me to ride. A natural, you called me." She couldn't

23

keep meeting his naked intent stare. "Oh, my father always wished I was a boy but would never let me ride. Told me it might…hurt me."

Adam stood next to her. "Are you back to stay, Margaret, or is this just a hello?"

"You asked if I were still single. I need you to know…" she felt him stiffen beside her but waited, quiet. She loved him even more for his silence. "I had been engaged to marry until a few months back. He died…trying to stop a bank holdup."

Adam brushed her check, his smile soft and sad. "I'm very sorry. I mean that." He chuckled as he stood back, giving her space. "So you were able to get over me?"

"No. I believed you'd never have me back. After Philip died, I had to find work, but I thought of you so often."

"And that's why you're here, now?"

"Oh, he's so intent—was he always? Can he read my mind?" she thought to herself. "Let's go back and dance, Adam. I am a little chilly."

They walked back in silence, with Adam's hand on her elbow to keep her from tumbling. At the corral she stopped to stroke a horse's nose, a big bay with a white blaze. She turned to him. "I'd like to stay, Adam, if I thought I had reason to."

* * *

In the moonlight, Adam could see the green in her eyes sparkling with hope, and as he returned the deep intent, felt a shudder pass through him and into her. He pulled her into his arms and gave her the kiss that spelled the longing of the past eight years when he remembered how good he felt with her in his arms.

"Meggie, I want you to stay. I want us to have the chance we lost." He wanted to say so much more, but a sudden fear gripped her. How did she know about the social? Why now?

"I want that, too, Adam. I couldn't believe Joe finding me and inviting me to come. I felt fate taking me by the hand."

Adam took a step back. "Joe?" That three-day trip to Sacramento wasn't about horse trading after all. An elaborate ruse—Adam had spent the day before Joe left going over figures and sales prices for breeds and ages, and even taught Joe his haunches technique. Joe came home empty-handed, and now Adam felt like a fool.

"Yes, your brother. He even gave me stage fare." She wanted to say more, but bit her lip. Adam had tried to clear his mind of sudden negative thoughts but she sensed them anyway. "Oh, I cannot imagine not being here tonight, with you. Does it matter how I got here?"

"Yes. No." Adam stared at the house. "We'll talk more, of course. Let's…let's go back inside, shall we? I'm thirsty for some of that punch." Adam recognized another of those dangerous moments when he could no longer think, only react, but further than that his mind refused to go. He wasn't surprised when Joe and Angela stepped out a second later.

Joe has been watching his every move, all night long. Adam felt sure of that now.

"Well, older brother, looks like you beat me. I hope you saved some of that moonlight."

"There's plenty to go around. If you'll excuse us…" Adam wanted nothing more than to get away from the smirk on Joe's face.

"Are you having a good time, Margaret?"

Adam stepped in front of Margaret. "Don't you think you ought to ask Angela that?"

"What? I'm just being polite."

"Then your priorities are screwed up. Excuse us." He pushed past Joe to the front door, hand firm on Margaret's arm.

"Boy, would you look at that?" Joe laughed to Angela behind Adam's back. "Older brother sure doesn't know how to show his appreciation for a good time."

Adam jumped off the porch and punched Joe in the jaw, not hard enough to knock him to the ground but hard enough to get his attention. He turned back without blinking to Margaret but Joe jumped on Adam's back and pulled him backward to the ground.

Adam believed in this unconscionable moment that he'd been set up, that Margaret didn't come here for him, just as likely to leave again. That kept him punching at a brother who knew enough to take a pounding and give back just as well.

* * *

Angela and Margaret stepped back, wondering whether to run inside for help, drawing unwanted but perhaps necessary attention to the brothers' dust and tumble argument, or try to break them up themselves. Margaret had the anxious feeling she caused this, and Angela thought Joe had maybe had a beating coming. They watched with varying degrees of helplessness and excitement, uttering occasional "don't, please," but otherwise figuring they'd stop soon enough. After all, they were brothers.

But as Joe and Adam fought the girls sensed this as more intense than usual, neither wanting to give, neither quite sure of their reasons, but getting madder as the pain intensified, neither meaning to cause harm to the other but instead reacting as part of a runaway freight they no longer controlled.

After what seemed to the girls an eternity, Hoss and Ben ran out, followed by party guests including Sam Clemens with his ever-handy notebook and pencil. Hoss ran between Joe and Adam and tore them apart and Ben grabbed Adam's arm when he could, as Adam didn't look near finished.

"All right, boys, you better have a good reason for breaking up the partying this way."

"Ask Adam, Pa, he threw the first punch." Joe wiped at the blood on his mouth and nose.

"Adam?" Ben turned his son to face him but at first Adam seemed distant, as though having escaped to somewhere far away. "Adam! Was there an argument that couldn't wait?"

Adam ignored his bloody mouth and cheek and looked behind him as though suddenly realizing where he was. Fear crossed his face when he saw people staring. His shoulder slumped as his head dropped to his chest. "I'm sorry, Pa. Please... extend my apologies to everyone."

He broke away from Ben and walked into the darkness, swallowed by the night and his own hurt pride.

"All right, what did you say to him, Little Joe?" Hoss shook Joe's arm.

"Oh, stop being a bully. I didn't say anything." Joe turned to Margaret. "Did you hear me say anything?"

Margaret looked into the darkness after Adam. "I'm...not sure..." and she ran off in the direction Adam disappeared.

Angela put a hand on Joe's arm. "Don't you worry none, Little Joe. Your brother already apologized. Let's go back inside, you could use some punch." She giggled. "I mean, something to drink."

Joe gave his pa a lopsided grin and nodded to several of the guests as Angela led him back inside.

* * *

Hoss started to follow, but Ben stood looking out into the dark where Adam disappeared. *So unhappy...so very...*Hoss grabbed his arm.

"Come on, Pa, you know how they are. The social ain't ruined, lest you want it to be. I ain't got all my dancin' done yet." Hoss, seeing his Pa not ready to budge, turned back to the guests and reassured them that there was still time left for food and dancing.

Ben listened but could hear nothing of Adam and Margaret. He wished, on the brightest star this night, that Adam could be more open about the pain he carried as part and parcel of his life. They shared a lot of experiences together but Adam was a different kind of person, sometimes so different that Ben couldn't figure him out. Not like a boy he raised but a boy who raised himself and alone, too.

Perhaps Adam learned Margaret agreed to be his dance partner for the night and nothing more. Ben thought that a little light romance could be good for him. Now he feared Adam's feelings for Margaret had been more intense than anyone, including Margaret, knew.

CHAPTER 6

Once inside, Hoss waved at the fellows to start playing. The fiddle and harmonica began to wail a hesitant waltz. But Hoss grabbed some punch to wash the dirt and memories of the fight from his mouth. He felt particularly dry and not in the mood for talking to Sam Clemens, who came over to him.

"I heard of a fellow who had five brothers. He got along with all but one of 'em. Not bad odds. But that one, whew! They couldn't look at each other without coming to blows."

"You ain't gonna print this in the paper, are you?"

Sam scratched his chin, as though thinking. "Well, you know, I always like a good story, even if I have to make one up. But what strikes me as peculiar is two brothers fighting over two different gals. Truth is often too strange to believe." He laughed, and Hoss couldn't help but join in. Sam, still laughing, got himself a punch glass and filled it with two scoops, just a little too full. He splashed some of the red liquid down his red wool vest. He got out a hankie and wiped at the spot that blended well and disappeared quickly. "Curious about that Adam. I never thought him as someone who couldn't hold his punch."

Ben slapped a hand on Sam's shoulder from behind. "Not telling him about your ghost, I hope, Hoss." Noting Hoss's dismayed expression over Sam's quick interest in another potential story, Ben moved in further between them. "Sam, I wasn't sure you'd get the invite I sent in time. I'm glad to thank you for coming."

"Please, Mark Twain, remember? I do tend to come and go a lot. Part of the territory, gathering news. No one wants to come to me, after all. Now about this ghost…."

But Hoss had slipped away to ask Lizzie to dance. The last thing he wanted was more gossip in the paper, especially about him.

* * *

"Adam, wait!"

Adam had settled back on the swooning bench, figuring to let her catch him. He couldn't go back to the social and was glad at least that she thought enough to come to him. Maybe something could be salvaged of the night, after all. At least she didn't see him as a total villain, or she'd be halfway home by now.He didn't like losing control, not in public and that's just what he did. He could explain his feelings away, rationalize each and every mood, but rarely saw a point in the exercise. He had to understand, too. And when Margaret sat next to him, Adam realized he *did* understand. He needed her. He needed to be married, to have a family, to be a part of something that he could lay claim to and not say "yes Pa" and "no Pa" the rest of his life. He wanted all of that with Margaret. But when he found out Joe's involvement, he feared this was all just a game. He didn't trust Margaret, he realized. Trust takes time.

"Adam, I think you misunderstood. Can I explain?" She put a hand on his arm.

Adam cocked his head at her. "I'm glad you're willing to, after the way I behaved." He leaned close, pressing her hard, willing her into his arms. "What have I misunderstood?"

She didn't back away. "I came…not *knowing* if you'd have me, but because Joe told me that you *might.*" She kissed him and he responded, not feeling the pain in his lip at all.

Margaret broke away with a small giggle and pulled out a hanky. She touched a corner of the cloth to her tongue and dabbed at his swollen cheek. "I'm sorry you got the wrong idea."

"Forget it. Bad timing and a little moon madness, that's all." Adam wrapped his arms around her. "You think we have one—a future? I'm ready, if you are."

"Oh, I am." She couldn't stop the shudder that threatened to tear her from his arms. "But there is something you need to know. Why I didn't come back years ago, on my own."

"Tell me and we'll put all that's past behind us. Nothing can be so horrible as to change my mind about you."

"Nothing? I wish that were true. I wish—on the brightest star in the heaven."

Adam felt a real sinking in his stomach but he held her tight and didn't want to let her go, even as he felt her pull away. "Tell me."

Margaret pulled away and wrapped her cape tight as she stood, as though his embrace had made her deathly cold. "I was all of 16 when my father moved me from here. You were older, but no one has ever been so gentle with me, not before…not since."Adam stood, longing to hold her.

"Please. Wait til I'm done. Then, if you still can…" She took a deep breath. "Oh, Adam. I doubt if I would have told you back then, even if I had the chance. We had to move because—I was with child."

Nothing could have prepared Adam for that moment in time. "Not…mine." His legs shook so he sat before she could notice. She had lived far enough away so they didn't even see each other all that much, certainly not at night or in secret. She had someone else even then, even when she pretended to love him.

Margaret laughed but with the opposite of pleasure. "My father's dead now, Adam, and I don't speak ill of the dead. But some things he did—were wrong. I have to live with these memories. I never wanted anyone else to do the same. I could lie to you, but—"

"Where's the child now?" Adam kept every muscle stiff, the desire to hold her gone.

"My father helped me deliver. And he…told me it was stillborn, buried it before I could see. On his deathbed, last year, he admitted…" she threw a hateful scream to the moon. "He told me he'd smothered it."

Adam supposed the dark enabled her to be so completely open, and also the dark that made his vision of her story that much more terrible. He felt as though everything he had just exploded and burned a hole into the ground. "Your…father…"

"Oh, I hated him after he raped me, hated him with everything I had. But I had nowhere else to turn. I had to stay with him."

Adam stood, staggered, caught himself. "No. You're saying…but…he…and my father …were good friends."

"Father had a lot of friends. That doesn't change the—"

"I don't believe a word of that story." Adam fought a sudden desire to leave.

"Adam, please."

"Margaret, you've concocted a brilliant story, but that's all. You come here on Joe's invitation to have a little fun but you had no intention of starting up with me now. This little story is your farce to keep me at a distance. Well, you can just go back and tell Joe…tell him he's won the wager. I'm through." Adam walked off into the darkness, leaving her behind on the bench to weep.

* * *

Glad he was, too, for the dark—he didn't much care to be seen on foot.

"Something throw ya?"

"Ya, a two-legged varmint this time."

For no reason Adam thought of the time Joe bought only one spur and used the rest of his money on sweetening. He told Pa after a verbal thrashing that he figured the other side of the horse would keep up. Adam allowed himself a brief chuckle remembering Joe's face when they told him one spur made him look like a sheepherder.[5] But laughter died a painful death. Same as a horse was a heart. Poke one end and feel the poking all over.

No family memory blocked that of how much he had loved Margaret once, feelings that had come back in an instant when she walked through that door. And to find out now, that even after he'd held her all those times eight years ago, that she could have been warm from her father's inappropriate advances…he felt little now but complete horror and disgust for all humankind. *Not a lie? Then she needs me…* but he kept walking.

He could go after her in the morning. When they could both see straight ahead again.

If he had known about her he never would have fought with Joe, but she had left him so sudden back then. She had meant so much to him, and he thought he meant as much to her. Why couldn't she have told him this years ago? What a difference this revelation could have made back then. Before all the hate set in.

Although, as Adam continued to walk to nowhere in particular, dodging trees and keeping his footing with the ease of the familiar in the slopped gravel trail, he wondered how he might have taken the truth back then—would he have killed her father?

Looking at the stars Adam guessed the time at around 2 a.m. but he didn't feel the slightest bit tired. Still, walking into the hills this way without a gun could invite trouble. Pa mentioned slavers and runaway slaves could be moving through these parts. If he had half the brains he professed to have, he'd head back. But that would call for explanations to a lot of people. Those darned socials sometimes lasted to dawn.

Adam squatted on the trail and looked up. The way the trees bent here gave him a clear idea of where he was. There would be the small cave not far from here where he and the boys played when Joe was little. Getting out from under the moonlight might just help him think.

He started to stand but a sudden rustling noise dropped him back down. Not quite like that of a horse, even though he had met some men foolish enough to take these hills at night. The difficulty was not so much in the horse's night vision. He trusted his horse enough times in the desert at night. But branches of trees seemed to come out of nowhere. No, that rustling sounded more like a bear, or elk.

Adam waited, holding still, but the critter must have moved on. He groped on the ground for a big stick, the best he could do for defense on short notice.

Served him right if he got into trouble. But he'd been there before. Mysterious old town, Trouble was—like a mirage in the desert, coming out of nowhere. Better to take his chances here than back at home. Things would look clearer in the morning. Always did.

He found the cave and crawled inside. "Can't look much worse."

CHAPTER 7

"Tobias! You can't leave us!"

His sister's voice seemed to follow him everywhere, bouncing off rocks and springing through trees like a nymph of evil. He had to leave her and her children behind but Jesse was old enough to protect them and, besides, separately they had a better chance of each making contact. He couldn't tell Sadie that—when he tried, she accused him of cowardice. Certainly he had a better chance alone, when he could run like the wind and had to, with that posse so close on their trail. Split up, one of them had better chance to get to a Cartwright. Split up, they had a better chance of getting away.

Tobias Wentworth ran as though the wings of his feet were like the wild mustangs he saw in the mountain plains here. He ran through the vague moonlight, looking both for warmth and a safe haven for the night. He felt the exhaustion in his pores but his mind kept his body racing, often tripping, slipping on the loose gritty sand or falling down the rocky terrain that had little mercy on unaccustomed ankles or eyesight groping for way through the dark. The bleeding on his arm had quit, anyhow, but they had got that close to him once, and that meant they were still back there, somewhere. He didn't have much time left.

They had been arguing too much anyway, four Negro runaways who, even in Lincoln's world, couldn't agree on anything. They may not agree together but separately they had the same idea. They had had good lives in New Orleans, but the war changed all that and now others must hear the truth. But just what was the truth, Tobias asked her. Do *we* even know?

Didn't matter anymore. They all knew the risks they had taken by running. Jumping ship two months back had been an unnatural reaction to Butler, to the Republicans and Union army control of their southern town—and especially against Lincoln, who Tobias came to see as the biggest outlaw of all. Tobias didn't see himself as being political. He only wanted the chance to live and work and eat same as anyone else. Not be sent away like he wasn't good enough to be an American. Sadie wanted something else, but he still couldn't figure out what. He only knew she wanted to get Lincoln's attention every bit as much as he, and others in his network.

From Utah, where the posse got on their trail, they found their way here thanks to some kind folk who knew these Cartwrights, and even agreed that they *were* the ones to help. Tobias knew those folk, who wouldn't give him their names, likely said that to be shut of pesky runaways. He wasn't born his mama's fool. But they knew the Cartwrights way over there in Nevada, so Darcy couldn't by lying as Tobias feared—these Cartwrights would be able to help, somehow.

Tobias had gotten used to hunting prey in the night, as at night slaves were allowed to find supplemental food for themselves. Still, seeing the man walk through the trees as though for no other purpose but self-contemplation had to be a gift from God. Who but a Cartwright would be walking on this land at this time of night, without any sign of physical distress? Tobias crouched behind a rock and watched, stealth his best weapon. And, keeping his distance, he followed the lone figure as potential salvation.

Tobias never fooled himself, not in this world, this white-man's world. He couldn't hide his skin color, not even in the black of night, and no matter who he was, no white man could ever really be trusted. Not even these Cartwrights. He thought the Republicans were going to end slavery. But now, what they had in store for the black man could be ten times worse than plantation work, work his daddy did, and his daddy's daddy. Getting a chance to choose his own line of work, without any slave obligation, that had been an exciting idea, at first—getting educated, being free to go wherever he chose—but promises were made that, perhaps he alone knew, weren't going to be kept.

Lincoln was no better than any of 'em—him and his whole Republican party, acting so high and mighty. All along Lincoln just wants to send them away, like they were immigrants who took a wrong turn somewhere! He thinks they can't learn to live equal with whites! Tobias's grandpa grew up here, and he wasn't about to be sent to some black colony somewhere just because his skin color made him fit for a certain kind of weather. The solution for the slaves being freed, who ran for protection to the Union Army—send them back to Africa!? Or some island called…Hayti?[6]

Tobias stopped and froze—the man he followed had stopped and listened, as though knowing someone was out there. This had to be a Cartwright, so close to where they were told they'd find the Ponderosa, and so alert to the goings-on around him, like he knew any sound out of place. Certainly not a slaver…that made him someone Tobias could potentially trust. He had little choice anymore, out here, alone.

Tobias figured, because Tobias liked to figure, that the North would not stop with the freed Negroes. Pretty soon, all citizens will be slaves to the government, with the big politicians telling them only what they want to hear. Like if him and his brothers were given their own plot of land and told they could control what they grew *after* they paid the rent of the land, and then finding out that no matter how much they grew they had nothing left after paying the rent on the land, which went up every time they grew more.

He watched as the man hesitated in front of the cave. A man dressed in party duds, oddly enough, in some kind of state to make him walk so far alone, at night, all dressed up. Sure enough, he crawled into the cave. Tobias waited until he nearly fell asleep himself...and crawled into the cave, too.

* * *

More rumors from the underground, sir—a plot to kill you.

President Abraham Lincoln stood in front of the heavy oak doors, closed now, with his shoulders slumped, trying hard to catch his breath. He didn't believe in rumors. Besides, dying now might be a blessing. *Just another casualty of war.*

Still, there were some who were going to make his life miserable, listening to rumors.

In the Red Room on the other side of those doors sat his wife Mary and four other people, all anxious to make contact with dead loved ones. He agreed just to pacify a wife who nearly lost her mind after Willie died—half a year ago? Felt like yesterday. So many dying. How could he deny God one of his own? But he missed Willie, too, a fact that Mary seemed unwilling to comprehend, too wrapped in her own grief that she won't even let him talk about his son. Memories help. But he kept them inside. Just as he had to keep his grief for all those dead soldiers inside (*numbers...more than Lee...we can lose more than Lee*). Keeping those dead soldiers buried inside him, way down deep. So he wouldn't go insane, too.

He couldn't find the energy to open the door. He wanted sleep bad, and ran here to escape another score of endless meetings. Mary needed his support, he told himself.

*That big gorilla...trying to win a war without supporting his army...*General McClellan's words rang in his ears, too, as well as his own, and scores of advisors, but Mac's words weren't distorted by traveling the war circuit because Lincoln knew just how Mac felt about him. Sure, Lincoln knew he had no real war experience, except for some militia work during the Black Hawk War in Illinois. Fortunately for Mac, Lincoln could look beyond his insolence to expect results. Lack of results he could *not* ignore.

McClellan, once so full of hope, had become insolent and slow to move his army, but even *he* didn't cause Lincoln's sleepless nights. Rumor swept through the White House that the war, and his recent Emancipation Proclamation, were merely political—wear down the Union troops and the public, and the North would be forced to compromise with Southern Rebels, as rumors say he's wanted, all along.[7]

He couldn't compromise, not even should they threaten his life, not on whether or not the country should be re-united. Other things, maybe. He could compromise on what to do with the Negroes. He never wanted to destroy slavery. But Lincoln couldn't have his presidency, the first Republican presidency, go down in history as the one that tore this country in half. Oh, those European bullies would love to see the United States become another Europe. They're still sore over Washington and the Revolution.

But now, more than a year after he'd ordered support sent to Fort Sumter that prompted the firing by the South, Lincoln felt as resolute as ever. This war was the right thing—for the railroads, western settlement, for the progress of the Nation! His Emancipation Proclamation will be the perfect tool to prevent the South from gaining the border states like Kentucky and Tennessee. Might even bring a few Confederate states back into the Union, like little lost sheep glad to see the herder. The war could be over by Christmas, as each southern state, one at a time, crawled back to Union to protect slavery. How they scoffed at him—*you ain't freeing no blacks, Abe! You's just freeing those you can't control in rebellion. And they knows it.* Could still work, he figured. He even added the part about compensating everyone after the war for the slaves they'd lost. Surely some of the Rebel states will return to the Union before January 1st.

But then, he thought offering to pay $500 for each released slave in the border states would work, too. A nice easy plan to make slavery end over the next twenty years, rather than all at once.[8] That could be a disaster, all at once, to a people not prepared.

The doors flew open and Lincoln, leaning, dropped his gangly frame onto the small quivering one of his wife's.

"You haven't changed your mind, have you?" She whispered, almost in tears, as she pushed him back up to his feet.

Lincoln put his warm hand on her shoulder. "Of course not. But I warn you, Mary, dear, I am only curious to see how this works, not believing you can make a toad out of water."

Mrs. Lincoln wheeled around and went back to the odd assortment of people at the table, the one man rising as Lincoln walked in. A round table had been placed over the round floor design, as though to double some kind of energy, and centered under the chandelier above.

Lincoln stared at the chandelier a moment. If he believed, he might have found the idea of sitting below something that could swing and fall a bit dangerous. The other, and more delicate, furniture had been moved aside and six chairs, from his council chambers, no doubt, had been placed around the table. He didn't recognize the table. He noticed a low burning fire in the fireplace and wished the grating could be placed a little closer to those flames, and then chided himself—*I don't believe in this nonsense.* But the eyes in the portraits around him watched him sit down.

Lincoln hoped he could concentrate. He had a scoundrel to catch, a live one operating in his White House, trying to belittle his program and his war by sending out information to the South. And those underground threats kept reminding him of his mortality, a more disturbing thought as he sat waiting to hear these people make contact with the spirit world.

He grinned and nodded at the people around him as Mary introduced them. When invited, he grasped the hands of those on either side.

"Yes, I'd like to see Willie, too," he said when asked if he believed.

Until he found that gopher's hole and drowned the little varmint, a lot more people were going to suffer, and more battles lost. McClellan was, as he has been reminded by his abolitionist cabinet, a Democrat. Who better to sacrifice as a gopher?

Once Lincoln thought that slavery could be cured by time, and that he would never be able to find another solution than time, should he live to be 100.[9] Now he'd torn even the Republican party apart by declaring slaves in the rebellion states to be free, but not in the free states. What kind of man was he? He answered to some people but not to all—but there wasn't any way to answer to all. Not in a world as divisive as this. He could do what he could do. He was a man, not a god.

If nothing else, he had to be a man of his word—or at least, appear to be.

As he closed his eyes, the ghosts of a thousand dead soldiers came for him.

* * *

All the guests were gone. Hoss wasn't tired so he tidied up some, which would put Hop Sing in a better mood come breakfast. He thought maybe he and Adam could have a little alone time—odd enough he wasn't back yet. Hoss thought to go out in another minute or two and look for him. He found some of the best leftovers were no longer good in the morning so he made short work of the food left in pans. The scraps of food from plates he dumped into the big bucket outside the kitchen door, fastening the lid on good and tight to keep the wild animals out.

Truth be known, Lizzie hadn't been as receptive as he'd hoped and he felt too frustrated and anxious to sleep. He didn't expect to give up on her, but he thought to work on his romancing skills a little further. He knew he had some because he's hung out with his brothers long enough. Some of their romancing must have rubbed off. Like helping ole' Hank woo Abigail, or the time Joe found a refined young lady in Carson City who had sworn to have nothing to do with a cowboy. Joe let Hoss sit at a different table in the restaurant to watch on his first, and only, date with her. Oh, Joe had done a fine fancy job in holding her hand and minding his manners and wearing his napkin but the next day she ran off with the town's opera singer.

Hoss thought he'd imagined the rap at the door. Much too late for visitors and Adam wouldn't knock. Figuring his older brother big enough to take care of himself, Hoss figured himself beyond sleepy. He blew out the remaining lanterns and headed for the stairs.

"Hello," a soft voice whispered at him.

"Hello," he answered back without thinking. And then stopped, swallowed nervously and looked over his shoulder. "Hello?"

"Yes, it's me." She stood in front of the fireplace, lit by the vague glow of dying embers. As Hoss fumbled to light a lantern she looked around. "Lydia." She walked over to the grandfather clock and brushed the glass face with her fingertips. "I hope you don't mind I came in. Your door was…"

"We don't much lock it." Hoss held up the lantern and walked over to the woman he'd met so briefly that he thought he'd imagined her. "Where'd you go before? You said you was in trouble and then you just…!"

"I'm sorry. But I have to be careful. If anyone else knows I'm here, I won't survive." Her dark hair glistened with streaks of red in the candlelight, which also made her face appear two shades lighter with embarrassment, in contrast to her ease of appearing right at home.

"Won't survive? Is that what made you skittish last time? You done ate and went outside and I thought you'd be right back and I went out to look but—"

"Shhhhh, don't tell anyone." She leaned close. "My husband's trying to kill me."

"Huh?"

"Poison." She walked to the back of the settee and stopped, as though she'd found someone standing in her way.

"Oh." Hoss scratched his head and grinned. "Ah, you're just funnin'. Why, poison will make you sick, or kill you right off."

"I'm tired of running so would you mind hiding me here?"

"Hide?"

"I know things he's done, bad things, things he doesn't want anyone to find out. When I told him I couldn't be married to him anymore, well, he took that as an excuse to kill me."

"But you got away."

"Did I?' She cast a dreamy look to the fireplace, and for a moment Hoss thought she forgot that he existed. "Oh, yes! And when he finds out, he'll be coming. Please." She laid warm arms against his chest, her fingertips brushing his neck and chin, her lips beckoningly close. "You're so big and strong. You can keep him from hurting anyone, I know you can."

Hoss backed away. "Yeah, but only if I know that you ain't just funnin'. Maybe you oughta tell me ever-thing straight from the start."

"Oh!" She yawned. "But it's late, and I'm sleepy. Could you at least allow me to spend the night? I'll feel so much better in the morning."

Hoss was about to tell her it was both early and morning when something thumped from behind him. Hop Sing had bumped into a chair, his eyes half open.

"Mr. Hoss! You do cleaning? I clean."

"Yeah, I know, Hop Sing, I'm plum sorry to wake you." But Hoss didn't think he made noise. "We have this lady…from the social and I was gonna let her sleep here."

Hop Sing looked around. "Where she is? I turn down bed."

Hoss in a frantic panic circled the room. "Where'd she go?"

Hop Sing peeked into the guest room while Hoss ran upstairs. He came back down, puzzled, while Hop Sing checked the kitchen.

When Hop Sing came back out, his round face had stretched into a quirky grin. "Mr. Hoss sleepee in his walk."

"No, Hop Sing, that's not…hey, what woke you, anyhow?"

"I hear noise."

"Like talkin'?"

"Not Hoss noise. Noise, like…baby make. A wailing sadness."

"Ya see, she *was* here! That was probably her cryin' before she came in." Hoss frowned. "Except I didn't hear her wailin' and her eyes didn't look red or nothing."

"How she disappear so qlick? She dead lady?"

"Huh?"

"She say what she want from you?"

"From me?"

"When dead lady walk, they request favor. If you talk dead lady, you must do favor. You don't do favor, they take you."

"Now, Hop Sing, she weren't no ghost. You're just trying to scare me."

Hop Sing looked around the room and leaned to Hoss. "Where she now?"

Hoss, startled, tried to laugh. "Oh, ha, you think, that she would, that she is…" He slapped a heavy hand over his eyes and sat on the settee. "Oh Lordy."

"Not to wolly, Mr. Hoss. My family hap for generation deal with dead Chinamen. They all same like live Chinamen. No mystery.[10] I hep you. Tell me everything she say."

Chapter 8

Frank blinked into the dawn's sun and pulled himself up on his elbows. He had been stretched out in the granite sand, his head wedged consolingly between two rocks, where he'd slept off another drunken night. But for a brief moment after waking he thought he was standing. Instead he'd fallen on a pretty steep incline, and only his head wedged in rocks kept him from sliding farther down. Every morning, another odd position. Every morning, another hangover and empty pockets. He had to stop this cycle of destruction but didn't know how. He knew he could win some of those poker hands if he didn't get drunk so quick. Every night he'd tell himself, just one shot, and every night, that one led to too many more.

He had promised Adam, but an empty promise, sure. He couldn't. Not alone. If he told Adam the truth, he'd have been sent packing right off. But unless he got that money back, he was dead anyhow, and then what? Gambling was the only way he knew to make the big pot quick, and damn, they kept that whiskey cheap.

At the sound of horses behind him Frank scrambled to safety off the trail. Four men on horses and two more driving two wagons came pounding down the road the Cartwrights had worn and graded through the Ponderosa. They came to the crossroad that led to Carson City, the one that Frank didn't remember taking last night, and slowed to a stop. One of the men jumped down and studied the ground.

"I think they split up. That's the best I can make of this trail, anyway."

"Never were much at reading signs, were you?"

"Come on, no time for that now. We have to split, too. I think one of 'em has taken off in that direction, leaving the other three to fend for themselves."

Frank peeked over the rock and ducked back down, holding his breath. From what he could see, two were off their horses and studying the ground.

"They're just a bunch of coloreds. No one's gonna listen to them."

Even at this distance the man's voice carried, like cannon thunder.

"Besides, they won't last long out here anyhow. We got southern boys in every town, most of 'em itchin' to do in a colored."

Frank didn't much cotton to the Irish, but understood his feelings toward freeing Negroes.

"Maybe the woman bitch and her young ones, but the older fellow, he's dangerous. And he's tricky. We gotta stop him, for sure."

"Too bad that bullet didn't do it."

"Ah, we was too far off."

"Well, if we get *them*, we can hold 'em til he turns himself in."

"Like hostages."

"Yeah."

"We'll make camp with the wagons and let the four of you move after them. Better get 'em before nightfall. If we lose 'em we're all in trouble."

The four horsemen rode off, splitting two ways, one in one direction, the other three in the other, while the two wagons moved toward the arroyo where they'd have a quiet camp away from prying eyes. Frank thought about getting the Cartwrights, but they might ask him too many questions he couldn't answer.

Besides, the law frowned on meddling with slavers. He was in enough trouble already.

* * *

Adam wasn't sure he'd slept, but felt slow sunrise light the cave. He winced, rubbed at his itchy stubble, and rolled over, not sure if he was dreaming. Sure enough, he could see outlines of the trees beyond the cave's ragged small opening. He'd gotten himself into situations before but nothing like this, at least not since he was 18. To wander away from a crowded house and stay out all night? How could he lose this much control?

Sure, Margaret had told him a terrible story. And he let her down by walking away. He didn't believe Margaret would lie, not about something that horrible. And that was the problem, hearing that, so plain and clear, and from a woman he loved—and had hated, for all the wrong reasons. She didn't abandon him. She ran in fear of her life. If only she had told him back then, he could have done…something.

He kept his hand fisted over his eyes. Still and all, while knowing better, he let his emotions rule his common sense. Ever since getting lost in the desert and tangling with that maniac miner, Kane…but no, he had a tendency to get riled before Kane. Just that…since that time in the desert, emotions tended to burn through his mind to the back of his eyes, blinding him. Whenever possible since then, he avoided confrontation for fear of what might snap inside him. He had come to terms with what happened, but like Pa says, some things are bound to have a lingering effect.

Margaret had been trying to show him that she felt the same about him by being honest and trusting him. He let her down.

I know I'm human, Pa, I make mistakes.

Problem was, he wanted a wife *and* a family. He was long past due. But would Margaret even want children now?

Pa met his wives far from here. The best thing for him would be to get far away, for awhile. Maybe head to New England for the winter. Not any warmer than here, but at least, far from here, and far enough from war madness.

He heard a snorting sound and sat up. Something, someone, was in here with him.

* * *

Five men sat around a blazing campfire, finishing the last of their morning coffee.

Marv picked up a pine needle and broke it apart between his fingers. "We better tend this fire careful, this area ain't seen rain in a year of Tuesdays." He spoke with a thick Texas accent that tended to surprise folk, as he was small of stature and sported a round belly. He wouldn't have lasted two minutes at the Alamo, thought people who'd met him.

The men had been on the road a long time. The trail showed on their faces and in their clothes. They fancied themselves government officials and military men but their look and demeanor were more vigilante than legal. Men in the border states, and even Lincoln himself, encouraged the return of runaways — especially those who felt betrayed by northern government ...those with a story to tell. Those who were a threat to national security.[11]

"Oh, like we care." Luke pushed burning embers around with the wet end of a stick in the silence his comment met. "Say, whose land you suppose we're on? Think we're trespassing?"

Cal's throat clearing was a matter of habit but with little effect. He didn't associate his gravelly voice with the near constant smoke he inhaled from cigars. "What if we are?" Cal hadn't shaved since they left Kansas and felt pretty mean. He was tired of trail grub but sheer hatred for their prey kept him going.

"Well, we might get spotted with a fire this big, that's all." Jimmy, new to the business, didn't much like Cal, and took every chance to argue with him. He wasn't happy with this job, but he needed the money to help his ailing pa.

"I don't know how one pack of coloreds can hide so good. Why would anyone give them critters shelter?" Luke tossed another stick into the flames and brushed at the sparks on his sleeve. "Can't believe those three could drop their tracks like that, in the middle of nowhere. Gotta be someone aiding 'em."

"Ah, you're just a lousy tracker," Cal muttered.

Marv laid back. "I doubt if anyone's helping them."

"Why'd Jake go it alone, anyhow?"

"Oh, you know how he is. Wants to be a hero. Rest of us was too hungry to argue, is all."

"Everybody shut up and let me think!" Cal poked at the beans in his pan with his stick. He spilled some of the juice, sending fragrant embers skyward.

Jimmy winced, watching the flames dance. "Somebody's helping 'em. That's right enough."

Luke groaned and kicked Jimmy's feet as he stood."I seen some tracks back there that need checking. I'm gonna have me a look."

Cal nodded. "You do that. Maybe run into Jake, help him out. But don't try and take three of them by yourself. Come back and get support." He reached into his vest pocket and pulled out a worn deck of cards. "Who's got a little left to lose?"

* * *

Joe and Ben met on the stairs the next morning—early enough considering the late night they all had. Joe finished buttoning his shirt, his hair still mussed, as he gave his pa a morose grin. "Pa, Adam didn't come home last night."

Ben looked over his shoulder at the front door. "You're serious? Well, good for him."

"No, he wasn't with Margaret. She left here in tears. But she didn't say why."

"Well, maybe he went after her. Or she after him."

"Could be, I guess. He was pretty mad, though."

Ben knew Adam will do things his way no matter what the rest of them thought. Still, Ben couldn't stop worrying when one of his sons went missing. "He'll send word soon enough. Guess that'll teach us for interfering." He chuckled and shook Joe's shoulder to show he didn't hold Joe responsible.

"Hey, Pa," Joe stopped short before the dining table, bringing Ben close behind him. "No food on the table, and…" he sniffed the air. "You smell that?"

"Nothing's cooking. The air smells like stale partying." Ben walked over to the loft outside the kitchen where Hop Sing slept and pounded. "You up?" He waited until Hop Sing mumbled a response. "Guess he had a bit of a mess after the social last night. Do you know if Hoss is still in bed?"

"Oh yeah, soundly snoring. He was munching on leftovers when I headed up after you."

"Well, breakfast won't be ready for a time yet. Hoss might make it…if you start trying to wake him now."

Joe giggled and sprinted back up the stairs.

Ben heard a rattle in the kitchen and figured on another half hour of hunger, so he put on a coat and stepped outside. The air was clear and crisp in the rising dawn and not a cloud anywhere. After a few chores in the barn related to horses and bug infestation, and a quick check of the grounds for his vagabond eldest son, he went back in the house to see Hoss sitting at the dining table drumming his fingers, as Joe poked a blazing fire that didn't need encouragement.

"Pa, Little Joe here told me Adam didn't come home last night."

"I swear, I didn't know how Adam felt about Margaret. Hoss told me that

41

back when they were young, he planned to marry her, before she ran off, without word. Hoss figured he had high hopes that she came on her own so when he heard what I did…" Joe shrugged.

"Awww, don't be hard on yourself, Little Joe. I agreed to the plan. Thought he wouldn't much care *how* she got here."

Ben grimaced. "I think there's more going on here. Maybe…your brother is taking his single life harder than we thought." After an unintentional frown at Joe, who turned to stare into the glowing logs, Ben sighed. "Now we're going to have to figure out how to mend this fence or lose him for good."

"You think he's took off, Pa?" Hoss didn't want his little brother to feel bad, either, but there were other things to think about.

"Not really. But I'll ride out and have a talk with Margaret. She's staying at the boarding house in Carson City until she can find a place to stay permanent. On the way I'll make note of the driest patches to send the water wagons out. We'll start wetting where we can. Hoss, you and Joe get out there and find Frank, have him help you water the winter herd."

"Ah, Pa, I'd rather stay here today."

"What?"

Hop Sing brought the breakfast out. His presence seemed to give Hoss courage.

"My lady—uh, Hop Sing says she's a ghost—she come visiting after the social." Hoss winced, braced for reactions.

"She not ghost, she phantasm!" Hop Sing hurried over at the mention of last night's spectacle. "Ghost not move furniture."

"Aw, come on, Hop Sing, don't tell me you're buying into Hoss's cock-n-bull story!" Joe stood with a look halfway between tears and laughter.

"Many stolly back in China about reality not like what you see every day. When person die in bad way, they want you find killer. When they die and not get lich burial, they come back. Dead Chinaman all same live Chinaman. No difflence. You bury wrong lay, they come back tell you bury light way. This lady she say, "you go catchee man that kill me!"[12]

Joe slapped his hand over his mouth to trap the laugh when Hop Sing glared at him.

Ben put up a hand. "All right, let's believe, for now, that Hoss did see someone here last night. Hop Sing, did you see her too?"

"No." Sadly. "Not see."

"Pa. I know what you're gonna say."

"No, you don't, Hoss. I don't for a minute think you'd say something like this to get out of work. I was going to ask, if you've seen this…lady…only at night, why do you think you have to stay home during the day?"

Hoss grinned. "Say, you're right. I didn't think you were gonna ask that." But his grin faltered as Ben crossed his arms. "Ah, Hop Sing?"

"Phantasm has otherworld connection to Mr. Hoss. Needs to connect with him when he 'lone. Hoss set trap while Hop Sing awake and we glab!"

"Glab? Ah, grab. Do you think you can grab a...phantasm?" Ben scratched the back of his head, wishing he was riding his horse in a rainstorm rather than have this conversation.

"Well, we can try. Pa, I swear, if she don't show up today, I'll... forget I ever saw her."

Ben frowned. Hoss came up with enough crazy schemes in a year to cost them a dollar or two, but not one of them had been a regrettable experience. There was, of course, always the first time. "All right. Just today. Little Joe, we'll ride together to the logging camp, and then split. I'll find Margaret and you'll find Frank. And Hoss, there is a list of things that need doing around here on my desk. Start doing 'em!"

"Yessir."

* * *

Mark Twain patted his notebook and walked into the saloon. Sam, the saloon keep, waved over at him.

"Hey, Mr. Clemens! What'll you have today?"

"Please, Sam, I told you, Mark Twain. Otherwise, people keep thinking I'm you." He chuckled but Sam looked puzzled. "I'm on duty, so give me one of your short beers and some information."

"Information?" Sam wiped out an empty glass and poured a particularly frothy one. "Sir, Mr. Twain, but I don't know that I know much."

"Not only do you know more than you think, but your word is gospel in town."

"It is?"

"My good man, I have always noted in my travels that the saloon keeper holds a shade higher rank than any other member of society. Your opinion has weight."[13]

"Really?"

"Have I never mentioned this? It is a fault of my own."

Sam leaned on the bar, grinning. "What do you need to know?"

Mark pulled out his notebook. "That Adam Cartwright, how many times a week would you say you throw him out of here for drunkenness? Just a round figure now, on average. Twice a week? Three times?"

"Adam Cartwright? Drunkenness?" Sam laughed so loud everyone in the bar stopped cold and looked at him. Sam lowered his voice and leaned close. "I would say...never."

"Never? Surely you jest." Mark shook his head. "Of course not. Your reputation as a saloon keeper and all. Never." Mark scribbled a few thoughts in his notebook. "Can't hold his liquor then? Maybe knows if he just has one, he gets rowdy?"

"Rowdy?" Sam clamped a hand over his mouth to keep the chuckle horse in the barn. "I'd say he's smashed my saloon a few times, but never without provocation. And he can hold his liquor just fine. What's this digging you're doing?"

Mark scribbled. "I see. Likes to have provocation. And now his brother, Hoss. How often is he given to seeing things?"

"Oh, all the..." Sam frowned. "What kind of thing are you planning on writing?"

Mark hesitated, and then tucked his notebook away. He picked up his beer and drank without stopping all the foam and yellowy liquid. "Ahhh," he said as he put the glass down. "I think that last night I might have witnessed the coming of madness. Thanks for your time, and very weighty opinion."

Mark Twain walked out on the sidewalk and looked at what he'd written. "Great title, too. "Madness among the Prominent Cartwrights.""

CHAPTER 9

A bear? A cougar? Adam didn't like the thought of either. *No quick moves now. There was that sound again. Easy.* He turned his head. At first saw nothing. Then laughed and as quickly frowned. There, curled up near enough to him, as though for protection, another man sleeping in the cave. But not a partygoer, this one. Adam could see that this was a black man, after a moment of staring. Ragged and dirtier than even cave sleeping allowed.

A runaway.

Adam brushed at his clothes as he stared. Definitely running. Appeared to go to some length to hide his skin color. He wore gloves with that ragged coat and had much of his face and head covered. The cave was about the size of a grizzly's den, enough to mother two cubs out of the rain, no bigger, but Adam looked around anyway. No sign of luggage or anyone else with him.

After a moment Adam leaned over and placed a hand on the man's shoulder. "Hey. You."

The man rolled and scrambled to his knees, bumping his head on rock because he forgot where he was. The bruise that would form on his head did not concern him as he eyed Adam, then relaxed. But only for a moment. He grabbed Adam's arm and pulled him as deep into the cave as rock allowed. "You gotta help me."

Adam considered the man's face, a fellow about his age, not much older. "I will, but let's get you to the ranch house first, where you'll be safe—"

Tobias tightened his grip. "Name is Tobias Wentworth, I figure I kin tell I'm a runaway. I runs from New Orleans with family but when they's surrounded by the nigger patrol I slipped away. Barely, too." He showed the patch of red on his arm where blood had dried.

Adam crossed his arms over his chest. Hop Sing says everything happens for a reason—but this? Both of them in the same cave, the same night? "How do you know you can trust me? Or, for that matter, how do I know you're telling the truth?"

"You're Adam Cartwright? I gits a description of you and where to look, but I never figgered to find you out here."

"Yes, I am, but—"

"You coulda been one of your brothers, but I was hoping you is you. Wearing them fancy duds in a cave ain't what I expected."

45

Adam made himself comfortable on a small rock ledge with the feeling this was going to take some time. "Why were you looking for me?"

"They says you the most Union-supporting man in these parts."

"Did you say New Orleans? Who sent you? Was his name Eduard Darcy?"

Instead of answering Tobias crawled toward the sunshine beyond the cave's opening and looked out. "Kin you get us back to your ranch without taking trails?"

"What kind of trouble are you in?"

"What kind?"

"You're not just an average runaway." Adam thought back to the most current slave law. "Seems to me no one has the right to return you to the plantation. You get away and you're free in free territory. Which this is. All I have to do is—"

"And they says you're smart, too."

"You come here with a name and a location…" Adam sighed, eyes closed as he pinched his nose, but the pounding in his head wasn't going anywhere. "I thought you wanted to hurry." He stood behind Tobias, also half upright, in sudden need of sunshine. "I don't have time for games. Follow me to the ranch, or don't." He got on his knees to crawl outside around Tobias's unmoving hunched form. He crawled out of the cave before Tobias could stop him.

Tobias caught up to him squinting into the blinding sun. "What if I tells you that Republicans don't care about us darkies and wants to beat the South so the North can have their railroads go the way they want? And us…us ex-slaves, well, we're going to be sent back."

"Sent back? To Africa?" Adam shook his head. "That's just an ugly rumor started by some northern Democrats to discredit the war."

"But what if they wants to colonize us in other places coz they don't know what else to do with us?"

"Look, everyone knows this war is all political trouble, a madness that no one could stop." Adam stopped when he realized that Tobias told him more than he commonly held as true. "What do you mean, colonize other places?"

Tobias nodded as he checked for signs of trouble around him. "Lincoln don't know what to do wit us when we're freed. So he's gonna send us anyplace that'll take us—Hayti, Cuba, even back to Africa. Adam, I ain't never even been to Africa."

Adam considered this. "I know Senator Doolittle of Wisconsin talked on the idea earlier this year. He said…uh…" Adam had to think a moment. "If blacks were living in the tropics, they would be dominant over whites. The Jeffersonian solution.[14] But that's just talk."

Tobias pulled a well-worn news article out of his pocket. "Here, read this."

"We need to get back…" Adam thought he heard riders but the sound disappeared.

"Jus' read that first. Then you kin argue."

Adam took the newsprint, careful not to rip it more. He read aloud: "But Lincoln said, "Even if slavery were abolished, racial differences and prejudices would remain. Your race suffers very greatly, many of them, by living among us, with ours suffers from your presence. There is an unwillingness on the part of our people, harsh as it may be, for you free colored people to remain among us."[15] Adam stared at the paper. "Dated this August past."

"Back in June, I escaped wit my family off'n the boat in New Orleans. I heard where we was going. We been running," he lowered his voice, "and spreading word about Lincoln."

"New Orleans has been in Union hands since May." Adam sat on a tree stump. "Look, I'm accepting your story, but I don't think the government was behind it. Lincoln may believe…this," he shook the newsprint, "but newspapers have a poor record of getting things right." He handed the paper back. "I don't believe he'd plot to send you all out of the country. As for the North controlling southern resources, I guess that makes sense. I felt that with the slaves free, more factories would be built and railroads would criss-cross the country. Is that a bad thing? The railroads and the settling of the western territories has been hotly contended for some time now. The South wants to keep the country in the dark ages. Sorry. I mean they think we should be farmers and nothing more."

"But is that worth all them boys dying over? All them civilians suffering? What if you could help stop the war, right now?"

"Stop war? What can one man, or two, do?" Adam walked over to the Ponderosa pine, one of the bigger, better shaped trees on their land, one they refused to chop down for that reason. He put a hand on the bark and pressed into the trunk to feel its deeply etched texture, a bit of the stiff bark coming off on his hand. The tree protected itself against the tough natural elements by developing a skin so thick in its adolescence that any twist and turn of the wind could not bring it down. Of course the trusting roots sunk deep into the soil made the most difference as to whether a tree would stand or fall. If the soil loosened too much, the tree didn't stand a chance. People were like that, needing thick skin, deep roots and strong soil to survive. "We can't always approve of what our government does. But we can vote them out, come election time." He leaned against the tree to face Tobias. "This division was coming, even before Lincoln got the Republicans to back him at the Chicago convention. No matter who had been on the northern ticket, southerners wouldn't have allowed a Republican ballot."

"You saying I should let 'em ship me away? Or be instantly freed with no one caring that we ain't educated to be freed?"[16]

"No. You'll need to organize for your own good, for your protection. But keeping the country together, that is a good cause, as is stopping slavery in this country, any way possible. Good noble causes often need bloodshed."

"What about caring for us once we're freed? Lincoln don't want to, so he's sending us away!" Tobias looked into the tree's massive height next to Adam.

"These are justified concerns, which I'm sure they're looking into. They aren't just going to throw you to the wolves of industry." Adam tried to see the top of the tree but the effort made his neck ache.

"You care a lot about other people, doncha, Mr. Cartwright?"

"Yeah. Let's get back to the ranch, eh?" He started walking, but stopped and Tobias came up short behind him. Adam wrapped an arm around Tobias's shoulder. "Ssshhhh."

Tobias stiffened. "You gots a weapon?"

"No. Don't you?"

"No tricks, move easy," said an unfamiliar voice behind them.

Adam contemplated their choices seeing the two men, the slavers, with rifles on them. Not too many options occurred to him. Bluff their way out? He could pretend Tobias belonged to him. Obviously slavers, they were dressed for stealth and travel, on horses that appeared worn, their dress a cross between frontier scout and gentleman army. They did this for a living and were paid darned well. Probably knew Tobias and any story he conjured wouldn't work.

Tobias whispered, "They's not after me cuz I's a runaway. They's after me cuz—"

One pointed at Tobias. "Shut up!" He strode up to Tobias and hit him over the head with his gun barrel, dropping him into silence on the ground.

Adam grabbed the man's arm and jerked him from the horse to the ground, knocking him momentarily senseless. Before he could react to the other man behind him, a hard barrel slammed against the back of Adam's skull as well.

CHAPTER 10

"I have the feeling we'll find Adam just over the next ridge with a filled water wagon." Ben settled on the most hopeful of reasons why Adam didn't come home last night.

Joe's laugh held little of his usual mirth. "I don't know what you did when he was small, Pa, to make him work more than eat."

Ben tried to match Joe's meager attempt at humor. "How do you think Hoss got to be so big? Too much food going to waste." Neither were much good at hiding worry, not when so much can—and does—go wrong out here.

The trail became steep before leveling off. They were headed toward Spooner Lake, the route that led to Carson City. They enjoyed their trips to Virginia City more because the distance meant staying overnight and having a little gambling fun, but for getting supplies Carson City made more sense.

Ben used to tease his boys as they were growing to stand straight, so no one would guess they grew to manhood in slanted hills. This lake area had some level land, some of their best grazing area for the winter herd, and because of that they made sure they had filled the water wagons here, as well as buckets in strategic locations around the lake, because ruined grazing stayed ruined for a year. With the drought, grazing had already spread thin, destroying some of the drier areas. Ben could figure out a lot of things, but never the weather. He told his boys to not even try, but Adam kept looking for ways to conquer its effects.

"Joe, look at that. Are you seeing footprints?" Ben reined and alighted to get a closer look. "Who on earth would go through this area on foot?" He pulled his horse to a tree. "Joe, let's follow these tracks. Leave the horses here."

"Something wrong, Pa?" The two men walked with their horses behind them to follow the human footprints.

"Maybe. Let's hope not."

The tracks faded out as the ground got harder and drier out in the open, but Ben and Joe didn't need them anymore—they could see smoke.

Ben leaped back on his horse. "I'm going back for the water wagon, Joe, you get some of the buckets. We'll have to tackle the fire from two directions."

Joe rode to the lake for the buckets, while Ben made sure the wagon was filled. He left Buck behind as he hand-pulled it to the far western section of the fire. They both had shovels and horse blankets, using anything they could that would help stamp out the blaze, which they could see ran along grazing land and jumped rocks into felled trees and debris.

Joe looked back. Ben waved him to go left as he circled around to the right, a more open location for the water wagon. Then Ben lost sight of Joe altogether in the smoke. Still, Ben figured the two of them could have this small blaze out. As long as the wind didn't pick up.

* * *

Joe threw his bedroll onto a runaway line of fire after hitting the worst of it with the water and then trenched with the shovel, throwing the sand and dirt on the flames. He made several fast-running trips back to the lake to re-fill his buckets but found that a futile effort and kept up the trenching and hit the flames near him with the horse blanket and more dirt.

After what seemed an eternity against a fierce enemy, Joe backed up, gasping. His legs weakened and he fell to his knees. His eyes stung as the heat made every hair on his skin stand on end. The heat and smoke in his lungs with exhaustive effort combined to slow his efforts and destroy the progress he'd made.

Eyes tearing, he looked over where Pa went—the meadow, they had to keep the flames from spreading to the cattle's winter ground! A lot of ground clutter, needles, broken branches, pine cones, dead stumps, dead trees, where the brush grows in oasis clumps. The bare ground fed out but ignited the clumps, making the fire burn hotter, easier to spread. Looked like Pa tried to contain the flames to that area because if the fire spreads beyond, they'd be in for a winter of lean cattle.

Coughing, Joe took off his shirt and hit at the growing flames around him. His hands began to burn but he moved, changed positions, sometimes almost flat on his back, kicking dirt to the fire while on his back to find air enough to keep breathing, but he couldn't move fast enough anymore, hardly able to catch his breath.

As he backed up he realized that this section seemed contained now. Nothing else to burst into flame around him, except maybe his skin, feeling so hot he rolled a few times to make sure he wasn't smoldering, too. Coughing hard, Joe got to his knees and staggered in the direction he saw Pa go, brushing at his flaming hot skin along the way. He stopped to trench in another area that might cause more trouble, but he didn't figure to hold out much longer on his own. Too much smoke. They needed help as the fire spread in two new directions.

"Pa..." Joe peered through the smoke and saw Ben wave at him. Ben had his kerchief around his mouth and he went back to trenching. Joe kept moving toward the figure mostly engulfed by smoke—reality distorted, at times thinking he saw a bear, or a deer.

As he staggered and fell, a bear wrap its massive arms around Ben, and then Ben disappeared.

"Paaaa….." Joe tried to get up again, but tripped over some rocks and nearly passed out. Low on the ground he tried to breathe deep, and with smoke rolling over him he started to crawl, disoriented, not knowing more than just moving forward.

The flames licked against his face as he groped his way to the edge of a cliff. Pa's horse blanket had caught on a tree. Pa was gone. The fire couldn't follow him down that rocky cliff. Joe hung his head over the side and passed out.

* * *

"Mr. Hoss?" Hop Sing crept into Hoss's room.

Hoss sat on the edge of his bed, waiting. He put a finger up to Hop Sing. "Either she's a ghost or she's plum tricky," he whispered. "But I think she's here somewheres."

Hop Sing held a container with some steaming liquid. "Potion made with roots and honey and boiling water make ghost disappear for good."

Hoss stared into the pot. He sniffed and stuck his little finger into the mix. "Hop Sing, that stuff's hot. If she ain't a ghost, she could get hurt."

"It cool down fast."

"'Sides, I ain't so sure I want her to disappear." He walked around the bed, trying to look casual, while still looking at her.

"Mr. Hoss like to be spooked?"

"Huh?"

"That mean…frightened. Nervous. Unsure of own fate."

"Oh, she ain't gonna hurt me, Hop Sing. She just wants help."

"If she ghost, you not trust her."

Hoss looked down at his feet and jammed his hands in his pants pockets. "Whelp, ain't no point sitting here arguing. She ain't here. You got any of the pork pie left?"

"Just enough for you, Mr. Hoss."

At the thought of food, Hoss burst from the room to the stairs and Hop Sing followed with a careful eye on his potion so that he didn't spill. He didn't expect Hoss to stop so sudden at the top of the stairs. "Ahhhhh!" they said together as Hop Sing ran into Hoss's back and spilled some potion on his shirt.

"Hey, watch it, Hop Sing!" Hoss tried to wipe the hot liquid off his back but couldn't reach. "Good thing I had my vest on."

"And we know you no ghost," Hop Sing said. "Why you stop?"

Hoss pointed down. Lydia stood at the bottom of the stairs, looking as fresh and genuine as a summer rain. "Follow my lead, Hop Sing. If I want you to throw the potion, I'll signal."

"If Hop Sing sense danger, he throw no signal."

Hoss walked down the stairs with Hop Sing right behind, both with eyes glued to the woman they felt could be a threat, or just disappear.

Lydia threw herself into Hoss's arms, appearing to Hop Sing as light as vapor but very real, warm and womanly. He crept closer, into the scent of the most marvelous of San Francisco gardenia gardens.

"Oh, Hoss, all my life I've searched for a man with arms that could protect me, make me feel so safe."

Hop Sing stayed hidden behind Hoss, holding the pot, ready for the first sign of danger... wondering if he'd recognize danger in time. He figured Hoss felt plenty spooked because he shook so much he dropped to a knee, yet Lydia clung so well to him she didn't come near to falling out of his big arms.

"You kin just stay right here until we find this feller and then—" Hoss pulled his big shoulders back and let her snuggle deeper into his chest.

"Oh, yes, please, tell me that I never have to leave you..." As she gazed at him her eyes fluttered and she slumped against him.

"She say never leave you?" Hop Sing scurried around to the front of Hoss and started to pour the water on her but Hoss gave him the fiercest of scowls. Hop Sing whirled around instead and put the pot on the table as Hoss carried her to the guest room.

"Dead lady same as dead Chinaman. Still like live Chinamen." He shook his head and waited for the time to be right to convince Hoss of potential danger, even while knowing the longer he waited, the more Hoss would fall into her spell.

* * *

Smoke swirled around Joe until even the cliff disappeared and Joe couldn't even see his hand, but he called over and over, waiting to hear Pa answer back, or—or was he dreaming? The more he called the more his chest hurt until he felt like his insides were blazing. Maybe Pa wasn't down there, maybe all he saw were illusions and even now he was asleep back home at the ranch.

Joe looked back over his shoulder where the smoke seemed out of control. He'd have to go off the cliff, too. Maybe...his Pa waited for him down there...Joe crawled forward, sending a rumble of rocks down the cliff. But something had his feet, pulling him...a bear, or...

"Pa...you're all right..." but as he laughed he coughed, couldn't breathe and passed out.

CHAPTER 11

Margaret went back to Carson City after the social and waited, wondering if Adam would come for her, wondering, after a day has passed, if Adam would ever come for her. She waited, torn by the desire to stay and the need to go. She had taken everything she had of value from Sacramento, hoping to move here. All foolishness, to think she was the same girl who first loved Adam. They were both different now, and love had changed.

Bearing her quiet room no longer, Margaret ran down, checked for messages at the front desk, and then walked outside, intent on booking a stage to San Francisco. She didn't make it that far. She froze, staring into Ponderosa hills, just as the alert whistle screamed. Men scrambled for their horses, grabbed shovels, blankets—she smelled the air and saw the smoke coming out of the woods high above Carson City.

"The Ponderosa."

She wrapped her arms around a wooden post and stared at the blackened sky. "Adam." He had a reason for not being here. She could wait a little longer, and could pray that he wasn't right now hurt in that fire. But more caring than that she didn't know how to give. Men pushed their way around her, but she didn't move. She knew these folks cared less about the Cartwrights and more about saving their own land in the valley, which, if torched, could destroy this whole town.

With fire and smoke above her, Margaret recognized that these men can love other property because they loved their own. As much as she needed to love someone else, she had to find a way to love herself, first.

* * *

First the jostling wagon shaking him, next the sunlight hitting his eyelids, and then the pain on the back of his skull, but Adam knew where he was and fought to keep still in the semblance of sleep.

"How far we gonna go before we do the nasty deed?"

Adam feigned the unconsciousness to listen, because the "what to do next" didn't want to register in his throbbing head.

"Just over the next ridge, looks like a fine place to dump a body."

A frightened young man and a heavy smoker, from the sounds of two voices. Different two than the ones who knocked them down. He couldn't

53

take down four even without head pain. They just kill someone? Tobias? Or planning to?

Adam blinked, shifted and looked up, allowing them to believe he hadn't heard anything. He moved too quick and whacked his head against the wooden slat of the wagon. The odor of manure forced him to back up a bit, feel his way with eyes shut—boxes, bags, little sitting room. Forcing eyes to open into sunshine Adam saw the ridge they had mentioned, a rocky climb to a parcel of trees, giving a brief vision of the mountain peaks beyond.

Resurgent memories of being a Cartwright, of timbering this section, of the cows that stampeded through here and tested Joe's maturity—Adam fought to keep an impassioned look on his face as he remembered how Joe for the first time figured out how to get five mangy steer to stop running, nearly getting run over in the process. But he had the right idea, all on his own, to stop the lead bull, and that was the main thing. *Stop the lead bull...*

When he saw the cliff where Joe had almost fallen to his death, Adam realized they were headed south and east. He counted five men, all to take a prize of one black slave back to his owners. A black slave with vast political savvy.

"Well, lookie, he's up. I suspect he'll be wanting to pee." Piney gave a cackle that reminded Adam of a leprechaun, for no reason he could think of. He knew he could outrun any of them, and he knew the territory, but escaping to get home on foot without supplies was the farthest idea away from possible hope, even if he did manage to keep from getting shot in the back. Southerners thought little of shooting northerners these days. He could pretend to be a southerner but no southern gentleman would be caught on foot. If they were northerners, operating legally, they might let him go. But then, why take him in the first place? And they sounded like southerners, too.

As he finished sitting Adam heard the clanging shackles they'd clamped on his ankles before recognizing the weight holding him down. Iron chains—like a common slave.

"Hey!" Adam saw Tobias curled up on the other side of the wagon. He hadn't stirred. Bracing himself for an inevitable outcome, Adam turned to one of the men riding alongside the wagon. "Where you taking me? What right you got?" He forced a kind of ignorant talk, to be ready to play his hand in either direction.

A rider, chewing on a cigar with a thin trail of smoke, pulled up next to him. "Okay, look, buddy, you just got yourself in the wrong place at the wrong time. We're taking you far enough away and leaving you on foot so that you can't go vigilante and come after us."

No...oh, no. Not again. In near panic, Adam raised his voice a timber. "I was jussa coming home from serving at the governor's party—I's a free man! You got no rights to me! You think I don't know what you are?" Adam waved the shackles at the back of the man driving the wagon. "You can't shackle me, I's a free man." The sun at Adam's back played in his advantage—and the fact that the summer sun already had its way on his dark complexion.

Still, the wagon driver, a Texan by his lingo, eyed Adam a bit too long, making Adam cower in fear. "You mean you're a nigger?"[17]

"I ain't no nigger. I's a free black man. Okay, my momma was white, but she done left me with my Pa. And my Pa worked hard to earn us our freedom."

"Ah, you're just joshing me. You're from the ranch back there."

Adam let his jaw go slack, his mouth gap open. "I was working there—they had a big doings and I was a …You gotta let me go! My master—I mean boss is gonna hide me again!"

"Well, you just wait a little longer, fella, and you'll get your freedom." The Texan hiyahed the team and the wagon moved on.

Adam leaned back and itched at the stubble on his chin. He felt Tobias lean over him.

"Adam, this ain't what kind of help I wanted."

"Titus," Adam growled, his gaze steady on the wagon driver's hunched back. If he had to, he could take that one down, at least, with one well-delivered bunch. "The name's Titus Black." When the time was right. They couldn't keep him shackled *all* the time. Could they? "And your plan might have been to be free a little longer. I was less than helpful there."

Jimmy and Luke, who had ridden ahead, came back at a gallop and surrounded them, guns drawn. Ahead the other wagon stopped to wait, its cargo hole for captive slaves empty.

"All right, what's the holdup? Why'd you stop?"

"Loud-mouth one back there, complaining."

"Oh yeah? Maybe he'd prefer a bullet in the brain instead of being allowed to walk for his life."

"Mebbe. But mebbe he'll fetch us a fine price."

"Huh? *Him* a nigger?"

"Says his mama was a white woman. He's got himself some education, too, from the sounds of his talking."

Luke rode to the wagon and used his drawn gun to force Adam to show a profile. "Got some darkness there, not much. Hair's dark." He reholstered his gun. "That true, boy? Your papa rape a white woman?"

Titus hung his head. "Ain't your concern," he mumbled. He looked up sharply. "And I'm a free man, not your boy!"

Jimmy pulled back on his dancing horse. "I dunno. He looks too white to be a muley."

"Come on, who would pretend to be a nigger who wasn't?"

"He's a nigger, like me," Tobias said with a defiant tone, his shackles rattling in emphasis. "Thought he could turn me in and get hisself like a reward. He don't know the South is hurting for *any* shade of darky right now."

"You're a liar, coon," Titus said without conviction.

"Probably thinks Lincoln is a god," Tobias added, the taste of disgust plain to hear.

"That's right, I do, cuz he is."

"Lincoln's a two-faced phony who jussa soon shoot us blacks as free us."

Titus blinked and then leaped on Tobias, knocking them both out of the wagon. They put on a good show, too, rolling and punching in the dirt, swearing and cussing as the men above them laughed and got on as though taking bets on who would win. Adam never fought with iron shackles before and tended not to duck quick enough to avoid an iron chain in the face, but figured getting a little beat up could work to his advantage. Tobias knew how to work those irons, too.

The more Titus struggled the more Tobias fought back, two niggers as divided against themselves as the country, even as the South was, two runaways running for different reasons but with the same goal, to understand and survive in a world torn apart. Adam forgot who he was and saw what he wanted them to see, a desperate black man believing in Lincoln's offer of freedom—just before feeling a heavy boot on his shoulder, kicking them apart.

"All right you two coons, knock it off before someone sees us out here. Get them loaded and shackle them to each other this time."

Adam sat back and wiped blood from his mouth. He had to fight, really hard, to keep what he thought might be a "muley" expression but he figured even a muley could look angry and beat up, which he was.

"You mean we ain't killing the muley?"

Cal eyed Titus a moment, as the two men sat agreeably near each other trying to appear unconcerned about bruises and blood. Cal spit a wad of tobacco at the mulatto's shoe, just missing. "Nah, he's entertaining enough, and he'll fetch a good enough price—if he lives that long." He pointed his gun at Titus. "Cause any more trouble, and you'll find yourself a free man, all right—permanent."

Before long they were trussed together and the wagon ran apace. Adam overheard they were headed to Kentucky, which made them more likely northerners, but maybe not, and even if he thought he could he wouldn't undo what he'd just done. He'd just leaped onto a runaway train—destination unknown, arrival uncertain. But compared to what he'd just left behind him—definitely stimulating.

Pa had warned him not to get involved. Pa should know—Adam tended to have his own thoughts about what he should and should not do.

* * *

Hoss laid Lydia on the bed. "Hop Sing, get us some water."

Hop Sing, behind Hoss but without potion, poked her in the arm. "She got body."

"Yeah, she's got a body, and it's good and warm, too. I think she's feverish. Now git us some water. Cold this time."

Hop Sing walked out of the room with an eye on Hoss kneeling by the bed. He bumped into the doorframe but didn't go far enough to take his eyes off Hoss. Finally, when Hoss looked back at him, Hop Sing grumbled and disappeared with his pot into the kitchen.

Lydia's eyes blinked as she looked at Hoss. "Oh, thank goodness, I thought this might be just a delicious dream. Please Hoss, you have to hide me. Where can I go to be safe?"

"You'll be safe right here, I promise."

Lydia sat and wrapped her arms around Hoss and kissed him deep and desperate. Hoss tried to pull away because the heat was so intense but Lydia pulled him down into the bed with her, her hands loosening his shirt buttons to caress the hairs on his chest.

Neither saw Hop Sing sneak back in with his potion. Alarmed, Hop Sing threw the entire pot on them both. Fortunately the water potion had cooled some.

Lydia screeched and howled in surprise, right along with Hoss. As Hoss wiped his eyes clear he started to laugh and Lydia joined him.

"Hop Sing, I think we kin say Lydia ain't no ghost."

Lydia's eyes widened in shock, and she covered her mouth as though about to be sick.

Hop Sing shook his head. "Potion not work light in this country. Some ingledients could not find, had to substitute. Need eucalyptus and—"

Hoss grabbed the servant's arm and led him to the kitchen. "Hop Sing, unless'n I tell you different, we are treating this lady like a guest, not a ghost, in our house. Now fix us something to eat."

Hop Sing jerked his arm away and swore at Hoss.

Hoss ran back to the guest room, in a panic fearing she'd be gone. But she sat in bed, having stripped off her dress, and used a dry portion of the bed cover to wipe her arms.

Hoss picked Lydia up. "I'm taking you upstairs, see if I can't find you some dry things to put on."

Hop Sing watched Hoss carry her up the stairs. "A tlicky ghost. But maybe...friendly ghost. Hope for Hoss's sake."

CHAPTER 12

Frank pulled up to the tail end of men riding hard for the Ponderosa to help with the fire. He could pass them all if he chose to, but preferred not to be noticed. He felt pretty sure those slavers had started the fire, a wishful hope on his part because when he's drunk, he often smokes, too. He could make himself a hero by leading the fire fight, and revealing who'd been through here, but Ben Cartwright would still learn that he had gotten away with four head of prime steer to feed a gambling habit, all to pay back a man who was—what? Nothing better than a lazy cowardly deserter trying to blackmail Frank into giving him the location of the entire herd.

He shifted and tightened in the saddle as he felt himself start to slip. Damn loose cinch. The world just appeared a little woozy—didn't mean he was drunk.

* * *

Joe woke coughing, stretched out on his back on the bare ground, surrounded by brush and reeds covering pole frames. He blinked to get the haze out of his eyes. Next to him sat a Washoe woman, wetting a towel, fragment of a blanket. She tried to hold the smelly rag over his eyes. Joe grabbed it from her before getting dizzy and laid back, rag over his eyes.

"What...happened?"

He couldn't understand the answer she gave him. He and his family learned some Paiute but the Washoe spoke somehow different.

"Where's Pa?" She shook her head. "Pa, where's Pa?"

* * *

Hoss tiptoed down the stairs. He glanced back over his shoulder a couple times before he reached bottom. "Hop Sing!" he whispered. "We got a problem."

Hop Sing met Hoss at the stairs, moving so fast and quiet that Hoss thought at first he had become a ghost, too. "Only one?" he mimicked in his best Adam voice.

"I ain't got no good clothes for her. You wanna borrow me some of yours?"

"Bigger problem. Mr. Cartlight and Mr. Joe not home. You go find them, you go now."

"Now?" Hoss looked at the front door. "Aw, Hop Sing, they're probably fine. I wouldn't know where to begin lookin'." He started for the stairs. "Bring me them clothes now, you hear?"

Hop Sing stared at Hoss's back. "Mr. Hoss no think. Mr. Hoss already possess by bewitch spell of spirit."

* * *

"Pa. My father. My...my pa..." Joe took the food and water they offered, but ate too quick and started a coughing fit that lasted a whole minute or even two. Trembling, he got to his feet. "Ben Cartwright. Ponderosa." He stumbled out into the open area where people sat cooking bits of some kind of animal over the fire. He tried to find someone who understood. "Okay, never mind. Just give me a horse, I'll go looking myself."

Several of the older Indian women pulled him to the campfire and made him sit. He couldn't figure out why right off. Various Washoe girls were led to stand in front of him. He gulped—they wanted him to choose one to take home?

Joe scrambled to his feet, shook his head and backed away. He looked for Cochise but couldn't find a horse ready to leap onto. "Listen, I appreciate this, I'd love to be a member of the tribe, really, but I gotta get home, I gotta find my...Pa..."

He ran off, away from the village, stumbled but never looked back.

* * *

Tobias's family, to escape the posse and the fire, had headed straight for the cliff and down, figuring no posse would follow.

"Ma!" Jesse yelled down, watching her and his sister climb down the cliff, another of the many new skills they'd learned on the run. "Is you okay?"

Sadie had her daughter's hand and waved him down.

Sadie watched him turn, thinking he headed down after them. He instead wrapped his arms around someone, or something, a tree perhaps, to keep from falling, but no, there they were, Jesse, with another man, and they were both falling, both...on fire...

* * *

"You's crazy as a mudhouse hen. You can't keep convincing them you's a nigger."

Adam—Titus—had his head back but Tobias didn't think he was sleeping.

Adam didn't look at Tobias but after a moment his mouth curled into a small and reflective smile. "Back when I was in Boston, 1849, there was this married couple, light-skinned folks, light enough to pass for white. They had escaped slavery in Georgia a few years before I met them. She cut her hair off to become a sickly old man going north for treatment accompanied by her servant, who was actually her husband. I met them when they took me in as a boarder for my last year of college. Two agents were sent to recapture them because they had gained some notoriety in Boston." When Adam looked up, for a moment Tobias saw Adam as the muley Titus. Adam's face lost all trace of reflective humor. "The town was—is—very abolitionist and the agents couldn't get to them, but some good people got killed in the attempt. In Boston, though, they vowed to resist the Fugitive Slave Law. Eventually the two agents realized their lives were not safe there and they left.[18] Ellie often passed me off as her nephew."

Tobias shook his head. "I's playing a dangerous game and now you've put yourself smack into it."

"I put *myself* into it?" He gave Tobias a comical smirk. "Well, my other option wasn't so joyful, either. So I help you in New Orleans, instead of here." Adam sat back against the wagon, eyes squeezed tight in pain.

Titus crawled over and sat next to him. "Thinking about your family, ain't ya?"

"They'll wonder. I promised always to leave word...don't know how, this time."

"We'll find a way."

"I can't let them worry." Adam took off a boot. "I always carry writing tools with me." He scratched his chin. "Wish I always carried a razor. Suppose they'll let us shave?"

Tobias patted his pockets, but all he had were news articles. "I got nothing either. Whatcha thinking to do with the boot?"

"I could write a note and throw my boot off to the side of the trail."

Tobias stopped him. "They's gonna make us do a heap amount of walking and such. You'd end up lame."

Adam stared at him, and nodded. He put the boot back on. "A while back I got lost in the desert. My family gave me up for dead, and just by accident found me wandering, out of my head. I couldn't at first get over the experience, and I'm not sure..." he looked off into the hills, as though begging Tobias to care enough to ask him to finish the story.

Tobias did.

When Adam finished the story he added, "I'm not sure they trust me yet."

"Sounds like you needs a chance to prove you gots your head together." They sat in silence, their heads swaying together in time to the jostles of the wagon.

After a time Adam laughed softly. "A few years back, my brothers and I together got in some dumb trouble, and Pa had to come rescue the three of us. We wanted to teach Joe how to round up some wild mustangs, and see how many he could handle alone. Well, he ended up driving them over a cliff—oh, four of them survived, we only shot the one—but Joe and his horse got tangled up and while we rescued him, our horses ran off for home. We couldn't walk that far without food and water, but we weren't about to stand around yacking, so we walked. The early spring sky was cloud-filled and we just got more and more lost. We huddled in a canyon that night, and Hoss, that's the middle brother, he caught us a rabbit but we couldn't build a fire so we…ate it anyway. Joe got himself a bad stomach ache, so Hoss went looking for water and I sat tending him. He told me that if he's gotta die, he's glad we were with him. I didn't like him talking that way and told him so."

"But now you kin understand."

Adam sighed. "Yeah. Better to be with people who care. To this day, I don't know if we ever told him those wild mustangs had been tamed down some by the buyer who'd come through and sold them to us."

"Sorry, Adam, this ain't like I wanted."

"Maybe. Or maybe this is exactly like you planned." Adam shrugged and shifted position to make the chains more comfortable, finally giving up. "Might be worth the risk to prove to you that Lincoln's on your side."

Tobias dug in his pocket. "Look, I got this here other news article here."

"They're gonna hear our chains rattling."

"They get so they only react to certain rattles."

Adam took the news clipping and read quietly:

> *Reckless persons intent on mischief, are trying hard to make political capital by the cry of "nigger." Because a few contrabands are coming north, to seek a temporary refuge from oppression, small pro slavery politicians endeavor to frighten the laboring classes, with the belief, that the negroes [sic] are about to overrun the north, and crowd laboring classes out of their employment. The Chicago* Times *and other Tory papers, are making great efforts to persuade the silly minded, that the north is in immediate danger of becoming Africanized. There are of course a few simple minded people, who can be frightened by such a scare crow; the street corner politicians perceiving this, improve the occasion by repeating the twaddle of the Chicago* Times *and the* Milwaukee News.*
>
> *A more ridiculous idea can scarcely be conceived, than that the negroes have a natural preference for the north. All the facts in case are to the contrary. The negro originally came from the tropics; his physical organization is adapted to the warmer latitudes, and his habits and tastes lead him to prefer the milder climates. Since the progress of the present war, volumes of testimony go to show that the negro has no desire to come north, if he can only be sure of protection on the soil of the south. This testimony not only comes from civilians but from numerous officers of the army, of various political antecedents. Of the thousands of negroes who came into the lines of Gen. Hunter in South Carolina, hardly a dozen asked*

for passports to go north; and even those few, would probably not
have desired to go north, had they apprehended no danger of falling
into the hands of their masters again.[19]

Adam folded the newsprint back up and handed it to Tobias. "Sounds like they don't want any Union soldier to walk off the front line. Don't want them fearing the loss of their jobs when the war is done." He eyed Tobias. "What do you think of Tahoe weather?"

"Oh, fine, just a might chilly—" Tobias laughed, catching on, but covered his mouth.

"Don't feel bad, I think so, too!" Despite themselves, the two men laughed, until the wagon driver told them to shut the hell up.

Adam kept his voice low, encouraged into talking by the loud clacking of the wagon wheels. "Listen, Tobias, I didn't ask to get involved. For the moment I either wear the disguise or die. But you've got me thinking. We need to get to Lincoln and convince him that blacks and whites can live together. He hasn't seen enough proof of that yet. Believing that, with this emancipation proclamation he talks about, why, the rest of the country will have no choice but to follow along."

"You might jus' find out you're wrong about him, too."

Adam gritted his teeth, and stared at the sky as though the only scenery he cared to see. "Huh. Guess so." He looked at the wagon driver's back. "The sooner we get away from these boys, the better, too. Problem with pretending, after awhile it feels real."

He scratched his arm and the chains clanked in agreement.

* * *

Roy Coffee came out of the Virginia City sheriff's office, stretched and yawned. He didn't know why, but sometimes he got to working so late that he just fell asleep at the desk. Chances were old Slim over at the saloon will let him use his facilities to get washed up. He didn't keep any here, except for the prisoners and he'd never stoop to using them.

For rubbing at his eyes to get them to open all the way, Roy stepped into the street and nearly got hit by a team of horses.

"Whoa!"

Roy jumped back and grabbed a post to keep from falling on his backside. "Oh, I beg your pardon."

"I'm terribly sorry, sheriff!" Roy couldn't see anyone around the team of horses.

"Not your fault, I wasn't watching a'tall." A slender, elegant man, dressed in fine Frisco clothing right down to the lack of gravel dust, jumped out of the wagon and ran to his side. "You're sure you're all right?"

"Nary a scratch. Say, you're new to these parts, ain't ya?"

"Yes, sir, Sheriff, I'm just passing through on my way to St. Louis. Thought

I'd take a couple days rest here, if that's all right."

"Well, yeah," Roy studied the man. "But Virginia City is hardly a direct route to Missouri. You had to climb a pretty steep mountain to find us."

The man let out a loud bray of laughter. "Well, that's true! But I got curious over all the mining ventures here and besides, I've got a couple of pretty sturdy old mules here to depend on."

Roy petted the nose of one of the monstrous animals. "You must have bred your mules with elephants."

"Ha! Well, these here are pure working stock, Belgians, we call 'em."

"Interesting. To name working horses after a people who don't much care for the idea."

"Sheriff, I love your sense of humor. I'm part Belgian myself and don't mind at all. I hope you don't mind if I check out the local mines and if perhaps I see opportunity here, I might even decide to forgo the move to St. Louis."

"Papa, are we there?"

Roy barely heard the child's voice but didn't miss the brief look of anger that crossed the man's face.

"Not yet, child, just stay put til I tell you different."

"I didn't catch your name."

"Nor I yours." The man smiled broadly. "I am Stephen Lawe, as in not breaking the. That is my daughter, Jodie."

"Well, you just keep it that way. Where's her mum?"

"Ah, Sheriff, surely you've lived long enough in the West to know how hard life can be on the ladies. I am determined, however, to give my daughter every advantage in the world, so she doesn't succumb to disease as her mother did."

"Well, there's a hotel right over yonder. You go and make that little girl comfortable."

"I thank you kindly, sir."

He jumped back in the wagon, and checked the road way for clearance before tipping his hat and moving on. Roy watched, and sure enough Jodie's head popped up to stare at Roy as they moved away. Roy hoped he imagined the fear in that little girl's eyes.

* * *

Adam felt feisty. He and Hoss and Little Joe (*not so little now, not so...*) had just knocked the heads off three chickens for dinner. At the sight of blood and headless chickens running about he wanted to work off some steam. Killing living things that were like pets didn't seem right to him and so he told Hoss and Joe to get their rifles, he wanted to teach them to hunt some pesky coons. When Joe laughed at the thought of hunting black people Adam threw his weapon aside and tackled Joe to the ground. Joe was just a kid, but before Adam could stop himself, he'd given his brother a bloody nose—

"Titus, wake up...Titus!"

Adam wanted to roll over because once his eyes opened he wasn't going to believe how the world had changed, but the rocking of the wagon made him realize that what he'd done wasn't going away any time soon. He always figured himself to be able to think on his feet and then something comes along and leaves him shaking his head at his own lack of understanding. For that, if nothing else, he was here.

He had been thinking of a trip east anyway, and how often does a man get a free ride? He shuddered with the realization—he couldn't get back home now, even if he tried. *Don't come looking this time, Pa, I can handle it*...and then wondered if that was true, at all. His initial pleasure at adventure dissolved into recognition—this was a helpless situation.

Once upon a time he thought there *was* such a thing as a free black, that a man like Fredrick Douglass would never get himself in a mess like this, so how could he? And yet here he was...with Tobias's hand on his shoulder, shaking him.

"I overhears 'em, we's stopping soon, and you and me, they's gonna make us steal food."

Adam sat, bumping Tobias's arm. "What?"

"Yeah, supplies is getting low, without even feeding you and me."

Adam pursed his lips. Being treated like a runaway. He didn't have the chance to realize what that meant.

"I suppose you ain't never had to steal no food before. Well, I have, and it's not shameful when you's hungry."

"Before I steal, answer me a question. You knew they were looking for you, and yet you didn't warn me how close they were. Darcy tell you to bring me back? This the help he wanted?"

"Mr. Darcy never expect you to claim to be a nigger! You done that alone. He gets us far enough to Nevada at his own risk, and says you are the only folk he knows in western territory what knows money, and you kin talk a skunk into spraying itself, you live in free territory and has influence and kin I convince you to come back with me. Somehow."

"Figures. Darcy never could stand not making trouble for my Pa. But that's not what rankles me."

"What then?"

"You going along with him, to involve people you don't know."

Tobias couldn't meet Adam's angry eyes and looked off into the rolling scenery, now more desert than hills. "Well, his overseer, that's foreman of the plantation, says to Darcy that if any family can see both sides in this here war, they would be the ones to help. So Darcy thinks of you. And we had nowheres better to go anyway."

"None of this is making sense to me, Tobias."

"Adam, these men is northerners. Ask 'em. They's on Lincoln's payroll. That's why they's legal."

Adam sat back. "You're not serious."

"They been chasing me for a time. I know them, right enough."

"If that's the case, then I can tell them who I am." He started to rise, but Tobias put a hand of caution on his arm.

"Don' try. They ain't to be trusted."

Adam eyed Tobias. "Are you hoping the South will win? Remain a separate country? Do you want to stay a slave?"

"No!" Tobias lowered his voice. "You gotta believe I believe in being freed. But not this way. Not being kicked out of a country because they don't want to take the time to educate me first. That ain't my kind of freedom."

"I guess not."

"Ah," Tobias thought a moment. "Something else, too."

"What now?"

"Well, them Republicans. They's making Lincoln do whatever the railroad bosses tell him to do. He's gotta have more guts than that. Stand up for what he believe. Unless sending us away *is* what he believe."

Adam remembered Kudwa, whose people would council and talk and not make any action until all had agreed on the course to take. The decision always ended being the one best suited to help the people to survive. Adam figured his government felt the railroad was the best way to help the country survive. "Well, from what I can tell, a politician is what his political party is." But every law the South opposed before secession, Lincoln has now signed into law. Did that mean this war was being fought for all the wrong reasons?

"Adam, these is facts I'm preaching, not fairy tales. By getting the South to secede, the North got what it wanted, and soon will have the South, too! What kind of thinking man would run for president knowing that the South won't even put his name on the ballot? The South had to secede when Lincoln was elected. They had no choice."

Adam watched Tobias with surprise. "You *are* well read. Sorry, guess that made me sound superior, eh?"

The wagon jerked to a stop near a meager homestead next to a muddy creek, barely a going concern.

"Adam, don't let them know you know they's northerners."

Adam thought about this. If the Union is hiring slavers, something of what Tobias told him had to be true. "I won't—not yet. Not until I feel this thing out."

Jimmy rode up to them. "All right, get down."

Both men got out of the wagon, Adam first but got his chains hung up on a pile of hay. Tobias snickered, watching him get loose.

"Thought hisself a free man," Tobias muttered, as he jumped out of the wagon, keeping his eyes to the ground.

Titus gave him a disgruntled look but also kept his eyes to the ground. Jimmy and Luke unlocked their chains.

"Now go steal us some food."

"Here? They don't have enough to—"

Cal, who had ridden up behind them, slapped a rifle butt across Adam's shoulders, hard enough to knock him to the ground. "You don't sass, muley. That's the first thing you learn. You keep forgetting you're not free no more."

Adam struggled to his feet, keeping his eyes down but never feeling a harder moment of self-control in his life. He hoped they couldn't see the steel in his jaw. "Yessir."

Luke gave them both a shove forward. "And don't think of running off. We'll be hiding, but watching your every move. And we are damn accurate in shooting. Get moving."

CHAPTER 13

Ben awoke to a world of darkness and the smell of damp stone. As his eyes adjusted, he confirmed that he was not at home but in some sort of mine shaft, and then he remembered getting here. He had emptied the water wagon when a burst of flames caught one of the wheels. Ben grabbed to pull the wagon to safety but a flame caught his hand. He backed away in pain, watching as more of the wagon began to smolder, and realized the fire was going to reach the edge of the cliff. He looked over the side, noting that there was little down there to catch fire, and began to work his way to a larger outcropping of rock lining the cliff, where he thought he could wait out the fire. Either that, or move to the far western edge and remove his shirt to beat at the flames. He strained to see Joe but there was too much smoke, and then he felt the arms around him from behind, and before he could catch himself, he was falling, on fire, and falling…

The fire in his limbs brought the pain back into his arm and head, and reminded him of that last conscious moment. For a blissful relief of pain, his surroundings were damp and cool.

"Joe!" he called out. "Joe, where are you?" Had to be Joe who pulled him to safety. Joe had grabbed Ben and leaped off the cliff with him to safety, injuring him, and probably Joe, too, in the fall. "Joe!"

Hands from nowhere touched his forehead, and a soft voice reassured him, "You's gonna be all right, massa."

* * *

Joe threw open the door of the house. "Pa!"

Hop Sing ran out of the kitchen and Joe felt reassured seeing him that everything was back to normal, but that second passed quickly. "Glad to see Mr. Joe, but please to not yell. We have guest, she not well. She ghost and possess Hoss, you help cure him." He held a bamboo pot he'd gotten from his uncle on his last trip to Virginia City like the lifeline to another world.

Joe grabbed the settee for support as his eyes blurred. "Where's Pa?"

"Last I saw he with you."

Joe dropped down in the chair near the fire, feeling the chill he thought he left outside. "Oh God." He faced Hop Sing but the effort made him sweat.

MONETTE BEBOW-REINHARD

"Hop Sing, we ran into a bad fire and now…get me some food, I gotta look for him."

Hop Sing grabbed his arm. "You see Hoss first. Talk him some sense."

"But Pa could be dying, or dead! You can take care of Hoss, can't you?"

"If you not know where you lose Mr. Cartlight, how you look? You leave, lose Mr. Hoss, too."

"Can't Adam help?"

Sudden dead silent stares between them broke only by their heavy breathing. Joe whispered, "Adam's not home?"

"No see Mr. Adam."

They heard Hoss yell, "Hop Sing, I need cold water!"

Joe glanced at the stairs. "That's Hoss? He sounds…"

"Spirit got him."

"I was gonna say strange. Listen, Hop Sing, I promise, I'll find Pa and bring him home and then Hoss and me will find Adam, okay?" Joe broke free and ran for the door, fearing Hop Sing might grab him with that tight grip again but Hop Sing hadn't moved. Joe held up a hurried one finger. "I'll find him, I promise, just…take care of Hoss, okay?" Joe grabbed for his hat, felt it already on his head, and ran out.

Joe rode hard and long on Adam's horse, leaving Hop Sing behind with more questions than answers. Adam still gone, Hoss possessed (whatever that meant) and Pa…Joe didn't want to think anything but Pa (and Cochise) being alive and safe, ready to be rescued.

As he rode, mostly by gut instinct because he focused on Pa being alive, Joe remembered without wanting to the day his mother died. Though he hadn't been much over a year, he could never ever forget the day…he ran outside into Hoss's waiting arms and Hoss swung him up. Joe's head hit Hoss's chin, as he often planned on purpose, making them both laugh. This time Hoss's laugh was different, so Joe grabbed his mouth to make him try to laugh right but instead he must have pinched too hard, because he made tears come out of Hoss's eyes.

Then Pa stood next to him and Little Joe, he was darned little back then, saw Pa crying even though Joe hadn't touched him and Adam couldn't even look at any of them. "Adam Adam!" Joe shouted but Adam only looked away, head down. Pa cried harder than Hoss, harder even than the time Joe fell out of the tree and Pa thought he was dead, harder…Pa took him from Hoss and showed him his Ma…lying on the ground as though asleep, but funny asleep, not on the soft bed she likes but the hard ground, and in her riding clothes, her hat still on, her eyes…her eyes open…but not smiling and reaching for him, never again.

Joe didn't know how much of that memory he was told and how much he remembered himself, but he went over that awful day so much in his mind that all of it felt like memory.

He spent the rest of that day covering old burnt ground, knowing the memory of his Pa's death would be guilt-filled, and all his. He found the burned out water wagon and a remnant of Pa's hat near it. He even found Cochise, nibbling on some burnt section. He rubbed the horse's nose. "Sorry, fella, but I'd trade you for Pa." He went back to the water wagon, to what he first thought were two tree stumps, charred to near nothing. He touched one, saw something that looked like bone and scrambled backward to the ground.

"Pa!?" He crawled back toward the stumps, his hand reaching out to touch but instead he dropped to the ground. "Oh, Pa...." Joe sat on the grassy plains, on the edge of the burned area, separated by a natural granite dry outcropping. Cochise came over and pushed Joe between the shoulderblades, but the tears wouldn't stop coming. Joe stood and wrapped his arms around the horse's neck.

Drawing courage, he picked up the charred hat and stared down at what he thought had been legs. He poked into the charred wood again. What had looked like bare bone was a single strip of unburnt wood.

Joe secured Cochise to some grazing so the horse woudn't follow and rode back to the Washoe village, a small community of related people in their wickiups, moveable grass huts that allowed them to hunt new areas for the sparse resources of a desert region. He tried to talk with them about rescuing him but could not communicate as well with signing as his brothers could. He spent the night there at the risk of waking up married, hoping to find a way to get his needs communicated. Surely they must know something about where his Pa went.

He couldn't sleep. He remembered times that will never come again, times when Pa and his brothers laughed around the dinner table. Times in the early days on the ranch when Pa and Adam had to protect Hoss and him from wolves and flash floods, and from Indians. Protection from Indians meant showing them that you were no threat. Pa always seemed to know the right thing to do, almost without thinking. Now Adam would have to take over running the ranch. Adam could be smart enough most times, Joe knew, but he wasn't Pa. He couldn't ever be Pa.

Little Joe, feeling two again, cried himself to sleep.

By the time Joe left the village the next day, he had pretty much pieced together what had happened. The Washoe fought flames on the western section, while he and Pa had worked from the south and north, and then townsfolk from Carson City came to the eastern side. Pa had moved easterly, so Carson City was Joe's next best bet. Someone must have found him.

Joe rode back to where he last saw Pa and retraced the edges. Where Pa went led to the edge of a cliff. Joe climbed down a little way, and scanned as well as he could from a near dangling position, off some less burnt tree material, but this section was pretty bad off, and Pa would never have survived down there alone. No sign of a body anywhere.

He knew one thing for sure. The longer Pa stayed away, the less likely he would ever be found alive.

* * *

Hoss heard Joe come in but Lydia gripped his hand so tight while she slept that he couldn't move. When she woke she told him terrible things, tales of marriage gone wrong that made Hoss's blood boil. Lies, abuse, mental torture, and as she talked her face became so angry that Hoss feared he'd taken a monster into his room, even as he understood her anger. When she told Stephen she was leaving him, he threatened her with every kind of killing death he could think of. She had to leave, she told Hoss, had to flee the stagecoach and run for her very life.

Hoss continued to keep her company, all that day into night, same the next day, nodding off sometimes and waking to find her gone. He'd wait and she'd return, with no explanation of where she'd gone. Hoss once heard a tale about an old fellow who walked the same length of Sacramento ground every day around sunset with his dog but no one could ever follow him or find out who he was.

Lydia couldn't be like that. But she would never answer his questions about how she could slip away or where she went. So he figured that gals like her needed some privacy sometimes. After all, Hop Sing's potion proved she's real. She's just…spooky.

He had asked Hop Sing what Joe wanted when Hop Sing came back into the guest room with cool water and towels but couldn't remember the answer.

On another of Hop Sing's entrances, when Hoss didn't know day from night, Hop Sing paced Hoss's room as Hoss watched Lydia sleep. "Mr. Cartlight missing."

When Hoss looked up, he felt like he couldn't see Hop Sing clear and wondered if he caught Lydia's sickness. "She's real feverish, Hop Sing. Think I oughta fetch a doc?"

"Doctor not help. Do what she need. Do qlick. Then she disappear back to other world. Then you find Mr. Cartlight."

"Ah, that's what you say. I can touch her, feel her, she's gotta be real. And you proved it with your potion, too." Hoss stood as she relaxed her grip on his hand. "Mind her for me?"

Hop Sing nodded. "She not the evil sort phantasm." He sighed. "Yet."

"I better get going then. She can't stay like this much longer. Keep an eye on her. She's a tricky little filly, can slip away like the wind."

"Because she—"

Hoss waved him off and left the room.

* * *

Ben's first response to strange voices was of suspicion and demand. "What's going on here? Who are you and what do you want?"

A male's voice blasted out behind him. "That's a kindly thanks for saving you's life."

"Enough, Jess. Go use you's magic now, your mama's hungry."

Ben tried to see who spoke but couldn't angle himself. "I'm sorry he's…angry. I didn't mean to yell—I'm just confused."

"That's my son, Jess, and he save you by pulling you from the fire. Both you fell down the cliff, but he's tough, he'll heal faster."

"Where am I?"

"I dunno, like a hole in de cliff, but too straight for Mama Nature to make all herself."

"Mine shaft, I suspect. All kinds of gophers digging for silver in these parts."

"We git it pretty well sealed, been here for day before fire, hiding."

Ben could see her eyes and then her form began to take shape. "You're…runaways?"

"Yes, Massa. I'm Sadie Duncanwood, and this is my girl Abby."

"Duncanwood?"

"Master named me after his plantation. After my man, he go away."

Ben liked this Sadie, sounding so southern and uninhibited. She reminded him of his trips to the islands so many years ago. Suddenly drowsy, he imagined himself drowning in the sound of her warmth. Before long, however, pain reminded him that he wasn't home. "What happened to him? Your husband?"

"My man? From what I hears, Massa, he kilt hisself. Gone loco."

"I'm sorry." Ben shifted and winced. "Please don't call me Massa. My name is Ben. Did you see any sign of Joe, my son? He was fighting the fire with me."

"Sorry, Massa Ben. Just you."

"How…how bad am I?" Everything hurt to move.

"Jesse done what he could to get you in here wit us but your arm is broke and you gots a bad bump on your head. Wasn't sure you was gonna come to. And your clothes was still smoldering from that fire. You was burning when Jesse found you."

Abby laughed. "Momma figgered smoke a good cover for our escape. But then we finds you and now we stuck here too." Abby sounded like a child forced to grow up too soon.

"Shush, child. I made a potion for ya but we's running out. Gonna has to figure out how to move you out of here. Get you back up the cliff—well, you gotta walk all on you's own."

Ben felt four hands on him, soothing his burning skin. "Who were you hiding from?"

"We is running from the slave traders, from New Orleans." Sadie said. "They started the fire."

"Slave traders. I was hoping they wouldn't dare come on my land."

"Your land?"

"The Ponderosa."

Sadie chuckled. "I tells you, Abby? We done reeled us in the big one."

Ben felt the pain knocking him out. "The big…"

71

Abby whined, "We needs you, Massa Cartwright. You owes us now, too."

"Massa...Ben, we runs from New Orleans and them Union soldiers because they... they won't makes us free. You kin help, I knows you kin."

"You has to help, Mr. Cartwright," Abby pleaded. "Darcy says you would. We's waited so long—and we deserve our revenge."

"Hush, child."

"Revenge? Darcy?" Exhaustion took its toll, and Ben let his consciousness drift away.

* * *

"Hoss!" Joe headed back to the cliff after getting nowhere with anyone back in Carson City. He veered off when he spotted Hoss headed in his direction. Back in town Joe didn't have the courage to say much more than, "is my Pa in town," or "was he fighting a fire with you?" because he didn't want to let on that Ben Cartwright could be dead. No one admitted to seeing him, which was the worst Joe expected and the most he needed to know.

Hoss didn't seem willing to slow up. Joe had to ride Cochise right into him. "Sorry, Little Joe, I'm in a kind of a hurry. Cayn't you wait til I get back to the ranch?"

Joe felt tongue-roped. "Uh. Just wanted to know...Pa back at the ranch?"

"Pa? I ain't seen him since..." Hoss scratched at his temple under his hat. "Huh. Well, since he left with you the day after the social. Don't you know where he is?"

"I, uh, was supposed to meet him...you go on, I think I know where he is." Joe braced himself for a "wait just a minute, little brother."

But instead Hoss tilted the hat back down over his forehead and rode off. Joe watched his brother ride off, remembering what Hop Sing had said about Hoss being possessed. "Guess that explains the funny look in his eyes." Joe felt for the rope on his saddle before reining Cochise toward the cliff.

When he saw riders head his way his heart pounded right up into his ears. *Pa's with them, gotta be.* His hopes raced even without seeing Pa's horse with them.

"Joe, glad to see you, kid. Dere's got a big problem," Salzar, one of the lead loggers, rode to him while the others stayed a mite behind.

Joe sighed and pulled up. No sign of any injured man with them. "Salzar, aren't you supposed to be with the timbering project?"

"Yessir, but dere's enough riding vence and marking logs, and someone had to report problem mitt the cattle count."

Joe sighed. Salzar butted in on other Cartwright interests too much for the family's pleasure, whether or not they could admit it. "What's the problem?"

"Oh, I tink I better talk on it mitt your pa."

"No, you won't talk on it mitt my pa, you'll talk on it mitt me." And in an instant Joe realized he was the only one Salzar *could* talk to.

"Den ride back mitt us. Dey's five head short and dis after beating de brush.

72

Including your new breeding bull. I suspect dat Frank fellow und his friends. Taking timber, taking cattle, making money und da side."

Joe put up a hand. "Only five? That could be nothing more than feeding the field. A few head always disappear." Although, as he thought about it, a few meant around three and never the good breeding bull. "Ah," Joe looked over his shoulder, in the direction of a much-desired cliff climb. "Yes, one of us Cartwrights ought to help with the count. But ah…" *No, there was no one else. What would Pa do?*

"Say, we saw dis smoke and thought about coming but figure by the time we got dere it would be either out. Or out of control."

"Yeah, I think—"

"And you gets another problem from us too. Des loggers tink that since none of you Cartwrights is around, that mebbe dey quit logging or be accused of stealing, too."

Joe nodded. "I'll…uh, send Adam out in the morning to the logging camp, okay?"

Joe grimaced as a headache cut a thin crack through his skull. He sure hoped Adam was home. And he'd have to send Hoss to go and talk to Frank, too. Seemed the last talking to didn't set. Every problem ended up on his lap— him just old enough to order whiskey. Which started to sound pretty good about now.

As Joe kicked his horse to keep up with the cattlemen, he thought, maybe not. Whiskey was the last thing he'd need right now. After this cattle count, he'd get back to the cliff, and quick, before dark. His eyes, his mind, his tears were filled with memories of Pa as Joe rode to the herd, which he realized he wouldn't have found on his own because the winter herd wasn't one of the projects he'd been involved in lately. Lately all Pa had wanted of him was to watch for signs of fire, so all he'd been doing was riding. While he was with the Washoe, he'd made out some words that indicated that the fire was the fault of the ranchers for not keeping brush cleared.

Bite back the tears, boy, these cowboys will see you.

As things go, he couldn't make the ride back to the cliff before dark. The herd was on the other side of the range, and he had little enough energy left to grip the saddle. Seven cows in all were missing and Joe sent several cowboys out to different areas where they might find some strays. He told them he'd be back in two days, with Frank in tow. How he planned to do that, he didn't know yet.

When he opened the door Joe saw Hop Sing tending something in a pot over the fire. Joe shut the door and dropped his gun belt. He picked it up from the floor to put it on the cadenza. He took off his jacket and then put his jacket back on, feeling the chill. He walked over to the fire and stood next to Hop Sing. Cooking roots? They smelled pretty good, like mesquite.

"What's that for? Like a Chinese air fragrance?"

"This is substitute for bai zhi root, cannot find here."

Joe nodded like he understood and turned to the door, waiting for someone, anyone, to walk in here and remove this burden of guilt, anger and loss.

Hop Sing waited, tending his stew. "Mr. Cartlight come, too?"

Joe's head dropped. He wrapped his arms around Hop Sing.

"Mr. Joe, what wrong with Mr. Cartlight? He die?" Hop Sing led him to the table and sat him down. He poured Joe a brandy and Joe drank it all. Hop Sing sat next to him and poured himself a brandy, too, while Joe helped himself to another.

"Tell all you lemember."

"Pa…and I… found a prairie fire and set to work fighting it. And I…lost him."

"Lost him?"

"Ahhhhh…he's gone."

"Where he go? To get help?"

"Ahhhh, no, we got the fire out with some Indians who helped, but they don't…and I don't know…Pa disappeared. I can't find him. I found his hat, burned up."

"His horse leturn?"

Joe got a sudden 'aw shucks' look on his face and beat Hop Sing to the door. The wind blew a sudden gust that took the hat Joe forgot was on his head as he raced Hop Sing to the barn.

"Buck!?" Joe ran up and down the stalls.

Hop Sing stood quiet, scanning the barn. "Horse not here."

Joe walked back outside and stood, hands on gun belt, his frown aging him. "That's odd, if Pa was gone the horse would just come back."

"Maybe someone steal horse," Hop Sing said behind him with a jerky nod.

"Yeah. Maybe. Or maybe Pa's been kidnapped!"

Joe stood, as though waiting for the horse to come prancing back in, paw the ground and lead him to his father.

Hop Sing took him by the arm and pulled him inside the house. "You not to blame. Mr. Cartlight love Pondelosa and die saving. If he here, he say, you not blame self."

Joe closed his eyes and let himself be dragged. When he opened them, he stood alone in the middle of the sitting room. "I hate when people disappear," he muttered.

* * *

Hoss didn't reckon he ever rode Chubby so fast down the mountainside to Carson City before—or that he could feel this strongly about a woman he barely knew, a woman so mysterious he did not even know if she were real. He headed for the doctor's house. He preferred Dr. Martin, who tended to be more discreet, but Virginia City folk kept him pretty busy. Carson City was a little tamer most of the time. As he rode past the hotel he saw Margaret sitting on a bench, looking like she'd lost someone.

"Hi there, Margaret." He tipped his hat and kept riding, until another thought made him pull back to her. "Where's Adam? He with you?"

Margaret leaped to her feet. "Hoss, I haven't seen him since the social."

"You mean he ain't? With you? But he ain't been home, neither. At least," he scratched at his sweaty forehead under his hat, "I don't think so. Maybe...I just been too distracted."

"Hoss, surely you'd know if he was there or not. What about Ben and Joe?"

"I...guess I ain't talked to them much neither. Excuse me, Margaret, I have to find the doc, I'm in a bit of a hurry, didn't realize how late it is." He rode off, with the feeling of puzzled eyes on his back.

Hoss remembered Ben telling him once that they were always there for each other, but that they each had separate lives to lead, too, that the family supports but doesn't suppress, loves but doesn't bind, and respects each other's differences and distractions. Like the time him and Adam argued about how to get a calf out of a muddy gully. Hoss wanted to jump down in there after it, but Adam says no, we gotta take this slow and easy or the poor trapped thing could panic and drown. Hoss pointed out that the hopping around it did meant it already panicked but Adam reminded Hoss that getting Hoss out of the muddy pit could be even harder than the calf and Adam knew darn well how Hoss could panic. They came to near blows arguing, too, because Hoss insisted he never panicked even though he was only 13. Then Little Joe came along, so they tied up his feet and threw him down into the muddy pit. Little Joe sometimes had the best solutions.

Hoss sure hoped Pa would remember saying that about being separate men with needs, because right now he cared only about having Lydia in his arms.

* * *

Margaret rented a horse at the livery, getting in just as the fellow was locking up. She didn't bother to change into riding clothes. She headed for the road that brought Hoss to Carson City. Guilt fit the spurs that moved her. She knew Adam was upset but that does not explain why he would stay away from home for so long. She didn't know what good she could do looking for him, but his being missed at least explained why he hasn't been to see her. Did he die in the fire after all? She didn't want to think so. And she'd be the only one who knew the direction he headed when he left her.

What she couldn't figure was how the rest of the family didn't care anymore about each other. They had seemed so caring the night of the social, and Adam had always talked fondly of them back when she was a kid, because she remembered she had so envied him for it. That fight between Adam and Joe, did that cause a rift that couldn't heal? If so, then maybe there was no such thing as family loyalty.

Margaret knew her own self-recrimination over what had happened between her and Adam that night had to stop. But could she have handled things differently? She kept going over her confession to him. She should have withheld the worst of that information until later—if ever. Had she been trying to drive him away? Maybe she felt she wasn't good enough for him. She kicked her stubborn horse but it didn't match its gait to these hills—might even stop altogether unless she coaxed it.

She lifted her head into the wind that had picked up with the setting sun. All trace of smoke in the air had disappeared, following that brief rain shower night before last. Not near enough for these dry hills but welcomed anyway. She had watched from the window in her room as the drunks came out and danced in the rain. A couple of them had spent a day fighting the fire that turned out to be more smoke than blaze. But any cowboy or miner knows that smoke with wind spelled disaster.

The idea kept reverberating through her head. *Not good enough for Adam.* Well, that was true enough. She wanted him to know the worst so that he'd know the truth. She loved him, sincerely and honestly but she felt he deserved better. *Love myself first.* She could get him back *if* she can accept that her father's acts did not diminish her worth. She needed Adam to know, at least, that she's working on it. Maybe...he'll even help her find her worth.

As slow as her plug was, the two men riding ahead as she rounded a bend were even slower. As she rode behind them, they stopped, and when one looked at her, she knew why—they were drunk. By their looks, had been that way all day.

The other rider Margaret recognized as a fellow who asked for a dance at the social, a man she had turned down. He had such sad eyes that she had almost said yes but he had smelled drunk and now appeared to be habitually so. Even at a complete stop, they both swayed in their saddles as though they were either asleep or challenging each other to fall off.

She stayed in Carson City because a woman alone was safer there than in Virginia City, where a woman was either married, a teacher, or a saloon girl. In Carson City there were a number of schoolteachers and women in other occupations, such as seamstress, laundress, and even a few business owners, and women alone were left alone, for the most part. Why these fellows had been drinking in Carson City instead of Virginia City was none of her concern.

Margaret spurred her horse to make a big circle around them.

"Whoa," one of the fellows called in her dust, "What's that? Looks like a little angel."

The other rider laughed. "I guess so. Maybe we can pray to her, whadda you think?"

"I think we kin surely try."

They rode harder behind her to catch up. She kicked her plug but got only a little faster walking out of the animal. She had two options, neither of which she liked.

With any luck, Hoss would come along before anything bad happened.

CHAPTER 14

Adam and Tobias crouched in the brush and stared at a huge barn a leap over a fence and a weed-prickly overgrown field away. Adam barely survived the last theft with his ego intact and they were immediately forced into another. "What we supposed to take this time?" He rubbed at his beard, having learned that asking for a razor was not worth the beating he'd get for it. Maybe this hairy face was better—maybe now he *was* Titus.

"I think we's after the corn crib, this time."

Away from the earshot of the slavers, Adam let up on his southern lingo. "Corn crib? That's hard corn. What are we supposed to do with hard corn?"

"They has to feed us, too."

Adam looked at Tobias with a bite that could snap a horseshoe in half.

"You take a kernel of corn offa that cob with your thumbnail, like so," Tobias motioned holding a cob and flicking a kernel in his mouth, "and you suck on the kernel til it's soft enough to chew. A few of them and your tummy fills right up."

"And this doesn't bother you?"

"Oh, sure it do, Titus. But you gots to know, we had much as little when we runned. Mostly just corn, some pepper, a warm jacket and knife. That's all. And runaways gots to keep stealing along the way, too. And we did, all the way to Utah, where we found some people to takes us in and helps us. Well, we thought they was helping us."

Adam pointed to Tobias's gunnysack. "I don't have one of those."

"We's gonna just fill the one. We won't have time for much more, before we'll has to hightail it out of there or gets shot in the britches."

"Well," Adam poked his head out of the brush, combination of sage and something prickly, and then up a little further. "I can't see the farmer around anywhere, so let's just get this thing done." He moved forward a little and then sat back on Tobias's leg. "Problem is, those cows are going to start making a fuss and that'll bring him running. Well, I've had my share of cows. I'm not worried about them trampling us. But I used to have a reputation for being calm in any situation. Until that last farmhouse, that is."

Tobias jerked his leg out from under Adam. "You done jawing yet? Let's git going."

After a quick count of three they leaped out of the brush, cleared the fence, rolled and crawled through the grass, while the cows mooed around them. Adam stuck his hand in a cowpie and blamed Tobias with another biting look before wiping his hand as best he could on the ground and following behind.

Surely this wasn't as bad as some of the things he's done as a boy, pranks they played on Pa and on each other. But someone close by could take a prank like this mighty serious. And he wasn't a boy, anymore. At least, not in *that* sense.

Tobias pulled him over to the corn crib where the chute opened and reached his hand in. "See, what'd I say. Not much."

Adam held the bag open and Tobias swept in as much as he could, some of the most awful looking dried hard corn that Adam ever cared to look on as dinner.

"Hey! Somebody out there?"

The farmer had been having lunch when the cows bellowed and at first was too hungry to do anything. Finally, with his napkin tucked in his shirt he picked up his rifle and ran out. That was as near as Adam could figure, anyway, by the gap in what he heard and saw.

"Come on, we'll take us another way." Tobias sprinted off across a hill where they could descend the other side and remain hidden before the farmer could round the barn to the silo.

As they lay on the side of the hill, panting, Adam figured they weren't spotted at all, and he started to laugh, more without knowing why than out of relief. The thought that they were also out of reach of the slavers never crossed his mind, either, until later.

Tobias held a corn kernel to him. "Hungry?"

"I sure am." Adam popped the kernel into his mouth.

* * *

Lincoln walked into the parlor to see his wife Mary standing at the window looking out. The table, where he expected half a dozen business associates ready to have dinner with him before taking the train to the war zone, was bare on all counts.

"Mary? Where's dinner? I'm hungry." He didn't care about seeing anyone or going anywhere, getting his fill of both every day without even asking.

"Well, you will just have to wait, dear. The maids are all outside at a rally."

He joined her at the window where he could see the large and colorful gathering of Negroes. "What are they rallying for? I already plan to free them."

"No, you don't, dear. Those are northern Negroes. You're freeing the ones you cannot control, remember?"

"All right, let's not get persnickety. I get enough of that outside this room." Lincoln wanted to walk away but had nowhere else to be at the moment. The paper published his proclamation over a week past and it had yet to have the effect he wanted. He felt sure the terms would convince at least some of the rebellion states to rejoin the Union to protect their precious slavery. But he also felt like a snake born with two heads—trying to please both sides of his party meant pleasing no one. He needed to find the courage to do what he felt was right, for a change.

"So what do they want?" He stayed behind her at the window. "Votes? Free Labor? Their own land?"

"Yes. What whites have." She sighed. "Probably want white babies, too."

Lincoln draped an arm over his wife's shoulder, his hand dangling in air. "Mary, can we talk about Willie? I want us to remember him. Not as a ghost, or some tapping on a wall. And I will insist to my dying day that I felt that lady's leg move."

"Oh, I'm sure you did, too." Mary pressed her face into his chest. "Not yet, please. I can't deal with death, just yet."

Lincoln bit back a retort. He dealt with death every day. Every day a lot of someones lose a loved one. So much at stake... *We have more men than the South. More men than the South...we can lose more, and will, to win...*

"Well, how am I going to get dinner? If I don't eat, I won't have the strength to hold up the Northern end of the battle, and then where will they be, tell me that." But Mary didn't answer. He meant it as a joke, but she wasn't laughing. "I'm as hungry as a—"

"Oh, please, Abe, none of your cute little homilies, I'm not in the mood." She walked toward the kitchen. "I can cook, you know. At least for the two of us."

Lincoln stared at the empty space she left behind. He wondered what real love felt like. He remembered he must have had that feeling once, long ago, even still remembered her name, although he felt like he'd long since gotten over the feeling, like the ague or something. Is one true love all we're allowed? And he had let her get away, long before Mary entered his life. He pictured her sitting somewhere with some bum, regretting letting an ugly joe like him get away, but that was little solace. Oh, she was a feisty one! Probably wouldn't approve of all this death and dying and war.

Now he was stuck with this little toad of a woman who has given him children but little else. She deserves better, of course. Could she feel his tears in the dark of night when he tried to hold her close, or was she too wrought up in her own regrets?

People asked him, during his somber spells, if the weight of the war got too burdensome. And he'd say yes, even though that wasn't always the truth. He had an army of people worrying about the war, and most of the time they didn't want him around. He liked to help them plan strategy, because planning made him feel in control, and that took his mind off the sadness that always seems to follow him around. And kept him away from that little toad of a woman.

The North would win, of course. That was inevitable and had been from the start. But if his cronies knew how he wanted to do things, they would probably kick him out of the Republican Party. This upstart young party replaced and eliminated the Whigs, but their theology could ruin this country, if given half a chance. Who do they think they are, controlling him without reason or sanity?

He had to tow the line, do what they tell him to do. He had ideas! But not with enough conviction to push them forward on the likes of Seward and the rest. They accuse him—him!—of having masterminded his nomination in Chicago. Well, he'd be the first to admit that the timing was bad, having the convention in his home state, but there had been little help for that. Why wouldn't he rally last minute support in his home state? Who wouldn't, in his shoes? Anyone in his shoes would just plain trip, that's all.

In the din of yelling and the clapping Lincoln realized they saw him at the window. He stared out over the expansive lawn to the courtyard just on the other side of the fence. Well, let them look, then. They might see a skunk rooting for dinner but that didn't mean they'd shoot.

Of course he knew the Negroes were human. But like his granddaddy used to say, "too many pigs for the tit."[20] They'd all need schooling and such before they could compete for jobs with whites, and the wonder of how to deal with suddenly loosened uneducated racially inferior people consumed him almost as much as bloodied and dying loved ones. How could his one shaky, war-broke government take on the task?

Hayti was still the best option, had to be, at least to lessen the load on him, poor mama pig. But his gut said something opposite. He was hungry. And he had a train to catch. At the moment he wasn't sure which was more important—his stomach or visiting that Democrat General to give him the scolding he deserved.

* * *

Tobias fell to the ground hard, and Titus thought at first he wasn't going to move, then prayed he'd stay down so they wouldn't hit him again. He could see the swelling on Tobias's forehead where an egg from the blow of the rifle butt began to form.

Tobias rolled to his back, blinked hard and sat up. "I means if'n you fellas is done gonna throw away the turkey legs anyways—"

Titus winced even before the loco Piney's butt hit home again. This time Tobias appeared down for the count. Titus knew he should say something, but Tobias told him that any nigger that comes to the aid of another gets the same treatment. And one of them needs to have his head straight. Titus figured his time will come when he says just the wrong thing. So far, to be safe, he hasn't said much at all.

Was that being safe? Or cowardly? Had Kane killed him after all, deep inside? Maybe he'd become a coward who played games to survive? But Adam thought maybe the truth went deeper than that—

because more went on here than he could see, and he wanted to know more. He and Tobias didn't matter, not in the great scheme of things.

Cal spit cigar juice on the fallen slave before turning to Titus. "Maybe you can teach him some manners, Muley. Like how to hold your breath before asking for white food."

"Hey, speaking of food," Piney took a drink from the whiskey in his canteen, as usual after he got himself worked up, "how come Jake didn't come back in to eat?"

"He rode on ahead to the next town to wire Mr. Smith about our progress." Cal lit his dirty wet cigar after some effort.

Jimmy laughed. "Yeah, Piney, ever since he got him that fancy horse on the trail, he's been volunteering to do all the riding duties."

"I wouldn't mind me a ride on that fancy horse. Like a show horse, with that saddle. Someone's hurting without it, that's for sure."

Laughing, the men walked away. Titus got the impression they knew how to hit a slave and when to stop. Or at least thought they did. Slaves often ended up dead after such beatings.

"He can't bring much if'n you kill him," Titus muttered. How can these fellows want to drag a slave back and deliver him unable to work? Or was Tobias worth just as much dead? He put a hand on Tobias's shoulder. "Are you okay? Can you sit?"

Tobias groaned, arm over his face.

"Just lay there awhile. I don't have anything that can help you anyway."

"You better be careful," Tobias murmured. "You sound too educated to be one of us."

"The more educated we are, the more likely to be freed. Or run away."[21] Adam winked at Tobias.

Tobias ignored the implication. He sat up sucking saliva inside a bloodied mouth. He leaned over and spit out a tooth. "Good, that one hurt anyhow."

"Oh now don't make me believe you riled him for tooth care."

"No, Adam, I mean, Titus, I is real hungry for that turkey we caught. Got me an idea."

Adam looked over his shoulder where the slave traders laughed and ate. "Don't know that I care to hear another of your ideas."

"You game for a little fun?"

"No."

"Guys like that like to bet on nigger fights."

"Luke." Adam nodded. "I noticed." He glared at Tobias. "Who you got in mind?"

Tobias ignored him. "One of us wins, but the loser eats better so he'll win next night."

Adam leaned back, caught off guard. "You're suggesting…Ah, you're already banged up. Wouldn't be a fair fight." But Adam remembered the last time he fought with chains.

"I want to lose. I'm hungry."

"Wait a minute, so am I. They're gonna catch on if we both throw up our hands and say "I give, I give."

"You ain't heard the rest. Guy who wins don't get whipped til the next time he loses."

Tobias winked and leaped on Titus, to the sound of chains clanking and "nigger fight!"

* * *

Margaret's horse struggled to climb even though the path had smoothed out. She figured she hadn't paid enough at the livery, so they gave her a nag — or they just took advantage of her because she's a woman. They must have given her the oldest horse in the stock. She had learned a lot about horse flesh from Adam and kept learning after she moved out of her pa's house, but she'd been in a hurried and trustful mood. Her learning didn't include getting a rise out of a nearly dead animal.

So Frank and this other fellow Frank called Stu caught up, even drunk as they were.

"Hey, angel," Stu said with a hiccup, "We could sure use some of your blessings on the chill of this mountain day."

"You're welcome to ride with me if you've a mind to," she responded, keeping distance to her tone, "and in fact, I would welcome a little protection from the deviants that I've heard are wandering these hills."

"Protection!?" Stu snorted. "Well, I guess we can handle that, eh, Frank?"

Frank stared as her, as though wondering where he'd seen her before.

"Normally I wouldn't ask two strangers, but you look reliable," she said with a nod at Frank. "And this horse they gave me isn't."

Stu guffawed. "We do. We look plum reliable!"

Stu's horse stumbled, and though drunk Stu moved quickly to rein up and jump down. "Think she's taken a stone. Frank, jump on down and help me out. This skittish thing will likely kill me as not."

Margaret had pulled up as well before realizing she'd been had. Stu turned from his own horse to grab her mount's bridle before she could think to hurry on.

"Hey, Frank, look what I caught. You know, I think she wants me."

Margaret laughed and moved as though dismounting but instead kicked her horse, knocking Stu backward, and rode off, her horse startled into a bit of a trot. Behind her the two men mounted and kicked their horses and she hoped they just meant to scare her, which they did, but they got alongside her, riding so close her horse slowed enough for one to lean over and grab the reins.

Helpless, she sat in the saddle as they led her off the road into the brush and then Stu forced her down, forced her to lay down, with Frank behind, and she struggled and spat and fought, but Stu was stronger, and she heard and felt him rip her dress and still she didn't scream but then her father's face came into her eyes as she felt the cold hands ripping down her petticoat, her stockings. Their voices faded into her father's and when she felt the cold steel against her leg she grabbed the gun and fired—

The smoke stung her nostrils and for a moment she couldn't breathe. Something warm ran down her bare leg, as the body on top of her screamed and rolled to the side, and she waited, her fear bracing her for the inevitable bullet to the brain.

When she got the courage to look, she saw Stu laying next to her, and no sign of Frank anywhere. Stu held his groin and she could see the blood, tons of blood, streaming from his wound. Where she'd shot him she didn't look close enough to see, but pushed him the rest of the way off and jumped to her feet. Stu's horse stood in trained obedience while her horse had likely gone back to town, running all the way.

She ran, stumbled, fell, but finally reached the reins of Stu's horse.

"Lady...you ain't gonna leave me here."

But Margaret knew she'd do just that.

* * *

The five slavers, including Jimmy, jumped up and placed bets. Two bet on the half-breed while three bet on the Negro. They all knew the rules of a slave fight, even though they didn't agree on all of them. They had enough food to feed the loser, but the way these two were going, they'd both expire before giving in to the other.

Jimmy, the most sensitive of the bunch, thought they should break up the fight because neither seemed willing to quit first. The others already called Jimmy too weak-willed for this line of work, which, short of soldiering, he found the only way to work for government. He wasn't about to go back to farming and break his back, like his Pa, who wasn't well enough now to do much of anything.

"Come on, Muley, pin 'em for God sake, you act like he ain't just took a beating!"

They were getting bloodied, all right, but neither seemed willing to play dead, both with too much pride for their color, Jimmy thought, and he got even more nervous when Piney, who wanted Titus to win, took out his gun and aimed as though to wing Tobias just for fun, but that would stick them with more work than any of them cared to do. After a couple of off-aim shots that got the slaves more excited, Piney holstered the gun.

"You stupid nigger, all you gotta do is grab his balls to make him play dead. Ah, we gotta change the rules like I says before, the winner should get the food instead of the loser, neither of them is trying hard enough to win," Cal said, chomping on a cigar no more than a nub.

"Yeah, and the loser gets whipped," Luke said. "Might make a better fight next time."

Cal all along told them that the fighting they encouraged in the slaves was stupid. Most often they could find one not hungry enough and wanting to win, but these two were taking all the fun away. They weren't even punching that hard, just rolling and wrestling in the dirt, the blood conjured by rocks they couldn't see to duck and an occasional chain or elbow in the face that couldn't be avoided, enough blood at least to keep them watching.

Finally Titus pinned Tobias by the throat, squeezing so tight Jimmy thought they were gonna be minus their biggest prize. He was, after all, worth more alive—or so Jimmy figured, not knowing as much as the rest. Marv, rooting for Titus, grabbed him by the back of the shirt and threw him to the ground, where Titus lay panting, unwilling to get to his feet even though he should have enough left in him after winning.

"All right." Luke stood and gave Tobias a kick. "Jimmy, take that muley to the creek and get him cleaned up while we try and get some food into this loser here. Be sure and explain the new rules to him."

Jimmy dragged Titus to what barely passed as a creek, more like a stagnant mud pond that had dried in spots only to pick up again further down. He sat back and watched Titus wash. There was something about him he didn't like, but couldn't figure out what. Right now, the way he washed, carefully cleaning his hands and splashing what little clean water he could find on his face…and those broad, straight, proud-looking shoulders…

"Where you from, Titus?"

Titus looked over his shoulder. "I's from Atlanta."

"You don't sound much like a Georgian."

"Neither do you."

Like a water viper Jimmy struck, pushing the muley forward into the water. "You got no right to question me, boy!"

Titus fell forward, startled, before he caught himself, getting dirty water splashed into his eyes. He shook off and sat back. "I's sorry, boss. I mean we got influences from places other than home. And you's different. You don't carry a gun like them."

Jimmy laughed, a little embarrassed. "They think I'm too inexperienced. But if they knew what I got…" he showed off the short gun tucked into his belt, under his shirt.

"You got more smarts than they think."

Jimmy nodded. "You, too, I reckon. Must be that white blood in you." Jimmy studied him, wondering how far to throw him to make the truth come out. What was he if not a slave? Could be something even more dangerous. Like a Copperhead. "Last thing I want is to tangle with more Republicans. You know, they come along, and all of a sudden the whole world is torn apart. They should all be shot, if you ask me. And will be, if Davis has his way."

"Well," Titus laughed, ending with an uncouth snort, "I's just glad to be seeing a way to be free and civilized and maybe even educated, some day." He sat back away from the muddy water and let the sun dry his battered face.

"Guess fighting in them irons is a little tough." Jimmy thought, too, that this man had too pretty a face to be a slave. Most of them he saw were already pretty beat up. This guy didn't even have a broken nose.

"You oughta try."

Too uppity for his station in life, too. "Oh, I don't think slavery would have lasted forever, way things were going. More of 'em getting free and educated all the time."

Titus scratched his head. "That why Lincoln's only freeing us southern slaves? Coz we're smarter?"

Jimmy didn't much glance at Titus, uncomfortable by this muley's odd way of talking. "Well, it's…it's a Republican plan, you see. Something that Lincoln and them Republicans devised back when Lincoln first got elected. We…they knew the South would secede after Lincoln got in—because of him not being on the southern ballot. All part of the plan, you see."

"Uh-huh." Titus looked like he just wanted sleep.

Jimmy watched the muley settle back quiet, feeling proud of himself for pretending he didn't know stuff—like how Tobias would be dead before they finished this delivery—because Lincoln didn't care how this rebellious slave was quieted, as long as he was quieted for good.

* * *

Adam laid on the edge of the stream as long as Jimmy would let him, until they brought him food. Leftovers again. Didn't take long for him to polish them off, and he couldn't see what he ate, anyway, for the pain in his eyes. Instead he played round and round with the idea that some other kind of rebellion rose up down South, leading northern men to go after runaways, and not just any but Lincoln-hating ones.

All Jimmy had to do was slip up with "we"—the way he said it and the way he caught himself saying it. These really were northern slavers.

Adam conjured all he could against Lincoln and realized the list was long enough. The Republicans were going after things they couldn't get before the South split off. That did, in some people's minds, make this whole war suspect. But then, since the days of the American Revolution, this has been an industrial country. Business owners such as timber men and mine owners got into politics because they were the most educated and wealthiest—Pa thought of politics a few times, himself. But getting their railroad route, passing the Homestead Act, were all great boons for the country headed west. And progress often came with a price, being paid by many now, like the Sioux Indians over in Minnesota who went rebel because of lack of money for treaty goods, killing people who didn't care the Sioux were being starved out.

This need for progress has made political government a hotbed for industrial leaders, like those railroad tycoons, to decide what government policies were enforced. And they would skew everything into profit for themselves. That means boys were dying for northern takeover of southern land and resources. Antietam, where the rivers ran red with blood—and McClellan, that Democrat General who let Lee get away, riling Lincoln's wrath. All of that for resources to keep industries making money?

Was Lincoln a pawn of a corrupt political party? Or maybe Tobias was playing with Adam's mind at a time he felt more vulnerable, leading him to believe things that couldn't possibly be true?

Adam didn't have to clean after eating but he made a process out of examining his fingernails, feeling Jimmy stare at his back. Jimmy was young, both suspicious and gullible. That made him dangerous. But why did they want Tobias? What kind of threat did he pose?

Jimmy grabbed Titus's arm and jerked him to his feet. He pulled his gun from under his shirt and poked it into Adam's gut. "Time to get back." He tucked the gun away again.

Adam realized what little resistance he could offer even if he'd wanted to. Lack of food did that to a fellow.

"We've been gone too long," Jimmy pushed him forward.

Adam got what he needed from Jimmy. But would he be as successful with Tobias? Northern slavers after one black—just who was the most dangerous here?

CHAPTER 15

Hoss didn't like going to the legal office. Sheriff Coffee shared his time between here and Virginia City but usually stayed in Virginia City because there were more disturbances to keep him busy—drunkenness, street brawling, mine ownership fights, and taxes to collect. Coffee called this the legal office, manned by a single deputy, a different fellow every week. Just when Coffee was getting used to one, there'd be a different one, he liked to say. Hoss never knew what to expect at this 'legal office.' But if there were a suspicious character in town, this would be the place to find out. And finding this Stephen who might be threatening Lydia was her best protection.

When Hoss walked in he saw this deputy, another stranger, busy writing. Dressed like he just came from a social. He looked up before Hoss could duck back outside.

"Yes sir?"

"You the deputy?"

"Oh," the young man with red hair and a flustered face to match jumped up. "Yeah. I mean…" he stuck out a warm hand and grabbed Hoss's to pump with enthusiasm. "I'm James Randolph, law clerk. They've put me in charge of this office now."

"No…deputies?"

"We keep several here, on staff, but they are out and about all day. Can't keep law and order if they're in here pushing pencils." He guffawed and snorted before wiping his face with the back of his hand and sitting.

"Dadburnit." Hoss turned to the door. *What's a law clerk gonna know?*

"Just state your trouble and I'll get someone right on it." James sat with pencil in hand and waited.

"Don't reckon I…well, I'm looking for a fellow who might be up to no good in these parts. New in the area, brought a wife with him. I met her. She claims he wants to kill her." Hoss spilled the story as James wrote. He thought he remembered everything Lydia told him but came up short on a description of the fellow, just that he was a dandy with a mean streak a mile high and potential thief. Hoss finished his tale, watched as James finished writing, and got ready to leave when James called him back.

"Hey, I know a guy sorta like this. I don't know his record on thieving, though."

Hoss felt his fists clench. He had no doubt of finding the man, because he believed every word Lydia said. He didn't know what he'd do when he found him, and that part made him uneasy.

"He went on to Virginia City. Found life here too dull. Voice of honey as thick as Mount Davidson but got nasty when addressing his daughter."

The air Hoss held in his chest whooshed out of him. *A daughter? Can't be right.*

"If he comes back here I could hold him for you. On a friendly basis, you understand. I have nothing to charge him with. Unless your lady friend wants to come in herself."

"Thanks, but he can go freely without knowing about me a'tall. I'll check him out in my own. Probably the wrong feller anyway. I do thank you kindly for your time."

Hoss took a breath of relief as he stepped back out and looked at the hills toward Virginia City, where an angry wind played devil with the dust. Had to be the wrong fellow, but didn't matter today. He had to go back to Lydia today.

* * *

Margaret, still breathless, nearly ran Roy over as she rode into the last turn before heading to the Ponderosa Ranch house. They both pulled up short, with horses snorting into each other's faces. But Roy looked like he was used to these near spills on this blind curve.

"Sorry, Sheriff. Ben should cut down this heavy thicket."

Coffee held his reins tight, grinned and tipped his hat at her. "Evening, Miss. No harm done." His horse didn't even acknowledge her horse snorting in its face.

Her horse, however, pranced back and tried to kick, acting ever since she mounted like it knew what she did to its owner, and wanted nothing more than to toss her into the nearest tree.

"Sheriff! I need your help!"

He thought she meant with her horse and jumped down to grab the bridle. Margaret jumped down next to him and kept a tight rein. Roy listened, quiet and respectful, to what happened to her back on the trail, except that his brows furled into an angry storm over his face.

"I suspect the wound isn't fatal, but I'll need to borrow the Cartwright's buckboard to pick him up. Come on, I'll ride with you to their ranch. Are you sure you're all right, miss?"

Margaret remembered Roy from years back but he hadn't been at the social so maybe he didn't know what had happened between her and Adam. She nodded, and they rode on together.

On riding into the yard they saw Hop Sing and Joe outside, going at each other with invisible swords, so intent they didn't turn when the two rode in. Margaret allowed Roy to take the lead. *Please let him get the buckboard and leave.*

Beyond this, she could see her last happy moment with Adam, and the fear of rape a moment ago rose into her throat, of her father coming after her, night after night, until she emptied all the whiskey in the house and learned to sleep out in the field at night.

When she swooned, she felt Hop Sing help her down out of the saddle. The other two men were too caught up in Roy's errand to pay her much mind.

"Joe, got a band of cattle thieves working these parts. Wanted to warn you. They work pretty close to the hide, too, have a way of getting hired on before doing their dirty work."

Joe frowned at something off in the distance before crossing his arms. "I suspect they've already been at work on the Ponderosa, Roy. Thanks for the warning, I'll... tend to it."

"You be sure your Pa gets the message, you hear?" Roy pulled back just as he was about to ride off. "Say, mind if I leave my horse here for the night and borrow your draft and a buckboard? Margaret here tipped me off to a problem that needs mending."

"Sure, that's...fine." Joe bit a lip and then his eyes lit with maniacal gleam. "Say, you might want to ask her where she's been hiding Adam out."

"It's late and I gotta pick up..." Roy looked over at her.

Margaret felt sure she was going to slip in a dead faint to the ground. How could Joe not know what Hoss knew?

"Adam's missing, you say? This got anything to do with that article printed in the Territorial Enterprise by Sam Clemens...uh, Mark Twain?" Roy turned back to Joe, who seemed intent on staring the truth out of Margaret.

Margaret couldn't stand Joe's expression and faced Roy instead. "An article, Sheriff Coffee? About Adam?"

"Is it true then, miss? You got him hiding out somewheres?"

"No. I..." Margaret bit her lip and glanced at Hop Sing.

Hop Sing took a step forward. "Mr. Adam, he go off on tlip to build windmill. Ground too dry."

Margaret and Joe looked at him in surprise.

Roy nodded. "Well, our friend Mark Twain reported on quite a social here, Little Joe. Says Adam got drunk and started beating on the guests as they was leaving. Now knowing Adam and this Sam feller, I figured it's just more of his tall tale telling. But some folks might not think so." Roy shrugged. "You send your Pa to town, you hear? Him and me will set 'em straighter on this fun tale telling."

"Let me help you with the buckboard, Roy." Joe walked Roy to the barn. He glanced back at Margaret. She saw open terror in those eyes. Or did she see what she felt?

Margaret leaned on Hop Sing and let him guide her to the house. "Thanks for covering for me, Hop Sing."

"Glad to see you, Miss Margaret. You say where Mr. Adam go?"

"Oh, Hop Sing," Her chest burned with a feeling like certain devastation might come heaving out. "I wish I could. But...maybe I can help Joe pick up his trail."

"Mr. Adam not leave if not important." Hop Sing sat her at the front porch in a chair that wobbled until she leaned back. "What happened to you clothes?"

She shook her head. "I need to see Ben."

"Mr. Cartlight gone. Mr. Adam gone. Not know where."

"Ben, too?" Margaret tried to stand but couldn't. "I don't believe it."

"You stay here, talk Mr. Joe. I finish clacking cicada...cicada easy part of potion, they everywhere. Dead this time of year, so I no have to kill." Hop Sing scurried inside.

Margaret sat catching her breath to make the world stop spinning. Adam and Ben both gone? She wondered if Hop Sing was one of those who hit the opium pipe a little too often. She waved as Roy rode off. Little Joe, after a moment of just standing there, came to the front porch and sat on the stoop.

Margaret looked up to see the night sky start its slow creeping across the blue. "Joe, I'm so sorry. It's all my fault."

Joe shook his head. "The fire's not. Although we could have used his help. Do you know where he is?"

Margaret couldn't hear him so she stood and pulled him to his feet. He felt very responsive to her touch, as though he's needed to be touched for a long, long time. "Tell me everything."

Joe pushed away from her. "A fire...has a way of changing everything."

She remembered seeing smoke but never expected that more than a little damage had been done. "Your Pa...died?"

"The preacher would say that fires have a cleansing effect. Where the world begins, fresh and new. I don't...want that kind of world." Joe collapsed to his knees.

Margaret couldn't hear him, but she could tell he was sobbing. She fell to his side and wrapped her arms around him. "Come on, we could both use some water. Let's go inside."

Joe hiccupped and let her lead. When Margaret got him into the settee, he pulled her down with him. "The fire killed Pa. I couldn't save him. And now Adam's gone and Hoss is distracted by a lady who isn't always there. I gotta run the ranch! Hop Sing is trying to stop me, but there is no one else. I'm a Cartwright, not Salzar." Joe leaped to his feet, wobbled, and looked around with the desperation of sorrow for something firm and possible to do to get rid of the helplessness.

She grabbed his hand. "Where's Adam, Joe? Was he in the fire, too?"

Joe looked, startled, as Hop Sing came out of the guest room and stared at them. "No, no, couldn't be! No, Adam will be back any time now, but until then I'm in charge."

Margaret knew Joe wasn't out of his teens yet and deeply saddened besides. What good could he do alone? This ranch was a handful for the most mature of men. "Maybe…Hop Sing knows some things you can do."

Hop Sing gave her a sheepish grin. "He not listen. I say lest for a few day, ranch not fall apart so qlick."

But Margaret thought of those two ranch hands, drunk and roaming without direction. These things going on—they're all connected somehow. She shook off the past with a shudder. "We could both use some cold water, Hop Sing." When Hop Sing left the room, Margaret sat next to Joe. "What will you do out there?"

Joe looked hopeful. "I didn't find Pa's body. Maybe…maybe he's still alive out there somewhere. I've got to climb the cliff! And I'll check on the cattle drive, see who's running things. And the loggers, if I can't find Adam, I have to…" But his voice dropped as he tried to figure out what to do first.

"Joe, I know that Adam went off into the night very angry at me. I know the direction. Maybe we can pick up his trail. And then…" she bit her lip.

"Why would he stay away? He's not like that."

"I know."

* * *

Hop Sing brought out two cups of water in cool metal and they both drank noisily. Joe finished first and sat back, exhausted.

"Hop Sing, don't you think that if Joe were just to check on things, make sure everyone was still working, then he'd feel better being busy? I'm sure Adam will come back, and—"

"I don't need Hop Sing's permission, miss." Joe's steely tone shook, just a little.

Hop Sing's narrowed eyes softened looking into Joe's glistening, wide-eyed ones. "He do what he must. I think he tly too much. I need to find flower like Magnolia, no time for you foolishment. No find flower in October. Be stuck with sagebrush. Yuck. Next time plan ahead." Hop Sing walked back into the kitchen.

Joe went to Ben's desk and ripped a book open. "Pa's got a ledger that shows all the men currently working and on what and how long the project is expected to last. And then I have to find the binder of contracts to make sure we're still able to deliver what we—"

Both of them jumped when Hop Sing crept up behind them. "She back! She in room! You come, come see light now!" He motioned them to be quiet and follow.

"Finally get to see the spook," Joe muttered and clamped a hand over his mouth.

As Hop Sing opened the door to the guest room, Joe caught images of all the guests who'd been here—Coffee on nights too late to ride back, the lovely French girl, the blind child at Christmas, and the night they put Adam here after being shot in the back. The girl in bed this time was as frail, vulnerable and beautiful as any he'd ever seen, still sleeping, and he feared taking a breath would make her disappear. She seemed to shimmer, like a fanciful play of light off the lake, but so perfectly human and fully formed that he did not doubt she was real.

Still, he reached out to touch her, filled with the urge but careful not to wake her. Before he could touch her Hop Sing pulled them both out of the room and shut the door.

"Who is she, Hop Sing?" Margaret whispered as he walked them back to the desk.

"She willow tlee in fog."

"Huh?"

Margaret grinned at Joe. "I second that. That's a little vague."

"I touch her. I know she real. But not real. Real like willow bendee and blowee in wind and hidee in fog. She live in fear of death, she is death and make Hoss love her is bad."

"What's a willow?" Joe seated himself behind the desk, figuring Hop Sing needed time to get used to seeing him there. The chair felt big, but comfy. He knew what he had to do. One of these jobs might lead him to finding Pa. He might have been kidnapped by the cattle rustlers, caught in the act, with only minutes more to live. Or Adam. He'll look for Adam, too.

Or he might find either one, or both, rotting on the ground. He dropped the pencil because his hand shook too much. His head sank down in his hands.

"Willow not live here. Long graceful branches reachee glound. Make good whips!" Hop Sing, embarrassed by his last statement, hurried off to the kitchen.

"Where'd she come from, Joe?"

Joe felt grateful for her warm hand on his back. "All I know is one night before the social Hoss started talking about this gal who came and went so mysterious like. And then after the social—he's been funny in the head ever since."

"I ran into Hoss in town. He was in an awful hurry. Is she ill?"

Joe studied Margaret, who could have been Adam's last great hope at happiness, at bringing new life to all of them. She stood there now, a symbol of death. "Where's Adam?" He stood and grabbed her arms. "What did you do to him to make him run off?"

"Me? You were the one who beat him up."

Joe stared at the stairway that led to emptiness. The whole house...empty...

"Oh, Joe, I'm sorry. I don't mean it's your fault." Margaret moved to the fireplace as though a sudden cold draft blew up the sleeves of her dress. "I suppose I better tell you everything." She turned back. "You're sure you haven't seen him since the social?"

"We talked about that the next morning, about him not coming home to sleep. And Hop Sing...hasn't seen him since. He's the only one who's been here all the time. Well, except Hoss, and I'm not sure Hoss was always here, either."

Margaret nodded. "I'm sorry, I...don't know what's going on around here."

Joe sat her down and told her as much as he could, which, by the time he finished, began to sound very insane, indeed.

* * *

Joe may be half out of his mind with grief, Margaret thought, but with any luck he still had the right half. "Let's go find Adam, Joe."

Joe glanced out the window over his pa's desk. "It's too late." Joe was just a kid, but a kid going through hell. He poured them both a brandy, which she gratefully swallowed. When he took the seat next to her, his expression had become cold and hard.

"Margaret, why did you come here? What do you want from us?"

Except that she knew this was Joe, she would have thought Adam was talking. "You invited me, Joe."

"What did you say to him to make him walk away like he did?"

"I told him...the real reason I left him, so many years ago. So sudden. He...I didn't expect he'd get so upset."

"Why are you still hanging around here? Why don't you just leave?"

Margaret hesitated. "I love Adam, Joe, and I want to help find him."

"It's too late."

"Stop saying that! I feel so guilty, Joe, please help me." Margaret grabbed Joe's arm and pulled him with her. When they walked outside the sky seemed lighter than on the inside. She could still make out the path to the moonlit bench. Beyond there, she had blurted out the worst confession of her life at the worst time. Like then, darkness crept closer, though the stars were still too far away. Nothing would be as that night had been—nothing ever again.

She didn't feel guilt over allowing her father to bury her newborn without even looking at it. Had that misbegotten child lived it could have spelled a horrible fate for all three of them. And she knew, with what little knowledge she had of the world, that she was not the only mother who ever felt unfit for that duty.

But trusting Adam with the knowledge so soon and when he'd just fought with his brother had been poor timing. And now to honor Adam and potentially his memory, his love of family and this ranch life, she would do what she could to heal this family before leaving on what may end up an impossible quest. To heal herself. She stood with Joe in the rising moonlight and pointed out the direction she'd seen him walk, the direction that took him out of their lives.

Both Ben and Adam missing. A tragedy incomprehensible.

As they stood at the swooning bench and Margaret pointed out the direction Adam took, they heard horses. Joe grabbed her hand and they ran back into the yard. They came to an abrupt halt to keep from getting run over by galloping horses.

Hoss leaped off Chubby and grabbed the reins of Dr. Jessup's horse.

Joe yelled at Hoss, though pleased to see him, Margaret could tell. "You know what Pa says about reining into the yard."

"Pa home?" Hoss helped a shaky doctor out of the saddle. "Sorry it's so late, doc, you're welcome to stay the night."

"Hoss, darned good thing you don't need surgery performed."

Margaret put a hand on Hoss's arm. "She's resting peaceful, Hoss."

"You saw her!? You see, Joe, you see? I told you she was real!" Hoss hurried the doctor inside.

Margaret felt the chill of the coming night and rubbed her arms, staring back the darkness so like the one that had swallowed Adam not so long ago. He had been darker himself than she had remembered, so well tanned from a summer of ranching that she nearly didn't know him. And wearing dark clothes, he fit in so well with the night.

Sure as I'm standing here, he's dead. He'd never do this to his family. "Doc gonna stay the night, Joe?"

Joe stared into the night like darkness was the salve he applied to his aching mind. "Maybe not. Carson City route is better than the Virginia City one, at least. Doctors get used to traveling for emergencies at any time."

"I suppose." Margaret wiped at her skirt and adjusted the hat that felt useless on her head. "I want to look for Adam, Joe. Can we try?"

"I'll get a lantern."

"I'll need a horse." She walked to the barn.

Behind her Joe made an exasperated sound and followed. As though knowing which horse was Adam's, Margaret headed right for it. "You'll never be able to handle her. We'll walk anyway, just til we can't see his trail no more."

Margaret had taken the horse's face near hers and stroked its nose. "She's wonderful. What's her name?"

"You know, I don't remember Adam naming her. Wait—Beauty. When he first got her, he said, "She's Beauty.""

Margaret smiled. "Well, he probably said "she's *a* beauty," but that's good enough."

"Come on, let's see how that trail looks you think Adam walked out on. Hoss wants some privacy, anyway."

Margaret followed Joe out the barn, with one lingering look at Adam's horse. "Joe, I have the feeling your Pa is fine. I just do."

Joe looked down at where her hand gripped his arm. "He's been missing before, given up for dead, had amnesia. Pa says he has this great resiliency. But this is the first time...I was so close. I should have sent him to get help, he was too...old...to help."

Joe didn't look like a little boy anymore—he looked as old as his Pa.

* * *

"Hop Sing! I brought the doctor! He'd like some tea!" Hoss stood the doctor outside of the guest room. "I'm gonna to tell her you're here. She can be skittish as a fawn and quick as a moth when the candle goes out."

"Hoss, that's perfectly poetic," said Dr. Jessup. "I'd say you're smitten with this gal."

"Ah," Hoss blushed at the floor. "She's easy to like, being so frail and all. Wait here. I'll git her ready...to be seen by you."

Lydia looked restless and anxious in her dreams. Hoss put a hand on her head and felt the heat. Her eyes fluttered open.

"Hoss. Oh, I had a dream that Stephen had killed you and I was alone!"

"I'm sorry, I had to bring you down here," Hoss blushed, "because it wouldn't be right for us...I mean...I need the bed...I mean—"

Lydia grabbed his arm. "Don't let Stephen hurt you!"

"No, Miss, but I think I found him."

"Oh, make him go away, please."

"Now you just simmer down, we got to get you well first, you're burning with fever."

"No. Hoss—"

"I got a doctor here to look at you, maybe give you some medicine."

"No! Hoss—"

When she struggled to get out of bed he held her shoulders down. "I want you well. Please. For me." Hoss leaned over and kissed her on the lips and the sensation, not unlike kissing a cloud, made him feel just as high.

When their eyes met he saw all the love he'd ever imagined in a girl's eyes who loved and trusted him back. "Now don't move."

But when he brought Dr. Jessup in, Lydia was gone. "Dadburnit."

Dr. Jessup searched the room. "I've dealt with shy ones before." He looked out the window. "But I think she's a crazy one, Hoss. Or a ghost."

"She ain't neither! I'll find her." Hoss ran outside, calling for her. He never dealt with this kind of girl before. He circled the entire house and when he got back to the front Dr. Jessup had already mounted.

"Sorry, Hoss, but I better get going. Remember we met Roy with an interesting one, a story I can't wait to hear." He looked skyward. "And enough light to get halfway down before my horse starts to slow up."

Hoss, embarrassed, tucked his thumbs in his vest pockets and nodded at the ground. Once Jessup rode off he looked back at the house.

Lydia stood in front of the door.

"Hey! Doc, hey!"

Lydia walked back inside and Hoss could do nothing but follow.

CHAPTER 16

Ben felt serious hunger. These folks had long since run out of their meager rations and scrounging the Ponderosa generally didn't prove fruitful, especially now, with much of the area around them burned out. Jesse had stolen from a few houses on the way to Carson City, saying he feared going to town because of his color. Ben knew that Carson City was better than most, but still, he might not be able to return once he got there. He tried to talk Jesse into going to the ranch house with a note for Hop Sing, but Sadie told Ben that wasn't a good idea. She couldn't say why, except that she wanted to see Ben healed a little more before his family attempted some crazy rescue. Since every muscle ached when he moved, Ben could see some sense in that. Still, his family, especially Joe, would be so worried by now.

Until this deep hunger set in, they managed to keep him very comfortable, giving him blankets and other padding from their wagon—transportation they kept hid, they said, but wouldn't say where. His hunger meant he had serious healing to do, and he wanted to get home to finish. And he was tired of this confounded dark. Ben could smell traces of blasting powder and some rotting timber, and the wet granite they had been blasting here had a distinctive odor. The mountains were peppered with abandoned mine shafts like this, but he didn't expect to find them on his own land. Didn't the fools know they were trespassing? All these mine shafts to follow a single trail of silver that invariably petered out.

Ben called out several times but no one answered. Left alone to do his private affairs. His arms and legs felt less dry and crackling than just the day before. Sadie was an incredible healer using unfamiliar plants, and she made him feel better just by singing to him. Soul spirituality, she called her songs. Ben found the bucket they'd left. They seemed to have no end of talent at self-preservation—these are people most whites believed were only smart enough for slavery?

The day passed and still no one returned—how could he even be sure the day passed? Alone in this perpetual darkness all moments seemed like the same one. Were they on the run again? Or had they been caught?

Ben got to his knees, not knowing how much area surrounded him. He reached out as he moved, feeling the area's depth, reaching through his pain, tight but bearable. He held his broken arm against him as he put one foot on the ground and forced himself up, good arm swinging up for barriers. He swayed and fell to one knee so he sat, finding first a wall to lean against, and careful, always, that he didn't tip the bucket.

Grunting, sweating, he scanned his surroundings to find in what direction the darkness abated, just a little. Thought he saw a light. Checked again. Yes. A slanted mine shaft, for easy in and out crawling. He could get out, but climbing a cliff with one arm? Ben sat and tried to figure the lay of the land around him. Maybe a little ways down the cliff he could find a trail. Possible.

They held him prisoner here—but why? Ben knew Darcy didn't much like him, but to plot against him this way? Made no sense. They took good care of him, and did admit to wanting more than just his help. Apparently Darcy told them Ben controlled a mountain of silver here. He could talk to Bill Stewart, of course, but just how much political influence did Darcy think he could muster? Ben felt certain Sadie wasn't done talking to him yet, and kept him here to convince him of something he might not otherwise care to do.

Still using just the one arm, he began to crawl. Now not only hungry but thirsty—that's how to tell how much time has passed. A few days without, and death, after agonizing delirium. Worries about home intensified as darkness tried to remove all hope and identity. He still didn't know if his youngest child was alive or dead.

* * *

"So how'd this young fellow get buckshot in his behind without any in the pants?" Dr. Jessup had the wounded man stretched out on his stomach in his office, and, having removed the lead, bandaged Stu up.

Frank shrugged. "Privacy moment. Forgot to put the safety on, I guess." He walked to the door and listened to the whoops and hollers from the saloon next door. "Gonna be much longer?"

Jessup eyed Frank's non-concern. "My father, bless him, always said, handle guns and women carefully. Both are dangerous. Guess that's why I became a physician." He put a hand on Stu's shoulder. You know you come seriously close to being sterile?"

Stu, still on his stomach, snorted at this. Since nothing on him kept shaking with suppressed humor, Jessup figured he sobered quick at the thought. As well he should. This was no accident, but neither man cared to be truthful.

Jessup let them both go but he made a note to himself in case some gal should come in with a pitiful tale of woe. For his part, he would keep his ears open for *any* gal acting fearful. Some won't say a word. Even worse—and this part he didn't know how to fix—if he attacked a gal and she shot him, that young fellow could want to get at her again.

Though the hour was much later than even a doctor normally kept, he feared his new worry would keep him awake and listening for strange sounds. Before he knew it, the sun blinked his eyes open, and he was further alerted by the shouting outside.

Jessup threw on his morning coat and stepped out the door. He remembered his fear for a gal's sake and Joe's concern over his missing father, and had offered to be on the alert for anything unusual. Sure enough, a crowd had gathered, and as Jessup walked to get a better view, saw the small worn wood wagon with the mangy cur, neither of which would be stolen if left alone for a day, and then took several steps into the street. They were black folk. He'd seen black folk before but not for awhile, not in this town. And not without being accompanied by whites. They appeared to be frightened, and, having no goods for sale or trade, perhaps even on the brink of starvation. Certainly without money to stop for goods at the mercantile, which was where they stopped.

Jessup hung back. Wasn't his concern, after all. He could fear for their safety, as the crowd accused them of being runaways, but he couldn't interfere. Not at his age.

The man—a boy really—jumped out of the wagon and helped the elderly woman down, leaving a young gal at the reins.

Ignoring questions and shouts around them, the two walked into the mercantile. Jessup wasn't surprised to see that no one wanted to stop them, by grabbing their arms or with some other such force. From what he'd seen in his life, people were downright shy of what they didn't know or understand. Instead the crowd remained outside, mumbling to themselves, watching, waiting and directing more loud questions at that poor young girl, sitting alone. One said to go for the sheriff. Jessup didn't see anyone respond to this.

Jessup wondered if she could be the girl he sought, the one who'd been abused. From what he figured, the gal this Stu attacked used his own gun on him. He thought to get closer, at least see her eyes, but before he could make a move that far, the woman ran out with goods in her skirt while the storekeep, not at all happy about being robbed, pulled the boy who had tried to follow back inside. Several more called out for deputies. The woman did not look back or try to save the boy but leaped into the wagon, spilling nothing, and the girl whipped the stringy mule into a trot.

Several shouted "Stop them!" but no one went near the wagon, as though they were diseased. No civilian was inclined to step in front of the mule even though the animal could be stopped easily by the slightest barrier.

Odd, Jessup thought, as he sat back at his desk. The town was more Republican than he thought. He had expected the two women to get gunned down as they ran.

* * *

General George McClellan sat in his tent alone, braced for the visit. Lincoln was coming to camp and Mac feared a nasty affair. Lincoln, that overgrown ape, never had a nice word to say about his army and Mac, who prided himself on every aspect of soldierly conduct, felt Lincoln was just a useless political mouth. Those Republicans were to blame for this war, and they expected him to get his boys killed for little to gain. Mac figured, instead, just cut off the South from needed resources and it would be on its knees in no time. He wanted Richmond.

What was the sense in getting all their men shot up? But that's what those Republicans wanted—to see how many soldiers they could kill on each side and then free the slaves to work for northern industry. Oh, they just call that a Democrat's opinion, but Mac thought it a pretty accurate one. Why else make him go after Lee when he was within seven miles of taking Richmond?

While riding through camp, Mac tossed off a wave or two at the men who cheered his presence. Camp appeared clean enough to his eyes, considering the sprawling of tents and needs of 100,000 men. Now he had to pretend to Lincoln that he wanted Lee every bit as much as Lincoln did. If Lincoln should learn what he and other Northern Democrats wanted... just to hold off, on the brink of war, until the South came to its senses, nothing more. That was the compromise that the Republicans refused to see. Blood-thirsty, that's all they were.[22]

Mac rode with several of his guards to meet Lincoln's boat at Harper's Ferry—the Maryland side, of course. The Ape Lincoln's recent proclamation was designed to give the South one last chance to negotiate for peace. By freeing the slaves in Rebellion states Lincoln thought he could starve off foreign aid to the South, too. And some called Lincoln the great emancipator. At least not everyone was fooled—not even those Parliament lunatics over in the old country.

Mac planned a counter-attack on Lincoln's so-called emancipation—one that would have to wait until after Lincoln's visit. Freeing the slaves, indeed. Why, they'd have to be educated first, and that took time. Time and money those abolitionists weren't willing to give. They wanted this war to become a moral war, but just in words, that's all.

The camp of the Army of the Potomac, however, was all in a buzz, when Mac returned with Lincoln's entourage. "Lincoln is coming!" The soldiers revered Lincoln, as well they should, him being president. The office, and not the ape, Mac reminded himself. Soldiers were excitable, like Henry, a recent German immigrant and new member of the provost guard. He was all for freeing slaves—but at the same time Henry worried that when the war was done, he might not be able to find a job. Such a balance of like/dislike most of these soldiers fought for. They went out on a limb, even dying, for the right to free slaves and lose their jobs! Mac figured he'll hear more of this growing dissention in the ranks in the coming months.

General Patrick, in charge of the provost guard, received orders to turn his brigade out for a grand review and the men stood in dress, with weapons at ease and each, like Henry, braced to catch Lincoln's eye. Henry stood with the proud bearing of the German military, chosen for the provost guard because he could already read and write, and his use of English had progressed better than some. Mac could see Henry's disappointment when Lincoln's eyes breezed right by him. *These are human beings, dammit!* But Mac didn't dare voice anything negative aloud. That's what his letters to his wife were for.

Mac watched Lincoln shake a few hands, proud to see that the men managed not to itch and scratch in front of him. Most needed a bath, dirty and filled with vermin, and Mac wondered—even hoped—that Lincoln, this close to them, would go home scratching, too.[23] He introduced a number of officers to Lincoln, and the discussion on everyone's mind was whether the South would now sue for peace, and if guarding the borders and starving the South into submission would be effective. Lincoln, to Mac's annoyance, kept proposing battle plans that for one reason or other Mac found ill-conceived.

Fully frustrated, Lincoln turned to the youngest of officers there, a bright blonde fellow named George Custer. "Are you, soldier, for peace or war?"

Custer didn't even pause. "So far as my country is concerned, I, of course, must wish for peace, and will be glad when the war is ended, but if I answer for myself alone, I must say that I shall regret to see the war end. I would be willing, yes, glad, to see a battle every day during my life."[24]

Mac groaned. A Democrat sure, but as bloodthirsty as any Republican. What strange bedfellows this war conjured.

By the end of the conference Lincoln reassured Mac that he had Washington's full support, except that he wished Mac would move even before he felt ready. Mac felt that was an odd thing to say and some of the officers agreed. They, too, would like to see Lincoln do something before he was ready.

Mac quipped, to general laughter, "I'd say this war and the presidency might both qualify for that." To himself, he added, "freeing the slaves, for sure."[25]

* * *

"You ever see such beautiful scenery in your life, Titus?"

The breaking dawn made Adam's hope for more sleep a futile one. "Yeah, back at the Ponderosa." They made good time, these slavers, and Adam knew that part of the reason was their monetary concern. Men who were hungry moved faster.

"Sure glad I was able to keep you from getting killed back there."

Adam grunted, thinking it the other way around. A bath and a shave, what he wouldn't give… He raised his voice, "I'd like to know what's going on back east. The war could be over, for all's we know."

The driver sitting above them snickered. They tended to trade off driving and riding and Adam didn't care which was who, just knew he had to be careful. "I tell ya, if it's a quick war, it's because the South is winning. A slow war and the North will get it for sure."

102

"I spect so, but what's your thinking?" Adam answered back in his best southern drawl.

"Because the South is on the side of right and mighty. And that's the side that wins a quick victory. Them what's doing the devil's work, well, they tend to stick a longer time and don't care how many fine boys die. If ole' Jeff Davis kin convince the North they's right about seceding, this war will end."

Adam was impressed by the clean thinking. True enough, if Jeff Davis could prove the Constitution allowed for slavery—so far each side interpreted it their way, however, so Adam had the feeling they'd never find an unbiased interpretation. "You well read, I kin tell."

The driver, Luke, got their attention over his shoulder. "They say Lincoln's over to visiting McClellan, says he's unhappy with Mac sitting tight and not going after Lee. But Mac's a Democrat, and that makes him one smart man. Now Lee, he's just taking a little time to do some recruiting and then he'll go after Mac, you mark my word."

"You taking us to Lee for his recruitin'?" This good ole' boy didn't sound like a northerner at all. *What's going on here?*

"Don't you wish? No, we got other plans. Doubt you'll see southern light past Brownsville."

Adam swallowed hard. "Texas?"

Luke lost interest when several riders came running back with the news that the trail ahead was a tough one.

Adam leaned over to Tobias. "I thought we were headed to Kentucky."

"Turns out the Confederate army from Tennessee has crossed into Kentucky, and now Buell has his arms full."[26] Tobias shrugged at Adam's gaping stare. "I listen good. So we gotta go to New Orleans instead. Don't be mad, Adam, that's a good thing for us."

"Not if they sell me off in Texas. Can't imagine how northerners would get through southern territory with their hides intact." Adam didn't share with Tobias what he had learned from Jimmy because he wasn't sure he could trust Tobias either. What he wouldn't give for Hoss's shoulder and ear right now!

"Oh, they's gonna sell *you*. I hear tell they can't wait to be shut of you. No northerner will shoot another northerner without a reason."

"You told them the truth?"

"Course not, Titus. I need you."

"Sometimes I get the feeling all you need is a northerner on your side. What you thinking of doing, using me to get Lincoln alone so you can kill him?"

"That's crazy!" Tobias leaned close. "You know, just might work." He laughed when Adam glared at him. "You jus' keepa thinking, Adam." Tobias stared out over the scenery.

Adam figured he could be mistaken but he sure thought that was fear running across Tobias's face. There was some charade going on here, all right. The slavers didn't anticipate picking a muley up along the way—or did they? So now nobody knew quite who to trust. Adam kept his smile to himself. That could be a good thing.

Now that he knew where they were headed, he recognized the trail…had been trying to figure it out but felt disoriented because he'd never seen the route from the back of a wagon before. They figured on taking the shortcut to the Santa Fe Trail? The Cartwrights did most of their traveling west to Sacramento, or east to St. Louis for a trip to New Orleans. But he knew enough about this shortcut to know few riders were desperate enough to consider it.

Adam remembered a time he and Hoss let Joe take them on a short-cut he'd just found. They'd been beating the mesquite looking for stray cattle when a sudden storm rolled in over the mountains. Hoss tried to explain to his little brother that sometimes shortcuts took them the long way, but Joe pointed at the urgency in the lightning and said he'd taken the route a lot of times. They spent the rest of that night huddled together under a rock outcropping, coats over their heads, shivering, wet and swearing. Joe said the trail looked different in the rain.

Adam saw the beginning of the shortcut ahead and wished for that rainy night again. A drop-off, with a ragged trail down to the valley where he could see a settlement and a road leading still farther south and east. The view took his breath away—or perhaps it was the danger. Shades of red and brown rock stacked high and pieced together with lines of silver and green—if the area was less dangerous miners would be here by now. A few trees managed to cling to the rock but for the most part withered and died soon after making a brave exit through the cracks. There had been some kind of earthquake here— on the valley floor sat a myriad of fallen rocks of the same colors, before clearing off to the path these fellows sought to take.

"We're going down there?"

"Have to," Jimmy said, riding alongside the wagon. "If we don't we just keep climbing, and end miles out of our way. Once we get down there, we ride safe and easy and fast for days ahead. At least until we hit the Navajo problem."

"Don't seem worth the danger for two niggers," Adam said, biting back his sigh.

Cal rode over. "Come on, enough jabbering, out of the wagon. We're going down. Jimmy, I'll take your horse. You get to the nose of the team."

Adam put out a shaky hand. "You's crazy? We can't guide a wagon down this here side of a cliff."

"The hill's got a bit of an incline, just gotta keep your heads together, that's all."

Adam could do no more arguing. The "hill" appeared to be death either way, if he goes or refuses.

Jimmy was none too happy either. "Why me? I ain't never done nothing like this before."

"You're better off letting them animals loose to follow us their own way," Adam muttered, a little too loud.

"You expect me to take the word of a muley? Unless you have more experience at this than you let on." Cal pulled his gun and leaned over his saddle toward Adam.

Titus threw up a hand in fear. "No, just thinking about the thinking that horses do good when they's loose, that's all."

"You'll do it our way. Now out!"

Tobias, next to him, didn't say anything. Adam sensed he was terrified. Still shackled, but at least not to each other, they climbed out.

Tobias cleared his throat and held up his hands. "You gonna take these irons off'n us?"

Cal laughed. "You got your ankle irons off. We ain't crazy enough to give you an extra chance to get away. Hand irons won't bother your work here."

Titus leaned to Tobias, keeping his voice low. "I know this route. Once below the first ridge, drops right off."

"You should tell them."

"All right, boys, out of the wagon. If you value your cushy seat, then you keep the wagon on that narrow trail and not let it go tumbling over the side. You're both smart and strong. Just guide the wagon on each side and follow Jimmy and them horses."

Titus winced. "Sheer suicide."

"You say something, muley?"

Titus closed his eyes. "No sir. We can do this, sir."

CHAPTER 17

Margaret had spent a sleepless night, after following a trail with Joe that grew cold in the dark. She watched the window in Ben's room, where she had chosen to sleep instead of Adam's, but sleep felt worlds away. As the light began to form shapes out of the black empty air, she threw off the sleep covers and struggled back into her red and black wool underskirt that had half ripped and would be tossed as soon as she got back to Carson City. She sprang out of Ben's room still lacing on her balmorals, one of which she found scuffed beyond repair, and found Joe pacing the sitting room quiet, like a panther. Wordless, she followed him outside, attaching her jocket hat as she went, thankful for the strap to hold her mussed hair in place. She knew she looked foolish, nice new clothes half ripped up and untended, but who around here would notice besides her, anyway?

Margaret insisted on riding Beauty and amazed Joe with her riding abilities. She sensed him watching her, wondering about what happened between her and Adam, wanting his disappearance to be her fault. Joe alighted at various points to have a closer look to be sure they were going the right away, but not often as the trail didn't tend to go anywhere but straight ahead.

He asked her again, "What happened between you and Adam?"

Margaret sighed, glad that he kept an eye on the ground rather than on her. "I told him the reason I left with Pa so many years before. He…didn't think it a sound reason. Thought…I was lying." She expected he'd want more and she would answer it if he asked. He took on enough blame for Ben and she could handle her own guilt. She had to.

Instead Joe kicked the horse into a trot. "I think I know where he went."

When Margaret caught up he had already leaped off his horse in front of a cave to study the ground. He pointed a cave out to her, as she adjusted her riding hat and dismounted, and found a number of foot and horse prints around the cave opening. Margaret realized Adam could have walked this far. The sudden stopping more than the distance riding had knocked her hat over her eyes.

"Are the hoof prints as fresh as his foot prints?" When Joe nodded Margaret clutched at the overcoat covering her heart. "What could it mean, Joe?"

106

"Nothing, yet." Joe lit a match and crawled into the cave. "Looks like someone slept here, all right. More than one. Maybe nothing more than bear cubs. Although wait—here's a match stub. Smells pretty fresh, too."

Margaret took off her hat and leaned over Joe's shoulder. "Adam must have met with someone here, Joe. Someone who kidnapped him, or...."

"As long as there's no body, we can still hope he's alive." As Joe paused, Margaret could hear him think the same for his pa. "But without more clues there's just no where else to go from here." Joe whipped out his glowing match to let the darkness back in.

"Let's look back outside, there must be some kind of tracks leading—"

They heard horses on the trail and ducked out of the cave to meet the riders. At first hopeful, Margaret stiffened and moved away. Joe paid attention to the riders and didn't notice her sudden unease.

"Frank! Is there a problem?"

Margaret saw now that any trail leading away from here in that direction had been erased by new riders. Too many days gone. Too many.

"Been sent to find you, Joe."

"Yeah?"

Frank paused to stare at Margaret. "Ah... something about wild horses needed picking up. Fellow named Amos."

"Amos Burnsby...that's Hoss's job, did you talk to him?"

"Hop Sing told me to find you, have you get 'em. I'm to go with you, and Charlie here."

Joe groaned but swallowed it down. Margaret stole a peek at Charlie, an old guy—probably hard working but good for next to nothing. She couldn't even half glance at Frank. "Maybe we should just wait until Hoss gets freed up."

"Can't. Amos says he's three days late already, and he's got someone else interested. They won't pay as much but anything's better than a Cartwright broken promise."

"Ah, Margaret," Joe shrugged. "You can find your way back to the ranch alone, right? And when you see Hoss, tell him..."

Charlie started to laugh.

Joe gave Charlie a look and continued to Margaret, "Tell him I'm doing his chores for him while he nursemaids a sick fog."

That shut Charlie up but good.

Frank tipped his hat to Margaret and three rode off.

Margaret, stiff as a board, waited until they were gone before relaxing some. She tried tracking Adam on her own from the cave, but felt ill when she found jumbled horse tracks in all directions, and gave up to return the message to Hoss.

* * *

Ben didn't get far in his crawling because he couldn't move fast. He heard their voices and sat back to wait, swallowing hard against the taste of granite. Because he'd crawled closer to the mine entrance, when Sadie and Abby reached him he could make out the outline of their faces, both lean and dark, with Sadie's hair starting to gray and Abby's in a wild mane about her face. Both appeared upset.

Ben tried not to sound mean. "I thought I'd leave, since I didn't know where you were and prefer not to die of thirst."

"Oh, Ben, I done tole you how much we needs you. I never do that to you. But I knew you need food to gets your strength back."

Ben devoured the biscuit she gave him after she told him where they got the food. "What did you use for money? I don't carry any on me or I would have—" He stopped when he noticed somber unblinking eyes in the dim glow of daylight. "Is something wrong? Where's Jesse?"

Abby started to cry until Sadie put a hand on her shoulder. "We had to steal. We couldn' lets you die, and you'll sets us right, I's sure of that."

"Did Jesse get caught?" Ben felt the answer they didn't voice. "You're right, I'll make sure he's okay, once we're out of here. All right, no choice now, but to try climbing that—"

"No, not yet."

"You can't keep me a prisoner here."

"Mama, let me tell him. Massa Cartwright, Mama's brother Tobias is running loose and looking to meanmouth ever-thing Lincoln do. He's one mean darkie! We was all on our way to Hayti out of New Orleans when Tobias gets us away to the coast of Mexico. We done fight Tobias who hate ever'body, and we needs help to get back. We asks someone listen to us. To help us be freed citizens, not freed slaves."

"Yes, I'm sorry. But you have to understand how much of my life, and my sons, I'm missing right now."

Sadie put a warm hand on Ben's arm. "Ben, they done want to ship us blacks out of the country, get rid of us slaves, people who been born here, to a land what the government thinks is better for us. They don' know what to do with us when we's free. Tobias am terrible angry, and is starting a Negro uprising agin Lincoln. That's why they is after us. But I think there's another way."

"What other way?"

"Come to New Orleans wit us. Butler will bring Lincoln to New Orleans if'n someone is there with money and power. You kin speak on our behalf. Butler likes silver, well, he likes any scheme what benefits him. You promise Lincoln that silver, Ben."

"Promise the silver to Lincoln? I told you it isn't mine—"

"We asks to be treated as Americans. You want you's sons shipped back to Ireland?"

"Actually our ancestors are from a variety of…no. Of course not. I can't believe Lincoln would sanction an idea like that."

"Then we kin count on you's help?"

"Where is Tobias now?"

"We dunno. He done run off on us. He say we needs someone bigger than a Cartwright, like the territorial governor, to tell him not to support Lincoln or the Union, but I don't know if he got that far."

Ben nodded. "Jim Nye's a good man, very anti-slavery. He'd listen, at least, until Tobias starts ranting anti-Union."

"Don' gets me wrong, Ben. Tobias ain't anti-Union. He's anti-Lincoln. He wants to see Lincoln blamed. And he's feeding anyone his venom who's a mind to listen. The more people he gets to listen, he figures, the more people will vote Democrat come election. So you'll help?"

"Of course." Ben wasn't sure they were giving him a choice. How convenient he just fell into their midst.

Abby handed Ben some more stolen food. "Come on, let's finish this contraband so we can git Massa Cartwright home and git Jesse out of jail."

* * *

Adam did some quick mental math as he got into position on the left side of the wagon. The path was so narrow that they would have to pick the wheels up off the ground at some points in order to climb down—plus having to keep the wagon from plummeting and take them all along for the ride. And except for one brief narrow stretch, there appeared a chance they could do this. If they kept their footing and if he and Tobias could work together on this thing.

As soon as both of them were in place on either side of the wagon, Jimmy took the noses of the team and started his slow crawl downward.

"Suicide," Adam muttered, and all human conversation died in the clanging of slave irons and screeching of wheels and horses' nervous sighs.

At first the path wasn't so bad, until Jimmy hit a sudden dip with the horses. The wagon pitched forward, and began leaning toward Adam as though Tobias pushed against it to keep from falling off the cliff. Adam felt himself standing on a single rock that wobbled, about to let loose. He yelled to Tobias to catch his footing and right the wagon, and Jimmy yelled at them to unhitch the team. But there was no one who could reach and the wagon flipped upward. Adam lost his grip—no, had the wagon wrenched from him, and felt his feet give way into open air. He threw his chained arms forward as though to grab the wagon but missed.

Unable to stop, Adam felt himself go over the side of the cliff, but he reached and grabbed for anything he could, the last clear instinct of survival and then screamed in pain as his iron shackles got caught in the rocks.

With feet dangling Adam struggled hard for some footing as his arms were wrenched from his shoulders, with his wrist irons caught up above him, wrapped around a tree and rocks. He could hear other screams and the wails of horses, and then rocks tumbled from above, knocking him out.

CHAPTER 18

Hop Sing stepped back inside the ranch house and looked down at his clothes. "Bling range in, too." He wiped at the dirt but to no avail. He knew he should count his blessings, that Frank and Charlie weren't that hard to find, having followed the cattle to a new water hole. "Too much to do." He went back to the table where some of his ingredients waited a sacred treatment, when the guest door opened.

Hoss looked glum and tired. "She don't seem to be getting better, Hop Sing, I don't understand."

"Because she not of this world, need different medicine." Hop Sing paged through his potion book and didn't notice Hoss's face light up.

"Hey, yeah. She'd get real happy if I done told her she wasn't in danger no more." Hoss went to the door for his hat and gun belt. "You tell that little brother of mine to put them mustangs in the north corral, you hear? I don't want him messing them in with the near broke stock. And Hop Sing!"

He had to wait a moment before Hop Sing looked up.

"You keep Miss Lydia fed. She's plum wasting away to nothing."

He ran out the door, trying to escape Hop Sing muttering, "That because she IS nothing." Knowing that Hoss would expect him to at least pretend he believed that Lydia was alive, Hop Sing went into the kitchen to cook.

* * *

Hoss hadn't been to Virginia City in awhile and forgot how long the trip was—down one side of the mountain, across the Truckee Valley and up another, a major undertaking for the Cartwrights no matter how often they traveled the route. He realized, too late, that he'd be there for more than just one night and didn't pack anything, not even food for the ride. He hoped Miss Sally would have some bread baking on the way. Stopping by to see how her hogs were doing wouldn't take him too much out of his way, either. And at least he had enough water in his canteen.

Hoss tried not to think about Lydia. Hop Sing thought she had him fooled but Hoss knew she was an odd sort of gal—the way she seemed to melt into nothing when he held her. The way she snuck around the house without him seeing her—one minute here, the next there. He had to keep moving her back

111

to the guest room because she wouldn't stay out of his bed. And tonight, just before he left she…

"Dadburn your ornery hide, you got a ranch and family to think about." But no matter how he scolded himself, Hoss couldn't get Lydia off his mind. Like Hop Sing said, she's taken hold underneath him in a way he never felt before.

Joe and Adam would say it's because he's had so little experience with women. He's known fewer ladies but his feelings for them were always intense. Like that gal as pretty as a spring morning until she told him she was dying. She became the wilted flower he could no longer hold. He nearly didn't get over that one but Joe and Adam gave him the space to mourn and encouraged him to keep busy. And there was that other gal, too, the one that first liked Joe but then he helped save her horse after it broke a leg. For awhile, that had been enough for her to love him on. When he tried getting romantic with her, he turned into a bumbling bunny and she ran home in tears. Joe, ladies man that he was, had the decency not to finish romancing her as she wanted.

Now with Lydia he didn't feel clumsy at all. Every move he made she had the right countermove. Romancing her was like a new dance that only he heard the music for, music that came right from her soul.

When he got to town he noticed Lizzie right away, and this surprised him because he kept an eye out for strangers, not people he knew. Of course all that waving she did helped. He had eyes for her at the social and now he didn't know what he saw in her. She was so big-boned he probably couldn't lift her at all and that brown hair never stayed tucked neatly under her bonnet.

Hoss tipped his hat at her and moved on. He had one mission in town and that was to find a certain fellow who needed a talking to.

"Hoss! Glad to see you in town." Roy had just left the restaurant with lunch tucked in his belly to see Hoss riding in. "Haven't seen any of you Cartwrights of late. You say hi to your Pa for me. I missed him last time I was to your ranch. Missed you too, now that I think on it. Adam get back yet?"

Hoss alighted and walked with Roy back to his office. "Yessir. Roy, I gotta ask you—"

"Say, that was some social you Cartwrights had. Wish I hadn'ta missed it. Joe and Adam got in a fight over that gal Margaret and Adam walked off?"

"About a feller…" Hoss looked out into the busy street but felt Roy staring at him.

"Adam—your brother? Mark Twain wrote that he got drunk and started laying into the guests." Roy took out his keys to find the one that unlocked his office. "Why, the very notion."

"Roy, I need to know—"

"Say, I'd keep an eye on that Margaret if I was you. She got into a peck of trouble all on her own yesterday. Your brother make it home okay?"

"Adam? Uh. You haven't seen him around here the past couple days?"

"No. Didn't I just say?" Roy opened his office and Hoss followed him in. Roy gave Hoss a puzzled once-over. "Say, you look a might peaked. Is there a reason you want to know if I seen Adam?"

"Well, I don't reckon I've seen him a'tall since the partying."

"But you're not sure?"

"Ah…"

"And that ain't why you come to my office, now, is it?" Roy gave Hoss's shoulder a shake. "You're looking funny, son. Why don't you go on home and sleep it off?"

"No sir, I just need to know about a feller, if he's been to town. Name's Stephen Lawe."

"Sure, I met him."

"You sure?"

"I don't rightly think I can forget a name like Lawe. What you want him fer?"

"Is he still in town?"

"He sounded to me like he wanted to stay a spell. You might try the International." Roy grabbed his arm. "You want to tell me why this fellow is more important than your missing brother?"

"Well, Adam ain't the only one missing. Pa's missing, too. So the way me and Joe figure," Hoss thought quick, because Roy's suspicious nature made him nervous, "is that they're off somewhere together and we'll hear from them anytime now."

Roy jerked upright in alarm. "Oh, now, boy, I cannot believe you're standing here—"

"But Roy, if there's one thing I *do* know, Pa and Adam can look after themselves. I got me a helpless lady to protect. One in fear of her life."

Hoss scurried out of Roy's office, knowing that Roy might just try to make more out of this than he should. And he had enough to deal with all on his own without Roy's worries.

* * *

Hanging from a cliff kept Adam from remaining unconscious. He bit back his screams when he saw Tobias staring down at him, with nothing but dead silence coming up from below. His wrists had begun to bleed as he tried to gain some foothold on the cliff to ease up on.

"Need some help?"

"Very funny." Getting his foot on one rock, he managed to loosen the pain by standing, just a little, until that rock wiggled and broke loose. He fell and choked down another scream.

"Being a slave comes in handy. You'd be dead for sure without those irons."

Cal joined Tobias, his expression more bemused. "Guess we better pull him up."

They got a rope around Adam's shoulders and together dragged him to a flatter position where he could pull himself up the rest of the way. Adam lay between them, between light and dark, conscious of the pain in his head and wrists. Sounds began, shouts and some creatures scrambling down the cliff. He couldn't tell what. Adam rolled over and tried to sit but found he couldn't.

"We lost Jimmy, a team of horses and your wagon. Guess you know what that means," Cal said. He coughed hoarsely and moved away.

Tobias touched Adam's shoulder. "Gitting down should be easier now."

Adam groaned. "Other wagon...make it?"

Tobias looked down. "Yup."

The two slaves slept in that same spot, as night overtook the rescue efforts below. Adam gave in to the darkness, fighting to escape distressed thoughts. He loved his country but for Democrat and Republican radicals to make a mockery of their political structure by using slavery to fan economics was difficult to consider. He and Joe fought over who's right and who's wrong in this war when nobody was either...and now this...this potential of getting killed for principles which might not be principles at all...Adam couldn't escape the dream that wasn't a dream but a memory...

"Political trouble is a madness, Pa. Suddenly something screams inside and you find yourself saying things you don't mean, things you don't even believe. Tell Little Joe I wanted him to know that, try to make him understand." He picked up his bedroll and tried to walk away, which became harder and more necessary with every step.

"These things that are packed here, what's all this, where do you think you're going?"

Adam bit back a sigh. "New England ought to be mighty pretty this time of year. I think I'd like to see it again."

"Oh, Adam, you can't be serious, use your head."

"Oh, Adam, come on."

"Hoss, things can't be the same between us anymore."

Ben stepped between the two brothers. "What are you talking about? What can't be the same? Why can't they be the same?"

"They just can't, Pa!" Walk away, clean and smooth, no more conversation. "There's no other way, Pa, can't you see?" Adam couldn't look back as he walked outside, knowing he was being followed, knowing they would try to stop him, and with everything they had. He thought he wanted to be stopped but that moment had disappeared.

"No, I can't see," and Ben's pain came through loud and wrenching. "I'm not going to stand by and watch my family flake away like rust off a wheel."

"Ah, use your head, Pa, not your heart. Can't you see the damage is already done? It's got to be little Joe or me. And he needs you more than I do."

Ben leaned against Adam's horse as Adam finished cinching. "Adam, I don't want you to go."

"You think it's what I want, Pa? Or even what Little Joe wants? This thing's gone so far now there's just no stopping it. You can't have two different points of view in the same

house, Pa, it just won't work, and that's all there is to it."

Adam tried to mount but Ben rushed to him and grabbed his arm. "Adam."

Adam could do nothing more to keep from sobbing. "Oh, Pa, leave me alone, will ya?"[27] *He may have pushed at his father too hard. He always tried to control his emotions but sometimes they got loose, and when they did, the impact was extra rough and hard to pull back. He had to get away before he started bawling for real. Emotions so easily got in the way of common sense...*

Adam awoke gulping in fear, needing to apologize to Joe—wondering if he'd ever get the chance.

* * *

Joe wouldn't let on to Frank or Charlie, but he couldn't remember the last time he herded wild mustangs. For some reason Pa always gave that task to Hoss. Maybe because Hoss could leap on a wild thing and wrestle it to the ground. Hoss never rode wild broncs because his weight just tended to drive a bucking horse into the ground, so he found other ways to be useful. Joe never herded any wild horses without Hoss or Adam around. He picked up a few more hands along the way because even Hoss always made sure he had enough help. Because there was just a bit of hurry involved, Joe didn't ask what kind of herding experience they had, but they appeared to be half-Indian and claimed to be Shoshone, so they probably knew a thing or two anyway.

When they got to Amos's ranch Joe at first thought the old man had gotten tired of waiting. They found Amos's corral empty and no one came running out of the house. Joe heard a heavy pounding and looked behind him. From what he could tell in a quick glance, Amos saw them coming and drove the horses down from the plateau where they must have been corralled. They were coming at full, dust flying speed and Joe wondered if he was supposed to stop them or just take over. He told his men to hold ground right in the path of the mustangs, figuring they'd stop.

But the mustangs didn't stop and as the dust flew around them Joe yelled to ask Amos what to do but his other men started running with the mustangs so Joe threw off a wave to Amos because he could no longer hold Cochise back.

"I'll run over the money tomorrow!" Joe held firm the belief that five men could steer eight wild horses at least in the direction of the Ponderosa. What on earth they'd do when they got there was another question, one he hoped he could figure out at a full gallop.

* * *

Sadie's sad old mule didn't make the trip all the way back to the ranch house. The two women and one injured man had to leave the wagon behind and walk. Ben hoped they'd run into someone but the range seemed quiet. Like everyone hid, and just watched. At one point near to the house, Ben became so exhausted Sadie and Abby had to prop him between them. They were strong women, even being as thin as they were, and being caressed by their warmth made Ben feel very secure. He felt Sadie was being kind to him just to get him to New Orleans with her, so he didn't understand his growing feeling of protectiveness toward her. Now that they were out of that infernal darkness and his eyes adjusted to the sun, both women appeared undernourished from their long travels, but with clear, bright brown eyes and muscular chocolate skin. Why they were called 'blacks' he didn't know, but then, whites weren't real white, either. And they were also as soft as cotton to the touch. He didn't have a lot of experience with colored folk and wanted more, much more.

He looked up to see the stable's corner sticking out from the path and felt his own pace quicken. "Come on!" He lurched into the yard before collapsing to his knees, catching himself with his good arm. Sadie caught up just as Hop Sing opened the door and ran out.

"Mr. Cartlight! You not kill. Mr. Joe say you burnee in fire." Hop Sing examined Ben's injuries while Ben knelt on the ground, and lifted him to help him into the house. He looked back over his shoulder at the women. "You come! You come, too!" He focused on getting Ben inside without hurting him further. "You must hear all happen here. Hop Sing going clazy. Now you home, maybe everything normal. Do you bring Mr. Adam? Mr. Hoss gone to Virginia City and Mr. Joe gone to get wild horses. Not see for whole day."

Hop Sing guided Ben to the settee and Ben was grateful for the chance to sit. Hop Sing's information made him dizzy.

"So Joe is all right then. Good." Ben gulped for breath, unable to bite down the pain. "Hop Sing, please go back and open the door so that our guests feel welcome."

Hop Sing ran back to the door, but stopped. "They stay? Hop Sing cannot keep track of one he alleady got."

"They saved my life, Hop Sing, we will make room." That wasn't exactly true but an acceptable enough story. Jesse's rescue of him stopped him from getting to another position of safety. He gave them the benefit, however, that they didn't know he wasn't in deathly trouble.

"Me alledy tellee them come in." Muttering, Hop Sing ran outside. Ben watched over his shoulder as the two women came inside with Hop Sing coaxing behind them. They stared at Hop Sing, who stared back—a facing of culture that amused Ben.

"Come in and sit down, we're all tired. Hop Sing, we could use some of your finest tea."

Hop Sing bounced between the women and Ben, clearly agitated. "No mean bad, Mr. Cartlight, but Hop Sing in middle of makee three cakes, beef stew and bewitchee potion, and glad you home but if just be good to sit, I have tea ready, take minute." Hop Sing dashed off into the kitchen.

Ben looked into Sadie's puzzled expression. "Hop Sing takes things very personally. He'll warm up to you. I'm not sure what he meant by making three cakes but...it's late. Let's get you both settled into the guest room and I'll get Hop Sing to go with me out to your wagon." He dragged himself to his feet, wondering if he could be asleep while moving.

"Oh, Ben, Lordy, you's plum tuckered. It kin wait til morning. Abby and I sure do cotton to something soft on our bones right now."

As he opened the guest door Ben was struck by an odd, sweet and spicy fragrance and the bed appeared to have been slept in but other than that, the room was empty. "I'm sorry, I guess...Hop Sing hasn't had time to clean in here."

"Mama, this is the sweetest, most welcome sight I ever seed." Abby leaped into the bed and snuggled under the covers. "Oooh, still warm."

"Ah!" Hop Sing stood at the door with a pitcher of ice water. "You see no one in bed?"

"Hop Sing, what is this about? I asked for warm tea, not ice water." Ben felt dizzy and leaned on the settee. "And where's Adam?"

"Mr. Hoss house guest but she...come and go, up and down, here and there."

"House guest? Hoss? I haven't been gone *that* long. Oh, you mean that woman who keeps disappearing? She still around?"

Abby jumped out of the bed and ran to her mother's side. "Mama, he done talking about a ghoul?"

Sadie crossed herself as she and Abby backed toward the front door. "I'm sorry, Ben, but we considers boarding with a ghoul to be...impolite. Kin we just nestle down in the barn? A blanket on some hay still beats a mine shaft."

Ben grabbed her arm, fighting the urge to stretch back out on the settee and sleep for a month. "No, there's no ghost in this house. Isn't that right, Hop Sing?"

"No. No, no ghost. Mr. Hoss friend Lydia, she spooky, but she real, real as some Chinamen. She not good eater, and always have fever, so I bling cold water, and I makee cake to find one she like, she not like...to eat...spices, so I make food after food." Hop Sing propped Ben up as he staggered. "I take Mr. Cartlight to his loom now to lest. You both go into guest loom. No ghost. You not wolly about ghost."

Ben knew from years of Hop Sing's service that he could pass out on the stairs and awaken the next morning dressed in his night wear. "Hop Sing, what's going on around here?"

Hop Sing talked as he got Ben ready for bed. He told Ben about Joe's anxieties over his father's death, and trying to run the ranch himself, of Hoss being so absorbed by Lydia that he couldn't think to do anything else. And then he asked if Ben knew where Adam was because he's been missing since the social.

But Ben had fallen asleep.

* * *

When Adam blinked awake, his head pain had eased and his wrists throbbed but the bleeding had stopped and his fingers still worked. He found he could get into a sitting position but with effort and dizziness. He looked over the side of the cliff. The supplies, the horses, a man's life, all for the foolishness of a shortcut. Jimmy appeared to have fallen against one of the horses but even the softer landing wasn't enough to save his life.

He saw Tobias curled up in the grass on the other side of the rocky path they once tried to negotiate. Above him, Luke stood with a rifle, staring down into the rocky canyon below.

Luke looked over at Adam, with a sneer. "I hope you niggers is happy. You lost us a week's supplies. Well, you'll just have to go hungry until we can scrounge us some more—"

Adam grabbed Luke's ankle, knocked him backward and wrapped his iron chains around the man's neck. "You think this is a game? A man died down there and all you can think about is food? Huh?"

From behind Cal knocked Adam aside with the barrel of his rifle, but not enough to knock him out. "We're all going to have to walk down there, and I can't have any man unable to stand on his own two feet. You keep it up, muley, and we'll leave you behind. Chain you high to yon tree dangling in air and let you die of thirst." Cal gave Tobias a rough shake to wake him and pointed the direction down for Tobias to lead the way. "Marv, Jake and Piney are down already, scavenging what's left. Come on."

Adam blinked, as he felt nothing left in his head but pain.

Luke, rubbing his throat, stood over him like one of those monster lumberjacks ready to squish him like a bug. "Don't forget, muley, you can die just like anybody else. Your hide ain't worth that much to me." Luke crouched down to Adam, his voice lowered. "See, I figure you'll make a good hostage, when the time comes. But don't bank your life on that kind of value."

Adam rolled over, feeling a slave's gratitude at not being hit again. But did Luke mean that he knew Adam was no slave? He took a quick look at the path downward, and followed Tobias, going down on hands and knees.

"You gots to be careful, Titus," Tobias whispered as Adam caught up to him. "Never woulda took you as a man with a temper."

Adam sighed, his breath whistling between his teeth. "We all have a breaking point, Tobias. When you reach yours, you'll know."

When they got halfway down, Cal yelled over them, "Jake's down there, waiting for us to move on. You two get to bury Jimmy cuz no one else will touch him. Keep moving."

Adam looked down—and had to blink. That looked like Pa down there, waiting for him.

CHAPTER 19

Margaret rode out from Carson City early and even her own father wouldn't have recognized her. She wore men's clothes and had her long brown hair tucked up under a heavy brimmed cowboy hat. She donated all her San Francisco goods and clothing to the poor man's shop—all the goods left from her life with Philip. After he died she thought to sell everything anyway but didn't because she wasn't ready to forget him.

Always best to move on, after the proper mourning of a week or two. Best to keep living.

She found men's clothes at the local clothier less than appealing, nothing with any more color than another shade of brown. Back in San Francisco men got to wear all kinds of colors and fabrics, wonderful silks and linens that got snatched from the Chinese shipping vessels, and with more laundrymen there, cleaning was cheaper, too. Here, colors just got in the way.

She packed a bag with enough supplies for a day on another livery horse—she checked its teeth this time—and rode back to the Ponderosa to try Adam's trail again, not stopping to get a Cartwright along the way because they all seemed too distracted to worry about where he might have got off to. Joe had an inkling of concern, but then, he had a ton of concerns, all pulling him in every direction. But what about Hoss? Not caring about Adam, or even his Pa?

This wasn't the family she remembered, but then, don't all families reach a breaking point over something? She felt skeptical enough about family to believe so.

Her biggest fear was that Adam had met with foul play somewhere on that path they'd found leading from the cave, so she wanted to follow those hoof prints, even jumbled, to see if they led to a body or a burial grave. She'd just travel and keep going, fall off the ends of the earth if she had to. That's how guilt spurred her. If he were dead, though, there were enough wolves in the area to keep a carcass from getting spoiled. She figured if that happened, at least she should be able to find some shreds of clothing. At least she could put an end to all their wondering. She could do that much. And then live the rest of her life in proper rather than imagined guilt.

Thinking of Adam as a carcass made her feel just as dead inside. Finding him as one could destroy all memory of his arms around her, his lips on hers.

After Joe left her at the cave, she rode Beauty back to get Stu's horse. She rode back to Carson City and returned it to the livery. She found her plug from her other adventure came back on its own and she had a partial refund coming. That gave her the idea to find Adam, or die trying.

Margaret spent the rest of the time planning, and talking to as many people as she could, all of whom knew Adam but none who'd seen him in the past week. Late in the day she had a break of sorts. A Southerner, thoroughly soused by 5 p.m., loudly proclaimed he saw some blacks come through town, talked about the young fellow still in jail and about another couple blacks who he'd seen being taken in irons east of here by a passel of ragged looking slavers. But he was new to the territory and the only one Margaret talked to who didn't know Adam from…well, Adam. He described the two blacks, saying one was lighter skinned, but definitely in iron chains. She had a brief conversation with the boy still in jail but he didn't want to say much. He didn't know any Adam, either.

As she rode back up the mountain, Margaret felt pretty confident that she could pull off being disguised as a man. With this came a sense of ease, and so she let her mind drift…

Adam had picked her up in a little buggy his third mother, Marie, used to drive around. He said the buggy hadn't been used in years and was just the right thing to take a pretty girl out for a ride to the lake. On the way she sensed a change in his mood, and when she asked, he told her that he had lingering bad feelings about how he used to treat Joe's mother, and how his Pa made him see he couldn't help these feelings, having already suffered so much loss. Did that make his treatment of Joe's ma right? Margaret told him that maybe he knew all along she was going to die, and he laughed and told her that her eyes sparkled a bright green, like the star that twinkled so near the moon last night.

That was the moment the boy who always seemed so reluctant to share his feelings made her fall in love.

Those tiny glimpses of love after that, as their friendship evolved—the times he wrapped his arms around her so lovingly she'd thought bliss was a word that could not begin to describe his particular state of heaven. He leaned down to kiss her once—just once, back then. He smelled rough, like the range but oh, so wonderfully rough, like a range angel, and even just the times when he held her hand as they sat in his favorite spot, a grassy knoll near a pile of boulders overlooking the lake with its fabulous shoreline, spoke so warmly of his love. He would tell her how the two of them would build a grand house right there on that jutty near the water, and they would raise so many children…and they would bathe and swim in its coolness every day…

At first she thought the pounding noise came from her heart, putting Adam and children together in the same consecutive thought that, even now, when she found him, he'd be ready to forgive her and take her in his arms...she recognized how she'd gotten him into this mess in the first place and knew to take all the blame...but the pounding continued and the dust flew, mesquite and sage brush breaking apart...

Runaway mustangs!

"Hyah!" She spurred the young livery horse upward, kicking hard but without hope of escape, not looking back, trying to get out of their way or be stuck running with them, far, far from where she needed to be...at first tempted to go downhill, but choosing the upward road momentum, hoping the runaways would take the easier path downward. She had a split moment to react and acted on instinct. She needed to get to the cave to start the search and wasn't about to give up for some mangy cur.

But the stampeders didn't take the downhill road. Instead they veered, as if relieved to find someone to follow. She caught glimpses of riders with the horses, one that looked like an Indian, but didn't have time to wonder further because the horses surrounded her and the granite dust blinded her until she no longer controlled the horse but just hoped it could handle the running, its nose getting bumped and swished by rumps and tails—

A hand reached out and grabbed hold of her reins, and she went flying backward.

* * *

Ben awoke with an appetite like he hadn't had in years, and not just for food. He stretched, tested his limbs, and his eyes closed as the bed beckoned him back. He wanted to see his sons, and found himself anxious to fit Sadie and her family into his life. She fascinated him like—well, like only three women had before. He's had a fondness for many others, but not like this. Just walking back with her, she reminded him of an uncatchable butterfly, as she'd talk about her early life and then go off into reflections of religion and philosophy that he never before heard out of an unlearned person. And politics—how one woman could know so much about politics!

Ben remembered warning Adam once about falling for a woman who had saved his life, how the feelings were just of gratitude, easily confused with love. He had been wrong, so wrong, to meddle like that. If gratitude becomes love, there could be little better reason for love that he could think of, and surely something that would last all his life.

A sudden thump brought him up on his elbows. Hop Sing tossed logs into Ben's fireplace. Ben had been relishing the cool chill of the room on his healing skin, but didn't admit this to Hop Sing, and sank back. "Bring food with that?"

Hop Sing jumped but continued, flustered, to get the fire going. "No Hoss, no Joe. No Adam. Lady come and go. Hop Sing kitchen explode with food

food food. No one eat. New guests not come out. You want food you get plenty food."

Ben throw off his linen cover and got out of bed, the act forcing his shoulders back as he adjusted his arm in the sling. Ben had thought to ask for a doctor to set the arm, but it seemed to be healing all right on its own. More of Sadie's magic—or he had only suffered a sprain, as Hop Sing figured.

"Hop Sing, forget the fire for now. Forget the guests and forget that ghost, because there is no such thing!" He ignored Hop Sing's look of angry consternation. "Right now, all I want to see are my three sons. Go out to the bunkhouse and send someone to find them and get them back here. Go yourself if you have to." He leaned on the reluctant Chinaman's shoulders and pushed him out of the room. "I'll help by cleaning out the kitchen of some of that food, and my guests will help me, and maybe I'll even get your ghost to tell me her story, so we can end this nonsense."

"Clothes just clean," Hop Sing grumbled as he ran the stairs and out the door.

Ben used the stair rail liberally as he took the steps down. Going down felt a little worse on his burnt legs than going up, oddly enough. "Sadie!"

Sure enough, after a moment the guest room door opened and Sadie poked her head out. She looked around before responding to Ben. "He gone?"

"Who, Hop Sing? I sent him on an errand."

Sadie sighed and reached behind her. She pulled her daughter out of the room. Both appeared well rested, but their clothing needed a good washing. "He scares me. Us. He's so quiet and soft...and white...and that hair...you sure he's a man?"

Ben made it, stiff as a two-legged goat, to the dining table and sat. "I'm sure. Yes, he insists on that traditional clothing. Sometimes I think he'd be more comfortable in range wear, the way I have him running all over. But there's no reason to fear him. Are you hungry?"

Sadie shuddered and let Ben wrap his arms around her. "Oh, you know hunger now, I kin see that, Ben."

Abby hovered in mad uncertain desire to run.

Ben stroked her arm to calm her. "Abby, why don't you go into the kitchen and see what looks appetizing." He showed her the direction.

Abby started to move and then screeched. "Momma, up there!"

Ben looked at the stairs and caught a quick movement of pink silk and frills. "Hop Sing! Go up and—" Ben shook his head. When he turned back he laughed at the white expressions on black faces. "Not a ghost, trust me. I wouldn't have one in this house. It must be Hoss's friend, and if I know Hoss, she's...shy, is all. Come on, let's have some food and talk, really talk."

Sadie followed her daughter to the kitchen for food, and Ben lingered behind a moment, catching sight of his three wives waiting on his desk for Ben to bring his sons home. But could he let his concern for them keep him from doing what was right for the country? And for Sadie? Could he sit idly worrying? Or get out there and do what was best for everyone?

He hoped, when the time came, he would know the answers.

CHAPTER 20

Hoss stood outside the International, breathing hard. He'd just run uphill a couple of streets to follow someone pointed out as Stephen Lawe. He realized he didn't need to run when the fellow ended back where he lodged, but Hoss wasn't sure that's what he'd do and anyway, as Joe would say, a little running never hurt him—although at that moment Hoss didn't believe that old tale.

Hoss decided on a little libation before he could bring himself to talk to a stranger. He stood in the street trying to figure which saloon might be the quietest but the Bucket of Blood appeared to be busting apart at the seams and he could hear the ruckus in the Silver Dollar from where he stood—gamblers again. He walked to the Comstock Saloon hoping to find the miners were not yet drowning their sorrows, and three fellows would have shoved him into the dirt when they burst out drunk and arguing over who had the better assay—if Hoss were shove-able. As it was they ended up bouncing around him without a polite word to him at all.

Hoss wiped off the cloud of dust that had settled on him as he walked in. "Glass of water, Charlie?"

"Need your head clear?" Charlie primed the pump and gave Hoss a good swallow. "Maybe try your odds with the cards." He needed over to the table.

"Need it clear, Charlie." Hoss wiped his lips after downing the water. "But I don't expect to do no gambling. Not on a lady's life." He walked back out, but hesitated. He was about to enter another man's world, uninvited. Generally the Cartwrights minded their own affairs, until asked. Lydia made this his affair, but Stephen might not think so. So far no sign of a little girl, so that red-headed fellow back in Carson City must have been involved in some mistaken identity.

Hoss stepped inside and at first thought the lobby of the grand hotel was empty. He didn't even see Vince behind the counter but he knew where the bell was. When he reached over to ring he saw the top of a small head behind the counter. Hoss peeked and saw a dark-haired little girl who pulled out drawers and dumped the contents on the floor, as though looking for something.

When she smiled at him, Hoss thought she was impossibly cute. "Well, hello, young'un. You the new desk clerk?" At the same time, Hoss felt himself gulping...did she belong to Stephen? And Lydia? He could see a resemblance, clear enough.

She smiled as though she had every right to be there.

"What you doing down there?"

She didn't seem frightened of a big strange man staring down at her. "I'm not taking nothing. Just looking."

Hoss laughed. "You better come on out, young'un, before Vince gets back—"

"Jodie! You down here?!" The man Hoss had been following, Stephen Lawe, came down the stairs in near panic.

Hoss glanced at the girl but she made no attempt to answer. He looked back at Stephen, pacing, wondering which way to look, where to go. He expected to dislike the man Lydia accused of trying to kill her. But Lydia never mentioned a daughter. A woman can't forget a daughter, even in fear of her life.

Hoss dropped his voice into a playful whisper, directed at Stephen. "I think she's hiding on you." Hoss pointed behind the counter. "But she made me promise not to tell."

"I did not!"

Stephen met Hoss's wink and crossed his arms. "Then I guess I'll have to go to the candy store all by myself."

Jodie stood and brushed off, like the lady knew when she was being bluffed but didn't want to take the chance on missing a treat. She kicked a few things around on the floor but made no attempt to pick any item up. She stood on the chair to read the names on the register and scribbled her own before strolling out.

Stephen walked to Hoss after taking her hand. "I'd like to thank you. Buy you lunch. This one, she isn't easy to raise alone. Mind of her own. Like her ma."

"I'd like to take you up on lunch, but best be going. What happened to her ma?"

"What makes you think—?"

"I done lost two mamas myself. If I kin help..."

"Oh, Lydia's not lost. She knows right where she is, buried six feet down, over in Genoa. Killed herself. Right in front of our little girl. Poor child still has nightmares." Stephen made no attempt to talk so that Jodie couldn't hear but Jodie acted bored with the conversation.

"She...that's...Lordy. Sad story." Hoss watched as Stephen led Jodie away. The little girl never looked back, never acknowledged Stephen's story...she believed what he'd said, or had been trained not to care.

Hoss plopped down on the circle couch in the lobby. Jodie could be afraid of her father.

For once Hoss was grateful for the long ride home. He had a lot of thinking to do.

* * *

Adam and Tobias ran on foot to keep up to the men on horseback, not allowed to sit in the other wagon, the one left that carried all supplies. Adam wasn't sure how much longer he could keep running. Lack of food, water…. They were in New Mexico territory, and Adam feared that this driving pace meant they'd be in Texas, and in trouble, before much longer. He used to think he was in a pretty good shape, but next to Tobias he felt as big and clumsy as Hoss.

Hoss. Did his brother, any of his family, wonder where he was? How could they even begin to look? That one lousy trail to the cave…Margaret could help, if she even remained in the area after he so rudely left her. Adam once read how all things happened for a reason. That meant mistakes we make aren't mistakes but deliberate opportunities for growth. Or shovels full of dirt leading to a grave all along meant for us.

Pa's horse—did that mean Pa was dead? Had Pa come after them and got himself killed trying to rescue his foolish eldest son? Had to be Pa's horse, the way the saddle glistened with silver. Adam found an extra burst of speed with clenched fists. This running, this pretense, has gone on long enough. There were some lives more important than one politician's.

At another incline they got to walk for a bit. Adam could barely swallow yet his mind raced feverishly. He realized he had been living in a sort of dream state since Margaret confessed all to him, and now that had to end. He had to get home, somehow.

Adam thought to strangle Jake for riding his pa's horse but after his last outburst they wouldn't let him survive another, and what good would that do?

"Tobias, we have to get away from them, and get to Lincoln ourselves." Adam needed to send a telegram home, at least. "I have an idea. We'll need precision timing, and I have to take Jake's buckskin, but I think we can both ride it, for awhile anyhow. You game for a little risk?"

"A little more, you mean? Massa Cartwright, as long as you go to New Orleans with me, I'll kill each and ever one of these fellows."

"Well, I hope we don't have to go that far. And don't call me 'massa.' Soon they'll find a town, and they'll want us to steal a wagon."

"And they watch us with guns ever minute, too."

"Right, but if I tell them I can steal them a horse to go with that wagon, I figure we can create a runaway situation, one with us on board."

"They'll jus' chase us."

"Not if we start shooting." Adam showed Tobias the gun from Jimmy's body that he'd stuck inside his shirt.

126

"Oh my Lord God!"

"Quiet. I saw where Jimmy kept this hidden and stole it while we buried him. I got some more thinking to do, and a lot will depend on where we find the wagon, but we're still in part of the territory I know, and I think I know a route home that will discourage them."

* * *

Margaret felt her body shaking and realized after a moment of tense fear that a hand on her shoulder and not runaway horses made her shake.

"Hey? You all right? Can you move?"

Margaret squinted as she dared to open her eyes. "Joe?" She sat up, but groaned as she did, feeling a cramp in her back. "What did you do? Those horses—"

Joe remained squatted next to her, a hand on her shoulder as though for support. "Honest, Margaret, I don't know how you got in the middle of that. I got you out the only way I could."

"The runaways, you were trying to stop—"

"No, they weren't runaways. Well, maybe they were for the first day, but now we got them going in the right direction."

"You've been herding them that long?!"

"We've been stopping to rest along the way, but yeah."

Joe looked aged to Margaret, irreversibly tired, and unable to figure out what he was doing. "But Indians...you had...they were...stealing?"

"No, they're darn good animal herders, Shoshone are, and they were counseling with the Washoe when I went looking for help. I told them to help me corral them at the ranch and I would like them each take their pick of one horse."

"But—where are they now?"

"Ah." Joe looked over his shoulder. "Well, I think they knew where they were going. But I guess I better find out."

"Joe, you didn't, I mean, any ranch hands?" Margaret hadn't gotten her breath back. She pointed to Joe's horse and he brought her his canteen.

"Oh, yeah. I better...will you be all right?"

"I...is my horse..."

"Oh, I tied him up over there. Good breed. Go on to the house and rest a bit."

"I'm looking for Adam."

"I know. But you're not going to find him. At least, not..." Joe dropped to the ground next to her.

"Joe...please, don't." But Margaret could hear him sobbing. She wrapped her arms around his shoulders. Those shoulders bore so much weight trying to hold everything together. "So what if some Indians stole your horses, Joe? They're just horses." But that wasn't the whole problem. She faced the youngest of a family that had just fallen apart, and there didn't seem to be any words to unite them. "Joe? How can I help?"

Joe pulled away from her and cleared his throat but he made no move to dry his eyes. He got to his feet and pulled her with him, and as she watched, he made an alarming transformation, his eyes dry and turning hard and cold. "Tell Hoss that in a couple days' time he'll get his chance to run the ranch alone. I'm going to find Adam. And Pa. And then go on a holiday. And Frank—if Frank shows at the ranch without me keep him there til I get there."

Looking at Joe became impossible—listening to him made her shiver. She nodded.

"Now I better go and find those Shoshone."

Joe helped Margaret to her feet, mounted his horse and rode off. With legs shaking, she wasn't sure she could mount, but the horse waited her attempts. She couldn't get the horse to run again, but she only half tried. Joe had his hands full with no one to help him. Well, no Cartwrights, anyway. She only saw them together that one night, the night of the social, but she envied them their closeness and their camaraderie. Perhaps that, more than anything, encouraged her to tell the truth about herself to Adam, expecting sympathy more than anger.

Now she wanted to find Adam alive and safe so she could move on with the rest of her life, anywhere but here.

At Spooner Lake she breathed a sigh. Not much further now. She had to take Joe up on that offer, rest for a bit before going out to search what likely was a lost trail. If Adam wasn't dead why hasn't he sent word? Any other possibilities? Arrested for a crime—no, he could still send word. Taken against his will perhaps, being held for ransom? Still there'd be some word sent, some money or other demand. Taken as a slave? Was he that light-skinned slave, now a captive headed east?

When she saw the wagon in the road she wondered why they were going so slow, before realizing it had been abandoned. She rode to the wagon and alighted. Whoever rode this had come a good distance. She peered at the faded red lettering etched on the side—New Orleans Shipping Company. The mule that had been attached to the wagon lay dead, still attached, pecked on by scavengers.

Margaret jumped back on her horse. The wagon pointed to the Ponderosa ranch house. Slaves. Runaways. Slavers. All on the Ponderosa, and all around the time of the fire. And Adam's disappearance.

"Hyah!" This time she made the horse run.

* * *

Hop Sing brought them dessert, a three-layer chocolate cake. Ben had been shocked to see it in the kitchen, thinking he'd missed a birthday. Hop Sing has been harried about cooking so Ben didn't press him further, especially with him so upset about not finding a single son.

Sadie continued to make her case about a trip to New Orleans—one she reminded him he'd already agreed to.

Ben held up a hand in submission. "We'll start in Carson City and get your son out of jail. But going to New Orleans takes a little more planning. And I need to see my sons safe first. We'd have to commandeer the stagecoach to get anywhere in any decent amount of time. This "War between the States" has halted all railroad progress, leaving us out here to fend for ourselves." He leaned forward and took Sadie's hand. "Sadie, stay here with me. We can have a good life. When the war is over, you'll be freed, I'm sure of that. Lincoln's made all the right moves in that direction, so far. When this war ends—"

"Oh Ben," Sadie's hand trembled as she covered her eyes. "If you coulda seed the eyes of them what didn' get away. They haunt me. I see them in a strange village, despaired of ever seeing home, and not even able to talk with people so different."

Ben wrapped his good arm around her. "I've often thought I could save the world, but as I got older, I felt I wanted more just to save at least my own piece of the world. Sadie, before long snows will close down the mountains. If I leave now, I might not make it back until next summer. I can't risk—"

They both looked over at the pounding of the door. Before Ben stood, the door opened and Abby walked in, followed by a breathless and disheveled Margaret, hat long lost to the wind.

"I'm sorry, Mister Cartwright, but this lady says she knows you."

Ben sprang to his feet, ignoring the burning in his thighs with the sudden movement. "Margaret, I am so glad to see you. Where is Adam? Did he come with you?"

Margaret stared at Ben before giving Sadie a good looking over. She sighed. "I'm glad to see you're all right, Mr. Cartwright, but I was hoping Adam was with *you*. My last real hope, I'm afraid."

Ben staggered backward, sitting. "You…if I remember right, you were the last one to see him. I know I've been gone, but…please sit and tell me what you know about him."

Margaret seemed preoccupied by thoughts miles away, fixated by the presence of the slaves in the house. "I'm sorry, I would not have intruded if I knew you had guests."

"Oh yes." Ben made the proper introductions, but sensed more on her mind. "Do you have an idea where Adam might be, Margaret?"

"I…might." She sat at the table and looked up to see three pairs of eyes waiting for more. "Ben, are these women runaway slaves? Related to that boy in the jail?"

Sadie stuttered in protest until Ben put a hand on her arm. "Some might consider them that. Why?"

129

"You and Joe were caught in a fire—the day *after* the social."

"Margaret, we have a lot to do today, so I would appreciate hearing what's on your mind."

Margaret walked to the fire, rubbing her arms as if a sudden chill blew through the room. "I've been staying in Carson City. A few days after the social—and fire—I heard talk about some men coming through the area on the trail of runaways. Said they moved on through the Ponderosa, were seen...Ben, this is no rumor! With two captured slaves in their wagon."

Sadie inhaled in pain. "Oh my. Then Tobias didn' get away."

"Tobias? Who's that?" Margaret stared at Sadie, but Sadie returned as good as she got.

"My brother."

"Anyone with him?"

But Ben exchanged silent recognition with Margaret when Sadie didn't answer. "Sadie, who else would be with Tobias?"

"No one, Ben. Jus' four of us."

Margaret held her breath. "They referred to one as lighter-skinned." She waited until she got Ben's gasp of recognition. "If Adam found a runaway in trouble, would he try to help?"

Ben stood but with very little strength in his legs. He grabbed Margaret for support. "Sadie, let's get to Carson City, get your son out and get us a stage to St. Louis. My son's on his way to New Orleans. Darcy, I might just have to kill you for this."

Sadie cried out and pulled Ben away from Margaret. "Oh, Ben, I is the happiest woman." She kissed him square on the lips and Ben responded hungrily before she pulled away, in one part embarrassment and three parts terror.

Ben's momentary passion for her rolled into the pain of potential loss. "I want to get there and back before the snows. Before..." He pulled Sadie close and held her, trembling, finding comfort in her return embrace.

Margaret put a hand on Ben's shoulder. "Has Joe seen you since you've been back?"

Ben let Sadie go and cleared his throat, hoping to clear his head at the same time. "I haven't seen any of my sons. Do you know where they are?"

Hoss burst into the room as though hearing his name. He stopped sudden, startled by all the people staring at him. Finally his eyes settled on Ben. "Pa!?" Hoss ran to Ben and gave him a bear hug. "Doggonit Pa, I told Joe you were all right but he just insisted you was dead."

Ben felt blessed by the sudden embrace of one of his sons, and so much better just holding on. "Glad to say that hasn't happened yet."

Hoss grinned and walked to the guest room but stopped short when he saw contents not belonging to Lydia. "Hop Sing!"

Ben studied his son's slouched back, as though the weight of his world had gotten too heavy to bear. He didn't ask about Ben's adventure, not like him at all. He grabbed Hoss's arm to get his attention. "Hoss, what's been going on around here. Where's Joe?"

"Ah, Mr. Cartwright?" Margaret raised her hand like a timid schoolgirl.

Hoss focused, noticing strangers. "Pa, who are these Negroes? Are they runaways? What they doing in Lydia's room?"

Hop Sing ran out. "Mr. Hoss, Miss Lydia, she still not eat. You sit down and get meal or food go bad. Throw away."

Sadie cleared her throat. "Ben, I thought you's wanted to get to the City. My son—"

Frank poked his head in the front door. "Excuse me, could I have a moment with Hoss?"

Margaret went over to Frank. "Frank, Joe wants you to stay here until he gets back. At least..." She looked around. "He said if I found you without him...he'd need to see you."

"If you found *me!* He was supposed to be herding with me! Sorry ma'am, I mean, miss, but I was herding some horses with him and then he disappeared and then the horses...well, they got sidetracked." He looked over at Hoss. "I thought maybe Hoss could come out and help."

Hoss shrugged. "I cayn't—got a puzzle to solve that needs immediate...questioning. Hop Sing, do you know where Lydia is?"

"All right, I want everyone to sit down and listen!" Ben waited until he had everyone's attention.

Margaret perched herself on the settee and the other two women sat at the dining table, while Hop Sing cleared the plates. Hoss, Frank and Ben confronted each other.

"All right," Ben continued, "I want to know where Joe is and what kind of trouble he's in. And then," he continued as Frank and Hoss started to talk at once. "I want to know about your ghost, Hoss, which—" He held up a hand as Sadie and Abby started to make excited gasping noises and moved toward the door. "—we know she isn't, because there is no such thing."

Frank started, "I already said—"

Ben shushed him with a wave. "I think Margaret has the floor to tell us about Joe. Margaret?"

Margaret explained to a willing audience about the horses that she now feared had been stolen, Joe's continuing devastation over his father's death, how he pulled her from the stampede and went back to look for the horses. How he needs to confront Frank on a number of issues. This made Frank squirm, but to her amazement, he held his ground.

"Hoss! Go on out there and find your brother."

But Hoss stared at the top of the stairs. "Lydia." He walked to the stairs.

"Hoss!" Ben started for him but Hop Sing put a hand on his arm. "What's he doing?"

"He see Miss Lydia."

Ben looked up the stairs. "There's nothing there."

"To Mr. Hoss there is. He is a man gu huò enchant."

"What? You mean in love?"

"No. Yes! He think so."

Everyone watched Hoss walk up the stairs, eyes on something only he could see.

Hop Sing shuddered. "She need him do something. Cannot leave living world when tloubled. He help. Is little different than helping live person."

Ben threw up his arms, exasperated. Sadie and Abby huddled at the front door, ready to bolt. "Ladies, go outside and wait by the wagon, we'll…uh, head to town. Frank, I need you to get out there and find Joe and bring him here. Whatever else you were supposed to do today, that's what you have to do first. I want him here within the half hour."

"I'll go with him, Ben," Margaret looked less than willing, like feeling an obligation, Ben figured, because of her role in Adam's disappearance. Otherwise, she didn't need to be here at all. "Joe asked me to."

"You don't have—"

Margaret whirled around at Frank, but kept her voice low "Yes, I do! Or believe me, I wouldn't." She barreled past Ben and outside, and Frank reluctantly followed, letting the door slam behind him.

Ben shook his head and turned to face an empty room. He stared up at the second level where a disheveled son had disappeared. "A ghost." He pounded the settee a moment, thinking. "Hop Sing, I need you to pack me a satchel of clean clothes, find something for the women, too, maybe some of Little Joe's smaller things. I'm taking them to Carson City and from there we're going to New Orleans." He stared at the door, fearing the worst. "Hop Sing!" Hop Sing stopped on the stairs. "I need you to take care of Hoss, try and get him…un-bewitched. And let Joe know I'm all right."

Hop Sing nodded. "Aleady have ginger and garlic and thyme for potion, need to find licorice loot and heart of gecko." He disappeared.

"Did he say…" he looked over at the women, who darted out the front door. "Of course not—please don't…" He sighed as he faced an empty room. "With any luck, Joe will be here before I leave."

His fear more than any other was how much luck he'd need to find Adam. Luck has a way of running out, in a country so big and so divided. And not even just in half anymore but in…pieces.

Like his family.

CHAPTER 21

Hoss called for Hop Sing to bring some of his special medicine upstairs. Ben, in his room cleaning up for travel, bit the urge to interfere. His rage at seeing Hoss tending an empty bed could do irreparable harm—to both of them. Hopefully Hop Sing can help, although the danged Chinaman and his foreign ways and bewitching potion, indeed, likely encouraged this on Hoss. And now he couldn't get Sadie and Abby back in the house so there was nothing more to do than hook up the buckboard and get started on their journey. At least he had a chance of finding Adam, and seeing Joe, on the way.

Ben put the razor back in the bowl with a sigh. "Adam? What kind of mess have you got yourself into?" Ben changed into travel clothes and headed for the stairs. *Should have paid more attention to the warning about runaways. Ah, hindsight.* He glanced in Adam's room, remembering the day of the social. He had pestered Adam not to dawdle, and Adam, bare-chested, still shaving, laughed and said that three Cartwrights were enough to get a party going. The memory faded and returned the room to emptiness. Ben closed the door, but then changed his mind and opened the door wide. If Adam wasn't given the chance to shave along the way, by now he'd be as cranky as a bear. Ben should feel sorry for the slavers.

He heard Hoss talking in his room and moved away. Whatever Hoss needed to do, he needed to do alone. Ben took the stairs and stepped outside into the cool air. Winter came on too quick for his liking, this year even more than the previous. The door to the barn hung slightly open. With a wry smile and a shaking head, Ben snuck over and peeked in to see Abby and Sadie huddled together in the hay. They'd eaten and changed in the house but had dashed madly out here again and now looked as though they'd been scaring each other with ghost stories. He sat down and wrapped his big arm around them, guarding his injured one.

"I'm sorry. I didn't know the whole story about...Lydia."

"Can we go now, Massa Cartwright? Right now?" Abby sounded about half her age.

"Right now. But I'll need your help to hitch up the buckboard, all right? Seems we're shorthanded around here lately."

When he stood with them he noticed Buck's stall was empty. At first he thought the horse had been pastured, but the saddle and bridle were missing as well. The fire. "Blast it, Buck's been stolen," he muttered under his breath.

Joe would be able to share more about how he got the fire out and where Buck might be. He could hope, anyway—but from what he's heard, Joe's not been himself since the fire and thinking his Pa's dead. He needed to hold his youngest in his arms, needed that more than anything at the moment.

What a mess, and now only a trip to New Orleans could straighten anything out. He sure didn't know how to help with a ghost—no amount of studying Charles Dickens would make a bit of difference. Ben wouldn't admit this to Sadie, but the idea of a haunting inside his ranch house made him feel creepy, as well.

* * *

Hoss had spent the night with Lydia in a kind of fog. He followed her into his room, but she had been so agitated that she moved in and out of the room, unable to settle down, unable to let him touch her. Finally, he stretched out on the bed and waited, because he knew a little filly couldn't be made to talk that didn't want to, and like some kind of spell settled on him, he slept sound and deep in his clothes. The next morning he spent a long hour with his Pa, getting all manner of instructions for while Ben was gone. After breakfast, Hoss made a mumbled excuse about needing something from his room. He needed some quiet time to gather his wits for confronting Lydia about a suicide, and a daughter.

When he stopped outside his bedroom door he sensed her on the other side waiting for him. He had to force, really force, memory of Steven and Jodie back into his mind to tense himself against her and make her listen this time. He opened the door. "Now Lydia, I gotta have you straight and honest with me, or I cayn't keep helpin' ya. You have a daughter—"

Lydia threw herself into his arms and knocked him staggering backward, as though she'd appeared from a hole in the wall. "Oh, Hoss, don't be cross. I couldn't tell you about Jodie."

Hoss held her, breathed in her liquid fragrance of morning glory and jasmine, and then took her hand and led her to the bed to sit. A brief flutter of fear crossed his mind that she felt and smelled different every time he held her— but the thought was nothing more than a pesky butterfly he brushed away. "You kin tell me now."

"Her father turned her against me. Hoss, have you ever heard anything so horrible? Oh, I feel so faint. I loved that child so."

"Loved? But you—"

Lydia lay back on the bed, eyes closed as she reached out and put a warm hand on Hoss's arm. Hoss leaned over and kissed her. She responded and with amorous strength forced him backward on the bed. Feelings stirred deep in him, as he felt her love penetrating his every pore, telling him that he would not get out of this room until he had made her a part of his soul.

She tore his shirt open and kissed his chest, a dry tickling sensation that sunk into his veins. He couldn't fight her. He believed in her loving him, with his whole heart and soul and now, unable to resist, with his body too.

They belonged to each other and nothing could separate them, ever again.

* * *

Ben couldn't delay the journey to Carson City any longer. Hop Sing packed them extra clothes and plenty of food and still no sign of Joe. Ben didn't hurry the team down the hill, feeling at times the ladies were ready to get out and run on ahead of him. But Ben spent every slow second scouring every bush, every rock, every tree, for sign of the two sons he'd yet seen. Even in the streets of the Carson City, he searched every face for recognition or potential guilt. Who to ask? And how?

Sadie and Abby refused to go into the jailhouse with Ben. He looked back at them sitting stiff and proper in the buckboard, and opened the door to the sheriff's Carson City office. He knew he'd be hoping too much to find Roy here but he hoped anyway. Sadie and Abby looked ready to flee, conscious of stares around them, and Ben realized with a startling thought how people became animals—when their rights were taken away, or in the case of slaves, never given to them in the first place.

James Randolph, law clerk, looked up startled and dropped several papers to the floor as Ben came in. "Yes, sir? You're not looking for me, are you?"

Ben didn't expect that kind of greeting, even though he's been told that on first acquaintance people tended to be intimidated by him. He kept his voice soft. "Ah, that depends. I'm here to bail out a prisoner."

"You want a prisoner?" Randolph walked to Ben with his hand out. "That's great! Wait, which one?"

"Mr. Cartwright?" Jesse's soft but hopeful voice came muffled from the adjoining room.

"Quiet, you, there's no Cartwright here."

Ben smiled. "I'm Ben Cartwright, and I believe that's the prisoner I want. Now if you don't mind, I'm in a bit of a hurry."

Randolph dropped his pencil in delight and grabbed Ben's hand. "Well, I'll be! I cannot believe this is the first time I've made your acquaintance. I met your son Hoss but he didn't mention you. Of course, I haven't been here that long, but still—"

"Yes, well," Ben looked through the open door at the women in the wagon, arms around each other, surrounded by gawkers staring and talking. "Tell me what I have to give you to get Jesse Duncanwood out of jail."

"Duncanwood? That Negro kid? That's a fancy name, ain't it?"

"Look, can you—"

"Hurry, hurry, I know. Everyone's in such a hurry. Listen, I got three prisoners in there I'm supposed to process for court date appearances and I don't have any help, plus I gotta keep track of all the deputies and what they do and where they go—"

"So I'll take Jesse off your hands and make sure he's back for your court date." Ben took out a bank note with sudden inspiration. "I hear his crime was theft. Tell me how much he stole and I'll cover every dime. Then the charges can be dropped, right?"

"Well, it's not just *what* he stole, he has to pay sheriff fees and court costs. Paperwork's already been filed, and all of that takes time—"

Ben sighed. "Just give me a price."

Randolph sat behind his desk and dug through the papers. "Give me a second."

Ben walked outside to a group gathered at the wagon. They badgered the women with personal and accusing questions. "These women are human beings, not spectacles for your sport. Move on about your business, all of you! They do not have to answer your questions!"

One drunk, not fearful of thunderous oration, tapped Ben on the shoulder. "We seen these women in town just a day or two ago, stealing from the store over there. We got a right to know what they's up to now."

"Do you know me?" Ben lowered his voice.

"I don't think—"

"That's true. I'm Ben Cartwright of the Ponderosa, a fourteen mile ride up the side of that mountain. That makes me your neighbor, and potential friend. And they stole that food because they were trying to save my life. Now I'm here to pay and to get them the justice they came here to find. Is that all right with you?"

The man's eyes had widened. "Ah, I guess, if you can vouch for them, I—" He dashed off to the nearest saloon, its grocer open for the women patrons.[28]

Ben patted Sadie's leg and looked at the sun. "Just a few more minutes and we'll get those stage tickets. Jesse's all right."

He went back in to see Randolph scribbling away, and sighed. "Would you say $250 about covers it?"

* * *

Margaret kept at a good riding distance from Frank, who seemed to delight in showing off some horse riding skills to her, making his horse rear as he rode, dancing around what appeared to be, to her, no obstacles at all, running and coming to an abrupt halt. She wasn't willing to forgive him, or even smile at his antics, after the attack such a short time ago. He should be plenty grateful that she didn't mention his name to the sheriff but he acted instead like nothing happened at all.

Frank hadn't attacked her but he made the attack possible. And Joe indicated that Frank might be behind some bad cattle count. That meant, whatever direction they were going, she didn't expect to get anywhere closer to finding Joe.

At the same time, Margaret found Frank intriguing. She knew the men had both been drunk and that makes men lose control. She thought that Frank seemed too reflective to be as villainous as Stu—and she couldn't have fought them both off, so Frank must have had second thoughts. He studied the ground as he rode, and sometimes veered off in a new direction, so she sensed he followed some kind of trail. Only he would know the direction the herd had headed when he left them, so she couldn't question him.

But she didn't trust him.

At the same time, she rode along because she wanted to know more about him. His sandy blonde hair seemed to always stay in place, and he had those wonderful piercing eyes. Sometimes when she looked at Frank, she could see him staring into eternity. While wondering how he'd look without a shirt on, she spurred hard to catch him.

"Frank?" He was younger than he appeared, she realized, probably younger than her. "Do you have any idea where you're headed?"

He laughed. "No. Do you?"

"You want to know why I insisted on coming?"

"I figure you want to get to know me better."

Margaret jerked her reins back. "You're arrogant, aren't you?"

But Frank looked over his shoulder in a different direction. "I thought I had a trail but it looks like the wrong one. So let's think logical. If he caught up to the herd after I left, and figured out how to handle them, then they should be at the east pasture. That would be the one closest to the corral the Cartwrights use for breaking horses."

He rode on and Margaret had no choice but to spur to catch up, wishing she had a map.

"I think the horses were stolen," she told him when she got within range. "After we check the east pasture, let's look for Joe with the cattle herd. Where would that be?"

Frank rode ahead so maybe didn't hear her, in too much of a hurry, and then his horse hit a hole, or something—it stumbled and Frank flew out of the saddle.

He landed hard on the ground. The horse had fallen but jumped up, kicking and running, and then stopped, waiting.

But Frank didn't move.

* * *

Joe thought he had been headed in the direction the herd ran. But at the old burnt area he slowed and realized he'd fooled himself. He wanted to look for Pa days ago and had been distracted by other chores. What will he do if Pa is too far gone now to save? He rode to the half-burnt water wagon, and jumped off. Everything was stone cold now. Everything…cold… he walked through the crunchy burnt vegetation and hefted himself up on a blackened rock, soot coming off in his hands. Over this cliff, somewhere—he could swear that's where Pa had gone, but as he stared down, his memory became cloudy. He had been so smoke-filled he wasn't sure of anything anymore.

Joe went back to Cochise for his canteen and told his horse to wait. Canteen with water for Pa draped over his shoulder, Joe grabbed hold of a tree trunk and leaned over, at first becoming gut-sick but holding position, forcing the sweat down his throat. "Pa!" There were signs of burning down the cliff, but then the vegetation gave way to bare roots and rocky outcropping.

Something else…he could see something else down there. Still on his queasy gut, he studied the odd mark sitting on a flat rock surface, an etching, a mark that some sort of tool might have made. Joe didn't like cliffs but Pa's life was at stake. He scrambled a couple feet to the left, where another tree hung preciously to rocks above a flat rock ledge. He wrapped his arms around the tree and swung over, without thinking, without breathing, and with great caution and some groans, lowered his body down until he could feel his feet touch.

For a moment he thought he could smell his father's pipe—a sweeter smell than vegetative ashes. He shook this off as wishful thinking as he relaxed his grip on the tree, but fell backward until he grabbed hold of a root. The stone was only big enough to hold one foot and only if he leaned against the cliff. He looked to the left and down. He needed to reach down and grab hold of a jutting rock in order to swing himself down to the next step. He grunted and reached but scratched his chin, making blood flow. He grabbed on as tight as he could… there was little down there to break a fall, although if he could move more to the left, there was enough rock to land on…he forced himself to stop thinking as he swung his legs down. He felt his grip loosen but kept his body tight against the rocky cliff, until his feet touched something solid…slipped, but then caught.

That's when he saw the opening. An abandoned mine shaft.

* * *

The horses weren't where Joe expected them, but he wasn't surprised, having gotten detoured along the way. So they'll pay for eight horses they never got. Pa would understand. He would say, *Joe, anything you have to do for family is more important.* And now, because of the traces of recent human occupation in the mine shaft, including bits of Pa's clothes, Joe knew Pa could still be alive. Maybe captive, maybe being held for ransom, but alive long enough to reach that shaft. Joe rode on toward home. Pa could be home by now.

Ahead a figure in the pasture bent over something on the ground. At first Joe thought to keep on riding by. He'd had enough for one day. But lately Pa's voice was never very far away, and Pa never left someone in trouble. As he rode closer he recognized Margaret, leaning over a body on the ground.

She heard him coming. "Little Joe! Oh, thank goodness. Can you go fetch a doctor? I'm afraid to move him."

"That Frank? Well, I guess, so but I don't think he's bad hurt, why not wait here and we'll see when he comes to." He'd serious horse tosses, and this didn't look like one.

"Oh, fine, Little Joe, by that time it could be too late. You just wait here with him, I'll be…" she looked around to memorize the location. "I'll be right back."

* * *

Once in Carson City waiting for Dr. Jessup, Margaret remembered that Joe needed to know that his Pa was still alive. When she saw the stage pull out she ran to the ticket office and learned that Ben had reserved that stage for his party alone. No help for it now. Joe will believe her when she tells him. He has to.

* * *

Frank had been lying on his stomach so Margaret couldn't see his face. Having Joe show up was a pure stroke of luck, combined with a bit of logical thinking. He'd worked for the Cartwrights long enough to know their routes between pastures and home. Timing, as his pa used to say, was everything in life. Ironic, though. Bad timing still killed his parents.

As Joe touched him Frank groaned and rolled to his side. "Oh, man, I landed hard. Margaret, are you…oh," he squinted at Joe. "Where'd Margaret go?"

Joe smirked at him and stood. "To get you a doc. Didn't think you'd need one but there's no stopping women sometimes."

"Yeah, like a freight train." Still grimacing, Frank sat, feeling his neck and back. "That's what women are. Gotta panic right away. If I could count the number of times I've fallen off a horse."

"You and me both." Joe helped Frank to his feet. "With any luck Jessup won't be free to ride back with her. And I'll keep my promise to stay with you until I know you're all right." Joe kept an arm and a steely stare on him.

Frank looked down at his boots. "You want to see me?"

"You might be able to explain our short cattle count."

"Yeah," Frank sniffed. "About that."

"Oh, you ready to tell me about where cattle's been going?"

"Well, Joe, maybe I better show you. You game?" Frank knew this day headed his way but he didn't feel like facing a hangman's noose for nothing more than saving his own hide. Kind of like self-defense.

Joe hesitated, and Frank could see he wanted nothing more than to go home.

"You'll ride with me to the herd and do your talking there." They mounted. "Why aren't you with the horses?"

"We had trouble, Joe. I lost you. Where'd you go?"

"You lost *me!* Where'd the horses go?" They started riding, though neither seemed sure of the direction.

"Actually," Frank thought about this, "I saw we were having trouble so I went to see if I could get Hoss to help."

"You were at the house? Did you see Pa there?"

Frank studied him for just an instant. "Your pa? No, why? Should he be there?"

"Did you talk to Hoss? Has he seen or heard anything about Pa?"

"No, Hoss thinks your Pa is with you. What's going on, Joe?"

Joe slumped in the saddle. "Nothing, nothing at all."

* * *

After Lincoln left, General McClellan dismissed his officers from his tent with a curt "leave me be" and sat on the creaking rocking chair he insisted on taking on every campaign. Finding alone time could be murder. They probably figured he was writing to his wife, but this time, he drew inspiration from Lincoln.

General Order No. 163, he wrote at the top of the page, after checking his notes to see which number to use to make this an order to be issued to the army. He wrote fast and he wrote hard, and when he sat back, felt very satisfied. Oh, Lincoln will hate him, but nothing new there. Someone had to officially speak out because desertions in the army were on the increase, and not enough being done to prevent them. Sure, many recruits signed on because they had no job, and deserted because the army wasn't the joy ride they expected. Some men thought shooting at another human being might be fun, until they were forced to do so. But once they learned they were fighting to free slaves, why, some of them just said 'to hell with 'em.' Many of them believed that they'd go home after the war to find the blacks had all the jobs. That was the number one reason most Irish fought for the South. Mac figured more people would vote for Democrats in this coming Congressional election to bring more opposition to Lincoln's war policies.[29]

He had a sudden thought—oh that Lincoln was so inspirational! With this natural bent Mac felt he had toward things political, he'd be so honored—and the Democrats so smart—if they nominated him to run against Lincoln in 1864. What a campaign that would be! Except that he could never call the war a mistake, not with men dying under him.

He tucked the order in his jacket pocket and stood, slipped his hat back into place and tilted it just so over one eye. That was two years away—war had to end by then, with him the hero, saving soldiers' lives.

* * *

"Roy!"

Roy saw Mark Twain, newspaperman, kicking street dust to catch up to him. He didn't mind trading barbs but since that review of Ben's social, rumors have been flying and no one knows how to answer them.

"Roy, I just heard—Adam Cartwright has turned up missing?"

Roy nodded but kept a determined stride to his office, hoping his hard heels pounding the wooden walk would deter the man.

"Wait! Is it because of what I wrote?"

Roy stopped outside his office, jangling his keys as he looked back. "Now ain't that just like a newspaperman? Think the world turns on your every word." Roy walked into his office, wishing he could shut the door on his face. No such luck.

"You're in a mood today. No one to arrest?"

"Day's young." Roy glared at him as he sat. "State your business, Sam."

"Mark, I told you, I'm using my pen name now, Mark Twain. Not hard to remember, if you just gave it a try. I hear Hoss Cartwright's having himself a bit of trouble. Know anything?"

"Not a thing."

"Odd, that is, when you know about everything in town, Sheriff. People wonder why I spread rumors and tall tales—I can't get my hands on the real stuff."

"Better you get in trouble than me."

"Look, Sheriff," Mark leaned on his desk, "I like those Cartwrights, and I want to help. How about I send out some telegrams to some of the other newspapers in the country? Ask if anyone's seen this missing Cartwright. I could go both east and west, have them print articles, people could keep an eye out."

Roy studied him, wondering over the catch, or how this might play in the paper. "You could do that. A serious piece. No foolishness."

"Now how about telling me a little more about Hoss?"

Roy stood, coming nose to nose with Mark. "Get out of my office. There will be no more news about the Cartwrights. No slander, no scandal. You print about how Adam drinks too much at parties and the next thing you know he's gone and now you're spouting to me that you have their best interest at heart? All you want is to sell copy! Now get out!"

"Huh." Mark pulled his jacket down and patted his pocket to make sure he had his smokes. "Guess I know where you stand on the bill of rights."

He walked outside and stood on the step, eyeing the street as he lit up. "Well, as they say, there's more than one cat to skin. Most everyone likes to read their name in the print."

* * *

Hop Sing pressed his ear against the door and held very still. "rù mó." He couldn't hear Lydia, just the sounds Hoss made, and, blushing, he backed away. "Very gu huò enchant."

Hop Sing spent the day putting food outside Hoss's door. He tried a couple of times to get Hoss to come out, but except for saying that everything was fine, Hoss made no response at all. This time, embarrassed by the noises, and with growing fear over what Hoss had become, Hop Sing ran downstairs into the kitchen. He opened his ancient recipe book to the back, to the instructions for using the bewitching spells. Dead were the same as living, seeking out those who can help them, a quest from beyond reaching into their former world. But if Lydia took all the control from Hoss, she might drag him into her world. Especially if she loved him.

She must be helped quick and Hoss must see her as a ghost to know how to help her. Only then could he help her *and* stay alive. Hop Sing hoped the substitutes he had to make for gecko heart and licorice root won't spoil the tea's spell-breaking effect. Hoss must have all his wits to cope with a wily she-ghost. One who could lie, even after death, to get revenge.

CHAPTER 22

They were still on foot, walking through some pretty dry land, skirting a grand and colorful canyon—which to the tired and hungry didn't look so grand. They hadn't found a wagon, or even a homestead to beg for food, and were rationed down to a few sips of water and hard tack, a soldier meal Adam never had inclination to experience but could appreciate now. It had a slightly buttery taste and sat in his stomach long enough to make him feel like he'd eaten something. There had been no opportunities to look for escape, none, and still, every day, they ran to keep up with the horses. Both of them bore the scars of whips when they fell and thought they couldn't get up. Adam figured he survived because of that experience with Kane. Because now he found himself nearly as helpless.

Finally the pace slowed to a walk. Both had been grateful for a brief rainstorm an hour ago, but their clothes had already dried in the heat.

"What about the plan, Adam?"

"I figure when I see the opportunity, I'll tell you the plan in just one word." Adam paused to gulp for air. "I know one thing, though, we won't get anywhere fast until they put us on horses. Just a matter of finding them already tamed."

"What word?"

"You'll know what word when you hear it." Talking was hard enough, with little breath to keep moving. Thinking was harder. "It'll be loud." Adam grunted. "Like a scream."

When Jake came riding back on Buck Adam felt a burning in his head drop deep into his chest. How he hurt not knowing what was going on back home.

"We got a homestead. Looks like a family of Mexicans. Want to send the slaves in?"

"We'll all go, and ask nice first. They're likely southern sympathizers. If not, I'm sure we can deal with them, not like there's anyone around to come to their rescue."

The homestead was nestled between two hills and along a scraggly riverbed that might be respectable in the spring but tended to sink into the ground the rest of the year.[30] They had colorful banners flapping from the crudely built shack, and an elaborate statue of the Virgin Mary in the front yard, surrounded by some foliage that tried to flower even in the lack of rain. But Adam didn't see any sign of living folk, and felt a gathering of unease.

143

They were in Navajo territory, where Adam knew the Navajos and Apaches remained in a sullen mood. He had experienced Apache anger once and wasn't too anxious to repeat it. Kit Carson recently signed on with the army to punish both bands for their unrest, but with reluctance, because Carson knew they were unhappy being surrounded by enemies—the Mexicans and the miners, all looking to get rich. Now all of their people would be punished for circumstances outside of their control.

The yard had been torn by hoof prints and one window shutter broken and left hanging. Adam leaned over to Tobias. "The army is after Navajos in these parts. Let's hope we get stuck in the middle, because that could be our chance to escape." But the signs of damage to the house and yard didn't bode well for any planning. They might be too late to be caught in the middle here.

"That your plan?"

"Always be ready for opportunity."

Piney came up behind them and gave them a shove. He didn't talk much, always smelled of whiskey, and they knew to brace themselves for this biggest bully in the smallest britches.

"Go on, you two," Luke shouted, like he wanted anyone inside to hear. "Go knock on the door and ask for some grub."

Adam held up his hands, not fond of the irons even after they'd saved his life because now the wearing just plain hurt. "Think they'd be more willing if we weren't wearing these?"

"They'll treat you kindly, believing you've been abused," Piney snorted in his ear. He gave Adam a push.

Luke added, "Go on in and act needy."

The slaves shuffled to the door and Adam leaned against the frame, nodding at Tobias to knock. He had another idea, one that depended on the decency of the people inside. As Tobias knocked and no one answered, Adam felt his pain deepen—the first encounter with real people since the abduction and he planned to use them.

"Just open the door," Luke shouted behind him.

Adam looked back at the four men watching them and regretted what he'd thought to try. Heaven help these people if they *were* still alive. At least Jake always rode ahead, so Adam didn't have to see Buck too often. Pa's horse made him feel crazy. But he couldn't risk the lives of the people inside for his own end.

Tobias opened the door and they stepped in, immediately struck by the odor of death. Tobias fell back into the doorway, terrified, but Adam walked into the middle of the bodies before he knew where they were.

Tobias behind him whispered, "Adam! Is they dead?"

Adam looked down and pulled his foot off a hand. He froze. They had been attacked by Apaches because Adam could see one still had a broken bit of lance in his side. As he stared, his side ached where not long ago he'd taken an Apache bullet.

144

When his family got him home to heal, they told him Cochise's story of the poisoning, and later, with the help of Sam at the newspaper office, he got his hands on the full story. Or what passed as the full story, an editorial published that was later discredited—Adam figured someone didn't like that the report sounded too true. Cochise had been employed as a woodcutter at the Apaches Pass stagecoach station of the Butterfield Overland line, but in 1861, after a raiding party drove off cattle belonging to a white rancher and stole a child of a ranch hand, Cochise and five other Apaches were arrested by Lt. George Bascom. Inexperienced officers like Bascom were quick to try to make a name for themselves and show authority over any Indians they could accuse of guilt—and friendlies were easier to capture.

During this arrest, the Apaches protested innocence, but in the struggle one was killed and four were subdued, while Cochise escaped by slitting a hole in the tent. He captured a number of white people and demanded the release of the Apaches, but Bascom retaliated by hanging six Apaches, including some of Cochise's relatives. This drove Cochise crazy, and he killed in retaliation.[31] They never even bothered to find out what kind of raiding party first stole the cattle—they could have been eastern army deserters, for all anyone knew.

And now here they were, driving right through the heart of this anger-torn land. What had these Mexicans done to deserve this slaughter? Adam wondered—perhaps they were thieving from Navajos and Apaches. Or perhaps they fired first.

Behind him Luke pulled Tobias out of the doorway where the slave had frozen and stepped in. Luke didn't step in far when he saw the bodies. "Huh. Find any food?"

"Place has been ransacked. Probably nothing edible." Adam felt the gun where he had it hidden, ironically sticking him near where the Apache bullet hole had healed.

"Listen, I know the truth about you." He walked to Adam and kept his voice low, as though trying to keep Tobias from hearing. "You ain't no muley."

"Why don't you kill me, if you think so?"

"Oh, I got big plans for you. But just so we're clear, I'm not telling anyone else, but watching you like an Indian on a snake, and can drop you just as fast." He gave Adam a shove. "My breath's choking me in here. You find us some food and don't come out empty."

Luke shut Adam in alone with the dead.

Adam scanned the room lit by a single window, careful not to breathe. Three people he counted, sprawled in various slaughtered poses. They didn't look too happy, but then, dead people rarely did to those still living. The smell sank into his pores, hitting his nostrils even when he didn't take a breath—the smell of death, decay, rot. And ghosts. They could still be here, filled of hate for whoever did this, or whoever was foolish enough to test them.

Focus, look for food, get the hell out. No such thing as ghosts.

Adam stepped over one to the table, and then to the cabinet next to what appeared to be a crude water pump. Dry. Just like him. He'd been swallowing so hard he wasn't sure he had much of a throat left. He poked around best he could, breathing short air through his nose, not daring to look back.

Until he heard a voice.

"You can't escape."

He froze. "Who's there?" *No, no, don't start hearing things, you don't hear things, that's Hoss, and even Joe, they might see ghosts, not me.*

Adam checked the first body. Man, older, a musket ball clean through the heart. Good aim. Gun at his side. Definitely dead. Adam picked the weapon up but it was too gangly to carry on him. Man was unshaven, mouth gaped open as though yelling. First signs of decomposition, skin flaking away. Adam backed away to the next one.

"Can you play the game?"

No, just in my head, is all. Sometimes we can't understand the trail life lays out for us. We just have to play along—a game, sure, where the rules keep changing. Win or lose.

The next was another man, about the same age, maybe, but with white hair instead of black. They were defending their home, their horses, beef stock, all taken anyway. Were these Indians desperate, or just mean? Hard to tell. Arrow went through his neck, another in his arm. One arrow taken, the other must have hit a bone.

When he grabbed the shoulder of the last victim Adam fell back in shock. A woman. Just as angry looking, just as determined to protect her home. She gripped a cast iron fry pan. Some believe their women were better off dead than taken by Indians. She died fighting. These weren't Apaches after all—they were Navajo, Adam figured, by the kinds of material on the broken lance and arrow, sheep strands rather than hide. She had a lance broken off in her abdomen, could have suffered awhile, except her throat was slit. Navajos were being surrounded on all side, by their enemies, because gold had been found and they were in the way.

These were Mexicans—probably squatting on Navajo land. Former Mexican land. *A sticky web this country has weaved...*a pouch hung from the woman's waist. He opened the bag to sniff the contents. With a grimace he wet a finger and tucked it into the pouch. Staring at the woman's wide frightened gaze, he hesitated, put the finger to his mouth, hesitated, and tasted. Sugar.

Pouches. He had to look for more pouches.

"You had all the breaks."

Adam recognized Kane's voice lingering in his head, speaking from dead lips. Kane demanded accountability—from him.

I am sorry that you felt you had to die. You didn't have to be a miner, few ever make it. I wish I could have helped you. I let you down, and I'm sorry.

Adam found a pouch of beans as the voice in his head faded away. There are no ghosts—only desires to change the past. But as he took the beans, sugar and oats outside, he felt Kane waving goodbye from the window.

He didn't look back.

* * *

Ben arranged for the stage to take the four of them to St. Louis, stopping for no new passengers, only to change horses. He doubted that Adam had been taken this way but without anything else to go on they had no other choice. At least he can get to New Orleans ahead of Adam, hopefully, and keep his son from fighting to the death to keep from being sold into slavery.

The first hours passed pleasantly enough as they distracted each other with talks of family and of the past, where Ben learned their lives were not always bad, even as they longed for freedom. He learned more of their dreams and hopes, having their own spread like his someday.

When their conversation dwindled into pleasant dozing, Ben let his thoughts drift back to home. He had hoped to see Little Joe before he left. Hearing he was all right was one thing. A person can be all right one way and not in another. Only a father knows his boys.

Adam accepted a disguise as a slave. Ben bit back a shudder. He believed his boy had recovered from his recent mental distress over the desert affair with Kane, but would he have taken on something like this if Kane had never happened to him? Ben remembered, with a sudden grunt that made Sadie look at him, back when Adam was a child, being asked a time or two by strangers if his dead wife had been an Indian or a black woman. Perhaps he got into such a bind with this Tobias that he had to claim to be a muley or get killed.

If he knew his son, and Ben expected he did, Adam had found a bigger purpose here. Similar to his, but unfortunately, much more dangerous.

"Ever-thing all right, Ben?"

Ben smiled at Sadie. "Just hoping Adam isn't taking on the entire world this time."

CHAPTER 23

Hop Sing heard the footsteps on the stairs and ran out. He had not been able to sleep much the past few nights and the movement made him dizzy, so he stopped and caught himself on the frame of the doorway leading into the dining room. He opened his eyes to see Hoss grinning like a little boy who'd just come from an adventure to a forbidden water hole.

"Where's Pa?"

"He...gone."

"No, Hop Sing. I know I've been kinda hiding out upstairs, but I saw Pa still alive."

"He gone with black women to New O'leans. Not be back some weeks. Months if snow come early."

Hoss pressed his lips together and wrinkled his wide face into a narrow frown. "Dadburnit." He jammed his hands into his pockets and walked to the fire. "Joe and Adam?"

"Mr. Joe not know Mr. Cartlight alive. Mr. Adam not know he dead. I not know you alive or dead." Hop Sing scurried into the kitchen.

Hoss corralled him there tossing pans about. "Hop Sing! You know better than that, doncha? I got big news—me and Lydia is getting hitched." His grin engulfed his face so comically that Hop Sing couldn't help but laugh. "I ain't joshing you, Hop Sing."

"Mr. Hoss cannot mally ghost. Only help ghost. She in other world." Hop Sing waved a rolling pin at Hoss. "You not careful, you go with her! I make potion. I makee light now!"

Hoss grabbed his arm. "She ain't a ghost. I swear that to you, what we done these past few days...well, I kin say she's real for sure. Now I gotta go to Virginia City and see if I can get her daughter to come here. Don't tell Lydia, 'cuz I want to surprise her. And I'll make sure that Stephen gives her up, pure and simple. You just keep her here, all right? Keep her fed. She looked pretty dadburned hungry when I left her."

He ran for the door as Hop Sing shook a ladle at him.

"I never want to be cook. I do laundlee, people either wear or go naked!" Hop Sing slammed the rolling pin against the counter. He had the tea ready, but darned if he could find a way to make Hoss drink it. According to his ancient book, Hoss had to be both naked and standing in an open window in the moonlight while he drank.

Hop Sing would settle for getting him to drink anywhere and take his chances. But even that appeared no easier than a fool's burden.

* * *

Frank had Joe riding in circles so long that Joe feared he and Cochise might fall off the ends of the earth. Every now and then Frank got off his horse and studied a trail, though Joe couldn't see anything at all. Then Frank made a compelling argument for the Washoe being the culprits stealing cattle, and where they'd find the horses, too. They had been making a circuitous route in that direction, whether by design, or Frank was right and the trail of thieves ended there.

Joe wondered why he hadn't seen this before. Why, just because the Washoe helped him put out the fire? What if they also made sure his Pa stayed dead? This used to be their land, after all. Stealing cattle would sure beat the heck out of eating grasshoppers, in anyone's lifestyle. Joe remembered going with Pa the day Pa offered the Washoe one cow per month for giving up their land to him. But the Washoe refused to become dependent for their survival on any white man. From what Ben could understand, they would let him have the land, as long as they could still use it. Ben was no ordinary white man, Joe told his pa later, after asking why they'd turned the offer down.

Maybe now they decided they wanted the cattle, after all. Because the Washoe were involved with the fire and because Joe wanted somewhere else to lay the blame for everything, he followed Frank to the village.

* * *

Tobias and Titus were kept apart for days, as the slave traders followed a trail of horses, hoping to find whatever Indians had done the plundering and steal the supplies they needed to keep going. Tobias was tied to Piney's horse, while Luke had charge of Adam's progress.

Something had happened to Adam back in that Mexican homestead, and Tobias wondered if his friend had become possessed by ghosts. Tobias never went into a house of dead people. He'd heard too many stories about what happened to people who did. He wished he could get a look into Adam's eyes. Then he'd be able to tell. He hoped they wouldn't find any Indians, either. He'd been taught that they were harder to kill than ghosts.

He caught sight of Adam running, trying to keep up with Jake ahead as Luke followed him a short distance behind. The buckskin horse seemed to recognize him, or liked him and deliberately tried to stay back by him, fighting Jake's whippings.

Tobias tried to walk toward him but Piney held one end of the iron chains on top of his horse and that horse didn't like Tobias much. But Tobias felt sure

Adam knew where they were headed same as he did. For a moment the horses and wagons stopped, as Jake pointed to a gully below, through a border of parched thicket. Tobias didn't care…he was just grateful for the rest. He perked up on hearing the others talking about a prize of food and horses, and then they were moving again, but more quietly, all cautioned not to talk. Tobias looked over at Adam. He could see Adams hands clenching and unclenching but Adam stared down at the ground and dragged his feet, as though at the end of whatever had kept him moving.

When they reached an intersection of gully and cliff, Luke jumped down and called Marv over. He led the two chained men to a boundary of rocks and gave them each a rifle. "We'll be standing behind the two of you, ready to shoot either of you in the back of the head if you aim at anything but Navajos. When I give the word, all of us will open fire, and with any luck, we'll all hit our marks. And don't go feeling concerned over them, neither, not after what we saw back at that Mexican ranch."

"Cochise."

Luke turned on Titus. "What did you say?"

Titus opened his mouth but shut it. Tobias had the feeling his aim wasn't going to be very accurate, and believed even less that Adam had a plan for escape or even an opportunity for a plan. He looked like a whipped man more than anything else, unable even to look Tobias in the eyes.

Tobias feared Indians plenty, but they couldn't hurt him like some of these slavers could. He'd care, or not if he shoots because Indians couldn't be killed anyway. But he could be killed for lack of effort.

Tobias used to think he knew what the slavers were up to, but he wasn't always sure. Only thing he *was* sure of—and that's hoping that he and Luke could enlist Adam's help for the final event. He told Luke that the first chance he gets he should wire ahead to Samuels—a scoundrel, but he could be their only hope in Brownsville.

* * *

Joe pointed ahead. "The Washoe village is just over that ridge. Remember, I do the talking. I won't have you making accusations that might just be unwarranted."

The ride took them past the burnout area where Joe had flashbacks of fear and devastation, at one point so dizzy smelling old burnout he couldn't breathe. But because Frank rode ahead of him Joe forced, really forced, his father's voice in his head—*I raised my sons to think without me*—and pushed Cochise through a blackened section, eyes closed, breath held, to the other side. *Pa's gone. There's nothing I can do about it. He's gone.*

When his eyes opened, Joe thought he had ridden back in time, back into the same fire and he nearly called out to his Pa. Instead he caught up to Frank. *"Fire!"*

150

Frank jumped off his horse and pointed. Through the smoke Joe could see Washoe Indians fanning the flames, sending the fire toward them, toward the burnout, where there was nothing left to burn. Joe and Frank moved their horses afoot to a safer and smokeless area.

Joe grabbed his shovel to help them fight the fire but stopped when Lucius, a half-breed Mexican who lived with them, rode toward him.

Joe hollered and waved. "Do you need help?"

"Likely a diversion, while they sneak off with more cattle," Frank said under his breath.

"No. No help." Lucius knew more English than most Washoe. "The people, they say land weak, must burn little soon or too much late."

"We had that fire," Joe pointed behind him to the black grass he knew so well, "because we didn't burn deliberately?"

"Bad fire. Not yours. Belonged to careless men."

"Careless? You saw them?"

But Lucius rode back to help guard the fire.

As Joe watched, looking from their controlled fire to the area that had burned out of control and took his Pa with it, Joe realized that they still had a lot to learn from the Washoe. And that learning could be worth a whole cattle herd.[32]

But not if they just *took* it.

Frank watched Joe watch the Washoe care for the controlled burning. "You're letting 'em sucker you. They probably buried your pa themselves. I suspect they started that fire, too."

"Now wait a minute." But Joe couldn't hear his pa's voice anymore.

"How else would they have gotten here to help put out the fire so quick?"

"We'll talk to them," Joe muttered. He didn't know who to believe, but felt the return of a need for vengeance—from someone. "With Lucius here, we'll talk to them real good." They rode on toward the camp. "Say, Frank, they might offer you a girl. Don't accept. They marry you off that quickly."

"Wouldn't bother me to get married. At least for a night."

Joe reined up. "Hey, I'm serious here. We aren't looking for that kind of trouble."

"Whatever you say, Joe." Frank spurred his horse into an easy gallop toward the village.

CHAPTER 24

Adam had only moments to think.

Slavers and slaves surrounded, as quiet as the sunset beating red off the rocks, a party of Apaches sharing what appeared to some of them to be stolen food. The slavers thought they were Navajos but they cared only about supplies they could get. Adam tried to figure out how to signal the Apaches without getting a bullet to the brain. He could see maybe half a dozen feeble looking weapons, while over half of them seemed either unarmed or carried bow or lance. They did seem to have some stolen goods, but stealing them and killing for them were two different attitudes. Adam felt sure Navajos had attacked that cabin, but in either case, no one had the right to execute people without proof.

The slavers didn't care a whit about guilt or innocence or identity, just about taking what these Indians had. Taking what could be had rather than working for anything proper. That's what these slavers did, regardless of their political affiliation. Adam knew he shouldn't judge but these men gave him that right.

Think! One bad move and Marv's gun against his back would go off. But maybe not. Marv has been the least violent of the bunch, and even argued to release the muley as they neared every town they skirted. Worth a risk? Adam tensed, ready to whirl around with an elbow to the gun at his back and start shooting, all right—at the slavers.

No time.

Guns exploded around him at the Apaches, gunfire deafening and powder stinging the nostrils and before he could stop himself, perhaps nothing more than the law of survival renewed by a gunfire in his ears, Adam closed his mind down and began firing—not aiming, just firing. Which could be just as deadly, the way the Apaches scattered and the bullets bounced off rock.

A few Apaches fell and the rest took positions behind whatever natural cover they could find. Adam didn't think they had workable guns but before long bullets began to take nicks out of the hides of rocks around him, following the arrows that had filled the air.

Cal yelled at everyone to spread out, spread out and watch their backs. Marv left Adam to take a new position along with the others. He left Adam with Tobias and just enough ammunition to keep loading.

Now, every man to himself, for survival. Last man alive gets the grub.

What men won't do to eat. Adam grabbed Tobias's arm, unable to think of a plan past escape, but Tobias didn't budge, eyes on Cal, waiting for Cal's orders rather than realizing this as the opportunity Adam wanted.

"Tobias!" Adam couldn't wait, couldn't lose timing. Believing he'd be more help to Tobias on the outside, rather than here, where the value of his life plunged lower every day, Adam feigned movement to a new position and fired off a couple shots. Over there, he'd seen horse tails twitching. Irons or no irons, he could still ride.

The horses had been hobbled in a grassy knoll by a small sputter of a stream. Adam unhobbled the closest, a bareback pinto, while keeping a sharp eye out around him. He leaped onto the horse but with the irons on he couldn't sit straight. Even before he got seated the chains frightened the horse. It leaped away to follow the drying stream as Adam grabbed hold of the mane and struggled to sit. Two men crawled out of the water toward him, one holding the other who had been wounded but alive enough to hold a gun on Adam. They spoke sharply to the horse and it dropped down on its front knees. Adam had no choice but to tumble off, getting a face full of mud and the irons twisting his lower body into an awkward angle. After a breath, a groan and a grunt, he sat to see the uninjured man holding a knife on him.

Adam could run but his back made a fine target. He would never doubt their accuracy in throwing a knife. They led him with the horse to a gathering of pinion pines away from the shooting. They talked to each other but Adam couldn't hear a word. He figured they'd let him go if he ran but his chances were better with them than Cal seeing him flee and gunning him down. They seemed to be talking about his iron chains, as they pointed and made gestures that he thought meant they knew what he was—or was supposed to be. Being a slave might save his life again.

The one who had been injured concentrated on staying on his feet and keeping a bloodied cloth pressed against the wound. The other helped him up on the horse Adam took and then hopped behind his friend. He indicated to Adam to grab the reins and start running.

Adam hesitated. Behind them an ominous silence had settled in, impossible to know who lost. He thought about finding Tobias, but once he got out of these irons, he could go back and have those slavers arrested—if, that is, he could find a court to issue warrants against the Fugitive Slave Law.

Barely had these thoughts emerged when gunshots rang out, so close that Adam ran, holding the reins tight behind him. One shot took a piece of his already tattered white shirt, and then the horse behind him stumbled and fell. Adam reached up to the Apaches but he was splattered with their blood and bits of rock from bullets biting the ground and he reeled backward. His irons got tangled in the horse's flailing hooves, as its pained squeals mingled with the dying wails of the Apaches. Adam fell, trying to untangle, and got pounded by horse hooves in the process.

In the seconds that followed, as all the sounds died around him Adam heard only his own staggered breath and felt new pain in his side. Dark shadows crossed between him and the bright Arizona sky.

"Looks like our muley's traded sides," said Cal. "Why don't we just put this miserable half-breed out of his misery?"

Piney raised his rifle but another rifle slammed on top of his, forcing his aim to the ground.

Luke addressed his anger to Cal. "What's wrong with you? A muley his age and intelligence could bring Quantrill a thousand, maybe five thousand. You think he'd appreciate having you blow that? You know how the South is hurting for financial support. Lots of men pay for his kind of breeding."

Cal waved at Piney to put the rifle down, and crouched down next to Adam. "Luke's got a point, as he usually does around you slaves. Hell, I don't even know what we're keeping quiet for around you. You're in as much trouble as Tobias, you know."

Adam chose to feign ignorance. "Is...everyone...is it...over?" Adam rolled, blinked hard, tried to sit, failed.

Luke pulled Cal aside for a silent discussion before Cal turned back. "Get him up. We're behind schedule. At least we got horses now so we'll all ride, and ride hard."

Behind schedule? What would they want a southern outlaw like Quantrill for? Dealing with that scoundrel meant they had to be southern slavers, not northern. Quantrill made his name causing terror on Union troops and supporters in Southern Missouri—stealing mail appeared to be his biggest joy—he wasn't likely the kind of fellow who would tolerate Union men trying to pass themselves off as southerners. Adam wondered if Luke had revealed his disguise and they were going to let Quantrill hang him, but nothing he could do now so Adam let himself be dragged and mounted. The dreaded irons came off his feet, this time for good because they were thrown into the bushes, but his hands were still chained. With signs of death scattered all over the desert Adam feared no Apache had escaped— if one had, these slavers could be in for a world of hurt further down the trail. Jake and Tobias, who learned the hard way that Indians can die, dug through the dead bodies for food. Tobias handed Adam a piece of jerk beef, and at first Adam didn't think he could eat—at least, not in the presence of dead Apaches.

"Don't weep for them savages. We lost Marv. Poor fellow. But at least there's more feed for the rest of us."

Luke brought Adam an extra piece, and a canteen of water. "Don't fall off now, they might not be willing to come back for you." He patted Adam's knee and went back to his horse.

Adam watched him. He was a southern slaver, maybe the only one of the bunch who was—and Adam realized that made Tobias other than he seemed, as well.

* * *

Lincoln hated cabinets meeting. More and more he had to call upon his sense of humor to calm things down, and humor became a harder reach for a longer arm every day. He called first on Eddie Stanton, to get a report on the War Department, because few other things were as important these days. When Harry Halleck protested Lincoln told him to shut up. The rest of his cabinet refrained from applauding Lincoln while Halleck slouched even further, his fishy mouth gulping for air as he fought to keep silent.[33]

These days, there were more opinions than there were soldiers, and war ran the width and breadth of the entire country now. No longer did Lincoln think he could concern himself just with matters east of the Mississippi. Stanton went on and on and on about Buell's army in the Perryville campaign in Kentucky and then started talking McClellen, with long and ponderous words even Bill Seward couldn't understand.

Lincoln got impatient as he often did when the conversation turned to Mac. "Let's hear about progress on the Texas/New Mexico problem."

"Well, as you know we replaced Canby with Carleton the end of last month."

Lincoln shot upright in his chair. "Vainglorious Carleton?! Did I approve this?"

A lot of hemming and hawing answered his question. Seward, in his no-nonsense way, got Lincoln's attention and told him what he already knew. "Canby thought only a few Navajos caused trouble. He didn't want to move them all. And Carleton needed a new assignment."

"Okay, so we had to move Carleton out of the eastern theater." Lincoln turned back to Stanton. "How he's doing on the western frontier?"

"Well, he reported that the Confederates under Sibley got the Indians, Navajos and Mescalero Apaches to commit outrages on settlements—"

"Just disloyal settlements, I hope?"

"Ah," Stanton rattled some papers. "Doesn't say, Abe."

Lincoln sat back. "From what I understand, Indians aren't fussy. Gotta be careful."

"He's ordered Fort Stanton to be reoccupied." Stanton seemed to blush at this. "With who?"

"He sent Kit Carson with five companies of the New Mexican Volunteers. Well, if he didn't, all the settlers would be gone by now. Most of them are anyway, and now we have to try and coax them back. One company will guard the supplies while the rest go after the Indians. If no one but Southerners live there—"

"Ah, they're getting so spread out pretty soon they'll disappear." Lincoln played with his iron Howitzer ball, rolling it back and forth on the table between his hands to keep focused. "So are you telling me that every Indian they find they're going to shoot? Without even an attempt to establish loyalty—I mean friendliness?"

More of Stanton's ruffling of papers. "All Carleton says is they have to be punished for their recent aggressions. He's got howitzers stationed at Albuquerque with two companies of the Fifth U.S. Infantry, with six other companies of the Fifth at Peralta, two miles south. He asks for troops from California to assist in Arizona. Says Canby asked for this back in August."

"Everybody wants more troops," Lincoln muttered. "Tell him no. Tell him I want him to go after Indians caught in the act of depredations and not just anyone he feels like. Tell him the snake must catch the rat nibbling on the shoe or suspect also the raccoon." But even as Lincoln said it, he figured someone was going to get him to change his mind. After all, they got Canby out of there without his approval. How they get him to say yes to things they don't ask him about was one of the mysteries of this office.

"Carleton also thinks he can employ some Mexicans as spies. Although Mexicans seem to be at great risk of vengeance by Indians if they're caught. They're often related, or part blood, to Pueblo Indians, who also aren't good friends with Navajos or Apaches, at least not right now. They use Navajos as slaves." Stanton waited but this brought no reaction from Lincoln. "He wants to hear from you if you want him to hold council, as he has already made the statement to his troops that there will be no council, just kill all men you can find, and take women and children prisoners. He drew the line at killing the innocents."

"What I wouldn't give for a good game of rounders right now."

"Mr. President?" Stanton looked perplexed.

"What does he plan to do about Confederate forces in New Mexico Territory and in Texas? You know, the ones who are stealing into Mexico and trading cottons for guns with those dastardly mercenary British?"

More ruffling of papers. "Ah, he seems to think the California troops are on the way."

"That's all he says? Like Californians care. Did you order them?"

"Well, I said if they could be spared. I believe they can. And," Stanton cleared his throat, "he suggested *you* take care of the British."

Lincoln sighed. He needed both Stanton and Halleck, but sometimes they could be so dense. "Well, it's true we need to tie Britain down to our cause, and soon. What can we bribe them with?" More papers shuffled but no one had suggestions. "How do we get Mac to move?" he asked to break the silence. "A win somewhere else will help us win over the British. And if we get them, they'll bring in support of Europe."

Stanton pushed a paper forward. "I took the liberty of writing a telegram to McClellan, giving him all the orders he needs, and if he does not move, you'll have every right to remove him. All you have to do is sign."

"Remove him? Before the elections? He's like a chicken in the rooster yard. I can't afford to lose any Congress seats to those Copperheads."

"Mr. President," Seward fidgeted in his seat. "You shouldn't give credence to that derogatory term by using it, even in private."

"I can't compare Northern Democrats to snakes filled with venomous poison? Since when?" Lincoln looked around at the rest of the faces at the table but they stared blankly back. *Bunch of pansies, all of them.* He read the telegram to Mac, relishing their discomfort in the silence broken by the rolling of his iron ball. He signed his name, but only after adding, "This letter is in no sense an order."[34] He sealed the letter before handing it back to Stanton.

He allowed the other cabinet members to give their reports. They were on the dull side, to say the least. Lincoln wondered what his presidency would be like without this war. If these reports were any indication, he'd sleep for most of it.

"Bill, tell me about New Orleans. Can I take my family there on holiday yet?"

Seward rose, as though to give a speech, but Lincoln waved him to sit. Seward just loved a good speech.

"Keep it short. I'm hungry as a dog on a cross-country journey."

"Mr. President...Abe, I'm happy to report that slavery is fast disintegrating in those parts of the Confederacy now under Union control. Butler's officers in New Orleans, however, report that some of the blacks are getting just a little too assertive for the comfort of the whites. An abolitionist officer has been encouraging this type of insurrection by issuing free papers to slaves expelled from their plantations for defiance."

"Wait. Is that legal?"

"Ah, freedom to blacks in insurrectionist states..."

"Not until January 1st. And not even then if they rejoin the Union."

This brought a burst of renewed anger from the abolitionists on his team, but Lincoln just sat quiet and let them run out of steam by feigning indifference.

When the quiet resumed, Seward nodded and scribbled a moment. "No more free papers." Content with his notes he sat back, ignoring the frowns of the other abolitionists in Lincoln's cabinet. "Butler has trouble with merchants not making a true return of goods bought and sold, so he suspects some activity still underground in furnishing the Rebels. He's taken the liberty of drafting an order that Halleck thought I should approve." He handed the paper order to Lincoln.

Lincoln read it under his breath and tossed the paper back. "More oaths of loyalty we cannot trust. Can we even trust Butler? Keep going, I'll tell you when you're done."

"Well, we have few other options." Seward cleared the makings of a cold from his throat. "At any rate, the abolitionists are hurrying in to New Orleans, and so I would say, no, don't holiday there just yet."

Lincoln grunted. "What a bother. Whatever happened to that Doolittle fellow's idea?"

"The one about sending them to colonies in the French West Indies and Hayti?"

"You're quick for a secretary of state." Lincoln took a long and noisy drink of water, ignoring the laughter generated by the gentle teasing of Seward. "Well?"

Seward tried to chuckle. "Well, for those of you who don't remember, back in April Senator Doolittle of Wisconsin claimed that if the blacks were living in the tropics they would be dominant over the whites, who would grow effete and degenerate. He pointed to their colonies in the French West Indies and in Hayti, where they are capable of maintaining civilization and free government. Of the 75 foreign countries with which we have commercial intercourse, Hayti stands 21st in her exports and 24th in imports. Doolittle believes that the repugnance of living side by side with blacks was not of prejudice but the true instinct of nature."

Lincoln nodded. "I believe at the time I agreed with him."[35]

"We had one experiment in shipping a settlement of blacks to the French West Indies, but only half of them reach their destination. A number of them jumped ship and drowned, while still others escaped even before the boat left the harbor and are still on the loose."

Lincoln waved impatiently. "And part of the insurrection we've sent a posse after. What's the progress?"

"Well, on the one family that is the most dangerous...yes, we have some of our best men bringing the older fellow in, and his family, well, they're still loose, but a woman and two kids, can't cause much trouble."

"Not much."

"So if they get away—"

"Because they are?" Lincoln waved an impatient hand. "When a fish gets off the hook we say we weren't hungry. Is it foolish to think the insurrection will die now?"

"Well, it should, with the big fish caught the rest scatter." Seward got laughs at this. "But we'll keep extra guards on you in the meantime, just in case. Also we're readying a location in Hayti for another group to depart before the end of the year."

"Throwing slaves in prison. Wouldn't the media love that? Can't he just be killed? You know, executed for raping a white woman or something?"

"You already rejected that idea, sir."

"Oh. I'm sure I had good reason."

He got the chuckle he hoped for, stealing attention away from Seward and loving every minute.

Until dead soldiers crept into his mind again.

* * *

Margaret sat, dinner half eaten. Drunken and loud men, anxious for food or to return to gambling, jostled her seat in the saloon's eating room, but she paid them little mind. Even the smell of stale beer and beef stew faded in her anger. She thought she could just forget and move on, but after three days, she couldn't stop being angry. Maybe Frank fooled her deliberately, maybe, but for Joe to go along? Were the two of them laughing right now? Poor Dr. Jessup, as old as he is, being dragged out there for nothing but her embarrassment. She could still remember what he said: "I remember the old days, when the Cartwrights really *did* need a doctor."

Margaret tried to concentrate on the voices around her to get her appetite back. She didn't know what else to do, but knew that she couldn't waste any more time trying to help the Cartwrights. She'd left Sacramento without looking back when she'd received Little Joe's invite to the social. She'd left San Francisco after her fiancé died to start over in Sacramento. She had nothing behind, and nothing ahead. Phillip had died so sudden that she hadn't known happiness long enough to remember the feeling.

Stop whining, she scolded herself *and look for signs in the real world.* And that's when she overheard two men talking about turning a borrasca into a bonanza.[36] Ah, a mine's name—The Borrasca—had stock at an all-time low. Rumor was its luck might just be starting to change.

So, she hoped, was hers. Margaret threw down the money for the food and walked outside. She checked out of her hotel and bought a ticket for the express stage to Virginia City, before heading to the bank. She'd already thought to move back to California because she couldn't stay here without a job. She had packed a day ago with no place to go.

Now, perhaps, she'd found a career.

* * *

"What do you mean when you call us Cartwrights lazy?" Joe asked Lucius and by reference the other Washoes in council. Frank wondered how Joe could spend two whole days here without worrying about the ranch. And now he even started to think like them, using Washoe words hardly without thought.

Frank was happy enough to stay here and not trail after stolen cows, but after a whole day and no woman offered to him, he got edgy. Frank thought that last question should be of anger but instead Joe had fallen into some kind of silly respect for these primitive people. Didn't help that they'd found Joe's wild horses here, already tamed, and offered back to him for a very small price for the taming.

"Fire start on your land, your trees, they shed, they die, they need to be cleared. You do burning when the weather is wet, prevent when weather is dry."

"But that doesn't mean we're lazy, just haven't...thought about it." Joe nodded, smiling. "To you lazy, to us, just haven't thought about it." He laughed at the pleasure of understanding, breaking another barrier of miscommunication.

Lucius nodded, laughing with him. After hearing the interpretation, the rest of the Washoe joined in as well.

Darned kid looked like he'd found himself a new family. The council between Little Joe and the Washoe had degenerated from accusations of cattle theft to one of pure unadulterated respect and admiration. Frank found himself admiring this youngest Cartwright son. Then the Washoe started to describe the men who could have started the fire. So Frank lit out, with some vague excuse about needing to check on…something. He had better things to do— like getting out of town before Joe found reason to hold him responsible for everything. He could have started the fire. He just didn't remember.

But he couldn't be responsible for all the problems on the Ponderosa. He just couldn't. Not everything. For a few maybe. For giving several of his Rebel friends the idea that they could take more cattle, more than just what Frank owed in gambling expense. Frank still didn't think they'd take the cattle. Stu talked big, but when sober he was about as quiet as grasshopper in prairie grass.

Frank knew the route he and his horse rode out on—he just didn't know where the trail led. Loose ends have a way of needing to be tied. With another day coming to an end, and with a clean slate for once in his life, Frank wanted to start over, somewhere else.

Time to head for California, after first settling a debt with one little lady in Carson City.

CHAPTER 25

Hoss figured on being in Virginia City for a day or two. Lydia had him so plum tuckered out he thought he might just sleep for that day or two. He figured to check on some town business so he stopped at the bank, and visited with Roy, and with Mr. Calhoun, Pa's attorney, but all he could find was a contract for some wagons and miscellaneous hardware to be delivered come spring. He stopped at the telegraph office to check for messages. Nothing from Pa or Adam.

Hoss walked to saloons, eateries, the usual haunts of men and boys but saw no sign of Stephen anywhere. He went to the International for dinner, hoping to find him there and solve his hunger problem at the same time, only to discover he wasn't hungry. He just missed Lydia.

He got to know her so well those past few days when they weren't...and Hoss blushed to think about what they *were* doing, most of the time. She told him that she had been married to a man other than Stephen and pregnant when he died in a stagecoach accident. She met Stephen and quite before she could help herself let him romance her. They married a short time later, before she could tell him she was pregnant. When she told him, she let him believe the child was his, even though she gave birth only six months after they were wed. But Lydia didn't feel shame not telling him the truth. After all, a child needs two parents.

She had wept hard when Hoss told her of Pa's wives. She was sensitive that way, and, until Stephen frightened her off, the perfect wife and mother. She didn't say that but Hoss could sense how much she loved the girl, once Hoss got her to start talking about Jodie. After awhile, as Jodie grew, Stephen started to believe she wasn't his and began to treat the girl poorly, but Lydia never admitted the truth to him.

Hoss wanted to get the child and hurry home but was too tired to figure out how. Good thing, too, because Virginia City on a peaceful day took some doing to get through, and on a bad day there were so many wagons and coaches jamming the sloping streets that no one could get anywhere. The Paiutes were active this time of year, walking the streets with firewood that they hoped people would buy. They knew they had willing customers with the Tahoe winter approaching, and hoped to sell to the best offers. Only yesterday two teams loaded with supplies, one of whiskey and one of flour and sugar, collided in the street and overturned, making a God-awful commotion and rioting as people tried to gather the goods, drinking whiskey off the ground, figuring the wreckage to be insured. There was still leftover damage to sort through and people scraped flour off the ground where it sat in diminished piles.

And more miscreants than he'd ever seen in the city before—panhandlers, drunks, and fistfights in the street. Two days earlier a whole herd of goats got away from some children goat-herding and practically tore up the town before they could be corralled. Hoss could see the chewed posts and goat turds in the street. All reminded him why he and Joe enjoyed their trips here more than to Carson City, where Adam and Pa preferred to go.

"Hey, Miss Angela!" Hoss remembered how Joe had spooned with Angela at the social, and felt bad that he hasn't helped Joe with ranch work so he could keep courting with her. She waited until he caught up to her. "Little Joe talks about you plenty, but he's been busy lately."

Angela brushed the sun from her eyes as smiled at Hoss. She had bags over her arms.

"That so? How's your brother Adam?"

"Oh, he's…around." Hoss tried not to stutter. "I'm sure Joe will be in town soon, to ask you…to a…picnic or something."

She put a hand on his arm. "Little Joe is very sweet. But I'm afraid I'm already taken. One of your loggers, I believe. Randy. We're getting hitched, you see."

Hoss took a sudden step back and fell half off the walk. "Really? That's…might swell, Miss Angela. Well, I'll be seeing ya. I guess." She waved and walked to the mercantile, where she glanced back once before disappearing. "Randy?" He frowned. "I don't reckon I know him." He shook his head.

Tired as he was, he figured a poker game might help get his mind off Lydia. He found one more than happy to let a tired rancher sit. By the third hand, he figured he'd been suckered, but at least, if Stephen showed, he wouldn't think Hoss was waiting for him.

"I'd throw that one in, too, if I was you."

Hoss saw Mark Twain grinning at him.

"Hey, Sam, sit down and join us."

"I'd love to." Mark sat. "But only if you remember my right name."

"Oh yeah. Mark Twain, ain't it?"

Mark accepted the deck, shuffled and put them down again. "Problem is I don't like to gamble. Life's short enough. I wonder if I might buy you a beer. Over here." He stood.

"I don't know that I should. I hear tell you called my brother a drunk."

Mark got an embarrassed "aw shucks" look on his face and crouched down next to Hoss so he could lower his voice. "I'm gonna let you in on my stylistic secret. Don't go sharing this or I'll have to quit the newspaper business. When I end my article with "and a good time was had by all," that means by me, too."

"Huh?" He waved off the deal as the cards went around and stood next to Mark.

"Means I'm joking. If I don't end the article that way, then it's not."

Hoss thought about this, and laughed. "Oh, ha-ha." But he frowned. "And if people still think it's real?"

"Then I can prove it isn't. How about it? A beer?"

Hoss nodded and left his spare change on the table. "What's on your mind, Mr. Twain?"

"Mark. I hear you're looking for a word with a friend of mine, Stephen Lawe."

"He's a friend of yours? Huh. Guess Adam was right."

"About what?"

"He says you can travel a circle about anywhere and find yourself starting all over again."

Mark laughed. "I suspect he was funning with you. Is Stephen in some kind of trouble?" When he noticed Hoss hesitate he leaned close. "Between you and me, of course. I'd like to keep him out of trouble, if I can."

"I kin only say that he and I have a mutual friend in common and it ain't you."

"And that friend's in trouble?"

Hoss leaned close. "She's terrified."

"Is she in town? I might be able to help, you see."

"No, no. I'm protecting her. And you kin forget about going to the house and talking with her. No one can see her but me. And Hop Sing."

"You mean, because she isn't really there?"

"Oh dadgumit!" Hoss took out some coins and threw them on the bar. "I'll pay for my own, thanks anyways." Hoss went upstairs to his room without looking back.

* * *

Margaret stepped inside the bank and held her breath. She had a good savings built up from her work as a bank clerk and Phillip's money came naturally deeded to her. And here she was, getting ready to toss his generosity and the little security she had for the future away. Maybe people became independently wealthy this way but some also became penniless paupers.

When the clerk waved her forward, she braced herself, and handed her satchel to him before he would process her request. They had a rash of robberies lately and he had to make sure she wasn't carrying a weapon.

"I'd like to close my account please, and take my funds in bank notes."

The teller mumbled something about being held up without a gun and laughed, but he processed her request, and handed her back her satchel with the notes tucked safely inside.

As she left the counter a fellow turned his back to her. Something about him made her feel uneasy so she left the bank to count the money when she got to the mining office, in front of witnesses. As she stepped outside she braced herself against the wind, the dust brisk for the valley, playing havoc with her hat strings. With her breath held she started toward the stage station to await the express to Virginia City, where her bags were all ready to be transported there. Since she got rid of most everything she had, packing hadn't taken long at all.

A gentle hand from behind took her elbow. She tried to jerk away but the grip tightened. At the sound of his voice she froze.

"Hello, my little ass buckshooter." Stu grinned at her. "Just happened to see you walk into the bank. And look at you, all dressed up. You going somewhere special that you need to close your account?"

"That is none of your concern." She struggled to get away but he pulled her into an alley.

"We have some unfinished talk. You get to pay me back for a little pain and suffering." He pushed her back against a quiet corner. "Give me the satchel."

"No. Please. This is all I've got. Take me if you have to, but allow me the chance to get out of town with some dignity."

"Dignity!" He leaned so close she could taste his spit. "You want dignity? How about having buckshot plucked out of your britches? I ain't leaving you nothing, honey, and that's all you deserve."

He ripped her hat off and pressed her against the building, and forced his lips on hers so hard he pinned her without breath, unable to struggle. He ripped the bag from her hand and tossed it behind him, and in the same move slapped her so hard she felt sideways to the ground.

"Any charge for this show?"

Stu grabbed her arm and grinned over at Frank. "You want a piece? Gotta stand in line, friend. And this time, hold my gun so she can't try nothing." Stu handed his pistol out to Frank.

"Gladly." Frank took the pistol and tossed it aside. He grabbed Stu by the shoulder, who first tried to shrug him off until Frank laid a good fist into his jaw, sending him flying backward against the building on the other side of the alley. "You know, I never liked you, not from the first, you and your phony story about bravery in Lee's army. You're a coward, and that's all."

Stu gave Frank a dazed look before slipping down the side of the building to the ground, and out. His head bobbled a little, making Margaret fear he'd try to get up.

Frank held his hand out to Margaret. She couldn't breathe, not knowing if she wanted Frank anywhere near her either, until she realized where she'd be at the moment without him. She took his hand and let him pull her to her feet, a little too close for her liking.

Still shaking, she brushed at the dirt on her velvet travel coat. "Thanks for the rescue. But this hardly makes up for that other incident."

"Other incident? You mean, you brushing me aside when I asked for a dance?" Frank pulled her into his arms but she broke away, finding anger a good medicine for the trembles.

"No, out on the trail. With Stu." She didn't expect him to want to remember and neither did she, but it had to be said. She leaned against a hitching rail until a horse nuzzled her hat.

Frank scratched his chin, thinking. "Huh. I ran into you when I was with Stu? I'm sorry, miss, I just don't remember that."

"I'll bet you—" Margaret gasped and stepped back, falling into the street. "My goodness, you really don't?"

"Could have been someone else?" Frank picked up her hat and handed it to her, while she clung to her satchel. "I'll walk you. Wherever you're going, if you like."

"I'm taking the stage to Virginia City. It's...not far." She frowned at him. "Besides, I don't care much for drunks. People who drink so much they can't remember anything they do."

"Whoa. A little harsh talk to a hero."

"A man always knows a time and a place. Why, Adam would—"

"You comparing me to that saint? No, thanks." He walked with her whether she wanted him to or not. "I didn't have the family he's got. You want to go comparing, you find someone who ain't had a mama who was a hooker and a pa who made money on her and beat us both."

"Oh, Frank, that wasn't you, was it?"

"I don't much cotton to making up stories, miss. Nor do I like to talk about my past."

People were boarding what appeared to be a full stage. Margaret handed them her ticket and made sure she could see her luggage roped in on the roof before turning back.

"Did you tell Joe his Pa is still alive?"

Frank looked down at his granite covered shoes before responding. "Yeah, sure I did."

Margaret heard her name called and stepped on the stage platform. "You can't tell the truth from the time of day. Goodbye, Frank." She got into the coach with help from the driver, and, once seated, looked back at Frank.

He looked so forlorn staring back at her that she couldn't help but smile.

* * *

Joe rode into the ranch house yard at full gallop. "Hop Sing! Hoss!" Without slowing his momentum he ran into the house and then came to a dead stop.

The house was empty. And even worse, it didn't appear anyone had been here for days. "Hop Sing?" He walked to the fireplace and put his hand on the inside stone. Cold. He looked in the guest room where he'd last seen Lydia. Perfectly clean and made up.

Joe flopped down on the settee and put his feet up. He heard his Pa's voice, *feet on the floor, Joseph* but didn't oblige. Pa was gone. He couldn't help what happened in the fire. But something happened to Adam, too. All he had to do was tell someone, put someone in charge of ... something, and then he could find his brother.

CHAPTER 26

Ben and Sadie found an easy, relaxed conversation, not fearing the silence, during which they'd watch Abby and Jesse playing hand games, singing spirituals, telling each other folk tales or cuddling. The four would converse, too, as there weren't many other places to stare when not talking, except at each other. Abby and Jesse seemed a little too friendly to be brother and sister, but Ben wasn't about to pry, and tried hard not to stare.

Runaways. During one of their quiet moments, Ben put his head back and closed his eyes. They came an awful long ways to find him, thanks to Darcy, who, it seemed, "employed" them, and who had Sadie's husband, too, until he'd…disappeared. Wasn't that what she said? Ben couldn't remember. His mind flipped between feeling used by her, and wanting to be used by her. She'd come with these two teenage children and a brother who seemed, as Sadie put it, "like a loose cannon." Darcy ought to be shot for allowing that kind of danger to these people. Runaways. If Darcy sent them looking for help, how were they runaways? Generally only the master wanted them found and returned. Instead, he wanted them in direct line of danger, just to get a Cartwright to New Orleans to talk to Lincoln? Seemed like a long shot, at best. The farther Ben got from home, the more he wondered.

Sadie, at least, seemed to have no regrets—seemed as capable of this kind of activity without second thought. Whatever Darcy's plan was, Sadie bought into it, heart and soul. Yet Sadie remained vague about those plans, just that they needed Ben to encourage Lincoln to come to New Orleans.

As they talked, Ben wondered what kind of relationship Sadie had with her children, and that husband she said was missing, or dead. Families of slaves were often torn apart, but many also retained a semblance of family life.[37] If they hadn't introduced themselves as family, he wouldn't have guessed it. For a mother, Sadie seemed aloof, and yet they communicated on a level that seemed spiritual. They had a familiarity and a…respect that demonstrated how love went beyond caring how one was feeling at the moment, to respecting individual thoughts and desires. He had the feeling she never sent them to bed, as he'd been known to do. He thought his parenting skills were good, but he could learn from her. But he puzzled more and more over Jesse, who didn't seem to be related to the ladies, either in looks or personality. He and 'sister' Abby touched more often than Ben found appropriate.

Thoughts, during lulls in conversation, kept him too busy to enjoy the scenery. They were making good time toward St. Louis, where they'd catch a riverboat to New Orleans. They had been required to sign waivers of non-responsibility toward the stage line in order to take them that far. Outlaws still caused trouble on the Missouri/Kansas border, and one, William Quantrill, had gathered himself a band of southern desperadoes and captured an entire Missouri town.[38]

Ben didn't think that they'd bother a stage carrying blacks, but to be on the safe side, he'd wired his funds ahead and carried nothing of value with him.

Sadie brushed his face with the back of her hand. "You don' wear whiskers, Ben. Ever-one I see wears 'em, 'cepting you."

"Never been one for trends, I guess. They don't look very clean to me. And none of my wives liked hairy faces." He leaned close to her, feeling her warmth but unable to make any more aggressive moves, even with her encouragement, well aware of the eyes of Jesse and Abby, who didn't try *not* to stare. "I suspect I feel pretty rough about now, and will sport that beard for you soon enough."

Sadie put her hand back down and sat straighter to look out the window. "Well, we's nearly through Kansas. Except for some far-off Indian sightings, I think I kin start to relax."

"Indians scare you?"

"We gets a little skittish is all. Well, coz they move like they live in the spirit world. We hears they's as hard to kill as ghosts."[39] Sadie sighed as she placed a hand on Ben's leg. "Kin I count on you, Ben? Truly? After all I done got you's family in trouble?"

"I'm still not sure what you expect from me." Ben didn't want to voice his *real* concern, not to her, not now. If he had to choose between knowing her and getting his son back, he didn't even hesitate. "I'm not sure what I can do there, besides look for my son."

"Oh," Sadie stared out the window, gathering her thoughts. "We's gonna get Lincoln to come, and you kin git him to talk to you private. You kin talk silver, and he'll listen." She sighed. "I know you knows that but…kin you tell him…not to send us away? And not to get rid of Butler. The worst part is…we gots to git to him before Tobias. Tobias plans…I hates to say."

Ben wrapped his good arm around her shoulder. "You're safe now. Anything you say is between us."

"Tobias thinks Lincoln don' care about us darkies. Jus' using us to win a war and the country 'tween here and Californee for them Republicans. We kin make Lincoln care, Ben."

Between here and California—a railroad… "But why worry about Tobias? If we're right, the slavers got him. And Adam."

"He ain't alone in his plans…Ben, this thing has done gone so far now, we might not git to stop it."

"Why don't you tell me everything? Start at the beginning."

Sadie took a big breath, and encouraged by the smiles of her kin, she took Ben's hands. "Well. I's raised in New Orleans, and freed when I's 19 and giving birth to my second chile. It was the massa's chile, I ain't ashamed to say, Ben. I was young and scared and he was kind and friendly. I thought he loved me. Then he done took it from me and sent it off and makes me free. So maybe he did love me, in a kind way, different way like they done back then. I spent some twenty years working as a laundress and facing long days and short food, and trying to git some education, Ben, and trying to find that child before I succeeded," she nodded at Abby, "and then I met Jesse's father."

"Wait, Jesse isn't that much younger than Abby—"

"He's his father's boy, but not mine," she told him.

Ben nodded. So Abby's a mulatto, which would explain a few of her more delicate features. They had a different kind of family, but still a loving one, so he wasn't about to compare them to his anymore.

"He weren't free, but we has us a wonderful relationship. But Ben, you kin look at me and see a slave, you can't see I's free. They sees you a certain way, and they expects a certain attitude. In New Orleans Butler says wrong, he say all the slaves would be freed come January 1st with the proclamation. Before he kin learn his mistake, so many slaves throwed down they's shovels or walks out of they fields, and won' go back without them getting some paid wages."

Ben hesitated, sensing other trouble. "And then they come to learn that since New Orleans is part of a Union state, then the slaves won't be free, after all."

"Yessir. Butler is gonna be in trouble with ole Massa Lincoln, and he been the best hope we has. Butler, he knows we need education to be truly freed, but Lincoln, he just wants us to go away so he don' gotta deal wit us."

Ben watched the scenery going by—beautiful hills and bluffs, trees of tall and gnarly shape and form, an occasional ranch with a self-dug pond for watering. He and Adam had often skirted around the issue of instant freedom's effect on an entire population. The ones they knew were freed were also first educated. "So they decided just to ship some of you off?"

"Yessa. And as I was dragged to the boat, I's screaming, I's free! But a lot of people was screaming that. Butler tries to control who goes or not but there ain't much he could do. They was some went willing to be freed and working. But me and my family, we knows better."

"What happened to Jesse's father?"

Jesse leaned forward. "They kilt him."

"We don't knows that for sure," Sadie said. She sat back and closed her eyes, as though exhausted. "Darcy says diff'ernt."

Abby leaned forward toward Ben until the stagecoach jostling forced her back. She seemed to be gathering her thoughts and grabbed Jesse's arm. "He followed and then he gone. That's all."

"Wait." Ben turned to Sadie. "You want me to help you find him?"

"No, Ben. I knows he dead. Darcy done tole me so, before telling me about you and you's silver. That's when we runs, with Tobias. Darcy give us little choice. Run or git back on the boat."

Ben bit his tongue, knowing his feelings about Darcy might not set right. He grunted with a nod, and allowed the conversation to dwindle. Now he had another problem. He'd have to control his temper once he finds out what Darcy, the scoundrel, was up to.

And Darcy might not even know his cousin Marie—Joe's mother—had died.

Almost as though they could read his troubled thoughts, Jesse and Abby started another spiritual, their voices low and so sweet that he felt his worries dissolving:

> I'se gwine on er journey, tell yo'
> I hyar yo' better go 'long;
> I'se gwine for de kingdom, tell yo'
> I hyar yo' better go 'long.[40]

* * *

They didn't stop to eat or drink but just ran, as though a contest to see who or what would drop first. As hard as Adam tried to outrun them, he always found himself surrounded and knew they would use those pistols on him if he were to veer off course. As good a horseman as he was, they were every bit as good. No conversation was possible.

For awhile the ride exhilarated him. Even his thoughts seemed to fly in the wind. Had the Apaches been guilty? Of what? For all he knew, those Mexicans could have been attacked by Apaches and not Navajos. Adam wasn't all that clear on what he'd seen in that dark shack.

The farther he got from home, the less Adam believed he'd ever see the Ponderosa again—and wondered if he could stay, if he did. The world cried out right now with war and cultural abuse, and poverty and hate and death. How could he live safe and snug on the ranch with all of this going on?

He'd once thought that with the wealth the Cartwrights had built up, they could use some influence to sway the government into kinder treatment of the natives, but now he felt that nothing they did from the safety of their ranch could be of any lasting help. He couldn't tell Tobias that, because Tobias seemed to bank on the Cartwrights promising silver to Lincoln.

Two of the horses gave out about the same time—Cal's and Tobias's. Tobias ended up in a patch of prickly pear and proved how tough he was by picking and eating it. They decided the day was late enough to camp for the night.

"Adam, feels good to have them irons off," Tobias said, picking his teeth with a thorn.

Luke and Piney nodded off near them, and Jake and Cal tried to find a way to make seven horses serviceable on the morrow. They had taken three extra horses with them, but all were showing signs of fatigue, drooping, unable to eat or drink. They'd made good progress that day, but might be on foot unless they steal again. They each dragged three horses in different directions to find grazing and more water in case they did revive, leaving Buck nearby to graze on what little was there. He remained in fairly good shape, considering.

"And to be riding." Adam stared at Buck, wishing the horse could talk.

"Still planning an escape?"

"Something about that Luke. I'd like to find out what. We've been gone so long now, I suspect we'll see this through to the end." Adam stretched back on the cold ground, the one moldy blanket pulled to his chin, not about to share his real fear, that of growing mistrust of Tobias. "I don't guess you want escape anyway." He yawned, keeping the thought casual.

"If you think I sets us up to get dragged back east in irons, you go on and think ahead, Mr. Know-better-than-anyone-else." Tobias flopped down and turned his back to Adam.

Adam looked at the sky but could read no news in the stars. "Listen, all right, I'm sorry. I didn't mean to sound critical."

Tobias stretched out on his back, hands under his head as he stared at the stars, as though to read a share of Adam's newspaper. "Adam, that Luke is a strange one. The other day he asked me what I'd do if he released me."

"Yeah? What did you say?"

"I asks if you could come, too." They laughed under their breath. "Adam, what would you say if I tells you that Luke is a southern spy?"

Adam blinked at him. "Spying on what?"

"He don't want me to get to Lincoln."

Adam propped himself up on his fist. Time to play with his confusion a little. "Let's say it's also possible that Luke is protecting your hide and won't let these northerners take you to Lincoln, who might have you thrown in jail. And let's also say that you're the head of a Negro Rebellion that plans to murder Lincoln."

"I ain't never met Luke before he shows up with these other guys. I jus' get a bad feeling about him, is all. Like he's one of them poor white trash allus looking to make trouble."

Adam studied him. "And, after all, if you were that dangerous, they'd just kill you. So Lincoln wants to talk to you, you think. Right?"

"No! You still don't get it. They will try to kill me. But with Luke here, they gotta make my killing look like an accident. He's the wild card. They don't know him." Tobias sat up, and his anger appeared as deep as his skin hue, even in the fading light. "I know you don't believe me, and I don't need you's help. You think you knows Lincoln, just look at his emancipation plan. He's using us. To win a war and to push industry to the west. He'll kill all them Indians, too, if'n you lets him. All I's telling you can be found out, Adam. All true. Like in newsprint true."

"You're calling Lincoln evil when all the other blacks think he's some kind of savior?"

Tobias sighed. "Too many wants freedom any way, and wants it too long. Few realize that finding freedom takes real effort, more than just a word of one man." He forced a smile, the contrast to his anger startling. "Makes me dangerous, Titus, don't you think?"

"No. Just delusional. You're a runaway slave, and they're bringing you back and that's all there is." Adam closed his eyes, but not for long. He looked back at Tobias. "You sounded just a little more educated than you let on. Who are you, really, Tobias?"

Tobias, at first, pretended to be sleeping, until Adam gave him a nudge. He sighed and squinted open an eye. "Adam, a lots of black folk like me is starting to get educated and scared to be freed. They's educated enough to know they don't know what to do."

"Only natural, I suppose." Adam fought with every inch of northern blood the idea that Lincoln and his party were anything less than noble. "Face facts, Tobias. Even though Lincoln and many in his party aren't perfect, Lincoln never wanted to see slavery expand beyond the current boundaries. He also pledged when he ran for president that he'd not interfere with slavery inside those boundaries. But war changes things. You know that." But that wasn't the point, and Adam knew it. For freedom to be true, and real, a number of factors had to be taken into consideration and planned, not... manipulated. "Just...get some sleep."

* * *

Hop Sing found the bank drafts and the pay for the loggers all dated yesterday. They would not wait long for pay before they up and quit. He had no choice but to take a wagon out alone, because he *was* alone, and run the pay out. He had been planning to find Salzar, anyway, and ask him to take over until a Cartwright was...of a right mind again. He hadn't seen Joe in days, either, and now Ben's entire life's work was at stake.

Salzar, Hop Sing felt, would jump at the chance, although he was a bit of a lunatic. At least, to Hop Sing, he talked too funny to understand, most of the time. Hop Sing couldn't let things fall apart. And he still had a lot of food that needed mouths. So he packed a buckboard with all the extra food, checked the map routes for the right location, and started out.

He didn't like going out in a wagon on his own. He didn't like how many people in these parts still hated Chinamen, even though his people took jobs they didn't want. He knew they hated him for not spending his money in their stores, but sending his income back home for his family to invest for him. There wasn't much in this country that interested him. The Cartwrights took care of all his needs anyway.

Most of the time. Except now.

Once out in the wind Hop Sing pulled his hat down tighter on his head and buttoned his coat under his chin. He hoped the Cartwrights were all dressed warm, wherever they were. Especially Adam, missing now for over two weeks, and wearing little more than his dress clothes. Joe, even though mourning his Pa, handled some of the ranch duties—hopefully, still was—and Hoss, well, few things grab hold of a man like a ghostly entity needing help. Ben promised to send a telegram every few days to report on his progress but Hop Sing would not go to the city to get them. All problems. Dry weather and missing cattle and bad timbering. Hop Sing hoped he would not find the men in a bad mood. Being paid and getting food tends to cheer them up, so with any luck none will feel the need to beat on him, just for fun. Ben told Hop Sing once that if he ever went anywhere to carry a rifle with him. He kept it loaded and ready under the seat of the buckboard.

Hop Sing wondered about Adam. Ben thought he got himself abducted by slave traders, but Adam did not look or act like those blacks he met. Why would they take him? Was Ben only hoping and they would find his body someday on the Ponderosa? Hop Sing hoped not today. He would be the saddest of all. Adam always showed him the most respect, the most gentleness, not wanting food like Hoss, or just to tease him like that rascal little boy Joe. Adam helped him when he was alone and lost in this wilderness, and got him this job.[41] So long ago. Without Adam Hop Sing figured he would be dead today. Hoss and Joe he loved, and Ben he respected, but to Adam he owed his life.

Hop Sing was about to make the turnoff on the trail to the lumber camp when he heard the pounding of hooves. Hoping against hoping that this rider was Adam, he waited. He would be grateful for any Cartwright face. Instead Hop Sing saw a man he thought he recognized as a ranch hand, maybe supposed to be with the cattle or horse herd, but he realized with growing fear that he didn't care to know and so got his buckboard moving.

Before he could even guess what danger he might be facing, Stu had stopped alongside the wagon with his gun pulled and pointed at the Chinaman's head.

"Get out of that wagon."

"I...just bling food to lumber camp. You hungry? You eat."

With the gun out, Stu rode around the wagon. "Yeah, get out. I'll take the wagon, you kin walk home."

"No walkee, too far."

"Got the pay here somewhere, don't you. I said out of the wagon, don't touch nothing."

"No, no." Hop Sing prayed a Cartwright wasn't far away. "Let me keep wagon. I give you wallet. Plenty bank note. Ah...negotiable. If I give you wagon I die."

Stu hesitated. "All right. Damn wagon and food would just slow me down. Hand the wallet over."

Hop Sing reached under the seat of the buckboard. As he held the wallet out with one hand, he pulled the rifle with the other, cocked it and fired at Stu only several feet away, all in the instant that Stu eyed the pay wallet.

Hop Sing flew backward with the force of the close impact shot, hit by flesh and bits of bone, thinking at first that Stu had managed to fire back. The ground moved under him as the horses reared in fear but the reins had fallen out of his reach.

The horses ran and the wagon swayed in runaway alarm. Hop Sing closed his eyes and flew into the air, feeling for a moment he'd grown wings until the ground leaped up and grabbed him, hard.

CHAPTER 27

Hoss waited at the telegraph office, but impatient, foot tapping the floor. When Sid waved him forward, Hoss explained what he wanted in the telegram to Pa. He learned that Stephen looked to invest in a silver mine and Pa has a part interest he might be willing to sell. That would give Hoss the opener he needed without looking suspicious, and he figured there should be only one liar in this relationship.

When he stepped back outside the telegraph office, a boy delivering papers put one in his hand. This plan to help Lydia took longer than he wanted, but no mystery was ever solved overnight, or else why call anything a mystery? He'd sure like to solve the one with Adam, too, but he can't leave the city, or Lydia, until he finishes what he started. But if he waits too long, would it be too late for Adam? He's had telegrams sent out to all the marshals, like Roy suggested, but it didn't seem to be enough, somehow.

Hoss understood enough about himself to know the real reason he was still in the City instead of going up and down and up and down to visit Lydia and make sure she was still safe. Because the longer he's away, the more he felt sure Hop Sing was right and she was already dead. That made what they did together—and Hoss gulped hard every time he thought this—a really really vivid dream. If he stayed away, he might even get a clearer-thinking head back. Which could give him answers on how to help everybody, all at once.

He sat on a bench, eyeing the street. Not much moving, everyone must be gophering. He sat back and read the paper, as he did, felt his temper shorten...

> Could Dickens be right? Murdered people DO come back for vengeance. Or so witnessed Hoss Cartwright, who says she—the ghost—is after a new citizen in town. But then, there seems to be a touch of madness in the Cartwrights lately, although this newest report could be little more than a touch of the old golden to be found in every shot glass in every saloon in town.
>
> To hear Hoss tell it, she's not a ghost a'tall, just a lady who likes to come and go without warning, a lady no one else can see. I've personally seen plenty of lovely ladies like that, and if you grab their arm to get the money back for their services, they disappear quicker than steak into a miner's gullet.

Hoss crumpled the paper and stood. Something's got to be done with that wily newspaperman, and he might just have to lock himself up before he could do it, too.

* * *

Roy walked out of his office, puzzling over another report of stolen silver from a stagecoach and witnesses unable to figure out what direction the robbers took. They seemed to vanish. He tucked the paper in his vest pocket when the boy handed him the newspaper. This he tucked under his arm as he walked to the stage station, where a stage had just pulled in. He recognized a lady stepping off but couldn't figure out why. He was only interested in the men, anyway. Few women came to town to cause trouble. Much as he disliked prostitution, these gals tended to keep the men gentler than they would be otherwise. She didn't wear the garb of a prostitute, but bore a proud stance, in an attractive and worn sort of way.

The men were the usual types, a disreputable lot all, but he had nothing to hold any of them on. All faces on his wanted posters were etched into his memory. Men in these parts could change their names and keep going, but faces get covered or uncovered with hair, and he trained himself to see through that.

Roy watched the woman walk to the bank. She held her satchel like she had something mighty valuable in there. He decided to keep an eye on the bank until she came back out, just in case. She stopped outside the bank as though weighted down by some mighty heavy thoughts. He'd seen her before, just recently —

"Hey, Roy."

"Oh! Hoss, you startled me." For a big man, Hoss moved pretty quiet. "Say, you've been spending a might bit of time in the City lately, ain't ya?"

"I'm getting close to solving a mystery and I think I just need a day or two more."

"Find any trace of Adam yet?"

"I got one response to a telegram saying they thought they saw some fellows like that, but they moved through right quick. I asked them to send some deputies out but ain't heard anything since. I'll try offering a reward, but at least I've got more hope now that they mean to keep Adam alive. But there's that other mystery..."

"That Stephen Lawe bugging you?"

"Yeah." Hoss glanced around and pulled Roy back against the sheriff's office window. "Say, Roy, how can I get a newspaperman arrested?"

"Fer what?"

Hoss pointed at the newspaper tucked under Roy's arm. "Take a look, just read it."

Roy opened the paper to where Hoss pointed and read, lips moving. Hoss felt the people passing, staring at him, some laughing. He fought real hard to keep his anger swallowed and embarrassment controlled.

Roy laughed and pointed to the article. "See here? Says he's joshing."

Hoss grabbed the paper and read, "and a good time was had by all." He handed it back, still feeling glum.

Roy shook Hoss's shoulder. "Can't arrest him for publishing things like this. Newsmen like stories like yours, encourages people to read. The other stuff, the criminal stuff, that's where they can cause trouble, when they get stuff wrong. Nothing I kin do. Can't keep 'em away from prisoners, courts, or the common citizen. I tried, son, I did." Hoss and Roy watched the street, knowing that if Stephen Lawe got wind of Hoss's real goal, this mystery would remain unsolved. "Well, at least no names were mentioned. If I was you, Hoss, I'd just laugh about it, like the rest of 'em."

"Laugh? When people are laughing *at* me?"

"Make it *with* you by laughing, too. You know, like when Little Joe plays one of his pranks. Most of them will know it's just another of Twain's jokes. The rest, well, they just don't matter."

Hoss felt little reassurance, Roy could tell by his an angry pout. "'Spose so."

"I will tell you one thing, though, Hoss. Mark did come through for your brother."

"Yeah?"

"He sent all kinds of articles out by telegram to different newspapers, having them keep an eye out for Adam. Get him to send out more, and include a reward. Tell him he owes you one for providing him a story."

"Spect I could." Hoss lifted his hat and wiped the sweat from his forehead. The heat of the day always did that to him, Roy knew. "And I'll tell him to leave my ghost alone!"

Roy noticed the little girl before Hoss did. "Hey, hey you there! Don't run out in the street like that!"

But Hoss moved quicker. He scooped Jodie out of the way of incoming wagons before Roy could even put a foot into the street. Hoss put her on the sidewalk on the other side and the woman Roy had noticed earlier came out of the bank and ran to them.

Roy wondered if he should put a ban on children in the streets of Virginia City. He looked down at the papers in his hands. *Now, where was I?* He wanted to solve the mystery of the silver robberies—almost like the silver was being taken to salt a mine in order to get folks to invest in phony stock. Well, he wouldn't put anything past anyone.

* * *

Margaret left Hoss caring for the vagrant little waif and went to the stock options house, a portion of the bank where mines were bought and sold. She looked at the posting in the window about prices and who and what was selling. She felt overwhelmed. Maybe there was something there even better than the Borrasca, she wondered, feeling discouraged by her lack of stock knowledge. She decided to walk in and listen to conversations for awhile.

She knew she should have told Hoss that Joe didn't know his Pa was still alive. But the way the Cartwrights have been acting, none of them cared about anyone else anyway.

No man was worth much for trusting anymore. Even those who saved her from herself .

* * *

"Jodie!" Stephen ran down the sidewalk to the mercantile where Hoss and Jodie munched on taffy. "I'm so sorry, Mr. Cartwright, did she give you any trouble?"

"She shouldn't be left alone. Nearly got run over in the street."

"I can't trust her to stay with anyone. I am at wit's end. I can't support her and take care of her at the same time."

"She's just a little girl. Why not take her with you?" When Stephen frowned, Hoss shrugged. "I was raised without a ma. My Pa took us boys nearly everywhere, or left us with Hop Sing. Our cook. There's a way if you look around."

"Wait a minute, you're that Hoss Cartwright in the newspaper, aren't you? That fellow seeing ghosts? Is that what this is about? You trying to get Jodie taken away from me by saying her mother is still alive?"

"Huh? No. That…that's just Mark Twain, writing some more of his silliness."

"It's in newsprint, isn't it? That makes it true enough."

Hoss pulled out the article Roy let him keep. "See, right here, where it says—"

"You just stay away from me, Mr. Cartwright, stay away from me and mine." He grabbed Jodie's hand and pulled her off down the street.

Jodie whined but quickly shut up. Hoss leaned against the pole. He had to get the girl away from him. Her father terrified her.

The same way he terrified Lydia.

* * *

Hop Sing winced when he heard the crash in the distance. With the smell and tickle of grass and dirt in his nose, he feared moving. He felt like every bone in his body had broken. He thought maybe just to lie here and rot. Slowly he moved one limb and then another. He pushed up on his elbows and then to his knees. He hurt all over, but he could move. He had blood all over his chest, but it wasn't his. No corpse in him today. He looked at the distance ahead to the wagon where its team had stopped because the wagon overturned and looked back at the man he'd shot.

The dead body had gotten to its knees. Hop Sing squeezed his eyes shut and looked again. No, a man had crouched down over it, and a pinto pony waited near him. Hop Sing sat crouched in a subdued position until Joe rode over.

Joe jumped off his horse and pulled Hop Sing to his feet. "Are you all right?" When Hop Sing nodded, Joe fingered the blood splattered all over his white clothes, and held the money out at Hop Sing. "Hop Sing, were you on your way to pay the loggers?"

"No want to see ranch fall down. Mr. Cartlight gone, Mr. Adam and Mr. Hoss, and you, too. Nothing left."

Joe laughed, but to the look of strong consternation from Hop Sing he stopped. "No, I'm sorry, Hop Sing, but we dismissed the loggers a week ago. They started to overcut. These bank notes are weeks old. They aren't any good."

Hop Sing gaped at Joe. "You not tell me this?" He paced back and forth in the tall grass, his arms waving as he cussed. "This man, he die for nothing!? He come back and haunt me!"

"Oh you and your ghosts," Joe muttered, chastised. "Come on, let's fix the horse and wagon and see if we can't do something for the body. Then maybe you won't be haunted." He leaped on his horse and held a hand down to Hop Sing.

Hop Sing refused to ride on the back of Cochise but followed, limping, behind Joe to the wagon. Joe hitched the horse back up proper to the wagon and started reloading it with the scattered debris.

Hop Sing leaned against the wagon to catch his breath and willed his limbs to stop hurting. He watched Joe salvage bags and boxes without paying attention to what he was doing. Hop Sing pulled one of the more damaged cartons back out of the wagon. "Much food no good. Was going to give loggers. No bring home, no one there."

"Yeah." Joe kicked at a bag that had started to leak. "Even Hoss can't eat this much."

"Mr. Hoss in Virginia City."

"I figured. I was just home. No one there." Joe helped Hop Sing into the wagon and together they rode back to the dead man.

In silent respect they stood over the body. Hop Sing stood in back of Joe, using him to deflect the man's angry spirit. The beyond should be the place to soothe the spirit but Hop Sing knew first hand that this didn't always happen.

"Should have let him take," Hop Sing muttered.

"No, you did the right thing." Joe squatted and rolled the man on his side, exposing the gaping high chest and neck wound. "Whew." He winced and closed his eyes a second before looking at the man's face. "Damn no good friend of Frank's. Gonna have Frank arrested, too. I think I can get him accused of cattle thieving." Joe handed the wallet back to Hop Sing. "I found out why the fire started, Hop Sing. I no longer feel so guilty."

"Why Mr. Joe feel guilty?"

"I thought Pa died because of me. The Washoes said that we need to learn better fire prevention. They see a lot of strangers go through our land so this fire was only a matter of time. There just wasn't anything I could do." Joe's voice trembled. Hop Sing could see he still felt guilty.

"Mr. Joe not hear good news?" Hop Sing got into the wagon and picked up the reins. "Mr. Cartlight, he not dead." He wished he could pull Joe's Pa from his coat pocket.

Joe jumped back into the saddle. "I think I know what happened to Adam, too. The Washoe say that black slavers moved through the territory around the time of the fire. Somehow Adam tangled with them and I'm going to go looking...what did you say?"

"You Pa, he take slave ladies who save life to New O'leans. He say he find Mr. Adam there, too. You not told this?"

Joe stared at him and laughed, a sound filled with doubt. "You're saying Pa came home...and left...more of your ghosts, Hop Sing?"

Hop Sing stared back. "Hmmph. If you not believe, I cannot help."

Joe sighed and looked off toward the mountains.

"You go Virginia City and leport killing. This man, you say thief, get sheriff, bring sheriff. You come back, check cattle." Hop Sing steered the wagon back to the dead body and retrieved a bag of garlic from one of his boxes. He sprinkled the garlic on the corpse. "Keep animals away. But you hully."

"I wish I could have seen Pa, Hop Sing. Did he blame me for—"

"Only blame for you is you. Now go!"

CHAPTER 28

In the morning, the men found a lake that had lost respectability and turned into a muddy pond, but to Adam the sight of water approached Nirvana. After waiting their turn, the slaves leaped into it head first, getting a face of mud but finding enough liquid to quench an undying thirst. Neither had slept well the night before, as the ground for sleeping had become harder and harder the farther south they went. They rode on, after first men and then horses, had a bathing. They rode on hard, but paused to wonder over the view of ancient ruins in the canyon below.

Adam wanted more time down there but had no choice but to move on. "Curtailing of inquisitiveness. This, too, is slavery."

Tobias rode to him. "Sleep well, Titus?"

"Well enough, Tobias."

"A man only lets his conscience plague him for so long before he passes out."

"There's nothing wrong with my conscience. I have not set my faith in my country in vain, as you seem to think. But...," Adam shook his head and wiped at the burning of the sun in his eyes. "Why do you think Lincoln would use your people for political gain?"

"He has much to gain. An entire western half of the country."

"Well, if you're right, he'll make Nevada a state without caring about the rules." Adam realized that would be the reason Lincoln might be willing to meet with him. "How can so many of your people be wrong about the northern cause? Most of them cheer Lincoln and union victory like their lives depended on him alone."

Adam and Tobias alighted where Cal indicated. They watched as the slavers argued over how to make a fire without matches until they were sent into the brush for some burning material. The two slaves ran to the only green they could see, along another muddy creek, and took a quick drink before gathering all the dead debris they could find.

"We done talked about this. We's been hoping for freedom for so long that many will take it no matter how it come. Only some of us thinks it might not be so good as what we got now. All depends on perspective."

Adam thought at times that Tobias seemed a little more educated than he let on, and even affected a southern ignorance in his voice as though figuring Adam might trust him more. "Well, you still haven't convinced me that Lincoln doesn't care about your people. I think we both know slavery was already dying on its own. He just gave it a political nudge." He kept his voice even as he picked through the muddy debris to find the dry.

The slavers yelled at them to hurry, so they gathered their armloads. "You's right about that. My people is killing our bondage ourselves."

They found Luke and Cal squaring off over some disagreement with Jake and Piney holding out pans and raw bacon, ready to cook. The two slaves dropped the burning material where instructed and cowered under Jake's whip.

"You two useless human beings think we have all day?"

Piney tended the flame to the brush until it got going good and hot, with the added help of a little gunpowder. The two slaves were sent with the horses to find them feed. Adam took Buck's reins, and several others and the two men walked off, with Luke keeping a watchful rifle on their backs.

"My sister Sadie and I was schooled privately. Virginia's got lots of freed slaves, freeing them before being forced into the Confederacy. And now they force us, by the color of our skin, onto a ship to be exported to some black island."

Adam and Tobias no longer feared being overheard. "I agree that was wrong. Just as wrong as forcing the Cherokees to go west, after they'd become as civilized as any white. I know this is a political fight, but I deny Lincoln would skew democracy into industry-owned progress."

"I says that?" When Adam looked at him, shocked, Tobias laughed. "Guess I did."

Adam smelled lunch cooking leading to the familiar ache in his gut. He figured he didn't weigh any more than Hop Sing by now. "But why are there so many Democrats in the northern army?"

"Because they knows the southern way of life is doomed."

Adam knew they'd get nothing but leftovers, and both were forced to remain with the horses until time to ride. Adam accepted his meager piece of bacon fat and single hard tack, and checked the cinch on his mount. He could feel the horse's ribs. This poor mustang won't make it far today.

"General McClellan, Lincoln's best general, is a Democrat, and he doesn't want to see his soldiers killed. He don't believe slaves should be freed this way, don't want his soldiers killed. Lincoln will remove him, but not til after elections. You wait and see. That's how political this war is."

Adam and Tobias moved up the rocky incline behind Jake and Cal. "I know one thing, Tobias, if you want to place blame, place it on the government and not one man, not Lincoln. He'd do more if he could. I'd bet my life on it."

"Real hero for you, ain't he."

Adam scratched his beard as he looked off toward the mountains they were expected to climb. Those heights were not as bad as the Rockies, nothing more than big hills, really, but they looked treacherous enough for poor horses. He didn't know this route, and that meant escape now would be tricky at best. He could use the gun and run any time he wanted, he figured, but he feared now what might happen to Lincoln if he lost track of Tobias.

"We'll be looking for chances to trade horses along the way," Jake shouted to them, "so be ready for some fast saddle swapping."

They reached an even trail and started the horses running.

* * *

Joe spent a sleepless night. He rode in late and woke Roy up, who'd fallen asleep at his desk. Working on a puzzler, he told Joe. Both took spare cells to sleep in, but Joe feared, the rest of that short night, that wolves had dragged Stu off and now he had nothing to get Frank arrested for. He got up when dawn broke through the jail cell window, and washed in the prisoner facilities before rousing Roy, who mumbled that he'd be right along.

Despondent over delays, Joe walked outside in time to see Hoss standing in the street, looking disturbed and lost.

"Hoss!" He ran across the street and grabbed Hoss's arm. "Boy, am I glad to see you."

Hoss saw Joe but then looked back across the street as he finished crossing. "Joe. What you doing in town? Who's running the ranch?"

Joe followed, unable to take his hand off his brother for fear he might disappear like everyone else. "Well, I hoped *you* were. I got a lead on where Adam is and I'm going out to look for him."

"Good for you, little brother. I hope you…"

Joe followed Hoss's gaze. "What's so interesting down there? Hey, what's going on?"

Hoss gave Joe another of his puzzled looks, this time distant and unfocused. "Look for Adam?"

"He's still missing. Hoss, what's wrong with you?"

"There's a little girl over there, I think she's in trouble."

"I think our brother's in trouble, brother!"

"Ah, something…check with Hop Sing before you go, okay?" Hoss started to walk away, but frowned. "Ah, Joe? I'm worried about Angela, could you give her a talking to?" He walked back across the street, crawling between the wagons that had jammed.

"Hey, Hoss! Hey…Hoss!" But Hoss waved him away and kept walking. He wanted to ask Hoss about Pa. But Hoss already forgot about him.

Joe never felt so alone.

* * *

Hoss had been hoping to see his brother later on and apologize, and tried to call Joe back when he saw his brother ride out of town with Roy. Bad timing. He had to get back on Stephen's good side so he turned his horse to the schoolyard where he thought he could get Miss Abigail...Mrs. Meyers...to talk with Stephen about enrolling Jodie, even though she was still a little young. She greeted him happily, glowing with news of her own, and because of that, he figured, more than happy to welcome another new addition to her classroom. Hoss rode back and after some cajoling, got Stephen to listen to the news. Hoss brought the father and daughter to Mrs. Meyers and waited outside for the results of their private session.

When they came out, Hoss refused to match their somber expressions with fear. "Well? What did she say?"

"She's a lovely lady, all right, Hoss, but when she gave Jodie a word comprehension test, says Jodie's too young for school. Wants me to work with her first."

Hoss fumed. Something didn't sound right. "Did you say something funny to her?"

Hoss that morning as they went to the school began to feel sorry for Stephen. He seemed as if he had a gap where the two parts of his mind should connect.

"Well, Hoss, there aren't very many women I'd call real ladies in this town. Ladies who would make a good mother for Jodie."

"Oh, you didn't ask Abigail Meyers for a date, did you?"

"Well, doggonit Hoss, she sat there looking at me so pretty, and Jodie needs a mother."

"But...didn't you notice...she's *expectin'*."

"Yeah, that kinda made me want her more."

Hoss took Jodie's other hand to keep from scolding Stephen further. Lydia called him a thief but maybe he had no real concept of right versus wrong. Hoss realized the three of them had been walking back toward the International in quietude when Stephen spoke.

"Hoss, be a friend and mind Jodie for little while. I've gotta go see how my stock's doing. Maybe take a trip down into the mine. I'm getting a little tight of funds."

Without waiting for an answer Stephen ran across the street, just missing the usual array of galloping drunks. Hoss for sure knew he never saw so much up and down in one fellow before. When Hoss looked down at the little girl, he saw her staring across the wooden walk at nothing in particular, but with tears in her eyes. He crouched down next to her.

"Why you so sad, young 'un? Because you cayn't get into school?"

Jodie pointed.

Lydia stood in front of the International House, watching them.

* * *

"If you says he was robbing your cook, Joe, I suspect I kin believe ya." Sheriff Roy Coffee stood as Joe stayed crouched over the dead man. "But self-defense means Hop Sing felt he would be kilt. Is that what you figure?" Joe didn't move. "Little Joe?"

"Huh? Oh yeah." But Joe made no move to respond to Roy's inquisition. Instead he stared at the mountain where Virginia City squatted.

Roy looked back over his shoulder at the City. Joe had been as silent as hanged horse thief all the way over and Roy wanted nothing more than get this done. But he put a hand on Joe's shoulder. "Now, Joe, I might not be the brightest when it comes to family, but is there something wrong 'tween you and Hoss?'

"Who, us? Nah. He's just in love, or something." Joe shook his head and tried to smile at Roy but faltered, as though wondering what they were doing here. He looked down and bit back a sudden surprise at the corpse at their feet. "Uh, this was self-defense, Roy. You know Hop Sing isn't capable of murder."

"Well, I'd like to think I know that. Do you know this feller? Hop Sing must have, to let him get so close."

"Yeah, he worked for us, friend of Frank's." Joe gave the man's leg a nudge, as though expecting to make him stand and be identified. "But I can't tell you his history. Maybe Hoss could. Frank, for sure."

Roy squatted down and grabbed a handful of hair to peer at the face. "Thought I recognized his lousy behind. He's the one got buckshot, I had to take him to Dr. Jessup." He waited but Joe didn't seem to hear. "Know when he first started working for ya?"

"Mmmm, could find that in the books somewhere." Joe didn't offer to get the books and Roy didn't press him.

"Come on, let's get 'em on the back of my horse." Roy grabbed Stu's left arm, leaving Joe the bloodied right side, but they made short work of hefting the corpse over the back of Roy's horse. Roy tied a rope around the man and fastened the corpse to his saddle with the look of years of experience. "Listen, Joe, I'd keep an eye out for that Frank if I was you. Appears we got thieves in the area, and this fellow here may have been part of that."

"You want me to bring Frank in?"

"No, no, don't make him suspicious. But if you can find out where he goes when he's not working, that could be the key to solving this mystery."

Joe leaned against his horse's saddle, watching Roy ride off. "Well, brother, guess that means I don't get to go looking for you this time. Odds were against me finding you anyways. Odds are against me finding much of anything. Alone."

CHAPTER 29

Ben never had much trouble dozing in stagecoaches, often nodding off without a moment's notice, but this time he slept. He dreamt of a time passed when his sons were young, when the pain of Marie's passing had faded, and they were building their cattle herd by trying to mate the cows every season, rather than just at their normal pace of quickening twice a year. He'd had to explain to Joe what breeding was all about and at first Joe seemed fine with the explanation. Then that night at dinner Joe had shouted—"Pa, is that where I come from!?"

Adam laughed but Hoss looked puzzled, as though he'd had the same question but was afraid to know the answer. "I don't think Pa means we come from cows. Do you, Pa?"

Ben awoke, startled by the soft head pressed into his chest, and then relaxed. He draped his good arm around Sadie's warmth as she slept on. Across the stage from him Jesse and Abby had taken more limber positions—all four slept with the warmth of a good station meal in them.

Ben learned everything he knew about parenting along the way. Every parent did. And communication didn't always come easy. Parents couldn't always find the right words, so sometimes he used comparison words to make up for the lack. Using cows to demonstrate where babies came from had been only a momentary setback and one that Adam teased his brothers with for years after. Ben wished humans were born with all the answers. But then, he supposed, life would miss all its ups and downs, and get pretty dull.

He looked down at the tightly kinked head, at once both strange and wonderfully familiar. As much as he enjoyed having Sadie in his life right now, he feared she wouldn't stay. She thought her husband had died, but to accept her story he had to believe Eduardo Darcy had changed his coat and become someone Ben could trust. He didn't know Sadie that well, either, and she could be using him, nothing more. But he owed her, so that made everything he could try to do for her fair and fitting.

Although a little dullness with my sons at the dinner table sure would feel nice right now.

* * *

Frank didn't go on to Sacramento as he'd planned. Something about Margaret stopped him. He went to apologize to her but then couldn't. She was perhaps the finest woman he'd ever met, and to apologize for a near rape would be to kiss goodbye any chance for making himself change. She thinks him incapable of being honest? Well, maybe he is—but nobody's perfect.

He headed into the canyon that took him on a short-cut through to Virginia City, and alighted. He knew this route well, its nooks, the crannies where a horse could easily get a hoof caught up. He'd taken this short foot path a number of times before with Stu. He didn't feel much ease going this way, but realized he'd made the decision on purpose…and sure enough, he heard the sound of another rider, and in the next turn faced two men in his path.

"Far enough, Frank."

"Hey, Randy, what you—"

"Shut up. Just listen. Found Stu dead today."

"Really?" Frank knew to hold his hand against his chest around these fellows. He owed them nothing anymore, but they didn't seem to agree.

"So you don't know how he died?"

"I didn't know he died. Why just a few days back—"

"All right." Randy holstered his gun. "Thought maybe you were turning on us. But I know how it is with the gals, eh? You and him, on the trail? Got his pants full of buckshot, eh?" Randy guffawed, and snorted before pulling his canteen for a swing. "Got me a pretty little one waiting to be carried off on my knee. So I know how it is with the ladies."

Well, I doubt that. But Frank smiled. "Yeah, he-he, guess so." How dare Stu even breath Margaret's name? "So what's the plan? Find his killer?"

"Nah. Will need to move up our plans a mite, is all." Randy eyed him with a squint. "Come to think, we could use another hand. You in?"

"Hey, you know me—a little risk goes a long way."

"Ha! I like that. Tell you what, meet us in the Base Draw, six miles east and south of this spot here in two days' time. We'll have our plans drawn up by then. Come alone."

"Randy, you gotta be more trusting. Or your little lady won't stick with you for long."

"Ha!" Randy disappeared behind the rock.

Frank heard them ride off, afraid to even breath until he couldn't hear them anymore. "What was I thinking?" He didn't expect to see them here now— Stu said they'd be here dusk or dawn only. Stu's death made some kind of difference, obviously. Frank knew they had a canyon hideout,[42] but not even Stu trusted him enough to give out the location. Frank wondered if Randy's telling him now might be a setup. He never joined them when Stu asked, just paid off his gambling debt and gave them some information about some cattle, nothing more. He got Stu that Cartwright job, but that was when he thought Stu was honest enough.

He could join now, why not? He didn't know why not, but some confounded gut instinct just wouldn't let him.

Self respect?

No, that wasn't it.

Frank continued on toward Virginia City, becoming surer all the way that either he'd either help them steal some cattle or try to get them arrested. No third choice. Once he reached the city he understood his decision—but not quite how he was going to proceed.

* * *

Margaret was about to lay her money down on the speculative Borrasca mine, based on her in-depth study of all the mines, when Stephen walked in. Instead of going to the counter, she waited to see what he would do. The entire atmosphere seemed to change when he walked in, as though he brought the key to her future. She didn't believe in love at first sight but there was certainly an aura about him.

"So how's my Crown Point?"

"An amazing amount of material coming out of there right now. So stock's at its lowest, right now."

Margaret stepped up to the second counter. "One thousand in Crown Point stock."

Stephen grinned at her from his position at the other agent's counter. "Pardon me, but I'm a part owner of the Crown Point and I want to thank you for your...confidence."

"Not at all. Just don't disappoint me." She turned back to the counter but felt him staring at her. As she walked to the door, he joined her.

"Allow me to escort you back to your hotel." He took her elbow when she nodded. "You have the nicest smile. My daughter...she's six...would enjoy your company. Do you like children?"

* * *

Hoss leaned down to Jodie as she stared at the hotel. "Do you see your mother?"

Jodie nodded. "She's a ghost and she follows you. I can smell her on you."

Hoss couldn't see Lydia. "You mean, little one, you think she's dead? Like your father says?"

Jodie looked at him. "He's not my father. I want my mama back!" She broke from Hoss and ran for the hotel, with Hoss jogging after her. He caught up to her staring into the hotel lobby, a little frozen statue, a child suddenly aged. He peered into the lobby of the hotel but couldn't see Lydia.

"Do you see her in there?"

Jodie shook her head and grabbed Hoss's leg in a gripping hug. Hoss could feel her tremble—at least, he thought that was her trembling. He blushed at the thought that Lydia was in his room right now, waiting for him, and forced himself to think of salt water taffy before he bent down to Jodie.

"Come on, let's go cheer ourselves up with some more taffy, and you can tell me about your mama."

Jodie reluctantly tagged along beside him—at times Hoss felt he dragged her. He had always prided himself on how well he got on with the young 'uns. But Jodie shied away from him, tugging away from his touch but still walking with him to the candy store for his favorite taffy. She wanted to stay at the hotel, he figured, but right now seeing Lydia might not be good for either of them.

With candy in had they walked on to the school play yard. "Do you like being here in Virginia City?"

"Uh-huh."

"Do you think your daddy's going to stay here?" Hoss waited to hear her say that he wasn't her daddy but she just shook her head no. "Why not?"

"He never stays nowhere."

"Tell me what happened between him and your mama." He blurted, no longer able to contain himself.

"She called him names. And then he…" She slapped her hands over her eyes and shook her head. "I was asleep. When I awoke she was gone."

"Where? Where were you sleeping?" Hoss knelt and grabbed her shoulders. "Is she still alive? Tell me!"

"Paaapaaaa….he got so mad…"

Stephen led Margaret toward them. "Hush now. It's all right." He jumped up and ran toward Margaret but with a cautious look over his shoulder at Jodie, who kept her face buried in disheveled dark hair. "Margaret! Nice to see you again!" Hoss grabbed her hand, pumping vigorously. "It's been a long time."

"Well, yes, Hoss, well, not *that* long." She pulled her hand away and shook off his enthused grip.

When Jodie approached Hoss put a warm hand on her head and she grabbed his leg. "He smells like mama."

Hoss laughed. "Oh, haha, must be my new…tonic water…"

Stephen ignored their 'bonding' as he slapped his hands together. "Looks like we have the makings of a party. Hoss, why don't you join us for dinner?" At the same time he signaled "no" to Hoss while Margaret cooed over Jodie, prying her willingly from Hoss's leg.

"That's plum swell of you." Hoss followed the three to the hotel, knowing full well what Stephen had been signaling and not willing to accommodate him. He knew what Stephen wanted with Margaret, and he didn't want to let Stephen get it. But as he listened to polite conversation, Hoss realized that he may already be too late. Margaret, charmed by him, had also invested in his mine.

Jodie seemed shy of Margaret, at first, and for awhile just kept looking around the International as though for Lydia. A few times during the dinner Jodie called out "Mama" and Margaret thought Jodie meant her. Hoss's heart about broke at the look Margaret gave Jodie when she did this. She'd brush Jodie's hair back and reassure her that she didn't mind. She wasn't able to take her eyes off Jodie after the second "Mama." Not all ladies took kindly toward being mothers, but Margaret seemed to want it just fine. Maybe, Hoss thought, she could make a difference with Stephen and Jodie. She seemed able to handle someone like Stephen, at least more than the fragile Lydia.

Lydia should have Jodie in her arms right now. Or Lydia should be in his...

"And then Jodie said, real loud, but daddy, the lady's face is on backward!"

Margaret broke out laughing at Stephen's joke and gave Jodie a hug, making her giggle. Hoss hadn't heard it all but laughed anyway. They stopped laughing before Hoss.

Hoss shrugged and gave Jodie's head a rub. "Jodie, your daddy tells me your mama is gone. Do you know where she went?"

Margaret looked puzzled but Stephen looked like he'd been slammed in the gut.

"You doing more meddling for the newspaper, Mr. Cartwright?" Stephen started with a mumble but ended on his feet, pointing at the door. "If so you can just—"

"No! He knows Mama." Jodie looked at Hoss. "Why does Mama follow you?"

Hoss had plans backfire before but never this badly. "Uh, no, Jodie. Why do you think I know her?"

"My wife is dead. But maybe you and that Mark Twain are in cahoots to prove I murdered her."

Hoss stood to face him direct. "All I know is a lady came to me for help and claims you want to kill her."

Stephen laughed and sat. "Well, she's wrong. Bring her over sometime so I can meet her." Stephen waved a waitress over. "My daughter knows that her mother killed herself."

"No! I was sleeping, remember? I know what you told me. But I don't know who you are!" A very grown-up voice came from a frightened little girl, sounding to Hoss like Lydia had taken over.

Stephen's red-faced angry scowl hadn't left his face though he tried hard to be civil. "Child, you don't know what you're talking about. Be quiet now."

Jodie looked at Hoss, a tear running down her face. "He told me she's dead. I never saw her dead. Sometimes I think he scared her away."

Stephen laughed. "Now sweetie, I'm your father, mustn't talk about me that way."

Hoss could see what Jodie wanted to say in her eyes but, to the credit of her intelligence, she didn't. Instead she grabbed her milk glass and took a swallow. "May I be excused?"

Margaret watched the whole drama quietly and Hoss wished he could read her mind. At no time did she look at Hoss, as though mesmerized by Jodie. At Jodie's question, Margaret stood. "I'll take her to her room."

Stephen shook his head. "She's not done eating. She knows the rule."

Margaret sat, after sending a despondent look to Hoss.

Hoss held up the pot to get more coffee and order desert. "I'm sorry. Dadburnit, I didn't mean to stir a fuss. Your relationship with your wife is none of my concern." Hoss turned to the gal who came for the pot. "I'll have the cinnamon cake. Anyone else?"

CHAPTER 30

Aam fell to his hands and knees after alighting. He'd had nothing to eat for two days or drink since yesterday, and now his legs felt permanently spread apart. The horses they'd gone through were good for little but shooting, except that Jake still had Buck, keeping it with him even when he changed horses to ride.

They pulled up at the boat landing and he and Tobias were led onto a ferry steamboat. Adam collapsed on the deck next to Tobias.

"Why couldn't we...take boats sooner?"

"Too exposed on those other rivers. They wanted to stay off...beaten trail." Tobias didn't sound much better. Adam figured his legs must be in even worse shape. He couldn't speak above a whisper. "Think...they'll get us...water?"

"I'm just glad to be laying still."

Someone kicked his leg but Adam didn't even open his eyes.

"Don't get too comfortable. We're on our way to Laredo and the Rio Grande. With any luck, our responsibility for you two will be over."

Adam recognized Piney's Irish, which at times he attempted but failed to disguise. Cal and Luke appeared to be working separate purposes, so he doubted this would end at Laredo. "Thought we was headed...to Kentucky."

Luke laughed. "What you think we is, northerners?"

Piney 's laugh died quickly, as usual. "Change of plans. Quantrill wasn't where he said because we weren't there when we said. Now we're outside Albuquerque, but no time to loll around."

"You get what you deserve, working with outlaws."

This got Adam a boot in his gut, and as he folded in half on his side he grabbed the boot and flipped the man backward. Piney landed hard on the deck, as weak with hunger as the slaves were, so he didn't give Adam fight. But Luke put a boot on Adam's throat.

"Give us just a little more reason to throw you overboard," Luke said. "Go on."

"No," Adam said, panting. "Sorry, boss."

When Piney finally got to his feet, he gave Adam another kick before walking away. "Come on, let's get us some goods for the boat ride. They ain't going nowhere."

"You gotta watch the temper," Tobias whispered.

"Yeah, well, sometimes," Adam coughed, "feels pretty good. What...was supposed to happen with Quantrill?"

"Not sure. Getting more runaways. Or..."

Adam didn't like the tension in the pause.

"We coulda been killed in a pretend ambush."

"Or the plan has always been just a ruse." Adam tried to sit, managing with gritted teeth and sweat beading on his forehead that he wiped with a shaking hand. "Come on, they think we won't leave."

"And we won't." Tobias didn't even try to sit.

Adam looked over at the shore—sure enough, two blacks guarded the boat with angry rifles. "Tobias, tell me what you want me to do—why you came for a Cartwright."

"Luke has a plan. He's on our side, Adam, you wait and see."

"Ha. He's threatened me a number of times, knows I'm no muley."

"Cause I told him." Tobias rolled away from Adam's temper but no need, because Adam only nodded. "Once we get to Laredo he's gonna cause a major fuss about these slavers being northerners. Then he's taking you and me to New Orleans."

Adam closed his eyes and winced. "This is all a set-up?" Only thing that mattered now was what lie ahead. And Tobias had the most confounded way of simplifying the most complex situation. Getting away from three slavers couldn't be that simple.

* * *

"Hey, Cal, what you reading there?" Luke and Piney joined him inside the mercantile, where Cal munched on what appeared to starving men an endless array of jerk beef.

"We got trouble." He held out the newspaper, showing them a sketch of Adam next to an article penned by Mark Twain. "Fabulous Reward for return of Wealthy Man's Son."

Piney grabbed the paper with a loud curse, while Luke remained silent but tensed. "What do we do with him? Turn him in like this reward says?"

Cal grabbed the paper back and Piney lost interest to seek out some food. "This is our muley, all right, but there's no fabulous reward. This Mark Twain, he's a news jester, I read him before. But he ain't jesting about the identity of our muley, that's clear enough." He folded the paper up. "What do you think, Luke?"

"I don't see this changes much. Means he's pretending, but he's still trying to help that nigger." Luke concerned himself with the goods.

"So you don't expect we should kill him, pretend we never saw him? We leave him dead in the bush somewhere and we'll be long gone afore he's found.

Can't have Lincoln implicated in anything more scandalous than this nigger we're bringing back."

Luke hesitated, pretending to read a can of lobsters. "True. But I have the feeling this Cartwright is up to something and we should wait and see what it is."

"You know what? I'm not sure, come to think, that I trust *you*. Seems you been easy on those two slaves, easier than I'd expect for our pretense of being southern slavers." They heard noises, shouts, and Adam could make out Piney's frantic voice.

"I think they'll be more cooperative with Lincoln if they ain't been beat up first, that's all. You want to kill this Cartwright, I can't stop you. I just think he's more valuable alive, for now. That's all."

"As long as you're behind me." Cal walked to the door. "And I mean, way behind me. When my decision is made, I expect 100% cooperation."

* * *

The boat gave a lurch and pulled away from the dock. Adam and Tobias sat below deck, chained to poles, where Adam stared at Buck, who'd been brought below as well—almost as though they were taunting him. Hoss and Joe...how were they handling this? Pa lost, their brother gone? If only he could find a way to send word. As the boat swayed, he began to feel nauseous and his eyes welled with tears.

From their safe position below deck, as the boat started to move, gunshots rang out. Adam's first instinct was to get up but he couldn't. "What's going on?"

"I think they's stealing the boat."

"From who?"

Tobias shrugged. Adam supposed, noting bales of cotton stacked around at the inner gut of the ship, that the Texas Rebels shipped cotton illegally, probably to British ships. They heard clattering noises, shouts and Adam could make out Piney's frantic voice.

"Come on, Luke, let's get some steam going here!"

Northern slavers posing as southern slavers being chased by British mercenaries who thought they were Confederate mercenaries? Strange war indeed.

* * *

Night came quickly this time of year. When the wind picked up Frank felt ice pellets hitting his face. He wasn't sure what his plan was, except to talk to the sheriff about Stu and lead a posse to Base Draw. He wasn't about to walk into a trap alone.

Frank found a high grassy outcropping surrounded by rock and snuggled in for the night.

* * *

After Roy left, Joe wanted to go back to the ranch and talk more about Pa with Hop Sing, but Frank was still out there, getting his gang ready to steal more cows. Frank lied to him about Pa not being home and that alone meant Frank deserved a beating. And that wild goose chase with the Washoe…they wouldn't steal five at a time. One, maybe two, to supplement their hunt but they rarely took more than they could eat at one time. He saw no sign of any jerk beef smoking at their camp.

Nor could they set up a cattle business of their own. Their land did not have the good grazing these cattle preferred. They had only the common sagebrush, which the cattle found too bitter to eat. White sage, which is what the Cartwrights encouraged to grow, became quite tender and nutritious after the first frost and cattle fatten rapidly, getting them in good shape for the winter when they would be driven down into the valley corral field.[43]

Hearing Pa was still alive controlled his thoughts. He'd come to terms with his mourning and guilt and to find out Pa was alive and hadn't made sure his youngest son, who was also caught in the fire, was all right…Joe had a feeling his relationship with his Pa had changed. He wished he had someone to talk with. Hoss ignored him and Hop Sing was caught up with ghosts and Adam…oh, if only he could talk to Adam. He'd take back every punch, every mean thing he ever said. He spurred his horse to catch Roy, to talk about catching a thief.

* * *

Hoss spent a helpless night watching Margaret with Stephen and Jodie. Whatever charm Stephen had, he turned it on Margaret full gallop, and Hoss could see how Lydia had been charmed by him. Hoss hadn't found Lydia in his bed that night, either, and knowing she was in town and hiding on him made him feel cranky. He wanted to prove she was not a ghost, once and for all, by grabbing her by the hand and bringing her to Roy. Or Mark Twain. Or someone who would listen to them. But she defied all his attempts.

Hoss figured Lydia planned to rattle Stephen into admitting the truth and wanted Hoss's help. At least, if Hoss remained close to Stephen, she'll have the courage to confront him.

Which could be all she's wanted from him, all along. The thought of love being nothing more than a woman's way of using him kept him tossing and turning in a cold heartless bed all night.

* * *

Frank rode into the city early that morning after sleeping out on the trail, his horse puffing to finish the climb. He alighted at the sheriff's office and tied his horse—hungry as a bear, but business first. Instead a street vendor hawking some goods caught his attention. Frank watched as the fellow promoted something he called a battery, an electrical machine that for one quarter would give a shock to your whole nervous system and make an old man feel young and a weak man feel strong. He shook his head and started up the walk toward the sheriff's office, but saw a little girl alone on the walkway and she appeared to be crying.

"Remember that electricity is life! It is what you, each and every one of you, require, and it is utterly impossible for you to live without it! Try the battery! Try the battery!"[44]

The girl paid no attention to Frank but seemed transfixed in her tears by the street caller. Frank didn't want to threaten her so he stood next to the little girl and watched with her.

"Silly, isn't it," he said to her.

"Yeah."

"Are you lost?"

"No. My daddy's inside that big building. He just told me to wait in the hotel lobby for a little while. I got bored."

"I get bored a lot too. That's sitting around with nothing to do, right?"

"Yeah."

"You know, next door there's a candy store. You think a sucker might help you be not bored?"

"Daddy wouldn't want me to leave here with a stranger."

"I'll go get it for you. What color do you like?"

"Red."

"I just knew it. I says to myself, Frank, that little girl is a 'red' girl."

"Your name is Frank?"

"Yup."

"Can I come and pick out my own sucker?"

"You sure can."

She took his hand and they walked to the candy store.

"Is your mommy with your daddy?"

"No. She's dead."

"Oh, I'm sorry."

"Daddy says she's dead. When we left San Francisco to come here she was still alive. When we got here she was gone. I thought maybe she ran away because I was being a brat. Daddy says I'm a brat a lot."

"You don't look like a brat to me."

"Can I have two suckers?"

"Sure."

Jodie took her time picking out two suckers. As he watched, she reminded Frank of the kid sister he'd lost when he was 10 and she was seven. So sweet and not deserving of her fate, getting run over by a runaway wagon like that. Frank had left home when he was 15 and never looked back, because his parents were so busy mourning they never even noticed him anymore. When they died together, he wasn't surprised.

Jodie smiled at him with the two suckers and he paid for three, and popped one in his mouth to join her. When they walked back Frank sat her on a bench and told her to stay there until he found her father. Margaret headed his way, her expression between a smile and a frown. Frank saw a man shouting behind her, and when he looked back at Margaret he saw a brief expression of distaste before she smiled and turned to him, as if she were reluctant to let the man get to Jodie first.

"Jodie, what are you doing? I told you to wait in the lobby."

Jodie wailed as her father shook her, her tongue red with sucker.

Frank grabbed Stephen's arm and then removed the sucker from his mouth. "She was with me. I wasn't going to let her get hurt."

"How do I know that? Who are you?"

"That's Frank." Margaret stepped forward. "Hello, Frank. Nice to see you. I thought you were on your way to California. It's okay, Stephen, I watched Jodie from inside and knew Frank wouldn't hurt her."

"Well, thank you for that. I'll still head out, after I take care of my business here." Frank pointed his sucker at Stephen as he addressed Margaret. "You with him?"

"I was. Am. Jodie, come on, let's have that walk to the livery now." Margaret took Jodie's hand and nodded at Stephen.

Jodie waved bye to Frank as they walked down the street.

Stephen pointed a finger in Frank's face. "You stay away from my daughter. And... from Margaret, too."

* * *

Roy invited Joe to spend the night at his house, where together they wrapped the dead man in burlap. The next morning they got the papers filed on the death, and Roy promised to keep an eye out for Frank as well, using the warrant Joe had drawn for his arrest.

When Joe could finally break away from his duty with Roy, he ran to the International, stopped outside the hotel to clean the horse dung off his boots, and walked in. He got Vince to give him Hoss's room number and found him still sleeping. With the biggest grin he could ever remember feeling on his face before, he leaped into bed next to Hoss, startling the big man awake. Hoss sat up, which at the same time knocked Joe backward to the floor. But Joe couldn't help it...he started laughing.

Hoss looked over the bed at Joe on the floor with a scowl. "What in tarnation you think you're doing, little brother?"

"I'm sorry, I'm just...you wanna have breakfast with me?"

"Yeah, git down and I'll meet you there. Git!"

Joe was about done drinking Hoss's glass of water when his brother finally plunked himself down next to him. At first neither of them spoke.

Joe held up the water glass for a refill. "So?"

"I'm sorry, little brother. But I prêt near got this thing with Lydia nailed down and I just gotta finish, that's all. I just gotta."

"You just gotta."

"That's right." Hoss threw down the menu when the gal came over. "I'll have what he's having."

After she left Joe giggled. "Oh, I'm just having coffee. I ate on the trail."

"Dadburnit. What you doing in town, anyhow? Don't you have anything to do at the ranch? Where's Pa?"

"Oh, you know about Pa then? That he's okay?"

"Sure I know he's okay. Why wouldn't he be okay?"

Joe wanted to shout out all his angst but Hoss's eyes got all glazed and funny, and then Hoss stood. Joe looked at what Hoss stared at, and saw nothing but some other diners paying them no mind. "Hey, Hoss, you can't be planning to take their food."

"No, Joe, Lydia's here, and I gotta go plan something with her."

Joe grabbed his arm. "You can't be serious. She's here?"

"Yeah, she's here, Joe, I gotta go. This is a real life or death mystery. You see her, doncha? She's real, right, because you seen her?"

Joe looked around the room and then tried to focus on the spot where Hoss saw her. "Yeah, yeah, sure, Hoss. I better, uh, leave you two alone. I'll go find Angela, and I gotta stop some cattle thieves. But don't you worry, you...you stay here and I'll come back and we'll talk some more, okay?"

"She ain't no ghost, Joe! I've been with her...I'm gonna marry her, Joe."

Joe stepped backward when Hoss's announcement landed its punch. Hop Sing had been sure she was a ghost. And Joe sure couldn't see her now like Hoss did, although he could swear he did see her once. He forced a grin and punched Hoss in the arm. "Well, that's swell, big brother." He leaned close. "But I gotta tell you. A gal that the rest of us can't see, well, this could just strain family relations, just a little."

Hoss stepped toward Joe with a scowl. "One of these days, Little Joe, I'm just gonna—"

Joe, seeing his clenched fists, ducked out of the dining room. But he poked his head back in. "I may be losing horses, and cattle, but you're losing your mind." He ducked out again.

Joe ran outside. *Pa IS alive!* He felt suddenly as if he could handle every problem in the world. He thought about checking saloons for Frank, but saw Margaret with some strange fellow and a little girl standing between them. She looked pretty upset. When he got close enough Joe overheard Margaret blame him for losing all her money.

"Good morning, Margaret. This man giving you trouble?"

"Oh! Joe, no, it's...all right."

"Aren't you going to introduce me?"

"This is Stephen Lawe. But I swear he just broke it."

"He broke…" Joe giggled. He'd just had an unbelievable weight lifted off him. "That's a good one, Margaret."

"He romanced me for my money, Joe! The stock I bought is worthless. Someone salted the mine with silver and now it's empty, gone, useless!"

"Pardon me, good man, but you know we all take risks in this silver business. Explain that to her. To accuse me of salting, well, Margaret, you have no proof." Stephen took Margaret's arm and tried to walk past him. "Excuse us, good sir, this is a private matter."

But Joe grabbed his arm and gave him a good fist to the jawbone, sending him to the ground. Stephen stayed there, rolled over, and tried to shake off the pain in his jaw, while looking very irate.

"Now see here, boy—!"

"Name's Joe Cartwright and Margaret is a good friend."

"That figures. A real curse, your family." Stephen struggled to his feet and dusted off. "I had hoped…well, until this unfortunate affair, that Margaret might make a good mother for my daughter." He reached a trembling hand to her. "You must understand I had no way of knowing. Why, I'm broke too. Well, not totally but I lost a lot and if you'll allow me, I can offer you a good life with me—"

Joe made a fist but Margaret stopped him.

"Stephen, I think we better discuss this in private. Excuse us, Joe."

Joe grabbed Margaret's arm before she could follow Stephen. "Do you know what you're doing?"

"Adam taught me something, Joe. Just because I don't trust men doesn't mean I have to live alone. Jodie needs a mother. And I," she sighed, "I think I need to be one."

Margaret caught up to Stephen, took his arm, and didn't look back.

Joe sniffed. "Women, never can figure 'em." He turned to the Bucket of Blood but at the same moment Frank walked out of the sheriff's office, mounted and rode off.

"Frank, wait!" Joe ran back to his horse and rode off after him.

* * *

Frank never figured the kid could outride him. Bad enough Joe tried to get him arrested on nothing more than suspicion. Before Frank had a chance to explain, Joe leaped off his horse and dragged Frank to the ground. Frank reacted the only way he knew—he fought back until both were lying, exhausted on their backs.

"What did ya jump on me for?"

"What did you run off for?"

"Ain't your concern."

"Stolen cattle are my concern."

"What makes you think I got 'em?"

"You act guilty."

"You're just a kid. You don't know nothing." Frank sat up. "I turned myself in to Roy Coffee, but when told him I think I can find him the real culprits, he realized he had nothing more than your suspicion to hold me on. Not enough, Joe. I left all my valuables with Roy, everything I own, to get him to trust me to do this. I may have taken a cow or two, Joe, to pay a gambling debt, but nothing more and not recent, I swear. Now will you or not?"

"Will I or not what?"

Frank sighed. "Trust me."

"Sure." Joe jumped back on his horse. "Let's go."

"What?"

"Can't trust you unless I ride with you."

"Joe, you can't ride with me." Frank checked his cinch and mounted. "If they see us coming together there's liable to be shooting. Me they invited in. They see you, they could kill us both."

"What's the plan?"

"I'm to accept their offer to help drive the cattle—they want my know-how, I guess—and once I find out their plans, Roy will plan an ambush."

"Hmmm, sounds dangerous."

"So you can't come."

"I'll be your posse, stay hid, watch your back." Joe pulled out his pistol and twirled it a few times before reholstering it

"Look, how do you know I didn't shoot Roy down back there?"

Joe rode next to where Frank sat mounted and with a quick hand pulled his gun from the holster. He sniffed it and shook his head. "Hasn't been fired."

Frank grabbed his gun and shoved it back in his holster. "You oughta know better than grabbing another man's gun." He sighed. "I could have overpowered Roy, shot him with his own gun."

"Can't. He keeps it locked in his desk drawer."

"He does?"

"Ah-ha!"

"Okay, okay." Frank put his hands up in resignation of the armed robbery of his story. "You still better not come."

"Do you even know where you going? If these guys are outlaws in hiding, like you say, then you need me."

"How's that?"

"Because I've lived here since I was a baby and I know the area better than you." Joe moved his horse next to Frank. "Besides, I still don't trust you."

"I told you the truth already!" He rode off and Joe followed.

"Ha!"

"All right! My fault I got into trouble with these drifters, these army deserters, but I didn't know what they were when I played faro with them. Once I paid off the debt and the bar bill, too, I stopped stealing just like I says. I even quit drinking. Ever since…well, that doesn't matter anymore."

They rode on in silence for about another mile and then Frank pulled up short and looked around. "To be honest, I'm not sure where Base Draw is."

"Base Draw? That's the eastern end of Six Mile Canyon. No problem…see that cliff with the smiling shadow off in the east? We head that way."

After a couple of hours they couldn't see anymore so Joe reined to a stop. "Right around here there's a cave we can stay in for the night. Old man Summers used it for his goat herd, until he got in a peck of trouble with Pa about…well, never mind that." Joe alighted and loosened his bedroll and canteen to carry on foot.

Frank pulled off his bedroll and followed Joe but he didn't like the looks of the dark around him. This kind of day turning to night made prime haunting for the goblins of his pappy's dreams back in Louisville.

Joe stopped and Frank collided into him. "Hmm, don't like the feel of this," Joe whispered. "Just a little unstable—"

The ground collapsed beneath their feet, sending both men into a deep, dark abyss.

CHAPTER 31

She disappeared again.

Hoss told the wait gal to run some food to his room and left the dining hall. Joe was right, for once. Enough was enough. Time for Lydia to confess all—why she's not going after her daughter, why she's been lying to him—if she loved him, he expected she'd be honest.

She'll show up, dadburnit!

Stepping in his hotel room, he reminded himself he'd been there nearly a week. He could sure use Hop Sing right now. Because of Lydia he didn't allow the girls to come in and clean, figuring they'd scare her off. The bedclothes were flopped every which way, and various assorted plates and drink ware tucked in every corner imaginable, with dirty laundry heaped to one side. For Lydia's sake, he took liberal use of the hotel's bathing facility and even bought a new set of clothes, in addition to the extra set he brought with him, but Lydia wouldn't like seeing him leave the extra clothes or all this other truck just tossed about.

Thinking perhaps sloppiness kept Lydia away, he cleared all the eating ware and took them down to the dining room. He met the gal with his breakfast and gobbled it down right there. Then he went back to his room and made the bed, a grunting effort but he got the bed looking fairly straightforward and acceptable. He walked his laundry downstairs to the Chinaman working on commission in the basement. Hoss scurried back upstairs. He felt better about Hop Sing slaving over meals in their kitchen—at least there he could see outside.

When he got back into the bedroom he noticed, in the dim candlelight that he was sure he hadn't lit, with curtains drawn he was sure he'd left open, a vague outline form under the covers. With a sly smile, he removed his boots and got under the covers with her.

He could feel her warm moistness against his neck as she snuggled against him and unbuttoned his shirt. This wasn't the time, he knew, but he missed her, "Oh Lordy, so much," he whispered as he pulled her warm body next to his so hard he felt she'd come inside him. And before she was through with him, caressing him top to bottom until he thought he no longer existed except as a fever of sweat and joy, he knew he could never ever let her go back to Stephen, and would never ever let any harm ever come to her.

"Hoss?"

Lydia stood over by the window as Hoss's eyes blinked open. He had somehow gotten fully dressed again. Or did she have some other kind of magic?

"What...time is it?" He couldn't see the wall clock. Hoss joined her at the window and she melted into him.

"I'd be so happy, Hoss, if we never ever left this room."

"But we have to, ya know. You need to get your daughter back. He could hurt her, or another woman."

"I'm so frightened. You'll stay with me?"

"You know I will. I'm going to marry you, Lydia! I done told you that!" He pulled her into his arms where she melted, becoming invisible and yet malleable in his arm. He got frightened, wondering at how her physical form seemed to fade away as he held her tight, and yet he could still feel her. Tears sprang into his eyes. "I love you, Lydia."

"Oh, Hoss, how I wish I had met you when I was..."

"Don't talk. I understand. We'll...figure something out."

"I don't know what Stephen will do. When he sees me. But you're right. We have to get Jodie away from him. He could kill her, too!" She wandered back to the window. "And you. And then, we could be together."

"Huh?" Hoss wasn't sure what she said and walked to her, reaching for her.

But she backed away. "You haven't been able to get him to admit to trying to kill me, have you?"

"Huh? No. He says that you're dead but that you kilt yourself. Jodie doesn't believe it." Hoss felt a growing unease. She didn't look like Lydia anymore. She looked like a stranger, filled with hatred and vengeance...burning...with vengeance.

Even the thought of her daughter angered her. "Dear sweet Jodie. Where was she when I needed her? Asleep?"

"Lydia, she's just a child. She thinks you're with me."

Lydia walked toward the door. "That's not so surprising. Children are very astute." The door opened for her as she held her hand to Hoss.

Hoss hesitated. He remembered what Hop Sing said. *Must to be careful, you could end up like her.* What he wouldn't give for some of that potion right now. He took her hand. If she wanted him dead, wouldn't he be already?

They began the slow descent down the stairs. Lydia's hand grew warmer as they walked, but Hoss felt her vengeance now as her sickness. She seemed to waver, as though her skin reflected the glow of the candlelight in the stairway, until Hoss thought she was nothing more than candlelight herself, burning with rage and vengeance. Toward the bottom he heard a faint buzzing and at first thought she made the noise, even though her lips weren't moving.

What if you die? What if I want to take you with me?

As he held her hand she changed, warped, got taller and stretched out, right in front of him, nothing more than a shadow on a wall. Hoss felt a terror that made him sweat but he knew there was no going back now. She possessed him, and would hold him, until this was over. When he accepted her need, he put his fate in her hands.

He heard voices, first Stephen and Margaret arguing, and then Jodie whining, but he couldn't resist the tug of Lydia's hand in his, determined to get to the bottom of the stairs, where all three—Margaret, Jodie and Stephen—stared at Hoss coming at them. Lydia knew they were here—she knew this was the time. Jodie screamed and Stephen, also seeing what he did not expect, backed up toward the door and pulled his gun.

Margaret, only seeing that Stephen pulled a gun and pointed it at Hoss, ran to Hoss to protect him. "It's all right, Stephen, Hoss'll listen when I tell him."

Hoss turned back to Lydia, but she had disappeared. Jodie and Stephen had seen, but Hoss could see on their faces they weren't sure, and Margaret had not seen anything. Lydia was dead, no more denying, and someone had to diffuse her feverish heat of vengeance. One wrong move and she would take someone with her.

Hoss walked from Margaret's protective stance to Jodie, frozen and staring, and touched her head. She cried out and beat on him. "Mama, mama, what did you do to her? Where did she go?"

Hoss picked her up and walked to Stephen, whose shaky gun still pointed at Hoss's gut. "Stephen, why don't you tell Jodie and Margaret about Lydia? Why cayn't you be honest, for once, so Lydia can rest in peace?"

Stephen stepped back, not letting anyone touch him, his grip on the gun firm. "No, you don't. That was some kind of trick. Lydia's not here, she's dead! Jodie, don't listen to him."

Jodie put a hand on her father's arm. "Did you kill Mama?"

Hoss pulled Jodie close and walked toward Stephen "He did, child. Your mama found out he is a thief and a liar, and wanted to leave him so he killed her. Tell her, Stephen. It's too late for lyin'. Lydia will haunt you til you tell us the truth."

Stephen started to sob. "Yes." He fell to his knees and wrapped his arms around Jodie. "Oh, I'm so sorry. She told me...she told me that this was my last chance...to make things right. Or she'd leave me. You were asleep in the coach, and no one else saw...when I pushed her out...of the stage..." Jodie pulled loose and ran to Margaret, holding her tight. "She was going to turn me in! She gave me no choice!"

"You're not my Daddy. You never were."

Margaret stepped forward, as though she'd broken some kind of trance with Jodie clinging to her. "Stephen, what are you talking about? What did you do?"

Hoss fell into a vision of Lydia's terror as she fell out of a fast-moving stage coach, could feel her body hit the ground and roll, over and over, left alone, to die…and now Margaret…he grabbed her arm and pulled them back, away from him. "He killed Jodie's mama. He steals silver and…he cayn't accept…" he glanced at the child, who seemed to have guessed the truth but that's as far as the truth would travel tonight, "that Lydia never loved him." He stepped in front of them, blocking them both with his body.

"Oh, Hoss." Margaret sobbed behind him. "I…had agreed to be Jodie's mother." Her voice dropped. "I had agreed to marry him."

Hoss looked at the stairs, expecting to see Lydia smiling at them. But she wasn't there. "Jodie still needs a mama." Hoss held his hand out to Stephen, still kneeling on the floor, gun loose in his hand. "Give me the gun. You don't wanna hurt no one else. Not now that you see what kin happen."

Stephen jerked upright, stood and backed away, gun pointed at Hoss. "No! You're not taking me to jail. Ain't gonna happen."

Hoss looked around the lobby of the hotel but with just Vince behind the desk, standing in petrified fear, there was no one around to help. He didn't dare go for his own gun. *Lydia, honey, don't let him…*

"Now, come on, Stephen, you ain't thinking straight. Why, all of us can forget you said anythin'. You don't want to do nothin' that'll hurt this little girl even more, do you?"

"This little girl? Do you know anything about Lydia? What a bitch she was?"

Hoss took a menacing step toward Stephen, as Margaret and Jodie backed up toward Vince's counter. "Who in this world of yours deserves killin', Stephen? Did you take a good cold look at yourself?"

Stephen's eyes squeezed shut as he grimaced.

Hoss took another step forward. "Lydia's watching you, too. She saw something in you once, something good. She's watching you now, waiting for you to do the right thing."

Stephen waved the gun at Hoss. "No! You want my little girl to grow up knowing what her father is? What kind of life is that for a kid? She deserves a chance at happiness. Margaret, she deserves…you…"

He pointed the gun at his head. Hoss leaped to grab the gun away. Behind him the girls screamed and hid their faces against each other as the gun went off.

Hoss, covered in blood, fell backward as Stephen drove a bullet hole through his ear and flew away from Hoss to the floor.

Jodie screamed and ran out into the street. Margaret ran out after her. Hoss, reeling backward from the explosion of Stephen's skull, looked into the smoky haze to see Lydia stand over him, laughing. She laughed so hard she grew as big as the room, and then disappeared.

* * *

Hoss went back to his room to clean up, hoping to see Lydia there. But he didn't expect to. The spirit world owes no goodbyes, he figured. They have their own rules. He stood in the room that only a little while ago had been lit with her presence.

"You're welcome," he whispered. He dropped onto the bed but received no loving response in return. He was so tuckered he thought he'd never get to sleep for forgetting how.

Margaret had taken the little girl to her room for the night, and Stephen's body was at the undertaker's. He'd had a long afternoon of explanations, of calming Jodie down, having dinner with Margaret, talking with Mark Twain for the official news report. Sleep was the last bit of business left after a very long week.

Could she leave him so easily? He watched the candlelight flicker against the wall, sending the shadows dancing through the room. He imagined himself dancing with her in his arms, the flame burning with the potential of love eternal, as his eyes closed.

Hoss drifted off into a world where the spirit blended with the physical, to linger there for just a little while longer.

* * *

Sadie taught Ben some of the folk songs and delighted in his rich baritone voice. The four took turns telling ghost stories and leading each other in song, until the stage came to an unexpected stop to the sounds of gunfire and shouts. Ben pulled Sadie close as they listened, and finally Ben poked his head out. Union soldiers questioned everyone using the roads, so Ben told them to sit tight and follow his lead.

A colonel with a guard rode up and demanded accountability—he threw open the door and looked around at the four, noting no weapons first, and then demanded their purpose. Ben said what he felt they would accept—he was a traveling salesman and these were his servants, freed and legally paid to travel with him. The colonel looked at the three who all nodded with big white grins. The colonel ducked back out. Ben heard some distressing military lingo and then some fast-talking by the driver. The colonel cleared the stage to move on but the cavalry company gave them escort for some miles ahead, while the four stage occupants exchanged smiles, frowns and some sign language with giggles but no words, all to ease the tension that they knew came at the Kansas/Missouri border.

After the military left them, Abby tried singing a spiritual but stopped, as none felt comfortable enough to join in. The silence deepened as they sat tight against their seats, all four with eyes glued out the window. Every once in a while one of them pointed out the window at the smoke billowing in the distance or the four recoiled, as though one body, from a distant gunshot. They had a stage stop coming and Jesse voiced a common wonder, if the station would still be standing, or which side, North or South, would be in control.

Even in the silence, the memory of the songs played with Ben's ears and lips. This last stretch could not erase the comfort he'd found in Sadie's presence, or the growing affection he felt for the two kids across from him, who, though young, seemed as smart as any aged adult he'd ever met. He had a sudden thought, startling—could that many whites believe in slavery because they felt threatened by a people who could well be smarter about humanity and the right way to live?

The sun had dipped to the horizon and he found himself wanting to nod off, but Jesse sat straight, squinting off into the distance.

"What is it, son?"

Jesse pointed but Ben didn't get the chance to look out at what Jesse could see, because the driver and guard sitting above gave a sudden shout and the stage brakes squealed. The four braced themselves for the jostling and then Ben poked his head out, gasping in the dust. Just as quickly he drew back in as one of the riders took aim at him.

"Who's in that coach!? Everyone out! Unarmed or be shot on the spot!"

"Ben, what's out there?"

"Shhhh, no panic. I think I know what this is. Just follow my lead. Like before, only this time…different." Ben leaned out again and jumped back when a bullet hit the side of the coach. "We're unarmed, for the sake of God," he hollered in his best southern drawl. He poked his head back out again. "I'm already late for the harvest thanks to these runaways of mine, and now this!?" He directed himself to the lean, sandy-haired fellow.

Quantrill rode up next to Ben and waved a gun in Ben's face. "You got slaves in there? Get 'em out."

Ben threw up his hands and turned back to Sadie but quaking with fear inside. What if he'd made a mistake? He thought there were only two options— they were Union and would respect his position as legally binding, or they were Rebel outlaws who wouldn't harm fellow southerners. But what if there were a third option—or a fourth? He stepped out of the coach and offered his hand to Sadie.

"Come on, it's all right," Ben said, and quickly corrected his accent. He put the hand on his hip and bellowed, "Come on, all of you lazy sow bellies, let them have a look at you."

Jesse got out first, stole a glance at the outlaws and then helped Abby out. The two of them turned to help Sadie. Sadie got her feet on the ground and then stared at the leader, frozen.

"Quantrill. You from the devil hisself."

"Do I know you?"

"You will!" she hissed.

Ben crossed his arms. "Can't live with 'em nor without 'em. You want something from us?" He caught sight of the guard, still sitting on top the coach, and the driver nowhere to be seen. Ben feared he'd see the man if he looked behind, on the road, but didn't dare.

Quantrill laughed, pushing his hat back on his face. "Well, aren't you just the polite one? You know, you're lucky I'm in a good mood, or your guard would be dead, and you too. I could use me some new slaves."

"I'm very glad you're in a right fine mood."

"I surely am – on my way to Richmond to visit with ole' Jeff Davis. Gonna make me a Colonel, is what. But now, I need financing to get there."

"You're welcome to everything, just let me keep my slaves." Ben waved his hands at the trunks on the roof of the coach. "I'm afraid you'll not find much of value. If you look up Eduard Darcy in New Orleans, he'll be glad to—"

"New O'leans!" Quantrill aimed his gun at Ben's head. "You know that's Union! What you trying to pull!?"

"Yeah, perhaps. But Darcy is as southern as they come. A lot of folk are there. I gots me a network you can use—"

"Shut up and all of you back off. Claude, you shoot either of these whities if they so much as flinches." Quantrill indicated to two other men to climb to the trunks. Two broke open after their fall to the hard rocky ground. The contents of clothing and small trinkets disappointed the attackers.

Quantrill rode up to the slaves and alighted. "You travel light, doncha? Excepting for slaves. You got three. Certainly you could spare one." He brushed a grimy hand over Abby's cheek. He grabbed Abby's arm and pulled her toward him, as she struggled and whimpered.

"Now just a minute!" Ben thundered, careful to keep his southern sound. "You can't mean to stand in the way of producing goods to help keep the South alive. Why, slaves have been leaving our plantation all along, ever since this blasted war started. You don't need them worse than me."

Quantrill stared in amazement at Ben's audacity, then threw his head back and laughed. His throat bone bobbed like an angry fish to get off a line but his laugh was more like the congenial picnic laugh. Still laughing, he mounted. "All right! You want to get to New Orleans? You, shaking up there, Mr. Guard, you can drive this thing?"

The guard nodded and grabbed the reins. He pushed the dead body to the ground, and Ben jumped out of the way to keep from getting bloodied, his impromptu introduction to the murder on this route. He allowed a brief remorse at their inability to give the man a proper burial.

"All right, now, the four of you have to the count of ten to get inside that coach, because when he hears ten the driver will whip those reins or get shot. One…"

Ben gathered the three together, and Sadie fell, in her fluster, to one knee. Abby, who by this time had a good cry going, jumped in the coach and put a hand down for her mother. Behind her Jesse pushed, in a spot Sadie would never have allowed otherwise. Finally Sadie sunk into her seat and Jesse leaped over her into his, as Ben scrambled up behind them…

"Ten!"

Ben hung on for dear life as the stagecoach rumbled away. He held an arm out to Jesse and Abby who tugged and pulled and got him inside on his knees, and Abby reached, missed, and reached again to get the door closed as the stage bounced away at furious speed.

The coach raced a game with the devil, as Quantrill and his man rode alongside them, laughing and shouting and shooting.

"At this rate the horses will die and we'll never get there."

No one heard Ben above the clattering noise of hard riding and Abby's screams. The scenery and the coach swayed in the speed not meant for any of them. As suddenly as they had appeared the riders disappeared and the coach rolled to a stop. The guard jumped down and opened the coach door.

"Everyone all right?"

They were all breathing hard, as though they, and not the horses, had been pulling.

"Yeah. Yeah. Just get us there...a little more slowly."

"I'm going to stop at St. Joseph and see if they have another driver available. Otherwise, you might find yourself stranded for a time, until another coach to St. Louis has room."

Ben took Sadie in his arms, as Jesse held Abby, who sobbed against him. "We'll get there, Sadie, we'll get there."

"You's good back there, Ben. I's ready to call you Massa."

"Oh, no, don't..." He accepted her kiss. "We had to take a chance..." but he felt dizzy and put his head back, as the stagecoach rolled on.

* * *

After the cries of surprise and yells of pain subsided, silence surrounded the mine shaft, until, "Shit. I remembered a mine shaft, not a cave."

"What in the hell is wrong with you, anyway?"

Joe offered no apology. "What is this soft stuff we're standing on?"[45]

"And that smell! Ugh!"

"Here, wait, I think I've got..." Joe struck a match.

Frank blew it out. "Are you crazy?!"

"What!? What did you do that for?"

"You could get us blown up! This could be one of them natural gas things you hear about, could be why they don't mine here."

"Ah, we don't have any of those around here. Anyway, it didn't blow up, did it?" Joe struck another match. "Oh, look. Dead goats. Some pretty fresh yet. Oh, yuck. Must be like," he counted aloud, "six of them. Oh wait, that's not a goat head that's..." His match went out and he lit another. He watched Frank bend close.

"Human. Goat herder, maybe?" Frank gripped the side of the shaft. "You said *you* was gonna hide. I think the point was not to hide *with* me. Joe, we gotta get out of here."

"I know. Got a rope?"

"Not on me."

Joe looked around but their canteens and bedrolls didn't make the trip down here with them. He looked into the vague impressions of trees and dark night. "Too high up to reach. I wonder who put rotting boards over that hole? Hey! *Anyone There!?*"

Frank jumped at Joe, startled at the loudness of his voice and pushed him harder than he meant. "Will you cut that out? You've got us in enough trouble."

Joe pushed back at Frank and pinned him against the rotting wooden shaft. "You think I like this? This isn't my choice of rooms for the night, I don't care how soft the floor."

Frank realized how strong Joe was. "All right, what's your idea now?"

Joe let him go. "Just remember, your thieving and drinking got us down here in the first place." He looked up. "I don't know. You got any ideas?"

"How about one of us gets on the other one's shoulders and gets boosted out?"

"Hey, that might work." Joe groped in the dark for Frank and grabbed his arms. "Okay, boost me up on your shoulder—"

Frank pushed Joe off. "Wait a minute. It's my idea, I'll stand on your shoulder."

"Oh, you think I can trust you helping me once you're out? Oh no."

"Come on, didn't I tell you I was helping Roy catch those guys?"

"Maybe. I'm still more honest than you, so I'm going."

"Nope. You got us in here, so you stay."

"I'm smaller."

"You're not, we're the same size."

"I'm younger then."

"Well, I'm older and smarter, so I got a better chance of rescuing you."

Joe laughed, pointing. "You sounded just like Adam there."

"Hey, is he still missing? You don't suppose…"

Even in the dark Joe caught sight of Frank looking down at the human corpse at their feet. With an ache he refused to name Joe peered down and lit another match. He jumped back and blew it out. "Oh geez! Why do I listen to you? Ugh."

"We're not getting out of here unless you boost me out."

Sadly, resigned, Joe nodded.

CHAPTER 32

Lincoln knocked on the door. Mary was in there with her ghost cronies and they didn't want him around. But he could use some of that salve they were applying to each other's minds—all about how the ghosts proved in the immortality of the soul.[46] He needed to know for sure that all those boys, dying to elevate a Republican way of life, weren't just plain dead.

Before the door opened Seward found him and dragged him outside, where he had to exchange barbs with newspapermen, Halleck and Stanton. After the newspapermen left, Stanton handed him a telegram delivered to him the day before. After a quick peruse, he grinned. Ole' Mac played right into the abolitionists' hands.

"And that, my dear friends, is why the skunk no longer roots in the dirt for ants." He waved his secretary of war and chief general off, and walked back up the steps before they could figure out what the heck he'd just said.

Lincoln walked back to his desk where his tea sat cooling in his cup. He didn't think much of anything had been in his hands, not since the beginning. Once the South broke off, he nearly said good riddance until the abolitionists on his team began to scream, "force 'em!" And then after that firing on Sumter, which was expected to happen when the North tried to get food to Union forces barricaded in a southern fort, they forced him to call out the militia without any attempt at compromise. These Republicans were crazy, but he had no choice. He joined the party of his own free will, after all. But they won't bring war to a vote in Congress, oh no—this was just an insurrection to be put down, nothing more. Now, over a year later, that's still what Congress called it—an insurrection. Fools, all of 'em.

But supposedly, as president, he had the free will to do as he liked. Free will. Like those shysters calling for ghosts, playing on Mary's weakness, getting her all lathered over Willie's possible appearance. Still and all, if she gets over Willie's death, can shysters be all bad? Not that he doubted ghosts *could* exist, he just doubted they could be called up *that* way.

Lincoln's mama raised no fool. He knew very well what was going on here, that the White House was bought and paid for by the railroads magistrates, disguised as abolitionists, who wanted expansion across the country *now*. No more tomfoolery with the South dragging their feet just because Congress decided slavery could not expand. So now those for Union want to hit the South in the one place where it would hurt the most. Destroy their way of living. That's what the war's been about, all along. Mac was right about that much.

And he played right into their hands, with that Emancipation Proclamation. He was proud of it—but now he wondered, what was he proud of?

Lincoln looked out the window at the early blanket of snow. Ha. Of course slavery couldn't expand. Well, then, the abolitionists were right and why shouldn't he listen to them? They wanted half of the colored population exported, and they wanted Mac out.

Lincoln shook his head, his breath steaming up the window. "Cheap labor, that's what abolitionists want. But the Negroes won't want to live in the North. So what should I do with 'em, eh? Send factories to the South?"

He sat and made some further notes for his Emancipation Proclamation, and then turned back to Mac's telegram. He took out another sheet of the crisp onion paper and started to contemplate a reply. "I have just read your despatch about sore tongued and fatiegued [sic] horses – will you pardon me for a asking what the horses of your army have done since the battle of Antietam that fatigue anything?"

He added a little syrup to the sting, and then decided to hold off sending the letter.

Lincoln ignored the knock at the door, but the courier had instructions to deliver and remained insistent. Lincoln accepted the telegram and sat back to read. *Nearing New Orleans Stop Need you there for conference Stop what to do with captured slave Stop Bringing Nevada silver Stop Meet with us or lose big Stop Luke.*

Luke? Who's this Luke? They knew they weren't supposed to contact him directly on this Tobias matter. What in the name of holy soldiers was going on now?

* * *

Frank poked his head out of the broken wood covering the shaft and pushed away at some of the timber, which wasn't going to support him long enough for him to heave himself out. "Walk a little to your left."

Joe grunted and did, and Frank's right boot toe hit his eye again. "You could have at least taken off your boots."

"Stop a second, wait."

More timber came falling down the shaft, grazing off Joe's shoulder. "Doggonit, Frank!"

"There just doesn't seem to be anything solid up here to grab on to."

"Then I'll put you down."

"Oh wait, hang on a second, oh, ah, oh no...."

Joe felt the weight lighten and then disappear as Frank's feet lifted right off his shoulders, as though he'd caught a ride on a bird. "Hey! Hey, Frank, don't forget to throw down a rope!"

"A rope? Yeah, sure."

Joe frowned, and then Frank talked to someone. *No, don't tell him who I am…*

When Frank laughed, Joe realized he was right about the scoundrel all along. After a moment a rope came sailing down at his feet.

"Give you something to keep you busy til you die," said the strange voice.

They rode off, leaving Joe alone to collapse in the black goat hole.

* * *

As anxious as Hoss was to get home, he feared the journey. He had to look for her body along the way, the worst chore he had ever contemplated. He thought about getting Roy to come with him, but Roy had his hands full with establishing Stephen's cause of death in the middle of tax roll season. Even with witnesses the death had to go through inquest proceedings. Margaret said she'd act as witness, and Hoss wrote out and signed his statement. To Hoss's great relief, Margaret filed adoption papers with the court for Jodie.

He thought Roy would wait until after he found Lydia's body to begin the inquest but Roy saw no need. Even finding her body would not be proof that Stephen killed her, and anyway, he was dead now too. He left Hoss the disturbing idea that she might have flung herself out of the stagecoach.

Hoss wanted to talk to Jodie more about the stagecoach ride, but Margaret asked him to please wait, so there was nothing more to do but head on home. He had no clue where on the route from Sacramento to Carson City they had been when Stephen did the deed, nor, after this much time, if Lydia's body would still lie where she fell. Still, he couldn't help himself.

He looked, with jumpy nerves, every step of the way, leaping off his horse at the slightest appearance of a non-natural leaf or tree stump, or odd depression in the brush. By the time he reached the ranch just after sunset he was thoroughly drained and hungry. Chubby hated the dark and Hoss had to get off and walk the stubborn animal the rest of the way.

But when he opened the door and smelled all those wonderful familiar Hop Sing smells, his mood perked right up. "Hop Sing! Got some dinner for a hungry fellow!?"

Hop Sing ran out. "Glad to see Mr. Hoss! No see Lydia—did Mr. Hoss make happy?"

"Yeah, Hop Sing, I…I'll tell you all about it."

"Lydia no return? I seek day and day for right potion to unbewitch you, I have to go out at night with torch, walk many miles…" Hop Sing placed a hand on Hoss's forehead. "Might give you potion anyway. No tell where ghost linger."

"I appreciate all you done, Hop Sing. Turns out you was right and I'm unhappy about that enough for both of us. Where's Joe?"

"No see Mr. Joe for days. Not with you?"

Hoss felt the stab of a headache he thought he'd left behind. Just fix one problem when another comes along. "Well, at least give me something to eat first." But Hoss didn't have a clue how to pick up Joe's trail in the dark. He feared, instead, he might have to ride back to Virginia City at the break of day. "Hop Sing? Maybe I better have a whiff of that potion."

At night in this house where the smell of Lydia lingered? With all his family gone? Hoss still felt plenty spooked.

CHAPTER 33

Joe figured he slept, but standing up. Whatever sleeping he did wasn't enough to erase the exhaustion. He kept throwing up the rope long after he could see where to throw. He refused to look down—the sound of bones crunching was bad enough. His arms ached, his legs from standing so long, his neck from looking up constantly—everything ached.

He thought it odd that he wasn't hungry. Or, as he got another whiff of the rotting smell, maybe not odd. When the sun broke through the opening, he squinted down at the soft floor beneath him to find the rope and picked it up with his boot—a pair of well-fitting boots he'd never bring himself to wear again—if he ever got out of here. With a sigh, and pain stabbing him from every direction, Joe tightened the noose and threw it up, hope against false hope to snag something tight enough to hold his weight.

* * *

Hoss met Roy halfway up the mountain. The inquest had gone well—the judge accepted the suicide and Stephen had been properly buried, all before Roy took breakfast. Yes, the little girl was fine. But then Roy made Hoss's hair stand on end.

"Turns out Stephen had been involved in the illegal theft of silver with a gang that's still operating in these parts. I sent Frank last night to go see if he could scout out where they hid, cuz he thought he knew, and then Little Joe rode out after him."

Hoss gulped. "Joe?" That week he took to nail Stephen had taken far too long, after all. If anything happened to Joe…

"I didn't get a chance to stop him…something wrong?"

"Joe didn't come home last night. I was gonna ride to town right away, but my horse is skittish in moonlight, so I left as soon as the trail lighted this mornin'."

"This Frank is a ranch hand of yours?"

"Yeah." Hoss shuddered. "Dagnabit! I thought I had Frank straightened out, and then I was gonna follow…but I got so plum tied up with…other things. If Joe's hurt…" All satisfaction of solving Lydia's murder vanished.

"Well, then I guess I'm glad we met when we did. I suspect they've gone off the main trail." Roy looked around. "But I don't know where to begin to look, Hoss."

Hoss sighed. "Me neither. But I didn't see no tracks going off into no wilderness on my way here and I was lookin'. So let's keep headin' up. You stay to the left of the trail, and let me know if you see anything at all."

* * *

Joe heard horses coming and futilely waved his arms. "Hey! Hey, down here!" He kept yelling, yelling and hoping, yelling until he felt hoarse and coughed from lack of water.

But the face that peered down was far from friendly.

"Randy. Can you…" Joe swallowed hard, "Help me out?"

"Well, you're still alive. Geez, Joe, you know, I'd love to but you just might spoil all our plans. Tell you what, I hate to see a man suffer, so I'm gonna fix that." He threw a board down over the hole. "Dangerous, having a hole open like this." He threw another board down, and another until the mine went black. Rocks were dropped on top of the fresh boards. "There, now I can't see anything!" Randy laughed as he walked away.

Joe fell backward against the shaft, unable to scream or even cry out. He was trapped, alone, in the dark.

And he wasn't ever getting out.

CHAPTER 34

"Going high, going low, going mighty slow, a little while to go. Bid em in, bid em in, the sun am high, the sun am hot, us got to git home tonight. Hearing at $200, say giving us $200?"[47]

The Laredo crowd seemed a little pensive listening to the auctioneer, as though believing the Union army would be right behind them at any moment. The slave traders, riding in on the ferry, gave good and somewhat false information on the mulatto and four other blacks they had to unload, but held a special Negro aside, already sold.

Adam had faced Cal's gun when they docked at Laredo. They gave him a choice, stand and pretend, a little longer, to be a mulatto or get shot in the back trying to escape. Adam, with few options, allowed the irons to be clamped on his ankles. He wasn't sure there could be a humbling moment lower than this, standing on center stage, waiting to be bought like a piece of meat. People were hesitant to bid on him, as though sensing him akin to illegal contraband. This made him feel not even good enough to be a slave, a feeling he tried but couldn't shake off.

These slavers knew who he was now, even used the name Cartwright at him, he didn't know how, but that didn't stop them from showing him as a slave to others. *Did this to myself. Now a Cartwright* and *a slave. My own doing.* Having his façade broken made all the pain and emotion of being so far from home, and so close to war, spread through him like a Tahoe avalanche. Cold. Nonexistent. He and Joe had once been trapped by an avalanche, on a January thaw day they were getting supplies from Carson City and tried taking a shortcut back. Joe had been 12 and trusted Adam like Pa, but that day and for awhile after, he accused his older brother of being reckless. Being accused hurt Adam worse than the cold had, and how quick Joe had forgotten all Adam did to keep them both alive.

They had ducked into a short cave, more just an indent in the cliff, as the snow collapsed and Adam dug so furiously that he warmed enough to give Joe his coat to huddle under. When more snow collapsed on top of him, he could hear Joe cry and kept moving his head until enough snow fell off so he could see and breathe. He encouraged Joe to push his feet, push him out, push harder, Joe! Until with his warmth and wiggling he popped out of the snow and formed a gully with his body for the two of them to slide to freedom.

One older fellow waved his sack in the air. "I'll give you $150 and not a penny more."

217

Adam had been lost back on the Ponderosa, thinking how the worst times were not as bad as this, when an elderly fellow grabbed an arm. Adam followed, head down, all thought of home dissolving. He felt hot, dizzy and had to be forced to keep moving at all.

Luke seemed despondent to Adam, like something had gone terribly wrong. All along they'd been changing plans, but this time seemed different. Adam didn't realize he hadn't been moving until a poker stabbed his back. The auctioneer had a cattle prod on him, forcing him to move. At the bottom of the platform stairs, two men took hold of him and led him to a wagon, where his new owner, Samuels, give him a big smile.

"Come a long ways, didn't you, boy?"

Still dizzy, Adam reached for the wagon to climb up but someone grabbed him from behind.

"You walk with the horses," Samuels told him. "You need to be taught respect right from the start, do you, boy? Letting that white in you go to your head."

When the whip came up Adam ducked and the whip caught his side and part of his arm.

"Oh, come on, you can do better than that. A whip stings less on your back, I guarantee. Now get up there and take hold off the horse's bridal. He don't much like to walk, but I figure with your help, we can get to the dock at Guerrero in no time at all."

Adam held his arm and blood seeped through the shirt. He looked over his shoulder at Luke and Tobias. But they made no move in his direction, and when the stinging started up in his back, Adam grabbed the horse's bridle and got the wagon moving.

At least he still had his gun, but as another wave of dizziness passed through him, doubted he'd be very successful at using it, for escape or anything else.

* * *

Hoss and Roy found a pair of fresh horse prints leading off toward Six Mile Canyon. By this time Hoss felt as jumpy as a jackrabbit falling off a cliff. Worst possible endings for Joe kept flashing through his mind. Adam and Pa were gone and he chased ghosts and that left Joe to do—what? The horror he'd begun to feel last night came back to throw a chokehold around his neck. He had Hop Sing give him the potion last night—even to the point of standing in the window in his skivvies. He wouldn't, not for any superstition, stand naked. Only for the thought of Joe could he stand even just like that for more than a second or two. And that potion was plum misery, too, worse even than his spring tonic. But for Joe's sake, he'd drunk it all, hoping to feel clear headed this morning. And doggoned if he didn't feel even worse than ever, fighting the feeling to concentrate on following tracks, but getting dizzier by the minute.

Because now Roy had a horror story about a gang of thieves, led by Stephen, no less, who had not only stolen silver from other mines and stagecoaches but rustled Cartwright cattle, and his gang of thieves included Frank. He trusted Frank!

Hoss looked into the sun, keeping his hat brim bent. "We don't have to follow these tracks anymore, Roy, I think I know where they got Little Joe!"

* * *

"Pa?"

The horse hooves faded off into the distance.

"Paaaaaaaa!?"

* * *

Frank was having a really good dream, even though he couldn't shake the headache that went with it. The steamship cruised out on the ocean and the stars were out and he had his beautiful girl in his arms, and they were dancing, and laughing…but a shadow rolled across the ship, like a fog, and then the boat began to sway back and forth and his beautiful girl fell overboard and he couldn't save her…

"No, no, wait, I'll come in, I'll jump down, I'll save you, Joe," and he leaped. When his eyes opened he found himself in Hoss's arms.

"Frank, Frank, easy, boy, easy."

Frank looked happy enough to see Hoss and Roy but then he groaned and held his head.

"Tell us what happened, son," Roy coaxed.

"Yeah, where's Joe? Why do you think you gotta save him?"

"Ah…did I say that?" Frank kept his eyes shut as memories returned. "They didn't kill me. Gosh…maybe they thought they did. Hoss, they're going after the winter herd! I said no. I said…and then everything went black. They left me here."

Roy nodded. "You're lucky they didn't kill you, boy. Well, Hoss, should we look around for Joe? I don't want to think the worst but—"

Frank struggled to sit. "No, he's not here. He's…oh, ugh. They left him rope. Maybe he got out. I had to pretend to go along or they would have killed us both."

"Where is he? Where's my brother? What's the rope for?"

"The mine shaft, the one with the goats."

"Can you lead us?"

"I think so."

Roy shook his head. "He needs a doctor, Hoss. I'll take him. Do you know of an old mine shaft around here?"

Hoss pursed his lips and shook his head. "Frank, did they take Joe's horse? Joe's horse always stays by him otherwise."

219

"I think…yeah."

"Come on, you'll ride behind me and hang on."

Roy put a hand on Hoss's arm as Hoss lifted Frank to his feet. "I think he should ride behind me. More room."

After an hour of following hoof prints and Frank's scattered direction recall, they heard an odd wailing. Hoss pulled up. "Like a calf stuck in a gully or mud pond or something."

"That's purely strange, Hoss, because we come this way before and didn't hear a thing." Roy looked behind him. Frank, arms wrapped around Roy, appeared to be asleep. "Frank! Are we close to this here mine shaft yet?"

"Wait a minute, Roy, shhhh." Hoss put up a hand and tilted his ear to the wind.

"Paaaaaaaaaa!"

Hoss spurred his horse on and picked up more signs of other horses passing through, until he found where the horses appeared to have stopped. "Joe! Are you here?"

"Paaaaaaaaa……"

"These timbers look fresh and rocks placed deliberate." Hoss flung rocks and boards aside. "Joe!? Are you down there, boy?"

"AH-ha-ha-ha, help me out!? Please!?"

"I'm coming, Little Joe, you hang on." Hoss grabbed the rope off his horse and tied one end to the saddle. He gave the reins to Roy, and crouched back down by the opening of the shaft. "God, what's that awful smell? Joe, are you all right?"

"Pa, is that you?"

"No, Joe, it's me, Hoss."

"No, no, no, no, Hoss is just a ghost. He's looney! Ahhhahahaha."

Hoss tied a loop on the other end of the rope and threw it down. "Joe, put your foot in that loop and hang on to the rope."

Joe stared at the looped rope he'd caught, and threw it up out of the shaft.

"No, Joe! Put your foot in the loop." Hoss noticed the looped rope on the goat-filled floor of the shaft. To be shut in there in the dark, like being buried alive. "Oh Lordy. Come on, boy, I can't get you out…look at those dead goats, come on, Joe, put your foot in the loop."

Hoss felt Frank's hands on his shoulders.

"Joe, I'm going to let you stand on me and give you a boost out, okay? Joe, listen, in order to stand on me you first have to put your foot in the loop. You got it?"

Hoss watched, amazed, as Joe put his foot in the loop.

"Okay, Joe, now I'm going to boost you up, but you gotta hang on to the rope."

Hoss waved at Roy who backed both horses up. When Joe got high enough, Hoss reached down and grabbed his arms and finished pulling him the rest of the way out. Roy helped Frank move back out of the way.

Hoss held Joe and tried not to breathe. "You okay, boy?"

"Paaaa, I was so scared, you died, and Adam was gone, and then Hoss was gone, and I had to do everything because I thought you would be mad…I don't want you mad at me, Pa."

"It's all right, Joe, Pa could never be mad at you. You're all right now, boy."

Joe shuddered in his arms and squeezed his eyes shut. At first Hoss thought he'd passed out. "Hoss?"

"Yeah, Joe?"

"Is Pa really alive?"

"Really, Joe. Come on, let's get you home." Hoss stood, picking Joe up with him as Joe seemed groggy and half-conscious, unable to move.

Then Joe saw Frank. Like a bolt of lightning struck into him he leaped on Frank, knocking them backward into sage. "You left me there to die! You thief! You scoundrel! I oughta kill you!"

Roy pulled Joe off as Frank didn't fight back. "Hoss, get your brother home. I'm gonna get Frank here to the doctor."

Joe glared at Frank but didn't fight Hoss's grip. When Roy and Frank rode off, Joe bent down to pick up his hat, forgetting that his hat was still down in the mine shaft. He fell to his knees. "Pa?"

Hoss picked up his little brother, who fell asleep as soon as his head hit Hoss's shoulder. "I'll take you home, boy, I'll take you to Pa."

* * *

As Hoss rode, with the taste of tea potion in his mouth and smell of goat decay in his nose, he wondered if drinking more potion would help him find Adam, too. He bit back more and more shudders rolling through him, over finding one brother half crazy and feeling he'd abandoned his other brother. Sure, Pa thinks he'll find Adam, but what if he doesn't? Not that Hoss doubted his pa, but Pa had been willing to give up on Adam once before. What could Hoss do now? What, but hope and pray?

"Adam, how can we be sure we're going the right way?"

"We can't. They ordinarily don't leave any signs to follow. Except for that arrow in the tree, there's no sign that there's been an Indian hunting party around. We play our hunches."

"You said they meant for us to find Joe's hat?" Hoss glanced over his shoulder, fearing they were being followed.

"A warning, I suspect."

"A warning? That means Joe is still alive?"

"I think so. Yes."

Hoss waited, but getting words out of Adam these last few hours was like pulling tics off a wild dog.

"We still have to get him out of there." Hoss saw Adam's jaw clenched. That meant he'd do it or die trying.

221

"But Adam, you're good with Indians, ain't ya? They'll listen to you because you know how to talk with 'em."

Adam pulled his horse up short, listening, smelling the air, feeling his surroundings with every muscle and nerve. Hoss imitated him, breathing in air past that of pine and sage and sweat of the horses to pick up a scent that they hoped meant they were on Joe's trail. Hoss had seen Adam like this maybe only once before, a sense like an animal coming over him when he felt such a deep sense of loss and guilt and knew he had to do something about it. Hoss supposed that's why Adam respected the Indians, the way they lived themselves. He couldn't feel the same, because they had killed his mother.

"Adam, did you ever hate Indians?"

At first Adam didn't answer. At first Hoss thought he'd stopped breathing. Finally Adam looked at Hoss. "Not that I remember. Why?"

"You saw my Ma killed. I thought maybe—"

"Shhh," Adam alighted. Hoss did the same and crept over to him. Adam led them off the path, through a rocky grown-over pass no longer being used because the rocks had loosened. They kept their heads low to avoid the sticky pine and watched their feet on loose rock, while the horses behind them tugged at their reins, anxious to get back where travel was easier.

"Adam, before, when you asked about Joe's ma, how come you don't remember much?"

"I wouldn't let myself get close to Marie, because I knew she was going to die."

"Aawww, how could you know—"

Adam shushed him but too late. They were stopped sudden by a dozen Bannock warriors. They seemed to appear from under the ground, six of them with bows pulled back, arrows quivering, with lances ready to throw. They were dressed simply, only the most painted wearing breastplates with their animal skin legging and bare-chested in weather that made most white men wear coats.

Adam glanced at Hoss, who had squeezed himself into a tight mass of pounding flesh, and put a hand on Hoss's arm as though thinking he might do something foolish. Hoss didn't think he could breathe, much less move.

How badly Hoss needed Adam now. Adam, his older brother, has been at his side practically every minute that they were growing up together and yet always knew when to back off and let Hoss handle things.

Somehow, as Hoss remembered his older brother, he felt Adam would be proud of how Hoss had solved Lydia's murder. Maybe only wishful thinking, but the thought kept him going, anyway.

CHAPTER 35

Adam lay on the boat deck on his stomach. He couldn't remember much more than that the beatings led him here, but then the beatings stopped and he still couldn't get up. When something cool and wet touched his back, he groaned and shuddered. The woman whose name he should remember leaned down to him and gave him a gentle smile.

"You. What do you want?"

She had drifted in and out of his consciousness like a ghost, bringing him water and tending his wounds. For days…how many days?

"Just to help." Becca Samuels continued to apply the salve to his wounds. "You've had yellow fever, you know. It's all the rage around here. Don't worry about me, I'm immune. Just lie still."

"Huh. Guess I'll live, too. You the master's daughter?"

"Don't call me that!" Her frown caught Adam's eye when he turned at the sharpness in her voice. "I don't believe in slavery but I can't tell my Papa that. Oh, I'm still a Rebel, all right, if that's what you Yanks call us."

"Yanks?"

"Come on, I don't believe you're a slave, not for a minute. I've seen your back, how white you are. What are you really doing here?"

Adam put his head back down on his arms. *Careful. You don't know her.* His gun was gone, too.

* * *

Ben felt well rested when they arrived in New Orleans but never so exhausted in his whole life. He and Sadie had spent their time on the Mississippi riverboat talking about what they're going to do when they get there. She wanted Lincoln and the Union army generals to understand that they don't want to be shipped anywhere, that they thought of this country as home, too. But Sadie also wanted to find out if Nate was still alive.

Ben's mind never strayed far from his passion, either, finding Adam alive and bringing him home—buying his freedom, if he had to. But with all her talking about Nate and how she got that happy smile in her eyes whenever she mentioned him, he began to wonder what parts of her story were real. She didn't act like a woman headed back to widowhood.

Ben drew his focus back to Adam, with the fervent hope that Adam found better purpose as a slave than in testing those who captured him. If Adam found Tobias, as they believed, then he got caught up same way Ben did, to prove Lincoln's concern for blacks goes beyond winning a war and reuniting a country.

But what if Lincoln doesn't care? Ben decided that all men, even presidents, must be given benefit of any doubt. With a boat ride passing in little consequence, the harbor of New Orleans came into view almost before they were ready. Vessels of all kinds crowded the harbor, all waiting to be either passed or sent away. The four watched, apprehensive, anxious to finish their journey, as the boat docked, and passed inspection. Ben led them into the waiting crowd to touch dry land.

Already having seen more of this 'civil war' than he cared too, Ben prepared himself for the sights and sounds of a "northern" New Orleans.

* * *

Hoss carried Joe to his room because he'd fallen asleep, and Hop Sing brought up a bucket of warm water and some tea. Along the way they'd pick up Cochise. The horse appeared to have gotten away from his captors and, unless Hoss didn't know horse sense, went looking for Joe because Cochise rode right up to them and tagged along behind, every now and again nuzzling Joe's hand. When Hoss got his brother inside the house, Hop Sing reeled from Joe's odor and insisted on stripping Joe naked and burning the clothes. Joe slept even through the washing. Hop Sing then insisted Hoss bathe, too, but Hoss couldn't smell anything anymore.

Hop Sing sat and sipped the tea he'd brought. "He bad when you found?"

"Didn't know me at first."

"Was bury alive?"

"In a mine shaft, totally dark, had dead goats—one dead man." Hoss accepted the tea from Hop Sing but sniffed it first. "You got more of that potion?"

"No, you drank all. Hard to find ingledients."

"Huh? Oh. Too bad. I wanted to find Adam next."

Hop Sing shook his head. "You find Joe because you smart."

Hoss clutched Joe's hand. "I had to do what I did with Lydia, Hop Sing."

Hop Sing put a hand on Hoss's knee and stared into his eyes. "Lydia gone?"

Hop Sing had tried to grill Hoss about her yesterday, but Hoss had been so exhausted he fell asleep on the settee, big frame half on and half off as he slept. By the time he got up, Hoss had left to find Joe.

"Lydia." Hoss sighed, a big terrible sound. "She didn't say goodbye. After all we been through. I'm glad she's at peace—but I…I cayn't say goodbye. Her body…bein' out there somewhere, along the trail, eaten by wolves, or…" Hoss fought to keep the tears away. "Hop Sing, she won't…I mean, when we die we go to heaven, right?"

"You believe this as Christian. In my country—"

"I just…don't want her meetin' him…up there."

"Believe she will not, she will not."

"I 'spect you're right. Dadburnit, Little Joe, wake up and be all right." He put Joe's hand back on the bed. "Hop Sing, there's a couple of hours of daylight left. I think we got danger of our winter stock being stolen. I'm gonna find…a couple loggers and see if we can get on their trail. Apologize to Joe for me, when he wakes, all right?"

* * *

Ben wasn't sure he'd find his way around this time. He hadn't been there in at least five years, and as he could see, much has changed since the war started. The streets, once before clean with flowers everywhere, had been stripped and littered with army occupation and lack of gentile care. Houses had lost their careful coating of paint and in some places, had been abandoned and shot up by drunks. *Or shot up and then abandoned?* But Ben found Darcy's house easy enough, would have even without Sadie's lead. The man who answered the door made Sadie squeal.

"Nate!"

Watching Sadie fly into the arms of a man she thought was dead, Ben felt used. She never had any romantic design on him, not from the start. As he thought about it, realized she never gave him that impression, either. She and her family felt comfort in being close. That kind of closeness he reserved for his sons, too, but only at those moments of sheer relief after the pain of near loss. As he watched Sadie with Nate, he began to feel another emotion, one that at first surprised him. He felt relief at letting her go, as though she no longer owned him.

Clearly Ben saw, the moment they arrived in the city, that Sadie belonged here. Not on a boat sailing to Hayti but right here, in whatever capacity she chose. Even the feeling of being used didn't erase the lingering affection for her, or concern of her plight.

Nate shook Ben's hand briefly, and gave Jesse and Abby big hugs. "I was so a'feared. But now you're here and I'm still…Sadie, they's still gonna send us away. Nothing's changed."

"Nate, I was a'fearing for you this whole time. I thought you done gone on without me."

Ben studied the two of them. "Where's Darcy?" He thought to give Nate a scolding, but realized that could come out as jealousy. And besides, Tobias should have been protecting them, so how could he blame Nate for letting them go?

"Oh, the master, he's…I don' like to say, sir."

"It's Ben, and I don't care where he is or what he's doing. Just tell him I'm here." Ben remembered this house well. How fitting now to lose Sadie to this same house where he had courted his last wife. He walked over to the credenza and opened the big silver and wood box. Sure enough, still had his cigars here. Ben sniffed one. Cuban. Was Darcy part of the ring operating to send blacks away, perhaps?

Behind him Sadie, just the two of them in the room, gave him that look. She was about to apologize and he wanted to make it easy for her.

When Ben held out his arms, Sadie ran into them. "Ben, I is so wretched about what I done to you."

"Don't be. I'm here freely. I have to find Adam, remember?" He breathed her fragrance for what he realized would be the last time. He closed his eyes and enjoyed the memory of how she had kept him hopeful for so long.

"But I should have said…if Nate still lived…."

"Or even if he hadn't. You didn't like the Ponderosa, did you?"

She moved away and shivered. "You could tell?"

"You'd be safe and protected with me. And warm, I'd promise you that." He looked out the window at the environment that Butler tried to make free for them but didn't seem free at all. "I fear what might happen when I leave you here."

Sadie stood next to him at the window. "I fears for you's son, too. But now that you's here, kin you stay and talk to Butler? And Lincoln?"

Ben wrapped an arm around her and brushed the tear out of her eye. "This country is affecting all of us, and we all need to be aware of the enormous transformation going on. Back at the Ponderosa, we hear so little. Sometimes it takes a fire to sear the blindness."

"Oh, Ben, let's sit. I's so tired."

"I'm tired…of sitting."

They laughed together, and Ben relished the sound and the ease on his aching heart.

"Still filling the ladies' heads with platitudes, eh, Ben?" Darcy's voice startled them.

Ben stiffened but kept Sadie's hand in his. "Darcy, you old rascal, still up to your old tricks, from what I hear."

"You mean owning and dealing in slavery? As long as I can get away with it. And they're not free here, you know that about your old friend, Lincoln, right?"

They shook hands but not in the least congenially. "Sadie tells me you're on their side. That you helped them run away to find me and a mountain of silver."

"I helped, yes, because I believed they had a right to stay and not be shipped away. Even enlisted the help of the local Anti-Slavery Society." He chuckled at Ben's astonished expression. "Oh, but it's hard for you to accept any nobility from me, isn't it? How's Marie?"

Ben didn't like to be caught so off-guard twice within as many seconds, but he reminded himself of the long and mind-draining trip. Sadie moved away from Ben to stand next to Darcy, a sort of allegiance realignment.

Darcy smiled at Sadie. "Did you romance him away from his wife, darling Sadie? I always knew Marie was too good for him."

"Ben, I didn' know, you's never…" Sadie gasped and ran from the room.

Ben jammed his thumbs into his gun belt to keep from making a fist. "Still know how to say just the wrong thing, don't you." Ben took the cigar offered but not the brandy. "Do you mind if we sit?"

"Not at all. But I don't have much time. Busy man and all. Got a plantation to run."

"I need to ask a favor."

"You? The rich and powerful Ben Cartwright?"

"My son Adam is missing. I have a feeling he's here somewhere, or headed here. With your Tobias. Could you keep an eye out for him, see that he gets home all right?"

"If he's with Tobias, he'll get here." Darcy puffed on his cigar, his expression pensive. "And then, perhaps you haven't noted the wanted posters in town. I've got him listed as a desperate character, a bounty on his head for being a deserter. Oh relax, Ben, reward says 'bring in alive.' How else do you extricate a white man from the clutches of a slave owner? Without him just being killed?"

Ben stood, both in alarm and amazement. "How did you know?"

"Fellow name of Twain has been spreading news around that there's a reward for a 'muley' slave who's a rich man's son from back in Nevada. I know your family, Ben. Marie wrote often enough. At first. Until you poisoned her against me, eh?"

Feeling weak, Ben sat. "Marie…is dead."

Darcy nodded. "Suspected she wouldn't last long around you. How?"

"Horse riding—horse fell."

Darcy laughed, but short and bitter. "Of course you'd say that. You found that her weakness, didn't you?"

"I owe you nothing," Ben kept his voice soft but firm, "but the truth about Marie."

Darcy poured himself another brandy. "You want to find your son, and I've done all I could. Now are you going to help us?"

"Ah, to the matter at hand…why you had me dragged here—and Adam, too, by the sounds of it."

"Unfortunate they caught two of you. But more as a guarantee that one of you would actually make it this far. You and me are going to the Butler ball."

"General Butler?"

"I hear he's a friend of yours."

"I knew him briefly years ago, my brief stint fighting in the Mexican army. What—"

"Good ole Spoons Butler, we call him here. I don't doubt you'll find he's changed some since then. Everyone in New Orleans knows if you invite him over, better count your silver when he leaves."[48] Darcy chuckled, and leaned forward. "You go to his event with me, and get him to call Lincoln here. Convince him you can give him Nevada's silver for the cause."

"I thought Sadie was joking when she said…" Ben studied the dirt under his fingernails. "All right. On one condition."

"That is?"

"You promise to give Lincoln extra security."

The two men glared at each other a moment.

"I don't like what you're suggesting, Ben."

"Too bad I feel the need to insist."

"I hope I don't lose my reputation as a good southern gentleman, sir, but I'm going to have to ask you to leave."

Ben stood next to him. "What's wrong, Darcy? Sadie says we're on the same side."

Darcy studied the swirl in his glass of brandy. "I've got you in over your head, I'm afraid. Go find your son and go home."

Ben grabbed Darcy's shoulder. "What's going on here, Darcy? Just what are you and your slaves up to?"

Darcy laughed. "Political upheaval must be strong, sudden, and violent. Like the French revolution. You know your history? Don't ask if you don't want the truth." He put his glass down. "I suggest you leave, before I accuse you of raping my servant."

Ben turned to the door, but tensed. He smiled at Darcy, made a fist and knocked the man to the ground before Darcy could duck. "I'll leave when I'm ready, and not before."

CHAPTER 36

Adam sat, arms tied behind him, alone in a dark shack. After they'd landed at Brownsville, he'd been hauled like so much meat off the ship and put "in storage," as Samuels told Becca. He'd been quarantined on the ship and now with the lingering disease in him, still left alone, with nothing to do but think. Adam thought back to his instincts about Becca. *I don't believe in slavery.* Perhaps she can be trusted.

Adam was tired of guessing. He wanted to *know*.

Becca hadn't responded at first to his story about being a Nevada rancher, his decision to trust her while still sick creeping out of a corner of him where sheer desperation lingered. After several more times insisting on the truth and hearing the same story, she gave up and went away.

When the door opened, letting in sunlight, he winced in pain. He didn't realize his hunger or thirst until Becca brought the cup and wrapped bread.

She placed his nourishment on the floor next to him and untied his hands. She watched him while he ate and drank, cautiously getting his appetite back, yet relishing every bite, every gulp. He waited for her first move, feeling a bit snake-like, ready to flee or attack. When he finished she waved her gun at him.

"Come on, outside. They want me to hold a gun on you while you relieve."

She led him away from the shack, for his privacy. When finished, she grabbed his arm and led him in a different direction. As they walked, he oriented himself, seeing the large body of water to the east where the sun had just broke on the horizon.

"Where are we going?"

She kept the gun pointed at his back. "Where you can be honest with me."

Adam could overpower her, if he needed to, with a quick diversionary move. But she intrigued him. He felt there was something just a little too 'shady' about her, like she could give him three different expressions in the same sentence, each one reflecting a different personality. He figured, tired, shaky, that this distrust came from finding out just a little too much about Margaret, a wariness he couldn't discard even after all this time. Still, he could feel Margaret's breath in his as they kissed, after all this time. And wanted to feel it again.

Becca walked him along the side of the cliff overlooking gulf waters, and the two watched their footing more than each other until they came to a trail hidden by some pulled-down brushy trees tied to mark the way. Adam noticed the tie-downs only because she pointed them out. This led to a small cave structure carved into the side of the hill. Inside was nothing more than some half-wood walls, clean and empty.

"What is this?"

"A safe place." Becca sat on the floor and Adam did the same but more slowly, feeling every ache. "Father will be taking you to New Orleans soon enough so I can't keep you long. Let's hear your story. You're not a slave."

"I told you my story. You choose not to believe it."

"That you're a rich ranch owner in Nevada? Come on. My father seems to know you and what he knows he doesn't like. Why did he buy you, and why treat you like a slave?'

"He doesn't know me. But I think he's part of the plot to kill Lincoln. With Luke and Tobias."

"What? That's...that's crazy." She stood and paced. "Do you have proof?"

He told her Tobias's story, of a slave uprising against the North, of the shipments of blacks to Africa and the islands. He told her that he believed in Lincoln's cause, and that Tobias himself denied this plot. But Adam believed there could be no other reason for the elaborate ruse to get him here. And besides, he paid attention to the slavers' attitudes. They weren't all northerners.

"Oh, you..." She sat next to him and stared into his eyes. "You're incapable of telling the truth, aren't you?"

Adam sighed and put his arm around Becca. "I'm not always sure what to believe, either. Look, the slavers that came after Tobias are, or were, northerners. Not southerners. Tobias says that Lincoln put a price on his head. One of the slavers is southern, and part of Tobias's plan. In a guise as a northerner, he protects Tobias, got them to travel through Texas and here the rest will be killed. Okay, that's all supposition. But his story of sending blacks to colonies is true enough, I've read about it. It's not hard to believe a ripple of discontent runs through a portion of the educated black community, related to what they're hearing rather than what's true. And it's a fact that Louisiana slaves are no longer free now that they're Union owned." He studied Becca. She didn't look at him as he talked but he could tell she listened, eager to the point of memorizing every word. "I think your father is part of it. I'll neither be killed nor released, but used to get Lincoln to come to New Orleans. Do you want to take that chance with Lincoln's life?"

"You always use logic like a whip?"

Adam laughed and shook his head. "Luke as much as told me I'll be a hostage, and in another breath he calls me a front. Tobias wanted me to come to New Orleans and convince Lincoln to meet with me about better treatment for them. I represent big silver."

Becca helped Adam to his feet, making him feel more of an old man than he already did. "All right. We have to get back." She went for the doorway ahead of him, slouching to get out.

Adam got on his knees to follow her. "You believe me now?"

"My father told me about a Negro conspiracy, but says it's against the South, not the North. Hard to know what to believe these days. I have to help you escape."

Adam had to run on uneven trails to keep up to her. "Escape? Lady, if I had wanted escape I would have. I need to get to Lincoln to warn him. If they don't use me, they'll find some other way. If Lincoln is killed while this war is going on, the whole world will explode."

Becca nodded, eyes shining with tears. "No one knows that more than me. Come on, I have to take you back, and please understand, if you try to escape without my help, I will have to shoot you. Keeping my profile secure is very important to me. And I'd rather kill you than my father, at least, right now."

Adam studied her. "Your profile?" He couldn't see himself getting romantic over her. She was young and had a certain boyish quality to her—a sort of half-pint woman.

"My father doesn't know much about me. I like keeping it that way."

"Why is he keeping me hid?" *Maybe Joe's type.*

She laughed. "People have a hard time believing you're a slave. He has a reputation to protect, after all. And you are still considered contagious. Possibly in more ways than one." She laughed again, and as they got to the port, told him to shut up. Once inside the shack she tied him, a most secure job. "I'll bring your supper soon. Adam, you're in Brownsville now. This is a very desired location by both the North *and* South. Even with the constant bouts of yellow fever here. You're one of the lucky ones to recover, by the way, and why you're not being forced to work like everyone else. Lincoln can't close down this port because of the Treaty of Guadalupe Hidalgo and the Mexicans favor the South, for some ungodly reason. Economic, I suppose. They do a lot of shipping to keep Jeff Davis's armies going in the field."[49]

"Why tell me all this?"

"Because I have it on good authority that one little itchy finger will get a North-South skirmish to happen right there, right as Papa gets ready to commander a ship."

"Commandeer?"

"Oh yes. He takes whatever he can, whenever he can. You might say he's a..."

"Mercenary?"

"Something like that. While he's protecting his ship from attack, you can slip away."

What's something like a mercenary? Adam shook his head. "Not a good idea. Let him take me to New Orleans."

"No! Listen, if what you say is true, you won't get that far. Stick with me on this. You and me, we can protect Lincoln in other ways. Okay?"

Adam sighed. Typical woman. "Well, why not. It's worth a try, right?"

The door started to close but Becca peeked in. "When you escape go back to that hideout…I'll meet you there."

Darkness closed around him again.

* * *

"Pa! Fire – Fire! Help me, Pa! I'm trapped!" Joe couldn't run or hide or wake, his arms beating back both fire and dead goats coming alive to eat him. When the dead goat herder's eyes opened, Joe sprung awake and sat up in bed. He could smell fire and goat decay, could see the man's rotting face flickering in the match's flame. The putrid smell burned his nostrils and traveled down his throat, until he ran to the window and puked out the little food and drink they'd gotten into him.

Shaking, he leaned on the window sill. "Damn you, Frank."

Hop Sing come into the room, and Joe felt hungry again.

"Mr. Little Joe, must get back to bed. Catch death from cold."

Joe noticed he hadn't a stitch of clothes on and leaped back into bed. He covered his head with a pillow.

"Bringee you nourishment. Mr. Hoss say you down there long time. Had to burn you clothes."

"I can't stop seeing 'em—I can't stop seeing 'em."

"You eat. Dead live in eyes long time. Think other things."

Joe sat when coffee pierced the decaying goat in his nose. "Where's Hoss?" He grabbed the food and proceeded to take Hop Sing's word, to get the strength to run away from here to anywhere.

"He gone to find cattle herd, see if stolen."

"Me too. I gotta, too." He didn't stop to chew but swallowed whole.

He wanted to find Frank. He wanted to make Frank pay for real this time.

* * *

Adam heard the unmistakable voices of his slave captors outside his shack. They argued and in such a tone that he figured a fight was imminent—between Cal and Luke. He'd know their voices anywhere. In the next instant the door of his shack flung open and Tobias, tied and gagged, flew into his lap. The door slammed shut.

"Geez, can't you find your own room?" Adam grumbled as Tobias used Adam's body to sit up on a little piece of ground next to him.

Tobias poked his way around Adam's back, nudging Adam to pulled the gag out of his mouth, which he did, and then said, "Shhh." He didn't need to.

Cal outside the shack rattled some paper. "We got our cover blown. Now everyone in these parts knows, or thinks, we're northerners! I say we just kill this Adam Cartwright and burn the body. No one will ever know."

"I say we stick with the plan to New Orleans, keep up the pretense. Say we didn't know the others were northerners. And take him with Tobias to see Lincoln. Maybe this Cartwright can convince Tobias and a whole slave rebellion of Lincoln's honesty."

"Lincoln can do that without anyone's help."

"But Cartwright's got a whole mountain of silver. And you went and sold him to Samuels, so how you gonna get him back now? You done spent the money. No, we stay close to Samuels, like we's southerners, too, and get us to New Orleans. Stop trying to head north, for now, but get Lincoln to come south."

Something had gone wrong, Adam realized. Northerners coming to a southern town. Of course—what could go right? Clever of Luke.

"All right, we can't kill either of them right now, anyway. And I prefer to get closer to Lincoln before hacking Tobias in half, if'n I gotta keep a part of him to prove he's dead."

"All this just to stop a Negro rebellion?"

"Only thing important is the north wins the war." Cal coughed and leaned against the shack as he tried to stop.

"All you gotta do is put blacks in soldier uniforms." Their voices started to fade as they walked away.

"Oh-ho, imagine that! We can put 'em on the front lines and get 'em all killed off! Wonder if Lincoln thought of that yet?"

Adam wasn't alone in the shack but he never felt lonelier. "Huh. There are more sides to this war than there are soldiers." Northerners wanting to free blacks and use them as body shields?

"Yup."

"Listen," Adam struggled with his ropes but Becca did a fine job there. "There's going to be a battle once we're taken aboard Samuels' ship and that'll be our chance to escape. We get to Butler in New Orleans and tell him to tell Lincoln to stay the hell away from New Orleans—"

"Ain't you listening? Butler's the one shipping us off to Hayti!"

"Well, if he's a true abolitionist, he'll stop that once he hears your story." Adam sighed. "Can't think of anything else, for now. We need to hear the rest of the plan."

"I know the rest of the plan," Tobias said, his face lower than a nest of rattlesnakes. "They're not ever going to free us, because they don't know what to do with us. I'll end up in Africa, trying to learn how to make huts out of grass."

Adam put a consoling hand on his shoulder. "Lincoln will do what's right, you can be sure of that. Maybe not this year, or next, but he will. Just give him time."[50] Adam looked at him, startled. "You learn that good English from hanging out with me?"

Tobias shrugged. "Guess we both had to put on an act."

Adam didn't have a chance to question him further, as sunlight blared into the shack and the slaves were pulled out. They spent the rest of the day out in the hot sun, helping to load the ship, but with irons back on. All this contraband, Adam thought, used to supply the South so they can go on fighting for independence. Whenever they got the chance for quiet talking, Adam told Tobias about the plan to attack the ship, only a few words at a time, but he figured Tobias was smarter than he let on.

"I think Becca's sincere. And I'll do everything I can to keep them from killing you. I don't want you to give up, not after all we've been through."

"You go on dreaming, Titus. I don't think either of us is getting out of here alive."

* * *

Hoss walked his horse along the Truckee Valley stage road that ran from Sacramento to Carson City. The route being so many miles long, he didn't expect, not knowing where to look, that he'd find a trace of Lydia's body. But he marked trees to indicate the locations of his search, to do a section today before cutting over to the cattle range. Would Stephen have done the dirty deed just before reaching Carson City? Hoss knew a man generally became most desperate just before something.

As he neared the spot where the horse trail went into the hills toward the Ponderosa, he stopped and bent down. Pink. He worked the piece out of the brush as though still attached to a body. Pink lace. Hoss ignored sounds behind him, thinking hard on the pink and lilac dress Lydia wore. This could be, he figured, a little piece of collar torn from the dress. He parted the brush and crept in a little bit, but whatever got her, got the rest.

"What you got there, Hoss?" Mark Twain sat on his horse, looking uneasy, as though Hoss might any minute give him a fist to the jaw.

Hoss held it up. "Here's where Lydia died. Right here. On the intersection of trail leadin' to the Ponderosa and over to Carson City. That's why she came to me."

Mark nodded and alighted. "Just came from Carson City myself, on the trail of the Stephen Lawe story." He reached over as though to touch the piece, but stopped himself. "Piece of a lady's dress, all right. Sure seems to be why she'd head your way."

Hoss looked at him in surprise. "You believin' in ghost stories now?"

"Funny thing about that story. I put it in as a lark, but there's quite a passel of folk who want to accept these spirits as real. So I guess I'll have to be more careful what I print for fun."

"Yeah. Do you think you could print, like, an epitaph for Lydia? I mean, I know her killer is dead and all, but I think she deserves a fittin' tribute."

Mark snuck over to the brush where Hoss had been standing. "You see sign of a body anywhere?"

Hoss shook his head. "I was hopin'…to give her a decent burial."

Mark put a hand on his shoulder. "We'll do that epitaph with the Territorial Enterprise. I'll even let you write it. But answer something for me I've been curious about."

Hoss glared at him. "Not if'n it'll end up in your paper."

Mark laughed. "Not this time, only curious. I've been with all you Cartwrights now. And you're different than the rest, in the way you think, even the way you talk. Why is that?"

"Huh? Oh, what Pa calls my 'lazy' talk. He don't mean it that way. He says because I tend to talk slower than I think, my words just come out—he calls it a little more "squished." And my ma, she was Scandinavian, so…"

Mark nodded as Hoss stumbled for more words. "I've heard of settlements where the folks talk a little different English. But I always thought it was because they listened more to each other." He mounted. "I'd get rid of that piece of lace if I was you. You never know, it might draw her back to you." He grinned as Hoss tucked the pink lace in his pocket.

Hoss stared down at the spot to the sound of Twain's horse riding off, and squeezed his eyes shut. He wanted her to say goodbye. He didn't need her to say thank you, but this all meant so much to him and then just…gone. A bad feeling that he'll get over, he knew, but…her last words to him…

"I meant it, Hoss. I love you."

Hoss opened his eyes. Lydia stood in front him, her eyes and lips as wide and smiling as the first time he saw her—no, even wider. Her lips didn't move but he could hear her voice in his head. He wanted to reach for her but feared she'd fade away if he did. She always had to make the first move, and she always did.

"I wish I could have waited to force Stephen's hand. Bad timing, to give him that easy way to kill me. I know you would have helped me to stay alive. Some things are not meant to be, Hoss. Not in this lifetime, anyway."

Hoss felt, or maybe just imagined, the soft brush of a hand against his cheek. "You're welcome." As he wiped his eyes he saw what was left of her, the pink lace lying at his feet. He picked it up, held it gently against his cheek a moment, and then tucked it away in his pocket.

CHAPTER 37

Hoss didn't quite know at what pasture the winter herd would be grazing, and worried as he took longer and longer to find it. He worried about how Joe was doing, and if maybe that dead goat herder's ghost mighta got him. He worried that he didn't have the time to go back to the City and wire out more telegrams looking for Adam, or send one out to Pa to let him know all that's been going on. Pa's last telegram did say that he figured Adam would be showing up in New Orleans, and if he could, he'd wait for him. But then Hoss wired him that Joe was missing, so he feared Pa would have to head on back now, with or without Adam. He hoped Roy would think to wire Pa, as Hoss let Roy know everything as everything happened. Pa also said he was going to trust Darcy to do the right thing and keep Adam safe. Pa couldn't say enough in the telegram, but he sounded pretty worried, to Hoss, anyway. Worst part was, he couldn't even say that Adam *was* safe, because he just didn't know.

They weren't at Pasture 1 or 2, but the trail showed they'd been there and herded to Pasture 3, where with relief he found the tail end twitching happily in some clover. These fellows, these thieves, must have found themselves over their heads, not knowing how to drive cattle at all without Frank, but trusting that with Joe trapped, they had plenty of time.

Hoss heard his name shouted and turned to see Salzar poke his head out from a tent hidden off under some brush.

"Hey, Hoss, whatcha doing dere? You be needing something from me?"

"Hey, Sally, you're a timberman, ain't ya? Where's Billy?"

"Billy is not a good boss. I am a good boss."

"All right, Sally," Hoss alighted. "I'll need a report. There's been some scoundrels in these part, wanting nothin' better than to get their hands on this young stock. I thought they might already be here. If we lose this stock, Sally, we'll be hurtin' hard come next spring."

Salzar grunted and pushed Hoss away from the bedding camp. "You tink you not trust old Salzar to watch herd? Sure I logger. But I know a little about many tings, Hoss, and that why your cook say mitt no Cartwrights around, I take charge. I take charge good and you go home, without worry."

He took Hoss up a bit of an incline, the land rising on a bed of rock where Hoss could see over the entire herd. "Dis where I do count. Dis morning count was 105. Pretty good, no?"

Hoss did a quick mental calculation. "That's about fourteen short from what we kept from the drive a month ago. What was the count yesterday?"

Salzar didn't hesitate. "107. We figger a wolf in the area so sent Billy out with rifle. We all okay here, Mr. Hoss. You have other ranch to run."

"Now hang on, Sally, I think I got here just in time. Sounds like someone's taking our herd, piece by piece. And from what Frank says, they's now gettin' bold enough to walk off with the rest at any time. I'd like to meet all the boys workin' here right now. No one, including you, had the authority to move the herd this far west."

"You Cartwrights need to learn who to trust. I put in charge. No cattle get stolen from me!" Sally crossed his arms and furled his brow and waited for Hoss to challenge him.

Hoss hated riling his good men. Heaven knows they can be hard to come by. "All right, just—give me the names of all the fellers here, and…I'll just come back ever mornin' to help with the count. Okay? But don't move them any further west than this without my say-so."

Salzar pointed out some of the men roaming the herd on horseback, and Hoss squinted down at them until he couldn't see them anymore. Sally took a painfully slow amount of time to come up with the names. Five altogether, including Billy.

"Sally, I hate to tell you this, but except for Billy, I don't know any of those four men you named. Come on, I wanna meet each of them, right now."

Sal walked them down the slope, directly into the path of three drawn guns.

* * *

Ben had to wait until the General's ball to meet Butler. The telegrams from home were becoming more and more disturbing, and as time passed he feared becoming trapped on this side of the Sierras. But all of Darcy's requests for a private audience were turned down—General Butler couldn't take time for any social calls. Ben had helped write the request himself, so he knew Darcy had done all he could. The extra time here could bring Adam to him, but every day's dusk ended in disappointment.

He missed Sadie, who spent long stretches of time with Nate going places that Darcy either didn't know or wouldn't say. So Ben spent useless days wandering the town, asking for any news, either about Adam or a mulatto slave in town, and at the newspaper office looking through old files and reports to get a feeling for how to approach General Butler.

Ben felt strangely odd being in this city where he had met and loved the lively belle Marie, and often found himself wandering into the past to remember her, starting with how she almost ran him down on her horse. Now Union soldiers bullied their way through town, rather than lovely young ladies on horseback.

The city had an air of both of celebration and insolence. There was music, yes, as there had been before. But with the Union in control of the city, while a happy occasion for Lincoln's army, the music had an air of desperation. The Negroes he talked with felt uncertainty about their future mingled with the happiness that now they had a future. Lincoln's freedom didn't pertain to any Union-occupied town. If slaves still worked on plantations weren't they still slaves? If they took a chance and ran to army protection, like as not they'd be put on a boat to a colony because the army could only work so much contraband. As Ben imagined Adam toiling in a cotton field, he realized something both startling and true—whites can be slaves as well. Simply by fear for their lives.[51]

Ben saw the most unusual sight of his life, an army corps of blacks put together by General Butler and headed by a white officer. Butler called them his Corps d'Afrique, charged with keeping peace in the streets. Not all the southerners who took Lincoln's oath of loyalty had any real desire to be loyal, to Ben's amazement and growing horror. Two of the Negro soldiers stopped a white man in the street to ask for his loyalty paper. At first the man argued with them, then started to walk away, was yelled at to stop, began to run— and they shot him in the back.

Ben took out his loyalty paper, a document he at first thought ridiculous but now understood as a symptom of a city, and a war, gone mad.[52] He had vowed to stay away from New Orleans until the war was over and understood why. This wasn't the world he remembered anymore. But for that reason, perhaps, he became even more dedicated to why he came now. And why, if Adam had tangled up the same way with Tobias, Ben felt he could be even prouder of his son. Perhaps Adam will finish whatever Ben starts here. One of them had to get back to the ranch, and Ben knew, as well as he knew his son, that his son would try to right a wrong at the risk of his own life. For that reason alone would he pretend to be a "muley." Not because Kane made him crazy, but because he'd always been horrified by the wrongs of the world.

People begging in the street, women and children dying for food, all symptoms of a wrong, with armies to enforce peaceful resolutions to desperation. Buildings had been torched in an effort to root out potential Rebel bases, and the streets were lined with filth. No, this was not Marie's New Orleans, a city of grace and culture. The city showed the results of war, the northern army's attempt to control a southern city.

At least, if Adam came as a mulatto, he should be safe enough. If they broke his disguise before he got here...but Ben shook his head—depends on the 'they.' Ben asked every black he could if they knew any mulattoes newly come to town. They introduced him to a few, always a dead end. A few of them he would never have taken as a 'muley,' either.

Sadie believed that *if* they could get Lincoln to visit here, he would make everything all right. But if they were still executing potential Rebels in the street, Lincoln would have to be suicidal to come here. Surely Sadie didn't want Lincoln to put his life on the line. And would Darcy get involved helping secure more equality for Negroes? Had he become a northerner after all this time?

Ben retrieved a few bank notes—horrified to learn how much of what he'd sent ahead had been confiscated in the name of Union—and went to the clothier. He didn't pack any dress duds, and even if he had Quantrill now had them.

* * *

The supposed 'ball' in honor of a diplomat's birthday was less than an extravagant affair, and Ben was relieved that the government money wasn't being hoarded by the rich here. Still, they had scrapped together enough food to feed five hundred homeless, and from what he could tell, about one hundred were here to make short work of the vittles. Everyone dressed in fine clothes, but Ben had seen finer even in a wilderness like Nevada—in fact, everywhere in evidence he could see war's thumbprint. He hadn't even been able to purchase fine duds and settled for cleaning up his one set of clothes, and no one paid his western attire much mind. The band consisted of three army soldiers who knew two slow songs. Ben stopped paying attention, and before long, the only music was one lady on the piano.

Negro servants made sure the food bowls were kept full, and could be seen sneaking bites but no one stopped them or complained. Occasionally a shout out on the lawn was quickly silenced.

He stood, punch in hand, waiting for an appropriate moment. Various people kept Butler surrounded and Ben didn't want to get squished in the crowd.

"He's not going to come to you," Darcy said, coming alongside him.

Ben grunted. "I'm trying to figure out how to trust you after all these years, Darcy."

But instead of answering Darcy walked to Butler, waving at Ben to follow. "Excuse me, General, this is the distinguished visitor I told you about. The first and still the greatest land owner and great cattle rancher from Carson City, Nevada, Ben Cartwright. Ben, this is the commander of our great Union city of New Orleans, Major-General Benjamin Butler."

"You may remember me from Santa Fe, years back," Ben said, hand out. But Ben wouldn't have remembered Butler without the introduction. His eyes were too beady and narrow inside that heavy face, making him look like he despised everyone he met.[53] He also had the kind of smile that made you want to keep your hands in your pockets at all times. "I'm very pleased to see you, General Butler. I believe you were a Colonel when last we met. I know that the Union army, and Lincoln, are very proud of your successes here."

Butler grabbed Ben's arm and pulled him aside, waving all others away. "Do you know this? Did Lincoln talk to you?"

"Lincoln? Uh...no, but..." Ben shrugged it off, but Butler didn't even try to remember Santa Fe.

"Because if he did, you can tell me. See, I get the feeling he thinks I'm becoming disloyal. Ha! Me! Jeff Davis himself has a price on my head!"

"I am glad to have this chance to talk with you. I've come a long way—"

"And I know that Lincoln's been giving your state great consideration, due to the amount of silver there. Gotta get more people to move there though. He needs money for this war, you know. I have had a lot of financial difficulty since taking over. The people were on the verge of starvation! I've had to find a way to feed them. So I tax the rich—many are foreigners and they complain! Can you imagine? You know what I found out, just today? Hmmm? In a most recent count over half of the whites being fed were foreign born—over half! Only 10,000 were Negro, and most of these are women and children because the men are all working at turning cotton plantations into feeding grounds. Hmmm? They get paid and buy their own bread. That's not slavery, right?"[54]

"I'm sure Lincoln understands your efforts here. The concern that brought me—"

"I'm sorry, Mr. Cartwright, how rude of me. What's the concern that brought you here? Hmmm? Hello, Mrs. Lawson, my, you are looking handsome this evening."

"Runaway slaves."

"Oh, they're no concern. The military puts them to work. We never return them to their owners, anymore, even here." He waved at another woman across the room. "Excuse me, I think I need to dance."

"No, wait. The runaways ran *from* New Orleans. They want me to bring Lincoln here to see for himself what you're doing to them."

Butler squinted at Ben, making his beady eyes even smaller. "What *I'm* doing?" He pulled Ben into a private corner. "Just exactly what am I doing to them? Hmmmm?"

Maybe bringing Lincoln here *would* work. Using his name sure made Butler take notice. "Some runaways ran all the way to Nevada territory, saying they jumped a ship you ordered to take them to another country."

"Jumped ship?" Butler laughed. "Oh, there was that shipment a few months back, where some blacks panicked and ran. But we were taking them to a sugar plantation that's crying out for labor. Actually they still are. I need to get something put together for this..." but he lost his train of thought as he waved to another woman across the room.[55]

"Their fear is that once shipped away, they'll never be brought back."

"Nonsense. Mr. Cartwright, have you ever been to New Orleans? Hmmmm?"

"Oh yes, many times. I met my wife Marie here. I haven't been back since the war started, however."

"Well, that explains a few things. Hmmmm. This is a war city now, Mr. Cartwright, and we are in the process of reconstructing it to fit the needs of the North."

The idea made Ben shudder, but he ignored a potential reason why. "Well, there is a particular Negro uprising that is serious about bringing this issue to the President's attention. They are organizing against you, feel you are trying to send them away, to get rid of what you see is the problem. A way to solve food shortages, eh?" A woman gave Ben some interesting looks, but business before pleasure. He also saw Darcy watching them from a distance. "They want Lincoln to come here and listen to them, as a group, make a plea for why they belong here, as U.S. citizens."

"Now just a minute, Mr. Cartwright. Yes, I'll admit to trying to get them to go work on a sugar plantation for awhile, but I have no desire to see blacks sent off permanent to Liberia or anywhere else. Lincoln is the one—he thinks they're not ready for citizenship, not me. Lincoln is the one who is only freeing blacks in rebellion states, and now that New Orleans, at least, is Union, they're not even free here. Hmmmm? I'm the first one who emancipated, back at Fort Monroe, me, not Lincoln! Lincoln has proposed postponing the final abolition of slavery until the year 1900." Ben started to speak but Butler hadn't finished. "Lincoln says that we should send blacks in big numbers so they'll keep each other company and not be reluctant to go! Have you ever heard such nonsense?! I'm also the first to dare to hang a traitor! Bet you didn't know that, hmmm?"[56]

Ben hesitated, but with Butler glaring at him, he pushed forward on Sadie's plan. "Then let's bring Lincoln here and get him to listen to the people he doesn't think should be U.S. citizens. They can get through to him as you and I can't."

Butler scratched his balding head. "Hmmm, you know, I don't think I've tried that. As far as I know, Lincoln occasionally meets with the niggers—I mean Negroes, when he visits the army camps, but they're different than here, they're all freed army laborers that he meets."

"Wire him tomorrow. I'll give my assurance that as the largest property holder in Nevada, I can sway the territory toward eventual status as a free state, with wealth enough to fund the rest of the war."

General Butler noticed others behind them clamoring for his attention. "Done! I'll show him all the good work I'm doing here to dispel his cautions about me for good and all. Let's meet at the telegraph office in the morning, first thing, hmmm? I'll be very interested to see if someone like you can get him to visit when I cannot. Now if you'll excuse me, I'm in demand this evening and must spread myself quite thin." Darcy bounded away in his enthusiasm for some female rapport.

Darcy handed Ben some punch. "No good, eh?"

"I'm not sure. I got him to agree to bring Lincoln here, but now I wonder. Darcy, what do you know about Nate and Sadie?"

"What do you mean?"

"Is Lincoln in danger if he comes here?"

Darcy laughed. "Lincoln would have so many bodyguards that the entire South would have to fire all at once to hit him. Come on, let's forget politics and enjoy some of this food, for tomorrow, we go back to rations."

"If what Butler says is true, then Lincoln is the one these slaves are angry with."

"Come on, old man, there will be time enough tomorrow to solve all the black problems of the world."

Ben got himself some of the punch, spiked this time and felt himself start to relax and even trust to Darcy, just a little.

* * *

Adam and Tobias were forced to spend a final night cramped together in the little shack, after loading the boat.

"How did you get here, anyway? I thought you were on your way to Lincoln's prison."

"Luke arranged an attack...Adam, this is a Rebel state and Luke spread the word about who Cal and his bunch are. Luke's got friends here, like Samuels. Piney was killed. Jake run off...took that horse you like so much and who knows where he ended up. Laredo, maybe."

"And now Cal has no choice but to follow Luke's lead."

"He won't last much longer, not if...Adam, they're putting us on Samuels' boat."

Adam clamped a reassuring hand on Tobias's shoulder. "We're going to escape tomorrow, before the boat leaves dock. Be ready—"

Tobias's eyes opened so wide that Adam looked off in that direction, ready to duck, before realizing they were still inside the shack. "My sister...Sadie!"

"Yeah?"

"She's the one! Adam, they think I'm the dangerous one. She's the one they should be after!"

Adam waited for Tobias to gather his thoughts. Both of them were thirsty and talking more than necessary wasted spit. "So I'm right? Lincoln's in danger?"

Tobias nodded and started to sob, dry, rustling sounds. Adam didn't know how to console him. This was Lincoln's war, and because of that Lincoln's life would be continually threatened. "Tobias, listen to me. You and me, we'll get to New Orleans and we'll protect him."

"I never wanted all of this, Adam. You got to believe me. I just want Lincoln to listen to us. But Sadie, she's crazy. She doesn't want the slaves to be freed. She's scared of freedom. You got to stop her."

CHAPTER 38

The two men were dragged to the ship before dawn the next morning. Neither had much sleep, as they kept bumping each other awake all night long in cramped quarters. Adam at first thought the pounding noise came from his head, as headaches and thirst seemed a way of life since the bout of yellow fever from which he forced himself to quickly recover. But when others already on the ship shouted and pointed, Adam looked behind them on the trail leading to town.

Tobias pointed, "Looks like a massacre," and the assaulters on horseback hidden in the dust storm began to fire. Adam pushed Luke aside and grabbed one of Cal's rifles. He took Tobias's arm and they ran to hide behind some barrels standing near the dock ramp.

The weaponry of the five men were no match for this volunteer outlaw band of Union men, an impressive and able group. Adam thought the leader looked familiar, small but well mounted. Samuels called his crew to the deck with guns but one by one they were taken down. Luke waved at Adam and Tobias to stay put, as Samuels loaded a small cannon. Adam looked behind him when the first ball fired and rattled the air over his head. The shot was off target, but one of the fellows lost his hat and that's when Adam saw her.

"Becca," he breathed. He thought to run to Samuels and reveal her profile to keep her safe, but kept firing as he backed up toward the boat ramp. The crewman had reloaded the cannon by the time Adam reached it, and he knocked the fellow out with a well-placed blow behind his head.

Samuels' second cannon went off and the 'boom' made Adam drop his rifle and hit deck, believing that it came from the Federal renegade attackers on shore but several men and horses went down as the cannonball hit close to Becca. A gun and a sword landed near Tobias, who remained hidden behind the barrels. He tried to pick up the sword but it burned his hand.

Luke grabbed Tobias's arm and motioned for Adam to follow them below deck. Instead Adam knocked into Samuels loading the cannon.

"You'll thank me later," Adam told Samuels, who took Adam's blow the hard way and was in no mood to hear anything at the moment.

As Adam ran off the ship and broke from Luke, Tobias picked up the sword and ran after him, even as the firing continued hot and fast. "Adam, wait for me! Adam!"

Another dust cloud in the distance headed straight for Becca's troops. Adam ducked behind barrels, believing escape had become impossible. When he saw Tobias out in the open waving a sword Adam waved him to go back, stay with Luke for God's sake, stay down—

But three bullets hit Tobias simultaneously and he fell backward. Adam couldn't even tell who fired at who anymore and remained hidden, yelling at Tobias and then at Becca to watch out for the Confederate soldiers coming up behind them, one aiming right at Becca…

"No!" Adam leaped up from behind the barrel and ran toward her but she turned her horse, her hat back on to recover her male profile. She waved for the few men remaining in her small band to flee back into hiding. Adam ducked back behind another barrel, expecting to see the Confederates chase Becca's army but instead they surrounded him on the dock.

* * *

No matter how far away Joe got from that mine shaft, goats kept returning in his head to haunt him. He had the sinking feeling that the next goat that gets in his path would be shot. He wouldn't be able to stop. *Goats! I can't sit! Goats! I can't sleep, I can't lay down, oh please let me just close my eyes!* He wanted to get to the cattle range but heard a pounding, like the hammer of an ax against bark, so he rode off in that direction. The last thing he remembered, the loggers had all been paid and released.

He found Al supervising the work of four other men, all men Joe knew, and in a section that had landslided not so long ago. That land had healed well and they were cutting the felled timber.

Al waved Joe over. "Found us a good solution to men who got their pay for doing nothing. I figure this'll keep us busy earning our keep."

I'll be darned—Pa did real good in getting loyalty from those guys. As he rode off Joe realized he should have asked Al if he knew where Hoss or Pa or Adam were, but how would that sound? Like a whiny orphan, which was how he felt.

After a couple more hours riding he picked up the cattle trail. They had been moved, and were moving west. He pulled up, wondering the purpose. Maybe Hoss and the cowboys could handle this. Maybe he should just go home and…and what? Hide? Scared of falling in a mine shaft the rest of his life? The hills were filled with them. He could run away, find a traveling gypsy band doing freaky snake acts, or—no. He wheeled Cochise around but couldn't decide on a direction. He could help the loggers… anything to chase those goats away…

"Joe!"

Ahead of him, coming from the trail to Virginia City, someone who knew his name. Someone he thought he should know.

"Joe, I'm so glad to see you're all right. I had to leave you behind in that pit to save both our lives, I swear."

"Oh. Yeah." *No, no more goats!*

"The doc said I was lucky Roy brought me in because I could have died. I got a bandage, see?" Frank lifted his hat.

Joe jumped off his horse and ran to Frank. He grabbed Frank and pulled him off his horse. "You left me there to die!" He punched him, knocking him in the jaw to the ground. "You left me there, the worst of all possible—" He jumped on Frank, pinning him to the ground, choking him. "They covered the hole, they trapped me there in the dark!"

Frank grabbed Joe's hands and pulled, laughing and coughing at the same time. "I'm sorry, oh, God, Joe, I'm so sorry. But I didn't have a choice, or they would have shot us both!" Frank tried to roll away and took a hit from Joe's fist to the back of his head. He lay groaning. "Oh, God, how did I ever get mixed up with you Cartwrights!?"

Joe sighed and stood, unable to stay mad at a man who didn't run away or fight back. He held a hand down to Frank. "Are they cattle thieves?"

Frank saw Joe's hand, gave him a well-deserved frown, then took the hand and got up on wobbly legs. "They wanted me to join them...steal your winter herd. I said no, that's like stealing a man's future. And when I wouldn't join them..." Frank motioned a hammer to the back of his head. "Left me for dead."

Joe jumped back into the saddle. "I'd apologize but," he shrugged, "you made me look at that goat herder's face."

Frank grinned. "Then we're even."

Joe grinned back. "Let's find that cattle herd. Hyah!"

* * *

Adam tried to get back to the boat but Confederate soldiers surrounded him, half of them Mexicans.

"Gringo. People say you are not a slave but a Union spy. Do you know what we do to Union spies? Like to your friend?" He pointed toward the boat.

Adam crossed his arms. "I'm in your territory now and I should just play along and say no, but to be honest, I think I should warn you that for every single western territorial neutral settler that is killed here that you personally shouldn't care about, another four Mexican women are killed by Apaches, waiting right over that ridge. They're watching you."

When the Mexican Confederate soldier looked in the direction Adam pointed, Adam grabbed his gun and knocked him with the hardest fist he could make to the ground. At the sudden blast of a rifle Adam squeezed his eyes shut, waiting to fall to his death.

"Call off your war dogs, Javier, now! Or answer to my father," Becca shouted, her rifle still smoking. She had shed her revolutionary disguise on the ride and returned, and no one questioned her steady aim. She'd hit a soldier in the arm, one who had drawn on Adam's back after Adam laid on the punch. "My father wouldn't be happy if you killed someone he paid good money for. You, muley—get on the ship." Becca dismounted and walked up close behind Adam. "Foolish, did you want to die?"

Adam glanced back on shore to see the soldiers ride off. "I was tired of all the guesswork." Adam grabbed her arm. "Samuels will figure you out, dressed like that."

"Keep going!" But she smiled when she added, "my father sees what he wants to see."

Adam dropped to his knees when he saw the blood trail on the deck. Samuels pointed to the water barrels sitting aft. Tobias had crawled back there, bleeding from a hole in the chest, square between the nipples, the other two wounds less serious but bleeding bad.

Adam found Tobias and grabbed his hand. He squeezed, but felt only a brief flutter of ife from Tobias in return.

Tobias grunted, tried to move, whimpered, "Bad...?"

Feelings and fears of the past month swept through him. "Worse than a snake bite, I guess." This wasn't the help he wanted Tobias to have, but then, nothing has been as it seemed on this journey.

"Kinda stings like one." He started to shake. "Adam, I want you to know... Lincoln ...not my idea...tried to stop Sadie...you...can save him..."

"Don't worry, I believe you." Adam rubbed his eyes. "You're going somewhere safe. Where you'll be free."

"I'll be free? Forever?"

"For..." but Adam could barely swallow, let alone talk. Tobias, someone he could never trust, became someone he respected, at the end.

"Halleluiah...."

Adam squeezed Tobias's limp hand as hard as he squeezed his eyes against the pain. He looked up to see Luke standing over him. "Now what?"

"Now we bury him."

Adam stood, squaring his shoulders with effort as he wiped emotion from his face. "What is this all about, Luke? Why did Lincoln want him?"

"You mean Cal, Piney, the rest of 'em? Lincoln told them to capture the runaway slaves, stop them, whatever it takes. A Negro Rebellion would look bad on his presidency, you see. Tobias was too educated and spreading too much talk."

"And now that he's dead, it's all over?"

"Oh, hardly. I'm part of Tobias's Rebellion, too. And our plan succeeded, to bring you with us. A western silver man, ready to offer Lincoln his support. I found out about the slavers and joined on to make sure they didn't kill Tobias."

"Not too good at what you do."

Luke looked down at Tobias. "Shame, too. But I'll take over from here."

"And if I refuse to go with you?"

"You can't refuse. You're property of Samuels now. And we need you to get through the New Orleans blockade. You'll come...or get thrown overboard."

Adam looked over where he saw Samuels and Becca arguing. "What does Samuels know about me? About all this?"

"Listen, Cartwright, if you think you can put an end to this, think again. You're just one man." He pushed him at the point of a bayonet to Samuels. "Think we better kept this one tied up. Getting right rebellious, he is."

CHAPTER 39

Sadie in the kitchen kneaded bread but with the poorest wheat flour Ben could remember seeing, with clumps and seeds and what looked like small pieces of insect. Ben flashed to a memory of the first time he'd had white bread—the matron of the boarding house said it was easier to keep clean. But clean, he knew, didn't mean nutritious. At the sound of Ben's voice calling her, Sadie froze, but she went on working. The kitchen was bright and airy with everything she could need around her. The floor could use a scrubbing, a sign of her exuberance in cooking. Except for that, and lumpy flour, Hop Sing would be jealous.

"How was the doings?" She took the rolling pin and whacked at the uncooperative dough a few times. "Blacks like me, you know, if there ain't a job for us, we don't go. Unless'n it's to a sugar field on some far off island."

"Butler said those jobs are just temporary. He'd never make you stay there."

"He said, he said. Who do you trust, Ben?"

"I used to trust you."

"We jus' want Lincoln here. Jus' a few minutes, so he can hear our complaint. We wants him to hear us, loud and clear."

"Butler and I sent him a telegram today."

Sadie smiled and separated the dough into four equal loaves. Her smile broadened and she started to sing under her breath.

Ben grabbed Sadie's shoulders and pulled her to him. "Do you plan to kill Lincoln, Sadie? Are you ready to gun him down because he isn't the abolitionist you want him to be?"

She laughed. "Poor sweet Ben. You mistrust us darkies now? How can we think of anything but love toward Mr. Lincoln? Go home, tend to you's ranch. If you waits too long, you won' get back at all."

"Don't use my words against me." Ben tightened his grip on her shoulders. "Sadie, you listen and you listen good. Lincoln is not your enemy. If you kill him, the next man you get will be worse—tons worse. You think Hannibal Hamlin will be any more sympathetic? He could turn everything around the wrong way." Ben didn't know much about the vice president and that made the point all the more valid.

Staring into his eyes, Sadie started to cry and wrapped her arms around him. "Oh, Ben, you just don' understand. We wait and hope so hard and now them Rebel slaves get to be freed and not us? Is all so wrong!"

"I know. But we have to be patient. Sometimes these things ask us...to be patient."

"You let her go." Nate growled at them from behind. "I sends her to git you, and now you just takes over?"

"Nate, Ben's on our side, he really is."

Ben turned to Nate. "Yeah, you sent her. Didn't you realize the danger she'd be in?"

Nate stood silent, unbudging, fists clenched.

Ben sighed and slipped his hat back on his head. "This war has enough violence. I understand your anger, and your impatience, but maybe there's a better way." Ben stood between them. "Will you listen?"

Sadie nodded. "I'll put on the tea."

Jesse and Abby came in, followed by two little girls.

"Mr. Cartwright, we want you to meet my sisters," said Jesse. "They're learning to read and write."

"Well, that's wonderful," Ben said as he pulled them to him. "Then I have a job for the two of you that I think Mr. Lincoln will appreciate."

"Mr. Lincoln?" Abby spat the name to the floor. "Mama, didn't you tell him—"

"It's all right, child. We'll listen to Mr. Cartwright. Maybe he's right. There's been too much violence in this war already."

The seven, with a whistling pot in the background, gathered around the table to plan.

* * *

"Darcy, I am glad I got to see you again." Ben stood at the front door with his satchel and an additional bag of trinkets bought from the local blacks. He also made a donation to Butler's Food for New Orleans program, after wiring for return funds from Carson City. "I cannot remember why I disliked you so much."

"Maybe because I forbade you to marry my cousin?"

"As if you had the right."

"I did have the right, as her oldest male relative. And I knew that your tough western life would kill her."

"You couldn't know. We all take chances. I don't think she regretted a thing." Ben opened the door. "When you see Adam, telegraph me, will you?"

Darcy laughed. "Can't believe you're leaving without him."

"I hope I made New Orleans a little safer for his arrival. I'll have to settle for that." Ben held out a hand to shake.

Darcy shook his hand and punched him in the jaw. Ben staggered backward but didn't fall. "Just a little southern hospitality."

Ben rubbed his jaw as he chuckled. "Come on, walk me to the boat."

* * *

Sadie watched out the window as Ben and Darcy walked away. "I has to agree with him, Nate, he's done been right, all this time. Good man with a good head. But how does we stop what's already going?"

Abby leaned her head on her mother's arm. "We can't. This thing's gotten too big now."

CHAPTER 40

Ben looked at the people's faces all the way to the dock, all manner of people, some he'd trust with his life, most he wouldn't, soldiers pushing people off the docks, making arrests, getting spit on by the girls. No sign of a lost son. But he knew he couldn't delay getting home, or chance never getting home. He'd sent telegrams to Hoss and got telegrams back and the last one, from Roy, said nothing has been heard yet from Adam. And maybe never will.

Darcy promised to watch for him, and keep him safe, if possible. Ben had to hope that would be enough. He'd already done everything one man could, following a cold trail that defied all logic. He had to be home before the snows, because his other two sons needed him. He sensed that much when he left. He could lose everything if he delayed.

His home, tore into pieces, just like this country. Not divided in half at all. But shattered. Ben was anxious to put his home back together—at least as much as possible in this excruciating period in the country.

Ben booked passage on a steamer headed up the Mississippi, and from the deck watched as ships attempted to get in the harbor from across the Gulf but couldn't break the blockade Butler had set up. The army inspected every parcel coming in and made sure none appeared suspicious or found its way into Rebel hands.[57]

"Sad. So many lives being ruined." But as Ben's steamer pulled away, he left a good feeling behind. He sensed that Adam's cover as a slave had already been broken and he was not now in any more danger than he could handle. That alone Ben felt he could live on.

* * *

As Samuels' mercenary ship approached the New Orleans harbor on the Mississippi Delta, ship after ship blocked the entrance to the docks, all waiting inspection and passage, or battle and deportation. Adam heard some distant shots fired and knew that this boat would not pass. Except for Becca, these were Southerners on board. And one dead Negro. But what did they expect him to do?

They had only a skeleton crew left since the battle, one in charge of stoking the steam engine. They'd never be able to force their way through, or give battle to the Federal army here. Samuels stood looking out over the scene, the smoke from his pipe a hurricane around his head as he sucked furiously. He once had a plan, Adam felt sure, one that went awry with Becca's attack. Such a relationship for father and daughter.

Luke stood to the side with the three others Adam didn't have the pleasure of meeting. Two of them didn't even bother to clothe halfway down, and one couldn't speak good English.

Becca pulled Adam aside. "I need to tell my father who I am. It could be our only chance to get ashore."

"No, that's too risky. He's been in a foul mood. He's as likely to throw you over as anything else." Adam wanted to wrap his arms around her, but a single glance from Samuels would doom them both. "I'm ah…sorry your escape idea didn't work."

"Who planned on the 14th Texas Cavalry? I knew they were stationed at Fort Brown but to get there so quickly? Someone must have warned them."

"Luke." Adam nodded toward Samuels. "Probably working together with your father. Are you still willing to help me save Lincoln?"

"If he really needs saving." Becca held up a hand when Adam started to argue. "I've not bought your story—yet. Lincoln made a pledge when he became president not to interfere with slavery, no matter what. He knew he had no constitutional right. But after war came, the abolitionist north forced his hand. *You're either with us or with them*, they said. *You either want slavery to exist, or you don't. You can't have it both ways, Abe.*"

Adam laughed at her interpretation of a pompous northern abolitionist. "So you think Lincoln's heart isn't in this war."

"I think Lincoln feels bad about the secession and wants the war to end in preserving Union. But it's all he wants and he doesn't care how he gets it. I think deep down he's a gentle man, Adam. Right now, gentle AND confused—and obsessed."

"Hmmmph. Could be his son Willie's death has messed with his mind a little, too. Messes up a man's thinking, losing a son.[58] For whatever reason, Tobias's Negro Rebellion sees him as an enemy."

"He might not be an abolitionist, but he's the best chance their people have. He's the symbol of their heroic movement toward freedom. You'll always hear of a few dissenters when radical change like this is underway, regardless."

Adam grabbed her arm and pulled her out of view of the others, contemplating their task ahead. "Say, did I thank you for saving me from Javier?" He leaned over and kissed her. When he backed away she wrapped her arms around him and demanded another one, longer, slower.

"You need to learn to say thanks properly," she whispered.

"But not here. Becca, were you going to kill your father?" She leaned back and laughed. "Are you always all business?" When Adam smiled she shook her head. "I don't know. We haven't gotten close enough yet to test that."

"Cartwright! Where's that boy? Somebody bring me my muley."

Adam wiped his mouth and Becca pushed him out, staying hid. Adam stepped forward, feeling he had to keep up the persona of a slave, at least for now. They can whip a white as well as a black, enslave a white, just as well. He wondered—maybe they never believed he was a mulatto, at all.

"Yessir, Mr. Samuels."

"Oh, cut the malarkey. You're going to get us through, act the part of commander of this ship—as a northerner. You reek of Yankee. They'll believe you when you say we've got cotton for Butler."

"Or?"

"Or I'll have Luke shoot you in the back. See, you aren't going to be much help getting us to Lincoln if we can't even get in the harbor. And besides, I don't much like you messing with my daughter."

Adam could feel the tension on the ship around him as former master and slave faced each other and he sought for the right response.

* * *

Adam, wearing Samuels' coat and hat, both too small, watched the military vessel approach. They had seen other boats chased away, only a few allowed to dock. Now Samuels expected him to convince the most skeptical army soldiers, people with guns who chase other people away, on the basis of his looks and a phony piece of paper? He looked behind him as everyone except a crewman named Lucky Larry took cover inside the galley. He could see eyes peering out at him, with Samuels' entire face plastered for the moment against the round glass window.

Lucky Larry next to him looked more like a Union man than the rest, and Adam figured this could work. As he stood on the bow of the main deck, five soldiers, two officers and three provost guard, walked across the platform. Adam glanced behind him at the glint of a rifle aimed at his back from behind the observation deck overhead. From the other side of the observation deck he caught the swish of a skirt. Becca. With the air of a captain making sure all was secure on the deck he continued his observation of his ship, with an air of cool calm. Becca peeked out and gave him a queer little nod of her head. He winked and turned back to the military with a sly smile that he concentrated to erase.

Within moments an army colonel faced him and asked for his credentials. Adam had been told everything to say, word for word, to get them to accept this as a union shipment and crew from Austin, Texas, and held the phony document ready. He hesitated, took a breath, and placed a hand on Lucky Larry's shoulder.

The colonel repeated the question, asking for credentials.

"My name is Adam Cartwright, Nevada Territory." He held the papers out. "This is phony. This ship is from Brownsville and Matamoras—"

At the gunshot and clatter of metal to wood, the colonel waved for everyone to take cover. Lucky Larry dropped to the deck with the gun of a guard at his head, while Luke leaped to the ground for the gun Becca had knocked away. Luke leaped off the ship as the provost guard, guns drawn, scoured the ship for anyone to arrest, shoot, or otherwise corral.

Adam ducked backward and grabbed Becca's hand. They nodded at each other and leaped off the ship, to the sounds of gunfire behind them.

* * *

Joe and Frank found one dead cowboy, Billy, and the cattle missing. "I think we're going to need some help," Frank said.

"Can't, no time. They might have my brother. I won't lose anyone else. I won't." Joe rode on to follow cattle tracks.

"Damn Cartwrights. I should leave while I have a chance." But Frank, after a moment's consideration, followed.

Night fell quickly in the hills this time of year, and light snowflakes drifted through the air, sensed only by the wet feeling on already cold cheeks. Joe's fears for Hoss were intensified by missing his Pa, and Adam, and the thought of spending an entire winter at the ranch with no one but Hop Sing—and maybe some of his ghosts—for company.

Joe had galloped home fast from the Paiute village with a gift for Adam's birthday. He'd had such a good time visiting there that he'd lost track of time. When he got home he found the house empty. Even Hop Sing was gone. He couldn't figure it—the cake and gifts were on the table, but everyone was gone. Didn't take him much longer to figure it out. They'd thought something had happened to him. He got on his horse, quick, and rode out in the direction he remembered having pretended he had headed, so Adam wouldn't catch on that Joe planned to purchase a special Indian knife for him, and sure enough, there was Hop Sing in the wagon, headed his way. Joe prepared himself for a scolding, but he didn't care. As long as everyone else was all right. He just hated being alone.

Frank, because Joe's thoughts were so far away, pointed ahead. "They've stopped the cattle for the night, Joe, right there, near the Truckee."

"Let's leave our horses here." They alighted and pulled the horses to a lone mesquite bush and tied them. "We need to see what we're up against."

"Well, I know there's five of them. And two of us."

"They might have kept the other cowboys, and Hoss, as captives. If we could find a way to free them first…"

"Even if we did, they wouldn't have guns. And they'll be kept under watch, anyway."

"What are you, a coward? We can do this. Maybe they'll be watching for a rescue attempt. But maybe they won't be watching for gophers." Joe spurred his horse to a hidden embankment with a little grass and water.

"Huh?" Frank followed and tied his horse, with a wary look around.

"You know, those little things that come out of holes, and are gone before you see them?"

"I know what gophers are. But—"

"Shhhh....just follow my lead."

"Oh-boy, down another mine shaft."

"Shut up!" Joe spotted one of the men on horseback walking the herd, and told Frank to find the other. "Take him down and get his weapons. I'll take this one. Then meet me at the river, behind the big double rock. Tie his horse so it can't wander into camp."

Joe waved him with a finger to the lips to head to the west and keep low. He never saw Frank again.

CHAPTER 41

"Where are we going?" Adam sat dripping on the sandy shoreline hidden from view by the once fragrant swampy tree line of cypress and magnolia, the few he recognized of the many of nature's beauty gracing the city. He and Becca sat just on the drier outskirts of the swamp. "I'm hoping *you* know, because I haven't been here since I was a boy."

"Shhh. They could try to follow." Becca shed herself of some of her exterior clothing and draped them on branches. "We have to go mingle with some people to see if anyone's knows if Lincoln's coming for a rally."

"Find us a telegraph office, too. It's past time I let my family know where I am."

They swam, she told him, through Lake Borgne and now she needed to get her bearings by walking north and west. She wasn't sure where they came out because she didn't recognize the surroundings. She shrugged when Adam raised a questioning eyebrow. "Well, how often does a city resident visit a swamp?"

They trudged through swampy waters and Adam, a country boy from near desert terrain, thought if one could drown without submerging, this is where it would happen. Even swimming a bottomless and dirty water like that lake wasn't as bad as this green stuff clinging to him. Egrets and pelicans flew overhead, and he couldn't tell what did what squawking but he feared the birds were trying to give their location away.

Adam shut down his tactile surroundings and focused on getting home. Save Lincoln, the country and be home by dinner. Well, not quite. He remembered another time he had high expectations, and with Becca remaining ahead of him and focusing on direction, allowed himself to go back to Nevada, to the desert and drier times...

Joe at age five was already a schemer. He wanted to give Pa a special birthday present, because every year on his birthday Ben remembered Marie's death. Hoss and Adam, because Joe had just found out again how his mother had died, went along with him—give Pa a boat ride on Lake Tahoe. The boys didn't have a boat, never had one, never had the need. They could fish from the shore just fine. But Joe had visited his Paiute friends and got a ride in a canoe. He wanted one for Pa.

The boys spent nearly a month, with the help of a Paiute friend, and got a canoe built. They used a Ponderosa pine that had fallen and was already half eaten with rot, and dug it out, fashioned both sides into a peak and protected the craft with some fresh tree sap inside and out. All three of them imagined sitting in the middle of Lake Tahoe where the fish get bigger than Hop Sing, sitting there and enjoying the quiet peaceful company of family.

Joe wanted to be the first to try the boat out so he pushed it off and jumped in and before his brothers could get to him, he'd gone too far off shore. As he floated away, he realized he had no oars. Hoss and Adam were laughing their guts out on shore, but then Little Joe started screaming and waving as the boat began to sink. The wood rot had sink too far into the wood and couldn't hold out in the water. Adam and Hoss swam out to save their brother but the boat sank to the bottom.

Pa really loved his new jacket and boots that year.

Adam was surprised out of further reverie by Becca's hard fist on his chest. He looked down to see his pants were green but dry, so they'd not been in swamp water all that long. Becca stopped them just outside the city square. They were near French Quarter now, Adam figured by the rich sweet smells that reminded him how deep hunger could go. Even with Union here, some things never changed.

"I have a feeling that the army has spread the word to watch for us by now," Becca whispered as she stepped into the street. "Maybe not, but we better go about this easy."

"Right, but we can't look like we're sneaking around town in broad daylight, either." Adam walked out ahead of her. He wondered why they couldn't tell the army the truth. "And look at you. You're a walking street vendor."

She gave him an unabashed smile. "All right, walk natural, but follow my lead."

Becca went up one street and down another until Adam felt they were going in circles, but at least the streets were deserted. At one point he headed for a telegraph office until she grabbed his arm and pointed out the army colonel inside. A different one, but still…

After another couple blocks she pulled him inside a darkened house and shut the door. "We'll wait here. Francois will tell us everything we need to know."

"And if he can't?"

"I trusted *you!*"

"You didn't *trust* me. You said you'd go along."

"Same thing."

Adam thought about this and nodded. And before he had a chance to think further, Becca leaped into his arms and demanded a kiss that deserved the privacy they'd found.

* * *

Joe reached the double rock first and got nervous waiting for Frank, where minutes seemed like hours. His man had gone down easily and Joe left him tied between sleeping longhorns. Joe wondered what might come of him if the cows started to move, but then, nothing more than he deserved. He feared, waiting, that Frank didn't have as much luck.

After waiting longer than he wanted to, Joe wandered toward the camp, keeping the rock in sight. The camp was somewhere ahead, he could tell by the smoke. The river was to his left, and he'd left Cochise due south of here. With these bearings in mind, he slipped closer to the fire, where the smell of something being burnt made him hungry. Joe kept his gun out and took a wild look around him. No telling who might be sneaking up behind him. These fellows made good time, nearly off Ponderosa land and headed to California. Caught in the act of thieving. As long as that didn't include the murder of his brother. The way Joe felt, finding Hoss hurt could just drive him berserk.

The campfire appeared well tended, but no one was around. The fellows seemed to have left this area in a terrible rush, and would be back soon. Maybe they were butchering Frank right now, piece by piece. Joe hoped instead Frank had caused some kind of diversion somewhere, making his own plans like the arrogant bastard he was. Couldn't trust him, even now. Joe circled the campsite, hoping—and then he heard the loudest snore ever.

"Hoss...Hoss!" Joe followed the sound and found his brother trussed on the ground, sleeping. Joe crept up to him, keeping a wild lookout around him. "Hoss." He didn't have any bloody marks on him, at least. Joe patted his cheek. "Hoss, come on." He untied the ropes, but with a cautious watch around him. Odd they left no one to watch the camp.

Hoss, groggy, squinted at him. "Joe? What you doing?"

"Rescuing you, big brother. Looks like you got soft, all that romancing you've been doing."

"Oh, I nearly had them but they called my bluff—"

"Tell me later. Here. Take this rifle. Frank is here somewhere, but seems I can't count on two fingers how much to trust him."

"And Salzar, he's gotta be here somewhere, too."

That's when they heard the shot, followed by the thundering of cattle hooves. "Hoss—the cattle—they're stampeding!"

* * *

Francois found them in his house, settled in each other's arms. Becca introduced her cousin. As he provided her with clothes, he told them the stunning news. Lincoln was in town. "He's coming to see a Cartwright. I wouldn'ta believed it at all." He glared at Adam, as though being from a silver district made him suspect.

"Oh, I don't know, Francois," Becca said, "in these times, the North will cling to any little help offered. Adam, had those soldiers had the chance, they would have escorted you to Lincoln, themselves." She touched Adam on the chin where a small cut lingered, showing his anxious shave moments before to remove the month-long beard.

Adam winced, fighting a sudden queasy feeling. Just lingering illness, or the long trip, but something was wrong, real wrong here. Too fast, too easy. Too...set up. Why then did they leap off the ship, when they could have just relied on the Union soldiers for protection?

Francois treated them both to a leisurely French lunch of croissants and wine and then took them to the fairgrounds, where black people milled about and set up camp to wait. "No one knows what's going on. They just expect people to start coming. Like you. Very impromptu."

"So we could be here a long time for nothing?" Adam hoped so, but also feared this rally could be a diversionary tactic and the real threat could take place elsewhere. He smelled picnic foods but little else. Obviously these people were trying hard to keep the area clean for Lincoln's arrival.

"Oh, no." Francois couldn't seem to mask his disgust for Adam's presence. "While you were at the telegraph office, I paid a visit to Butler. Lincoln had been snuck into town and kept safe with Butler waiting for word that you had arrived. Your silver impressed him a great deal, Mr. Cartwright. I never would have thought one cowboy could have that much effect."

"Ah...yes...the silver." Adam frowned. "Cowboy" had never been pronounced like "slave" before. Someone must have sent Lincoln a phony telegram and signed his name to it. He watched as three young black girls climbed the wobbly stairs to the makeshift stage. Their mother—or some authority figure—remained on the ground, and started playing an oboe, to which the girls sang a spiritual in beautiful, high-pitched perfectly harmonized voices. When the girls finished and left the stage, Francois grabbed his arm. "Come on, you next." Francois, with Becca behind him, guided Adam toward the stage.

"Me?"

"These folks need to be kept entertained until Lincoln arrives. You can tell everyone what you plan to say to Lincoln, and maybe guide their speeches to him."

"Tell them what to say? I'd never presume—"

"Adam," Becca put a hand on his arm. "This is what we're here for, remember? What better way to keep an eye on Lincoln and the crowd than from the stage?"

Adam grimaced. He looked at the crowd. Some were looking their way. Very few whites in the crowd. Any white would stick out, like a green frog in a white lily pond. He thought a southern sympathizer most likely to pull the trigger. But if these were dissatisfied slaves, seeing one black hand on the trigger could be impossible. Tobias? Had he been their hired gun? His dying wish was to see this stopped, but perhaps Tobias's dying wishes couldn't be trusted, either.

259

"Well, why not?" Adam walked on stage to a light smattering of applause. He cleared his throat. "Ah, I'm Adam Cartwright, from Nevada Territory..." A number whispered to each other at this and some others applauded. "I'm here to meet with Lincoln, to support his efforts to reunite this country. I don't have much to say to you, but I think you might have a lot to say to him. I hope we'll see him here today, so that you can let him know why you've gathered here. He needs to hear how well all of you have fought for your freedom, freedom now being kept from you."

At this a roar of approval with a smattering of applause stopped him. These people don't want to kill Lincoln, just talk to him. From his point on the stage he could see five buggies on the road, off aways. What Tobias said about blacks wanting to stay slaves—what kind of game was that?

"When he gets here, let him speak and then ask him questions. Ask the same question three different ways at three different times and you'll uncover his honesty. A man can lie the same way once, but he cannot lie the same way three times. I promise you this—that unless he satisfies you that he offers you freedom and education right here in this country, he will get no silver from Nevada."

Adam didn't like saying this because it was not his to promise, but he felt reasonably sure of Lincoln's intentions. Volatile times sometimes called for a maneuverable fuse.

Adam felt his breath getting tight so he said no more, realizing he was about to meet the president. He and Pa have met dignitaries before and he'd even been to a Senate debate while going to college, but nothing like this. A few soldiers walked alongside the buggy containing the lean figure wearing a stovepipe hat, and Adam noted, to relieve his own tension, how the roof of Lincoln's buggy seemed higher than the rest. Adam supposed General Butler and some of his staff were in the other buggies. One after another and then groups of five or six got to their feet as the buggies approached, the slow cheer reaching a crescendo.

The buggies stopped and richly suited men were helped by soldier escorts to the ground. Adam watched Lincoln from the stage, but then a glint of sun caught his eye. He looked into the crowd and saw a reddish-brown head in a sea of black. Luke. With a rifle. He tried to get Becca's attention without looking suspicious but her eyes were glued to the buggies as well.

A Southern plot, not black at all.

Adam leaped off the stage, yelled "protect the president!" and ran directly at Lincoln's lean form. He knocked them both to the ground as shots fired—several just missing him, one taking a nick out of his shoulder. People screamed and fled but the army soldiers who had escorted the buggies surrounded the area and soon had the potential killers on the ground—five in all, all with guns out, and Adam reeled back in shock—

two of them black. All had been ready to fire and likely did, a concerted effort that should have worked—and almost did.

Adam, on the ground on top of the president, gave a bit of a laugh and got to his knees. "Sorry, Mr. President, didn't know how many…" Adam stood and held a hand down. He squinted. "Wait, Mr. President? Are you…all right? You look…different." Adam knew the war was hard on him and news photos did little justice to one's looks.

"I am perfectly fine, young man." He cleared his throat. "So what's this about silver?" He appeared ready to say more but they were surrounded by soldiers who escorted Lincoln away. He looked back over his shoulder and waved. "I thank you kindly, sir!"

Adam watched him get into a buggy before putting a hand on his shoulder and finding blood. Just a knick, he figured, nothing more. He went back to the crowd with his hand pressed against the wound to stop the bleeding. Luke sat with his hands tied behind him, and then Adam saw Becca sitting on the ground, guarded by two soldiers, along with three others who'd been captured. She didn't see him come up behind her.

"Damn that Luke, why didn't he wait? Damn him," she muttered at the ground.

Adam stared at her as the guards jerked Becca up, tied her hands and led her away.

CHAPTER 42

Butler invited Adam to a grand luncheon in honor of saving their 'special guest,' but no sign of Lincoln. He asked Butler if he could have a few moments of Lincoln's time in private.

"Lincoln, oh, ho-ho, yes, gone back already, didn't get to hear a lousy word from any of the blacks, thanks to that ruckus out there. You're a brave lad, eat up! You look famished."

Adam found his appetite returning with extreme gratitude. He tried not to think about Becca. If he hadn't heard her muttering, he might have believed they arrested her on false suspicion. But all along, to be part of the plot herself? Still Union but anti-Lincoln? How many sides could one war have? As he ate and laughed with the dignitaries he felt surprisingly at home with the understanding that Lincoln was simply a man doing a hard thing in a terrible situation. Nothing more. A man who makes mistakes in fervor for Union.

To be called to the prison to see Becca did not surprise him. He thought to refuse to go, but then the military made it an order. Adam found her ranting at the guards in a dank cell barren of any comfort whatsoever.

"I'm Union, damn you! I lead an infantry regiment in Texas, we work underground—oh, Adam! Vouch for me. Tell them I'd never kill Lincoln, I'm Union. I was helping you."

"Yes," Adam said. "She helped me get here, defied her father, all part of a plan. Not just of one group, but of two. To kill Lincoln."

"Adam! Then you were part of it, too! He wanted to see Lincoln dead, too! He's lying."

"If knocking a man to the ground and shielding him with your body is a form of murder, then yes, I'm guilty. I heard her, Colonel. Obviously Luke didn't like the change in plans, and wanted to get Lincoln before he reached the stage. I'd wager the problem was that both sides couldn't work together."

"No! Adam, you're part of this. I heard you, you said Lincoln wanted to ship blacks away and didn't care about them at all. It's because of you I got involved in my father's scheme! It's your fault!"

Adam shook his head. "You misunderstood me, that's all." But he realized how easily words could be misconstrued in an emotional time like this. "You need to learn to listen to your heart more, and other people less."

The Colonel, a shaggy bearded young fellow, nodded. "This woman surprises us, as much as anything in this war can. That Luke was the one we wanted. Had our eye on him awhile, but then he disappeared." He saw that Adam couldn't take his eyes off Becca, nodded with a brief hand on Adam's shoulder and walked away.

Becca slunk down to the ground and dropped her face into her knees. "Why did you have to ruin everything? Men, just can't count on them."

"Are you Union? Or was that attack just another disguise? Why attack your father? Why kill Tobias?"

"Yeah, I'm Union, so are my men. You're so smart, you know you can be for Union but against freeing slaves. You can be so abolitionist, too, that Lincoln doesn't do enough. Lincoln promised, when running for President, he wouldn't interfere with slavery. He lied. He says he cares about ending slavery. Lied there too. You can be for Disunion and want to see blacks protected. This war, all of it, all his fault. Tearing my family apart."

"Well," Adam scratched behind his ear, "war can do that...but only if we let it."

He walked away, ignoring her tears. To think killing one man would change an entire political atmosphere. Just another symptom of a country gone mad. This was a messy world and he was no longer sure what help there was for any of them. But Adam knew where he stood, unwavering after all this time, and realized that's all that's expected out of any man.

Outside the prison a driver in a buggy waved to him. An elderly man jumped out, limped a bit and then strode to Adam.

"Butler told me you were here. Adam Cartwright?"

"That's right."

"Eduard Darcy. A pleasure to meet you. And I will say I can see why some might take you for a mulatto."

Adam grunted and grabbed his hand, shaking pleasantly. "My father has said so *little* about you."

In playful alarm, Darcy backed up a step. "You're not going to hit me, too, are you?"

"Relax. I'll wait until you're not ready."

Darcy laughed, and waved an arm to his buggy. "Please, you must be exhausted. Be my guest for this evening."

Adam found the idea pleasing, and accepted.

After a lavish dinner during which they exchanged pleasantries, Darcy took him into the parlor. Adam kept waiting for Darcy to explain why he was here. "Let me introduce you to the people who saved your father's life."

Adam stood in complete surprise as four Negroes walked into the room.

"You missed your pa by a couple of days. These folks here..." Sadie took over from Darcy the story of Ben's rescue, his worry over his son, how he wanted to stop the attempt on Lincoln's life and the shipment of blacks to

Hayti and other colonies. Adam had forgotten about that part of Tobias plan, and in a halting, emotive tone he could not control, told them in return how Tobias's story had ended.

In growing anger, Adam addressed Darcy. "This was all your doing, wasn't it?"

Darcy stayed seated for his own protection. "I'm not a young man anymore. I thought I had just one more chance to make a name for myself, as your father has done. Killing Lincoln could have changed everything for the South. And for these people, who deserve better than that phony Emancipation Proclamation."

"But to tell them the Cartwrights had control of Nevada's silver?"

Darcy took a deep breath and struggled to his feet. "I'll admit I alluded to that idea to a lot of people, yes. New Orleans is suffering, Adam. And you live surrounded by wealth—all that silver, your cattle, your free and open land. If you think I wasn't jealous, think again. I thought if you could see what's going on here, see how we live, you'd understand. You are Nevada's first family, are you not? Convince your father to run for governor, Adam. Give that silver to the south when this war ends, so that we may do what's right for these people, as Lincoln will not."

Adam wished he could have been given ten minutes with the man whose life he saved. He would have told Lincoln...the man whose life he saved...

"Adam?" Darcy held out a brandy.

"Oh! Sorry." He took the drink Darcy offered. "About Pa being governor...I don't think..." he looked around at all the hopeful faces in the room, and sighed. "I'll see what I can do."

He hadn't saved Lincoln's life, after all. Lincoln had. The crafty devil.

* * *

Joe and Hoss dragged themselves toward the front door of the house after dropping the horse saddles to the ground and setting the animals loose in the corral to find the feed trough.

"How long's it been since we been home, Joe?"

"Oh, I'd say about five days."

"That long?"

"Well, let's see..." Joe looked skyward while he counted in his head, "catching steer, looking for missing ones, getting Salzar to Carson City for a doctor, sleeping for two days..." He shook his head. "Six."

Hoss pointed at the ground. "Snow. Wasn't there before."

"Yeah. No."

"Say, Joe," Hoss grabbed his arm. "I plum didn't get a chance to tell you this. But Angela...she's getting hitched."

"Angela? My Angela?"

"Yeah. To Randy. Well, I 'spect that wedding's off now, since he's dead and all."

"You mean one of them outlaws?" As Joe scratched his chest he noticed that two of his shirt buttons were missing.

"Yeah. I reckon that means she's available, only I wouldn't go after her if I was you."

"No?"

"Even though she did save my life."

"Yeah? How's that?"

"Well, she done told Randy that she couldn't marry him if he killed a Cartwright."

"She said that?" Joe laughed. "Big brother, after all I've been through, Angela is the least of my concerns." He slapped a hand on Hoss's shoulder.

Ben stood watching them on the porch, a big grin on his face.

"It's about time my two vagabond sons got home!"

"Pa?" Joe felt Hoss smiling at him but everything became blurry. "PA!?"

Ben ran and put his arms around Joe. "I don't know when I've seen a better sight. The two of you, talking and laughing."

"Pa…I'm so sorry…" Joe collapsed in tears into Ben's arm.

"Joe, what do you have to be sorry for?"

"The fire, I lost you…I thought…I'd killed you."

Ben laughed. "I'd say you and me have a lot of catching up to do."

"When did you get home, Pa?" Hoss led them into the house.

"Just this morning. I was getting ready to come out and rescue you two."

Joe laughed as the two sat at the dining table. "We were in Carson City too. But we just woke a little while ago."

Hop Sing poked his head out of the kitchen. "Hop Sing, bring us some tea."

Hoss spoke, his biggest fear resurging in the still partly empty dining room. "Adam… what…?"

Ben sat back, as Hop Sing, reading their thoughts, had the tea ready for them. "First thing I did when I got to Carson City was look for telegrams. I found five, and he's sending them to Virginia City as well. He's on his way home."

CHAPTER 43

Adam booked passage back to Brownsville. Butler tried to convince him to go up the Mississippi instead, but Adam had to retrieve some personal property in Texas. When Adam tried to ask about Lincoln not being Lincoln in New Orleans, Butler went off on a tirade about how the scoundrel thinks he's not doing his job there and will replace him with General Nathaniel Banks, and then ran off after one of the house servants. Adam was less surprised by the replacement of Butler with Banks. Darcy told him that Butler was a little too hard on the population of British and French in the city,[59] who Lincoln courted to remain neutral.

Since his family knew he was safe, Adam was tempted to stay longer. After all, he'd had a hellish time getting here. But when he went into the bank to get some bank notes the calendar told him that the passes to the ranch were closing. Time to go home or not until spring. He couldn't wait that long for home.

And he had a horse to steal.

* * *

Adam made a brief stop in Laredo to get the bullet out of his arm. When the doctor asked him how he got himself shot, Adam shrugged. "After this long journey, too tired to duck."

That would be the closest he'd ever admit to horse stealing.

* * *

All along the way, Adam sent telegrams and read newspapers. He read reports about snow in the Tahoe mountains and braced himself for a winter in the valley, away from home. In the election of 1862 the Democrats picked up a number of new seats in Congress. A Democratic newspaper reported:

> As we can probably expect, the Copperheads bitterly assailed the
> emancipation policy, accusing Lincoln of "bowing to the pressure
> exerted by the abolition wing of the Republican party." Lincoln
> had been given a qualified support by Moderate Democrats, only to
> have this support removed with the freeing of the slaves. This
> November, 1862 election was considered a "repudiation of the
> Lincolnian policy."[60]

A day later, McClellan was fired from his job as General of the Army of the Potomac. Adam wished he could hear Tobias say, "I told you so."

He wished even more he could be on a stage headed home, because he could go so much faster and sleep all the way, but he couldn't leave Buck behind.

He read all news he could find about New Orleans because he wondered what might happen to Becca, and then gave up on reading political news altogether when he read that she and Luke and someone named Arnie had taken the oath of loyalty and were released just before Butler left and Bank took over, and that the President wanted to amend the Constitution to delay freedom for the slaves until 1900. He didn't know what to believe, except about Butler being put in charge of raising Negro troops for the new campaigns come spring.[61]

"Sure enough, Tobias. Black soldiers can die as well as white soldiers for their freedom." Adam knew he could never forget Tobias. He never wanted to.

* * *

With less than two weeks left before Christmas, Adam and Buck walked into Carson City, side by side because the horse was tired. He had heard that soldiers could outmarch the cavalry and learned how true this was. Buck couldn't eat very well while walking, while he could. Adam looked up at the hills of the mountain where the ranch lay hidden by clouds of white, and his heart burst apart at the stitched-up seams of pain and loss. There appeared to be too much snow for him to make the journey the rest of the way. He wondered when his Pa got the last telegram before he could no longer make the trip down into the valley and alighted at the telegraph office to check.

"Adam? Adam!" Margaret ran down the walk toward him. Well bundled but smile still visible, she had her hand tightly clasping that of a young girl's. Behind her walked Frank, looking both pleasantly surprised and a little confused.

Adam held his arms out for Margaret, and gave her a hug.

"Oh, Adam, we've been so worried. Oh my, look at you. You haven't been eating well, have you?"

He laughed. "I'm fine." The hug felt different and he didn't know from whose side the difference came. He stepped back in relief, like a spell had been broken. "Who's this little one?"

"This is Jodie. Frank and I," and she waved Frank to come over, "have adopted her. We...we're married."

"Well! I have been gone a long time."

"Do you have time for a story? I'd love to hear yours."

Adam looked toward home. "I guess I do."

"Oh, Adam, before I forget, apologize to your family for me."

"For what?"

267

"I thought that none of you cared about each other anymore. I know better now. By caring about each other, you can care for others even more."

Adam understood her at that moment. She never trusted anyone, until now. "Frank, you ah…you seem to have turned your life around."

Frank wrapped an arm around her. "I owe my life to her."

"The right woman can do that."

Margaret laughed as she looked at Frank. "Would you believe he told me that his mother was a whore and his father used to beat them both?" She teased him but with love evident in her smile.

"Oh now, I promised never to lie to you again, didn't I?"

Adam leaned against a hitching rail. He felt Margaret's hand on his back.

"Are you all right? Adam, you've had a long trip. You should take a night's stay here at the hotel."

Adam shook off the recurring dizziness. "No, I've got to get home. Got to try."

* * *

Ben went outside to measure the snow. If another few inches could melt in this warm spell, he'd try his luck heading into the valley. He longed for another telegraph from his son, and maybe, maybe Adam was down there even now, wondering if he should risk the ride. He missed his horse, but that wasn't near as painful as having only two sons home for Christmas. Any day of the year, actually.

He turned back to the house, but slow, reluctant. Ben knew and knew too well how special every day was with his three sons at the breakfast table. Someday they would all have lives and loves and homes of their own. That's what made the telegraphs so important. Just hearing from him and knowing he was all right had to be enough.

He walked back to the house and reached for the door, fighting the empty feeling that came every time he stepped back inside.

"Hello."

Ben at first didn't turn, knowing his mind has played enough tricks on him lately.

"It's good to be home."

Ben saw what he thought was a ghost, a man wrapped in unfamiliar warm blankets and just his nose and upper lip peaking through. Ben walked back toward him as Adam threw off the blankets and eased himself out of the saddle, a look on his face like he'd never walk right again.

"Adam!" Ben grabbed his son in an embrace that spoke of longing and loss, and received a returning embrace, each of knowing that life had more control of them, than they of it. Someday the return will never happen. But at least that day wasn't this one.

"Glad to make it up the hill. Wasn't sure I could," Adam backed away to take in all of his father's tearful joyous face.

Hoss and Joe ran out of the house. Hoss nearly knocked Adam over with his enthusiasm. His older brother would need to compete with him for bigger portions of food to gain back the weight he'd lost.

"Hoss…" Adam wrapped an arm around his big brother, "you don't know how often I thought about your strong arms and calm head." He was about to say more but saw Joe, eyes shining, behind Hoss.

Adam wiped at the instant moisture in his own eyes. "Joe," he grabbed his little brother and gave him a big bear hug. "I'm so sorry…" but as he sniffed he pulled back in alarm. "What happened to you?"

"Oh," Ben laughed to divert Joe's painful memory. "He had a bad night in a mine shaft, is all. All behind us now." Ben could barely speak above a whisper, seeing his sons reunited made him feel more painfully happy than he could remember since…well, for some time.

"Smells like someone died."

Joe backed away and rubbed at his head. "I can't get this smell out!"

"We'll try a sulfur bath next." Ben saw Adam's puzzled stare and winked at Hoss. "His mine shaft needs to be sealed, although mine saved me from a fire."

"Mine shaft? Fire?"

Hoss chimed in. "Yeah, and my ghost got her murderer to kill hisself."

"You mean that lady…she *is* a ghost?" Adam looked from one to the next in confusion. "But Pa…we don't believe in ghosts."

Ben laughed. "Of course not. Let's go inside. Hop Sing is cooking something special."

They met Hop Sing coming out, carrying a big pot. "Mr. Adam, velly good to see you. Velly good. Will cook something special. But this not to eat."

Adam leaned over and sniffed. "Oh, I'm glad. Even as hungry as I am, I won't eat that."

"Ha! You should see the tea Hop Sing made me drink. Plum curl your toes."

"Hey, Adam," Joe's voice squeaked, "your windmill designs are in. You owe me $5."

They all laughed at this, and Adam gave Joe's jaw a tender slap.

Ben held Adam back as Hoss and Joe walked inside. "What did you find back there?"

"New Orleans? I hear you were there, too. Sorry I missed you."

"Lincoln? Did he come?"

"Let's just say…he knows more than we give him credit for. Pa," he draped an arm over Ben's shoulder. "We face a torn apart country and sometimes can't be sure what to believe. What's important, I think, is to always remember what *we* stand for. And that no matter what else happens, our house never divides." He patted his pa's shoulder and walked inside.

Ben, smiling, nodded at Hop Sing and followed Adam into a very warm house.

* * *

All safe at home. Hop Sing waited until they were inside. He'd saved this potion for precisely this moment. He carried the pot of liquid to the far side of the yard and drew a heavy wet line in the snow with the liquid, walking and chanting lightly under his breath. "Away you stay, we pray, today." He repeated it in Chinese, and then back and forth from English to Chinese until he'd made a complete line from one end of the yard to the other.

He would have preferred surrounding the house, but this was the most he could make with the ingredients he found.

Ghosts might still come. But Hop Sing believed they would not and that would help them all sleep better tonight. And they will all still be in the house come morning.

* * *

In New Orleans a group of nearly a thousand Negroes presented to the newspaper and to Mr. Lincoln a petition asking that they be allowed to remain in their home country, the U.S.A., and not be shipped to other countries.[62] Lincoln sat with the petition in front of him, alone at the window looking out into the falling snow of a tired, quiet winter, and thought about all the immigrants making this country home now. He decided to let the deportation idea die a slow death. He had also removed the part about holding off complete freedom for blacks until 1900 in the Emancipation Proclamation before he issued it that January.

"Sometimes desperation has its place, to make us see clearer." Lincoln penned a few notes to himself, grateful that the Negro Rebellion—the one that could have torn the Union hopes to shreds—had convinced him to remember blacks as people, not property. Some even thought that the blacks were doing the freeing all by themselves. Though Lincoln himself might agree, admitting that could be politically damaging. He wanted to think he had a future, beyond this war.

He got up to follow Mary's voice. Sounded like another of Willie's visits. At least he hoped so, and not more ghosts of bloodied soldiers that swarmed around him at night when he tried to close his eyes at night.

The End

FOOTNOTES

[1] The Civil War Diary of Rice C. Bull, edited by Darcy Bauer (New York: Berkeley Publishing Group, 1988), 14.

[2] The episode "The Crucible" aired in April, 1962, so I've placed the date in April 1863.

[3] James McPherson, *Battle Cry of Freedom: the Civil War Era* (New York: Ballantine Books, 1998), 262. General William E. Doster, "Free Negroes, Contrabands and Slaves," *Civil War Eyewitness Reports*, ed. By Harold Elk Straubing (Hamden, Conn.: Archon Books, 1985), 73-74.

[4] "Courtship and Marriage," *A writer's guide to everyday life in the 1800s* (Cincinnati: Writers Digest Book, 1993), 203.

[5] Ramon Adams, *The Old-Time Cowhand* (Lincoln: University of Nebraska Press, 1961), 55.

[6] Geoffrey Perret, *Lincoln's War* (New York: Random House, 2004), 199.

[7] Tom Wheeler, *Mr. Lincoln's T-Mails,the Untold Story of how Abraham Lincoln used the Telegraph to Win the War (New York; HarperCollins Publishers, 2006)* 83. Bruce Catton, *Terrible Swift Sword (New York: Doubleday, Inc., 1963)*, 466 and 475. Ruth Painter Randall, *Mary Lincoln: biography of a marriage* (Boston, Little Brown & Co., 1953), 292-293.

[8] Geoffrey Perret, *Lincoln's War,* 197 and 218.

[9] Robert P. Jordon, *The Civil War* (National Geographic Society, 1969), 27

[10] Dan De Quille, *The Big Bonanza* (New York: Thomas Y. Crowell Co., 1947, by Alfred Knopf), 292-294.

[11] James McPherson, *Battle Cry of Freedom,* 497. Geoffrey Perret, *Lincoln's War,* 196. The Fugitive Slave Law was not repealed until July of 1864.

[12] Dan De Quille, *The Big Bonanza,* 292-294.

[13] *Mark Twain in Virginia City, Nevada* (Las Vegas: Nevada Publications, *1985)*, 155.

[14] *Oconto Pioneer,* April 3, 1862.

[15] James McPherson, *Battle Cry of Freedom,* 508.

[16] General William E. Doster, "Free Negroes, Contrabands and Slaves," 73.

[17] From Anson Mills, *My Story,* edited by C. H. Claudy (Washington DC:

Byron S. Adams, 1921 2nd Edition), 94: "We had three brigades of colored troops in the command, and the Doctor was of so dark a complexion as to almost suggest a mixture of blood."

[18] James McPherson, *Battle Cry of Freedom*, 81-82. Recognition of mulattos as light enough to pass for white can also be found in John W. Blassingame, *The Slave Community: Plantation life in the Antebellum South* (Oxford University Press, 1979), 84, where white women would have affairs with black men, give birth to children that they then passed off as belonging to their white husbands.

[19] *Oconto Pioneer*, 31 October 1862.

[20] Shelby Foote, *Civil War, A Narrative: Red River to Appomattox* (New York, Random House, 1974), 375. Used in this source to refer to incessant office seekers.

[21] Henry Louis Gates, Jr., editor, *Classic Slave Narratives* (New York: Signet Classics, 2002), 1.

[22] Tom Wheeler, *Mr. Lincoln's T-Mails*, 83. Bruce Catton, *Terrible Swift Sword*, 466 and 475.

[23] *Inside Lincoln's Army:the Diary of Marsena Rudolph Patrick, Provost Marshal General, Army of the Potomac*, edited by David S. Frontis Sparks (New York: Thomas Yoseloff Publishing, 1964), 155-156.

[24] Jeffry Wert, *Custer* (New York: Simon & Schuster. 1997), 59.

[25] This was General McClellan's attitude in this time period and should not be construed as a direct quote or an attitude of the author's.

[26] T. Harry Williams, *Lincoln and His Generals* (New York: Vintage, 1967), 182-183.

[27] From the episode, *A House Divided*, written by Al C. Ward, that aired January 16, 1860.

[28] An interesting feature of combined business in Virginia City. See *The Big Bonanza*, 274.

[29] Jacob Cox, Major-General, "Battle of Antietam," *Battles & Leaders, Vol. II* (edited by Staff of *Century Magazine*, Castle a division of Book Sales Inc. nd.), 659. Tom Wheeler, *Mr. Lincoln's T-Mails*, 85. Shelby Foote, *From Sumter to Perryville*, 748. Noted Lincoln returned to Washington on October 4th, (749.) *War of the Rebellion, Official Records WROR*, Making of America, Cornell University web site, 1.32.II, 411 and General Order No. 163, October 7, 1862, *WROR*, 1.19.II, 395-396,

http://moa.cit.cornell.edu/moa/browse.monographs/waro.html

Report, Provost Marshal General's Bureau, March 17, 1866, *WROR*, 3.5, 609-610. *Green Bay Advocate*, October 9, 1862.

[30] Dan De Quille, *The Big Bonanza*, 4.

[31] This was referred to as The Bascom Affair, and in Bonanza history, would have led to the episode, "Honor of Cochise, that Adam refers to as the time he got the bullet in the side that nearly killed him. "Cochise, Geronimo and Mangas Coloradas," *Desert USA*,

http://www.desertusa.com/magfeb98/feb_pap/du_apache.html accessed October 7, 2007.

[32] Stephen Barrett, *Fire Management Today*, Spring2000, Vol. 60 Issue 2, p23, 3p, Item: 6599474, from Carson Valley Public Library, accessed 6/26/2004.

[33] T. Harry Williams, *Lincoln and His Generals*, 136-137.

[34] Brig-Gen. James Carleton to Brig.-General Lorenzo Thomas, September 30, 1862 and Carleton to Col. Joseph West, HQ Dept. of New Mexico, October 11, 1862, *WROR*, 1.15, 576-581. *Civil War Chronicle*, edited by J. Matthew Gallman (New York: Gramercy Books, 2000), October 13, 1862, 242-243. Jay W. Sharp, "Desert Trails: The Long Walk Trail of the Navajos," *Desert USA*, http://www.desertusa.com/mag03/trails/trails09.html accessed 10/7/07. Bill Harris, "Justice of the Fleece," *Wild West*, August 2008, 45.

[35] In 1863 the U.S. sponsored the settlement of 453 colonists on an island near Haiti, where starvation and smallpox decimated the colony. A naval vessel finally returned the remaining 368 to U.S. in 1864. James McPherson, *Battle Cry of Freedom*, 509. Geoffrey Perret, *Lincoln's War*, 343.

[36] Dan De Quille, *The Big Bonanza*, 115.

[37] John W. Blassingame, *The Slave Community*, 79.

[38] James McPherson, *Battle Cry of Freedom*, 784-785.

[39] Richard I. Dodge, *Our Wild Indians: Thirty-three years' personal experience among the red men of the Great West*, (Freeport, New York: Books for Libraries, Press, 1882), 30.

[40] John W. Blassingame, *The Slave Community* , 72.

[41] For lack of the real story of how Hop Sing came to them, this comes from the first story in author's "Cartwright Saga."

[42] Dan De Quille, *The Big Bonanza*, 100.

[43] Dan De Quille, *The Big Bonanza*, 208.

[44] Dan De Quille, *The Big Bonanza*, 297.

[45] Dan De Quille, *The Big Bonanza*, 103-104.

[46] *The Victorian Supernatural*, 45.

[47] Andrew Ward, "Fearful Cry of Freedom," *American History*, August 2008, 48.

[48] Geoffrey Perret, *Lincoln's War*, 193.

[49] *Fort Brown, Texas: A new frontier*, http://www.nps.gov/history/seac/brownsville/english/index-3.htm confederates, accessed 10/17/07. WROR, 1.15, 587.

[50] Andrew Ward, "Fearful Cry of Freedom," 49.

[51] David W. Blight, ed., *Passage to Freedom: the underground railroad in history and memory* (Smithsonian Institute, 2004), 219-220.

[52] Shelby Foote, *Fredericksburg to Meridian*, 393. *Sarah Morgan: Civil War Diary of a Southern Woman*, ed. By Charles East (New York: Touchstone Books, 1991), 409.

[53] Probably a kinder description than "cross-eyed cuttlefish, squat and

squinty." T. Harry Williams, *Lincoln and his Generals*, 214.

[54] *WROR*, 3.3, 430.

[55] *WROR*, 3.2, 808.

[56]"Emancipation in the Border States," *Oconto Reporter*, 7/31/62. Civil War Home web site

http://www.civilwarhome.com/lincolnandproclamation.htm

accessed August 8, 2008. Geoffrey Perret, *Lincoln's War*, 195. Geoffrey C. Ward, *The Civil War*, 179.

[57] *WROR*, 3.2, 725.

[58] T. Harry Williams, *Lincoln and his Generals*, 194.

[59] *WROR*, Vol. 3.2, 947.

[60] Barbara and Justus Paul, The Badger State: a documentary history of Wisconsin (Eerdmans, 1979), 206.

[61] T. Harry Williams, *Lincoln and his Generals*, 215.